Golden Shores

a story in the
RomantiSea Serenades
series

J.D. Harbor

Ebook ISBN: 979-8-9921213-9-1
Paperback ISBN: 979-8-9921213-5-3

Cover Design: J.D. Harbor
Editing and Proofreading: Nicole Kincaid, Naughty Nook PR
Formatting: Nicole Kincaid, Naughty Nook PR

To my children, the real life inspiration behind Marty and Emmett,
You redefine possibility daily, turning challenges into stepping stones
with courage that leaves me breathless. Your laughter is my favorite
sound, your victories my greatest joy. You've taught me that strength
isn't measured in ability but in spirit.
This story exists because you showed me what unconditional love
truly means.
You are my greatest adventure.

Preface

This story is about healing. About second chances, quiet courage, and the kind of love that offers something better than fixing. The kind that sees every broken piece and stays anyway.

It's a celebration of found families, messy beginnings, and learning to trust the soft places again after life has hardened you.

While *Golden Shores* explores these hopeful themes, it also touches on deeper topics that may be difficult for some readers.

That said, I didn't want this to be a heavy book.

So, in the midst of the hard stuff, you'll also find humor, flirtation, awkward karaoke, swim-up bars, mischievous best friends, and one very memorable singles cruise.

Because even the most meaningful stories need room to laugh, to breathe, to dance barefoot on the balcony at midnight.

If you're carrying weight of your own, I hope these pages offer something honest, something hopeful ... and maybe even a few moments of joy.

Welcome aboard.

Content considerations include:

- Combat-related PTSD and associated symptoms (flashbacks, hypervigilance, nightmares)

- Past miscarriage (referenced, not graphically detailed)

- Parenting neurodivergent children and navigating disability support

- Military deployment and its emotional impact on relationships

- Grief, emotional withdrawal, and the slow work of reconnection

Prologue

The park glowed softly in the late afternoon, bathed in a dreamy golden hue that spilled gently through the branches overhead. Sunlight slanted low across the grass, catching flecks of dust suspended in the warm air, turning them into tiny sparks of gold. A soft breeze carried distant laughter along with summer's signature scents of grass, soil, and sunscreen. Nearby, the pond lay perfectly still, mirroring the cloud-streaked sky like polished glass, its surface disturbed only occasionally by the softest ripple.

Marty sprawled in the grass, giggling breathlessly as his younger brother circled him in wild, noisy loops. His yellow tank top was askew, stained with grass and joy. One shoe dangled loosely from his foot, forgotten. Marty's laughter rose brightly each time Emmett crashed dramatically into him, all curly hair and mischievous eyes narrating every imaginary move.

"I'm the rocket ship and you're the planet! Watch out! Lava coming through!" Emmett shouted, tumbling forward and planting a loud, exaggerated kiss on Marty's cheek. "MUAH!"

Marty's giggles cascaded through the air as he squirmed and batted his hands in a halfhearted attempt to escape the tickling. Jerry remained a few feet away, resting on his haunches, wonder etching itself across his features at the sight of his son, lost in pure delight.

With quiet expertise, the photographer repositioned herself, each deliberate movement followed by the soft whisper of her camera capturing another moment. She paused briefly, lowering her equipment as her expression warmed, turning partway to face Jerry.

"They're really something, aren't they?" she asked warmly, lowering her camera just slightly. "You must be exhausted at the end of the day."

Jerry's soft laugh carried affection as he kept his eyes on his children. "Without fail. But just look at them. It's impossible not to savor every moment, isn't it?"

"It vanishes before you realize," the photographer said, tweaking her camera settings. "Both my girls are in high school now. Believe me when I say embrace this stage."

Jerry met her gaze momentarily, a silent understanding flowing between them. "I'm holding on tight. These simple days are everything that counts."

She gestured toward where the path disappeared around a bend. "That perfect light will only give us about thirty more minutes. Should we try those trees for our next shots?"

"I'm game." Jerry stood, easing the tightness from his limbs. "Operation Next Photo is a go. Everyone, collect your gear."

Emmett jumped in a flash, already racing toward the next activity.

"Hang on a minute," Jerry said, tilting his head toward their previous position. "I think a certain someone is about to be left behind."

"Oh!" Emmett's eyes widened with sudden concern, as if Jerry had prevented a tragedy. He scrambled back, scooped up the beloved orange toy, and nestled it carefully into his small blue backpack. "He says thank you," Emmett informed them with solemn sincerity.

Jerry knelt gently beside Marty, brushing away a blade of grass from his cheek. "You ready, bud?"

With arms outstretched, Marty beamed, and Jerry hoisted him up with a soft grunt.

The chair welcomed him like second nature. Jerry fastened the buckles, then leaned in to fine-tune the headrest, each movement calm, practiced, sure.

Just as Jerry reached to push, Emmett stepped determinedly in front, small hands grasping the wheelchair handles firmly.

"I wanna push him," Emmett declared, meeting his dad's eyes with quiet determination.

Jerry tilted his head, smiling gently. "Think you can handle it?"

Emmett nodded emphatically, puffing his chest out a little. "I'm really strong today. I ate two bowls of cereal."

Jerry's smile widened, his heart squeezing softly. "Alright, tough guy," he said warmly. "Go ahead."

With a determined shove, Emmett pushed the chair forward, his shoes squeaking faintly against the sun-warmed concrete.

The wheelchair rocked once, then glided into the glow.

Marty turned back, his expression soft and open, a silent exchange of trust passed between brothers like a secret they didn't need words to share.

The wheelchair dwarfed Emmett as he pushed, its handles nearly level with the top of his head. His compact frame vanished behind the substantial metal chair, requiring him to stretch his neck constantly to navigate. Occasionally, he would peer around one side, momentarily visible as he surveyed their route, his blue backpack bobbing against his small shoulders with each step. Despite the size disparity, he continued forward with deliberate movements, his face reflecting both effort and satisfaction.

The photographer quickly knelt behind them, framing the moment.

Click.

Jerry kept pace several steps back, observing as the pathway wound ahead, bathed in golden afternoon light. He noticed Emmett duck to the side of Marty's chair, then quickly correct his course, his posture betraying unmistakable satisfaction with his task. From the partially open zipper of the blue backpack, Orange Cat's ear peeked out, catching the waning sunlight.

For one fleeting, perfect moment, everything in Jerry's universe aligned in beautiful simplicity.

KAPOW

Jerry snapped awake, the tranquil park scene vanishing as darkness and chaos invaded his senses. Reality shattered the moment with brutal speed as rocket alerts screamed their high-pitched warnings and counter-measures launched into the night sky with violent mechanical growls.

BRRRT—BRRRT—BRRRT.

Each interceptor blast shattered the night with concussive force, the sound waves traveling through Jerry's chest and into his core. The bunker walls, rough and utilitarian, caught the staccato light show in fleeting illumination, casting erratic shadows that leapt and retreated with each explosion. Overhead, the darkness erupted in violent bursts of amber and brilliant white as defensive systems found their targets, transforming incoming rockets into celestial shrapnel that rained across the black canvas above.

He flattened himself against the rough wall, the chill seeping through his gear like ice water.

The gravel beneath him was unforgiving, sharp edges biting deep into his hands with every shift.

His breath stuttered, caught beneath the suffocating press of body armor.

Fingers curled tight, he braced against the shake in his limbs, adrenaline burning through every nerve.

Next to him, Mac had settled into his usual pose of combat nonchalance, elbow hooked over the concrete edge like he was lounging at a pool instead of hiding from rockets.

The gravel gave a faint crunch under his boots as he shifted, unbothered by the grit or tension.

He gave Jerry a quick once-over, smirking like the whole situation was a private joke.

"Another encore from the midnight mortar orchestra, huh?" Mac said, his voice raised above the relentless alarms and the rhythmic burst-fire of the defense system. "Seriously, they need new material."

Jerry's breath came out uneven as he coaxed feeling back into his hands, the rough stones having cut into his skin. "Those blasts keep getting louder."

Mac snorted, amused. "Nah, man. You're just going soft."

The laugh came out ragged and uninvited, just enough to crack the static in Jerry's chest.

Above, the bombardment eased. One last echo rolled across the sky before the sirens blinked out like dying stars.

Silence rushed in fast, dense as smoke, leaving him braced against it, breath caught mid-lung.

Mac nudged Jerry's boot, the gravel scraping audibly beneath his shifting feet. "Might as well hit the gym early. Beats waiting around for the next wave."

Jerry groaned, pushing himself upright, gravel crunching loudly beneath him as he stood. The sharp stones shifted uncomfortably under his boots, adding to the dull ache already radiating from every joint. "Let me guess ... leg day again?"

Mac pushed away from the bunker wall, stretching stiff shoulders with a casual grace. "Every day's leg day, Jerry. You gotta stay strong for those boys of yours."

A quiet ache settled behind Jerry's ribs at the thought of Marty and Emmett, their laughter still flickering in the back of his mind.

He scrubbed a hand over his face, exhaling slowly.

"Go easy today," he muttered. "My calves are still filing complaints about Monday."

Mac smirked, gravel crunching sharply under his boots as he stepped toward the bunker exit. "If it ain't sore, it ain't working."

Jerry shook his head wryly, following Mac out into the pre-dawn darkness. The gravel pathway beneath their feet was even more uneven and loose, rolling awkwardly under every step. Each footfall was uncertain, ankles straining slightly as they navigated the uneven ground in near darkness, illuminated only by the distant security lights casting pale circles of illumination across the base.

Jerry glanced at the ghostly outline of trailers, their metallic shells dull and unwelcoming in the faint glow. He sighed again, imagining the scorching heat that would soon overwhelm those thin metal walls.

Beside him, Mac moved purposefully, boots crunching on the unsteady gravel pathway without hesitation. Watching Mac's steady stride, Jerry straightened slightly, reminded of the strength he needed to stay sharp, to endure, to eventually get home. For Marty and Emmett. For the life that lay waiting beyond the chaos.

Reaching the cluster of metal trailers, they split toward their individual units. As Jerry navigated the gravel path, each step uneven and annoyingly loud, he muttered softly, "Can't wait to move out of these tin cans."

To be fair, he'd seen worse. Jerry had endured deployments in tents battered by windstorms and flooding. Still, what soldiers aptly nicknamed tin cans baked like ovens beneath Iraq's brutal sun, these metal trailers easily hitting 110 degrees on a mild day. Every power outage, each flicker of the unreliable generator, turned their living spaces into stifling metal boxes. Air conditioning was less a comfort than a fleeting miracle that rarely worked as advertised.

Jerry pushed open the flimsy metal door to his trailer, stepping inside and exhaling with relief as the door clicked shut behind him. Almost immediately, Jerry spotted his roommate from the corner of his eye, standing partially obscured behind the dividing wall of metal lockers, suspiciously quiet.

Jerry's breath escaped in a quiet rush as he battled a flash of weary amusement. He lowered himself cautiously onto the thin mattress, the bed frame announcing his presence with an indignant creak. Opening his laptop to find some temporary escape, he immediately noticed the missed Skype alert from his mother waiting on screen.

Hovering the cursor over the call button, Jerry hesitated, raising his voice slightly with playful caution. "Hey man, you're not spanking it over there, are you?"

A surprised laugh burst from behind the wall of lockers. His roommate cleared his throat, voice tinged with amused embarrassment. "Nah, dude, wrapped that up already. You're clear."

Jerry chuckled, shaking his head in mock disgust. "Thank God. Last thing I need is my mom overhearing something that'll traumatize us both."

His roommate snorted. "You're good. No trauma here. My little soldiers are safely back in their bunks."

"Appreciate the colorful analogy," Jerry muttered with flat sarcasm, clicking to start the video chat. "Truly the wordsmith of our generation."

"Anytime," his roommate replied, a laugh still clear in his voice.

Jerry's mouth twitched with affection as he repositioned himself, watching the pixelated blur resolve. Seconds later, Maggie's face came into focus, her expression tender and grounding, suddenly shrinking the vast distance between deployment absurdity and the sanctuary of his real life.

"Hey, Mom," Jerry's face brightened at the sight of her. Then he noticed her condition. Maggie's normally precise hair stuck out in several directions, and faint circles had formed under her eyes. "Everything okay? How are the boys?"

"Oh, everything's great," Maggie answered quickly, her voice almost too bright. "Boys are fine, I'm fine … everything is perfectly, wonderfully fine."

Jerry lifted an eyebrow, skeptical. "Mom. You look … how do I put this nicely?"

"Wrecked?" Maggie supplied dryly, smirking as she brushed a strand of hair back behind her ear.

Jerry chuckled, nodding gently. "Little bit, yeah."

Maggie released a long breath, her expression warming. "Don't worry about it. Your boys are absolute darlings, but they run in perpetual motion. Makes me marvel at how I managed with you and your brother and sisters."

"That's revisionist history," Jerry countered with exaggerated virtue painted across his features. "I was practically perfect in every way. A role model for the ages."

His father's understated laughter drifted in from somewhere off-camera.

Maggie rolled her eyes dramatically, shaking her head. "Oh, please. Marty and Emmett are little angels compared to you at that age."

"Fair enough," Jerry admitted, grinning despite himself. "But seriously, how are the boys?"

Maggie softened instantly, her voice gentle. "They're good. Emmett is practically counting down the minutes until kindergarten starts. He keeps packing and unpacking his little backpack, practicing for the first day."

Jerry smiled at the image, heart twisting gently. "Sounds like Emmett."

"Marty's good too," Maggie continued. Her voice turned reassuring, clearly anticipating Jerry's unspoken question. "We saw the neurologist today. She said he looks great. They're adjusting his seizure meds a bit since he's growing, but it's all routine. She wants to see him again in six months, after you're back."

Jerry felt tension release from his shoulders, nodding gratefully. "Thanks, Mom. I appreciate you keeping up with all of it."

"Of course," Maggie said gently. "We just wanted to fill you in, make sure you're doing okay over there."

Jerry hesitated, glancing toward the trailer's thin metal wall, recalling the harsh cacophony from the mortar attack just minutes earlier. He forced a casual smile, shaking his head slightly. "I'm fine. Just counting the days until I'm home."

"Not the only one counting," Maggie replied softly. "Boys miss you like crazy."

"Are they around?" Jerry asked, hoping for a quick glimpse.

Maggie shook her head apologetically. "Sorry, honey. We just finished wrangling them into bed a few minutes ago."

Jerry's dad chimed in dryly off-screen, "Wrangled is putting it mildly."

Jerry chuckled. "Rough night?"

"No worse than usual," Maggie assured quickly, throwing a playful glare toward her husband off-screen. "Just excited boys. But they settled eventually."

Jerry started to reply when three sharp knocks cracked against his trailer's metal door.

CRACK. CRACK. CRACK.

Jerry jumped as sharp knocks rattled his trailer door, Mac's voice cutting impatiently through the thin metal walls. "Jerry! You alive in there, man? Let's move it!"

"Alright, alright!" Jerry called toward the door. "Thirty seconds!"

He turned back to his laptop screen, offering Maggie an apologetic smile. "Sorry, Mom. Duty calls. Mac's dragging me to the gym whether I want it or not."

Maggie laughed gently, warmth filling her tired eyes. "Go on, sweetheart. Tell Mac to keep an eye on you out there."

"He always does," Jerry said softly. "Give the boys an extra hug from me tomorrow morning."

"Promise." Maggie smiled softly. "Love you, Jerry. Stay safe."

"Love you too," Jerry murmured, the words catching briefly in his throat. He lingered another second before ending the call, Maggie's face replaced by his reflection on the blank screen.

He closed the laptop gently, exhaling as reality settled back around him. Jerry quickly changed into gym shorts he'd left draped over the bed and slipped on worn running shoes, tying the laces hastily. The shorts were still faintly musty from yesterday's workout, but they'd have to do.

Another knock, louder and more insistent this time. "Jerry! Seriously, move your ass!"

Jerry yanked open the trailer door, revealing Mac leaning casually against the frame, arms folded, looking annoyingly awake for three-thirty in the morning.

"Thought you'd fallen back asleep," Mac remarked, eyebrows lifting slightly.

"Have I ever been that lucky?" Jerry shot back dryly.

Mac chuckled, stepping back as Jerry joined him outside. "Come on. If you hustle, we might actually get breakfast afterward."

"This had better be worth it," Jerry muttered as they navigated the rocky terrain toward the gym. The loose stones caused their footing to waver in the murky hours before sunrise, with identical housing units forming shadowy outlines under the distant floodlights.

As they rounded a corner, a familiar figure approached from the shadows. Corporal Barrett gave a quick nod of acknowledgment, clearly alert despite the early hour.

"Morning, Sergeant Duncan. Morning, Mac," Barrett said easily, falling briefly into step beside them. "Almost didn't recognize you two without coffee in your hands."

Mac flashed a tired grin. "We're aiming to fix that after the workout."

Barrett turned toward Jerry, her voice casual. "Hey, Sergeant Duncan, Sergeant Major Vega asked if you could swing by her office sometime today when you have a free minute. Said it's nothing urgent."

Jerry nodded, curiosity briefly flickering in his eyes before fading into resignation. "Got it. Tell her I'll swing by after the morning brief."

"Will do." Barrett smiled faintly, continuing past them toward the trailers. "Good luck in there."

"Yeah, right," Jerry muttered under his breath as Barrett disappeared into the shadows. "No one enjoys leg day."

Mac chuckled, nudging Jerry's shoulder lightly. "Gotta stay strong, man. Marty and Emmett aren't slowing down anytime soon."

Jerry let out a weary laugh. "Trust me, those two already run circles around me."

Mac gave a knowing grin, stepping slightly ahead. "Then pick up the pace, sarge."

Jerry rolled his eyes, but a faint smile appeared on his face nonetheless. He squared his shoulders against the chill, following Mac toward the dim glow of the makeshift gym, bracing himself for the workout and whatever Command Sergeant Major Vega had waiting for him later.

One

Time slipped by in a blur of alarms, backpacks, and spilled juice. Jerry had returned from Iraq, but some days, home didn't feel like a return. It felt like a reassignment. Different battlefield. Different uniform.

Baghdad's grueling shifts had lasted twelve, fourteen hours at a stretch, armored up and adrenaline-wired, but they'd had structure. Here, back in Killeen, in a cookie-cutter subdivision just outside Fort Cavazos, the days blurred together in a rhythm of logistics, exhaustion, and relentless devotion.

His four-bedroom house looked exactly like every other on the block: tan brick, trimmed lawn, the same set of shrubs out front. Inside, everything screamed builder-grade beige. Beige walls, beige tile, beige carpet. It had all the charm of a shipping container, but it was home. Emmett and Marty each had their own room, while Mac had claimed the guest room when he'd moved in as Jerry's roommate and best friend. Jerry's bedroom stayed neat, efficient, military tidy. But the rest of the house was always one step away from cheerful chaos.

The alarm blared at 4 a.m., blasting the University of Utah fight song through Jerry's phone speaker. He groaned and rolled over, the melody cracking through the still house like a bugle call. Once motivational. Now, just loud.

Sleep hadn't come easy since his return. When it did, it was shallow, restless. But there was no time to dwell. The boys needed him.

Muscle memory kicked in and Jerry moved fast, padding down the hall barefoot with the beige tile cool beneath his feet. A hallway nightlight cast just enough of a glow to guide him to Marty's room first. His eight-year-old son was already stirring, his limbs shifting slightly beneath the covers.

"Morning, champ," Jerry whispered.

Marty responded with a soft hum and a drowsy, delighted grin.

Jerry flicked on the bedside lamp and knelt down beside the bed. Dressing Marty was a practiced routine. Gentle hands, slow movements. He helped guide stiff limbs into a T-shirt and elastic-waist shorts, carefully threading his feet through socks and checking the alignment on his ankle braces. No complaints. Just the occasional giggle as Jerry made exaggerated faces or narrated each sock like a mission briefing.

They made their way to the kitchen, where the scent of cereal and overripe bananas filled the air. Jerry settled Marty into a chair with extra support cushions and opened the fridge to retrieve the familiar green yogurt cup.

"Alright, meds first," Jerry said, scooping just enough yogurt onto a spoon to bury the crushed pills.

Marty wrinkled his nose slightly but opened his mouth when prompted, accepting the spoonful without fuss. Jerry watched him closely, waiting for the swallow before offering another bite and chasing it with a sip of water in a bright blue straw cup.

By 4:15, Emmett had come racing down the hall, already narrating a dinosaur invasion while digging through the clean laundry pile for a 'socks-that-match-my-soul' combo.

"Shoes first, then second breakfast," Jerry called, holding up Emmett's sneakers.

"Roger that!" Emmett chirped back, one sock already missing again.

In the garage, Jerry loaded Marty's folded wheelchair into the bed of the truck, securing it quickly with the nylon strap he kept clipped to the rail. Then, he came back inside and hoisted Marty up into his arms with a quiet grunt.

Marty melted into the hold, clinging loosely to his dad's shoulder. Jerry carried him out to the truck and carefully secured him in the back seat, buckling him in.

By 4:42, the morning battle was nearly won. Both boys were dressed and fed. Backpacks zipped. Meds done. Jerry hoisted Emmett into the truck, gave Marty's belt a final check, and climbed into the driver's seat.

Maybe there was time to grab a gas station coffee on the way to the babysitter's.

Then, from the back seat …

"Dad! Dad! I forgot Orange Cat!"

Jerry closed his eyes. No swearing. At least, not out loud.

He turned the truck around, flicked on the hazard lights, and pulled back into their driveway. "We'll be fast," he muttered, mostly to himself.

Emmett had his seatbelt unbuckled before the truck came to a full stop.

"Hurry up," Jerry called after him, "we're already late. Marty, you good?"

Marty's response was a full-body wiggle of laughter. Even strapped in, even at five in the morning, his joy buzzed like static. Jerry smiled despite himself.

Two minutes passed.

Jerry's fingers tapped the steering wheel. Then his thigh. Then back to the wheel. The porch light flickered faintly above the garage, buzzing against the still-blue morning sky.

He opened the driver's door and headed for the house.

"Emmett? You find him?"

A small voice echoed back from the kitchen. "Yeah! He was thirsty, so I'm getting him some juice!"

Jerry exhaled hard and checked his watch. Of course.

"Drink quick and let's go!"

But instead of returning, Emmett padded around the corner with a paper towel and headed straight toward the laundry room.

"What now?"

"I spilled some juice. I'm cleaning it up," Emmett answered cheerfully, unaware of the time crunch.

Jerry ran a hand over his face. "Mac!" he called toward the hallway.

"Yeah?" came the reply from the guest bathroom, water running.

"Emmett spilled in the kitchen. Can you wipe it up before you head out?"

"No problem!"

"Thanks. See you at formation." Jerry turned back to his son. "Em, Uncle Mac's got it. Let's move!"

Emmett zipped back into the kitchen, snatched up the aging Orange Cat whose fur had faded more gray than orange, and sprinted for the door. Jerry followed close behind, corralling him with one hand while locking the door with the other.

"Bye, Mac!" Emmett shouted as he climbed back into the truck.

Jerry climbed in after him, buckled his belt, and checked the time.

Five minutes behind schedule.

Survivable. But just barely.

Running five minutes behind wasn't unusual for Jerry, and he always built in buffer time for surprises like the Orange Cat Incident. But there wasn't much wiggle room left this morning, and any more delays would throw the entire day off balance.

The truck pulled into Ally and Simone's driveway just as the horizon began to soften with pre-dawn light. The porch light was still on, casting a warm glow across the beige brick and short walkway. Through the front window, the flicker of cartoons hinted that the morning routine was already in motion inside.

Jerry shifted into park and turned to the back seat.

"Alright, mission drop-off. Let's roll."

Emmett unbuckled himself with dramatic flair and wrestled his backpack over one shoulder. Jerry opened the rear passenger door and unfastened Marty's belt, then gently scooped him up.

"Got your stuff?" Jerry asked, glancing toward Emmett.

"Yep! Orange Cat, backpack, shoes, and extra snack ... double check!"

Together, they made their way up the short path. Jerry adjusted his hold on Marty and knocked once.

The door opened almost immediately. Ally stood in the doorway, wearing leggings, fuzzy socks, and a "Caffeine and Chaos" sweatshirt. She smiled the moment she saw them.

"Morning, chaos crew," she said, stepping back with her mug of coffee. "Survived the jungle out there?"

"Barely," Jerry replied. "But we've made it intact. Juice spill and all."

"I won't even ask." She reached out to ruffle Emmett's hair as he darted inside, already aiming for the couch. "Shoes, please!"

"Already off!" Emmett called as he kicked them behind the door.

Jerry carried Marty over the threshold and into the living room. The beige carpet was already cleared for him, the play mat and pillows set out beside the television. Marty laughed with delight as Jerry settled him down gently, stretching out comfortably with his arms flung wide.

"I figured he'd want to go full free-range," Ally said, sipping her coffee. "Let him be a floor goblin while you're off getting sweaty."

"You know him well," Jerry said with a grateful smile. "Thanks again, Ally. I'll be back after I shower."

"You always say thanks. You really don't have to."

"Doesn't mean I'm gonna stop."

Just then, Simone appeared from the hallway, tugging on the cuff of her PT jacket. Her hair was pulled back, and like Jerry, she wore a gray Army T-shirt tucked into black running shorts, the reflective belt cinched around her waist. Her sneakers squeaked softly on the tile as she approached.

"Morning, sergeant," she said with a small nod.

Jerry gave her a sideways look as they stepped back out onto the porch. "Simone, how many times do I have to say, 'when we're at the house or outside of work, please call me Jerry.'"

"Yes, Jerry. But I reserve the right to switch back if you start getting bossy."

"Deal," he said, leading the way toward the truck.

Just before she followed him down the steps, Simone leaned in and kissed Ally on the cheek, soft and casual.

"I'll be back in an hour," she said.

"I'll have the second pot of coffee waiting," Ally replied.

That earned a grin from Simone. "You really do spoil me."

Jerry shook his head lightly as he unlocked the truck. "You get coffee kisses. I get spilled juice and cardio. Not sure who's winning here."

"Definitely me," Simone said as she slid into the passenger seat.

They pulled away from the curb, the early morning quiet broken only by the hum of the tires and the distant bark of a neighbor's dog. The sky was just beginning to shift, casting long shadows over the quiet streets.

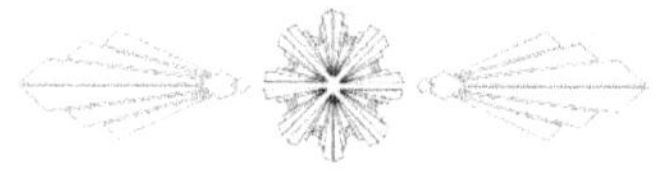

Ten minutes later, they arrived at the field. A few soldiers were already stretching, but Mac was front and center, grinning, bouncing on his heels like he'd been waiting all night.

"Morning, troops!" he called out. "Hope you brought your lungs and your regrets."

Jerry gave him a flat look. "You get weirder the earlier it is."

Mac tossed him a folded napkin. "Toast. Buttered. You're welcome."

Jerry caught it with one hand. "Remind me to promote you."

Simone smirked. "Only if he runs the warm-up too."

Mac gave a mock salute. "Gladly. Let's suffer."

PT was brutal. Sprints. Circuits. The kind of burn that lingered long after it was over. Jerry pushed through it, one rep at a time, his thoughts drifting: Marty's appointment. Getting the kids to school. Briefing. The speech draft. The never-ending to-do list.

When it wrapped, they walked off the field drenched in sweat and squinting into the brightening sun.

Jerry looked over at Simone. "Let Ally know I'll swing by in about thirty to pick the boys up?"

Simone nodded. "Will do."

Mac, already tossing his gym bag over his shoulder, motioned for her. "I've got room. Let's roll."

She gave Jerry a quick wave as they headed toward Mac's car. "Tell Emmett I'm stealing his cereal next time."

Jerry smirked. "Good luck. That kid's got snack radar."

They peeled off, leaving Jerry to climb back into his truck. He headed straight for the gym.

The base gym was quiet, the locker room mostly empty. Jerry dropped his gear on a bench and moved quickly. Uniform out, shower on. No time to linger.

Steam filled the tiled room as he stepped under the water. The heat hit him like a wave, loosening the knots in his shoulders. He stood there for a beat, not moving.

Margaritaville played softly from the speaker on the bench.

The melody about salt-rimmed glasses and pointing fingers slipped from his lips before he cut it short. The unsung truth of the chorus weighed on him.

His marriage had been over before it ever really started. They'd tried to make it work after Marty was born, and after his diagnosis … but it was like holding together two broken pieces that never really fit. Emmett had come along during one of those fragile, hopeful lulls. But it wasn't enough.

She hadn't stormed out. The relationship just … faded. Jerry didn't fight for custody initially. *How could I manage to be a single parent when I'm deploying all the time*, he had told himself at the time.

Then, a couple years after they divorced, he got a call from protective services. They had intervened in the kids' welfare, and before Jerry could decipher the situation, she was gone, and the boys were his.

He didn't dwell on it often. But some mornings, it crept in like steam, filling the quiet places he usually kept locked up.

He scrubbed down fast, dressed quicker. Pulled on his uniform, tightened his boots, checked his phone.

A message from Mac.

Mac

> **Coffee's waiting. Take a minute to breathe.**

Jerry smiled. He wouldn't have time to stop by the house today. But Mac always knew when to check in.

He pocketed the phone, squared his shoulders, and headed for the truck.

Next stop: Ally and Simone's house. Then the doctor's office.

Still a full day ahead.

Jerry picked up the boys and made it to Marty's appointment with two minutes to spare. It was a routine checkup ... blood pressure, reflexes, weight. The doctor was pleased with his progress and adjusted his meds slightly, but no red flags. No changes to the bigger picture. Just a quiet kind of progress.

Afterward, he drove them to school, checked them in at the front office, handed off Marty's medical update to the nurse, and made sure Emmett's snack hadn't been flattened in his backpack again.

By the time Jerry arrived at the office, it was just after 10 a.m., a full hour past the standard start of day. No one batted an eye. By now, everyone knew Staff Sergeant Duncan's mornings came with their own set of rules.

He'd make up the time tonight once the dishes were done, after story time, after Emmett finally stopped talking, and Marty drifted to sleep. Like always, everything else came first.

He headed upstairs to drop his things at his desk before proceeding directly to the command leadership offices.

At the admin desk outside Command Sergeant Major Vega's office, Corporal Barrett was entering log data, eyes flicking up as Jerry approached.

"Morning, Barrett," Jerry said. "Is the sergeant major in?"

"She's all yours," Barrett replied, flashing him a quick smile.

Jerry knocked once on the open office door.

From inside, without looking up, Vega called, "If it isn't my favorite pastry. Jelly Donut."

Jerry sighed through a smile. "Morning, sergeant major."

Vega finally glanced up, arching an eyebrow. "You look like hell."

"Sorry, Emmett was a bit more than his usual self."

"Mm." She leaned back in her chair. "Marty's appointment go alright?"

"Routine check. Slight med adjustment, but no concerns."

"Good. Tell Emmett I said hi … and that he still owes me a rematch at Uno."

"I'll pass it along."

She tilted her head. "And my speech? How's that coming?"

"I've got a meeting this afternoon with the chairman. I'll have the structure locked in by tomorrow and a draft to you by the end of the week."

Vega smirked. "You know I'm going to change half of it."

Jerry grinned. "Wouldn't have it any other way."

"Good." She gave him a nod of dismissal. "Go. You've got enough on your plate."

"Roger that, sergeant major."

He stepped back out into the hallway, passing Barrett on the way. "She's all yours, corporal."

"Thanks for nothing," Barrett responded quietly.

Back at his desk, Jerry finally sat down, logged in, and stared at his calendar. Training coverage. Article draft. Photo uploads. Speech outline. He scrolled through his inbox, already triaging what could wait and what couldn't.

A ping popped up with a message from Mac.

Mac

Don't forget the range tomorrow. Article due Friday for next week's paper.

Jerry smirked, typing back his response.

He hit send, then leaned back in his chair.

It was only Tuesday.

And the week had just begun.

Two

The soft creak of the mattress gave way to a contented sigh as Jerry pulled the blanket up to Emmett's chin. He gave it one final tuck on each side, then reached over to adjust Orange Cat where he'd been unceremoniously dropped near the pillow.

"You're all set?" Jerry asked.

"Uh-huh," Emmett mumbled, already sinking deeper into the covers.

Jerry ran a hand over his face, letting out a long breath. His back ached, his feet hurt, and it had been a sixteen-hour day—again. But this part? This part grounded him.

He took a step toward the light switch.

Click.

Emmett bolted upright.

"I forgot to brush my teeth!"

Jerry paused, hand still on the wall, eyes closing for just a second longer than a blink.

"Seriously?"

"I meant to, I really did," Emmett said, flinging off the covers and hopping down to the floor. "But I was getting Orange Cat and then I was tired and then I just ... didn't."

Jerry turned the light back on.

"Convenient timing."

"I *can't* get cavities, Dad. It's a school day tomorrow."

Emmett darted through the doorway into the small bathroom just off his room, grabbing his toothbrush like a soldier going for his weapon. Jerry leaned against the doorframe, arms folded, watching the child-sized chaos unfold.

The faucet started running. Water splashed. A squeeze of toothpaste missed its mark and landed on the counter, unnoticed. Emmett began brushing like he was chasing plaque for a bounty.

"Don't forget your back teeth," Jerry called out.

"I *know*, Dad," Emmett replied, the words muffled around the brush. "Ugh."

Jerry raised an eyebrow. "When did you turn seventeen?"

Without missing a beat, Emmett yanked the toothbrush out of his mouth and said, "Six. I'm *six*, Dad," before going right back to brushing.

Jerry smirked, shaking his head. "Right. Thanks for the clarification."

Emmett spit dramatically into the sink, rinsed, and looked up into the mirror with a final flourish of his toothbrush.

"Mission complete," he declared.

"Then march back to bed, soldier."

Emmett gave a mock salute and padded past him barefoot, heading back toward the glow of his nightlight. Jerry followed, flipping the bathroom light off behind them.

Once Emmett was tucked in again, for real this time, Jerry lingered at the door just long enough to watch his son curl back under the covers, arms wrapped tight around Orange Cat. Within seconds, his breathing slowed.

Finally, the house was still.

The soft whir of the dishwasher was the only sound greeting Jerry as he stepped into the family room. The chaos of the day had finally gone quiet, with no footsteps, no cartoons, no Emmett bursting into conversation mid-thought.

Just stillness.

Mac sat on the couch, legs stretched out, a chipped ceramic mug resting on his thigh. Steam rose lazily from whatever was inside. The warm smell of tea hung in the air. Peppermint, maybe. Or lemon.

The coffee table in front of him was mostly clear except for a crumpled napkin, a half-empty bag of trail mix, and a glossy cruise flyer that looked suspiciously well-placed.

Jerry walked past it without comment, heading to the kitchen for a glass of water. His bones felt like they weighed twice what they should.

"Teeth brushed?" Mac asked, not looking away from the mug.

"Eventually," Jerry muttered, filling his glass at the sink. "He remembered right after lights out. Like clockwork."

"Kids always develop perfect memory the second they're trying to stall bedtime," Mac said, glancing over. "It's a gift."

Jerry returned to the family room, lowered himself into the armchair with a quiet grunt, and took a long sip of water. His head rested against the back cushion, eyes closing briefly.

Mac sipped again, then let the silence settle just long enough to feel intentional.

"Long day?"

Jerry cracked an eye open. "They're all long."

"Sure," Mac said. "But today looked extra."

Jerry didn't respond right away. He just sat there, thumb running along the condensation on his glass.

"You know," Mac added casually, "if someone offered you seven days where nobody calls you Dad or Staff Sergeant ... just Jerry ... you wouldn't be wrong to say yes."

Jerry opened his eyes fully this time, glancing at the coffee table.

"I see the flyer made its way back out."

"It keeps finding its way back out," Mac said, with a half-smile. "Maybe it's trying to tell you something."

Jerry huffed a tired laugh. "Not the week for a singles cruise, Mac."

"It's not about being single. It's about not being on edge for five minutes."

"I don't think I'd know how," Jerry admitted. "My brain would probably start calculating who needs meds, or if the laundry's done, or whether there is any food in the fridge for dinner."

Mac nodded. "Sounds like someone who really needs a break."

Jerry let his head fall deeper into the cushion, eyes closed, limbs heavy. He let out a long, exaggerated sigh. Not the kind that asked for sympathy, but the kind that signaled *done*.

"Dude ..."

Mac didn't flinch. Just gave a knowing hum as he set the mug down on the coffee table with a soft clink.

"I know. Timing's crap. Life's full. You've got two kids, a workload that never quits, and a sleep schedule that's mostly fiction. I'm not saying it's easy."

Jerry didn't look at him. He just rubbed at the corner of one eye like the act of staying awake was slowly becoming negotiable.

"You're not saying it," he muttered. "But you're definitely circling it."

Mac's voice stayed even. "I'm saying you've spent the last year and a half proving you can survive everything. Maybe it's time you remember what it feels like to live a little."

Jerry cracked an eye open and gave him a sideways glance.

"You rehearse that in the mirror or just whisper it to yourself while you made tea?"

Mac grinned. "Microwaving popcorn, actually. Felt like a good moment."

Jerry scoffed under his breath. "Yeah. Real *Hallmark Cruise Line* energy."

"Thank you," Mac said with mock sincerity. "I'll be here all week."

He leaned into himself, spine curved and shoulders low, as if the hours behind him carried more gravity than usual.

"You really think dropping me on a ship full of bad decisions and overpriced cocktails is the answer?"

"No," Mac said. "But I think not dropping you might be worse."

Jerry let that sit. He didn't push back, but his silence wasn't agreement, it was fatigue.

He looked down at the flyer on the table, eyeing the palm trees and turquoise waves like they belonged to someone else's life.

"I can't just check out," he muttered. "Not when the wheels are barely staying on as it is."

"I'm not saying check out," Mac replied. "I'm saying check in ... with yourself. Just for a minute."

Jerry didn't answer. He leaned back, arms crossed now, eyes closed again.

He didn't touch the flyer.

Jerry's phone buzzed against the arm of the chair.

He blinked slowly, a weary smile forming when he saw the name on the screen: Mom. He tapped the green icon and leaned back, bringing the phone to his ear.

"Hey, Mom."

"Hey, sweetheart," Maggie said warmly. "Did I catch you at a good time, or are you still chasing Emmett around?"

Jerry chuckled softly. "Finally got them both down. Emmett conveniently forgot to brush his teeth until exactly one second after the lights went off."

Maggie laughed. It was a gentle sound that carried comfort. "Sounds about right. Marty doing okay today?"

"Yeah, actually. Had a checkup today, just routine stuff. They adjusted his meds a little, but he's doing good. Still smiling as much as ever."

"Oh, good," Maggie said, relief evident in her voice. "And you? You sound tired."

Jerry straightened slightly, his shoulders automatically squaring as if she could see him. "I'm fine. Just a busy day."

There was a short pause, filled with the quiet static of a mother's intuition.

"You always say you're fine," Maggie said gently. "And I'm sure you are. But you sound wiped out."

Jerry sighed lightly, smiling despite himself. "I'm good, Mom. Really."

Just then, Mac's voice carried from across the room, intentionally loud and clear:

"Mrs. D., tell your son he needs to take a vacation!"

Without even looking, Jerry grabbed the nearest throw pillow and hurled it across the room. It smacked Mac squarely in the face. Mac just laughed, snagged the cruise flyer from the coffee table, and sauntered out of the room with exaggerated innocence.

Jerry shook his head, rolling his eyes. "You two are in cahoots, aren't you?"

"What?" Maggie asked, failing spectacularly at feigning innocence. "I have no idea what you're talking about."

"Uh-huh. Sure you don't."

"Jerry, honey," she started, her voice softening again. "You know you're such a good dad, right? But you can't pour from an empty cup. You need to take care of yourself sometimes."

Jerry rubbed his forehead, feeling his resistance slip just a fraction. "Mom, I get it. But I promise you, I'm handling things."

"I know you are," she replied, warmth radiating through the phone. "But you're allowed to let go once in a while. You don't have to carry everything all at once."

Jerry sighed again. He didn't respond immediately, just stared at his feet, bare against the beige carpet.

Maggie filled the silence. "Anyway, how's work?"

"Busy. Nothing new. I have a speech draft to finish, some training coverage tomorrow ... you know how it is."

They talked a little longer, about nothing in particular: Emmett's latest adventures, a new recipe Maggie had found online, ordinary things. Eventually, Jerry glanced toward the hallway, exhaustion settling heavily again.

"I should probably get some sleep."

"Okay, honey. Call me tomorrow if you have a chance."

"I will."

"Oh, and before I forget ..." Maggie paused, her voice suspiciously casual. "Maybe think about going on that cruise with Mac. Might do you good."

Jerry sat upright instantly, eyes narrowing as a tired grin tugged at his lips. "Ah-ha! I *knew* you two were conspiring."

"Gilmore. Paul. Duncan." Maggie's voice had taken on that soft, steady, unmistakably maternal tone, and suddenly Jerry felt thirteen again, adrenaline spiking through his chest at the sound of his full name. "Just because we're conspiring doesn't mean he's wrong."

Jerry exhaled slowly, the faint grin lingering despite his best efforts. "Busted."

"Thoroughly," Maggie agreed, satisfied. "Sleep well, sweetheart. I love you."

"Love you too, Mom."

He ended the call and sat quietly, the phone resting against his chest. Eventually, Jerry pushed himself out of the chair and shuffled toward his bedroom.

When he flipped on the bedroom light, the cruise flyer on his pillow was impossible to miss, placed there with deliberate, unmistakable intent.

Jerry shook his head, a quiet laugh escaping him. "Yeah, that's real subtle, Mac."

Mac's voice drifted down the hallway. "I wasn't trying to be subtle, Duncan."

Three

The cursor blinked.

Jerry's fingers hovered over the keyboard, poised for another round of revisions. His world had narrowed down to words, structure, precision. The glow of the screen. The click of the keys. The hum of the computer.

Everything else was static.

His chair was stiff beneath him, but he barely felt it. His back was curved forward, elbows braced on the desk, shoulders locked in a posture that should have been uncomfortable, but he wasn't registering discomfort. His thoughts were deep in the trenches of phrasing and cadence, trimming excess words, smoothing out transitions.

His right hand moved automatically to his coffee cup, but the moment the ceramic touched his lips, his brain barely registered the bitter cold of it. He took a sip anyway, swallowed, and set it back down without looking. His other hand scrolled through the document, cross-referencing notes in the margins.

Rewrite. Delete. Rewrite again.

The speech was good. It was so close to perfect.

But close wasn't good enough.

Vega needed to be able to stand at that podium and own every word as if she had written it herself. Not too scripted. Not too formal. Direct, impactful, no fluff.

Jerry exhaled sharply through his nose.

Tighter opening. Stronger transitions. More punch.

His eyes flicked over the screen, rereading the last paragraph. Something was off. He backspaced. Rewrote it. Reread. Adjusted a phrase. Sat back just an inch. Stared.

The words on the screen started to blur slightly. His vision sharpened again as he blinked, rubbing his knuckles briefly against his temple before refocusing. His head had been aching for a while now. It didn't matter.

His knee bounced under the desk, restless, a silent metronome keeping pace with the thoughts churning in his head. His breathing was steady but shallow, as if his body had dialed down all unnecessary functions to make room for more focus.

Another revision. Another tweak. His fingers barely lifted from the keyboard, scrolling back and forth between sentences, rearranging words, tightening the flow.

His body ached, but he ignored it. His stomach was hollow, but he ignored that, too.

Just a few more edits. Then I'll stand up.

Time didn't exist right now.

The office around him? Didn't exist.

His focus was too deep, tunneled in, locked on the task in front of him. Every sound in the office had disappeared into background noise. The shuffle of feet, the murmur of voices, the distant hum of the printer, the occasional burst of laughter might as well have been happening in another building.

Even when chairs scraped against the floor and doors swung open, Jerry stayed locked in. His fingers moved. His mind worked. The clock was an abstract concept, meaningless.

Another line. Another edit.

Almost ...

CLANK.

The sudden slam of metal against wood sent a sharp crack through the room.

The desk jolted beneath Jerry's arms.

His fingers froze over the keyboard. His pulse thudded, a brief jolt of adrenaline hitting him square in the chest as his body registered the noise before his brain caught up.

His eyes snapped up for the first time in what felt like minutes. Maybe hours?

Keys.

A set of keys dropped right in front of him, the impact still ringing faintly in the silence that followed.

Jerry blinked.

Like resurfacing from deep water, Jerry felt the world rush back around him in a flood of sound. Fluorescent lights buzzed overhead, the nearly empty office hummed with quiet energy, and somewhere in the background a chair scraped against the floor.

And standing across from him, arms crossed, one eyebrow raised in an expression far too amused for Jerry's liking, was Mac.

Jerry stared at the keys, his heart still thumping from the abrupt interruption. He rubbed his eyes and sighed heavily, trying to shake off the fog of intense focus.

"What?" His voice cracked slightly, throat dry from hours of silence. He cleared it quickly. "What's up?"

Mac nodded toward the clock, eyebrows lifted in exaggerated patience. "Five o'clock, Duncan. You know, quittin' time? They're not paying us overtime here."

Jerry's eyes flicked toward the clock on the wall. 5:02. His chest tightened instantly, panic rising through him. Papers rustled beneath his frantic search for keys suddenly gone missing. "Dammit, I completely lost track of time. Ally's probably wondering where I am, and the boys ... God, I'm already late."

Mac raised both hands calmly. "Hey, slow down. They're at Ally's; they're fine. Listen, let me swing by and grab them. I need to chat with Barrett anyway."

Jerry hesitated, halfway out of his chair, the strain obvious across his face. "Mac, you've already helped enough. I can't keep leaning on you like this. Just let me ..."

Mac shook his head with a knowing smile, cutting him off. "Jerry, relax. I've got it. You finish your stuff, then swing by the pharmacy drive-thru on your way home. Everything will work out."

Jerry's jaw tensed, a silent war of stubbornness fighting gratitude behind his eyes. Accepting help felt far too close to admitting defeat.

"Mac, seriously."

Mac leaned forward, plucked Jerry's keys off the desk, and deliberately replaced them with his own. "We'll trade cars today. Marty's wheelchair needs the truck anyway. Consider it strategic."

Jerry let out a slow exhale, finally sinking back into his chair. His shoulders eased slightly, the rigid tension softening into resignation. "Alright. I owe you big time."

Mac grinned, heading toward the door. He paused, looking back with exaggerated sincerity. "Just don't take forever. I don't want to make us a nice dinner tonight if you're just going to let it go to waste. Honestly, Duncan, sometimes it feels like I'm cooking for one."

Jerry laughed softly, shaking his head at the affectionate jab. "Noted. I'll hurry."

Mac flashed a playful wink over his shoulder as he left. "Good. Otherwise, Uncle Mac is loading those kids up on ice cream, and you're on your own."

Jerry's tired smile lingered as Mac's footsteps faded down the hall. He took a deep, steadying breath and turned back to his screen, determined to finish quickly before Mac could cause too much damage.

The office was quiet now, an empty stillness settling around Jerry as he hunched forward, eyes glued to the screen. With Mac gone, the only sound was the distant hum of the building's air conditioning, a steady whisper of white noise behind Jerry's rhythmic tapping.

One more paragraph. Just one more.

He leaned in, eyes fixed.

The glow of the monitor held him fast while the clock blinked unseen in the background.

His breath slowed, shallow but steady, his heartbeat finding a quieter pace.

Footsteps approached softly, unnoticed until a familiar voice cut cleanly through his concentration.

"You planning on bunking here tonight, Duncan?"

Jerry flinched hard, heart jumping sharply as he snapped upright, automatically springing to his feet, arms rigidly clasped behind his back. "Sergeant Major."

Command Sergeant Major Vega stood casually in the doorway, arms crossed, her sharp eyes quietly appraising the scene: empty coffee cups, scattered papers, and a clearly exhausted staff sergeant standing at parade rest at nearly six on a Friday evening. She wore civilian clothes now, her bearing softer but no less authoritative.

"At ease, Duncan," she said with a subtle smirk. "Relax."

Jerry shifted slightly, dropping his stance into something less formal but still respectful. "Sorry, Sergeant Major. Didn't hear you come in."

"Obviously," she said dryly, stepping closer. Her eyes studied the disheveled workspace again, then met Jerry's directly, her expression shifting from mild amusement to genuine concern. "Jerry, when's the last time you actually looked at that clock?"

His attention flicked toward the digital numbers. 5:48. He sighed, embarrassment creeping into the edges of his tired smile. "Lost track again."

"Clearly," Vega said, her voice firm but gently compassionate. She leaned against the cubicle divider, fixing him with a sharp but understanding stare. "Look, Duncan, I appreciate dedication. Hell, it's what makes you good. But whatever you're working on? It's not a combat op. Nobody's going to die if this waits till Monday."

Jerry swallowed tightly, shifting his posture. "Just want to get it right, Sergeant Major."

She exhaled slowly, shaking her head with quiet understanding. "Sergeant Duncan, you're not in Iraq anymore. Stop working like you still are. You don't have to prove yourself every minute of the day."

He nodded stiffly, words catching slightly in his throat. "Understood, Sergeant Major."

She straightened, stepping back toward the doorway. "Five minutes, Duncan. If you're not right behind me out that door, you and I are gonna have a different kind of talk Monday morning."

"Yes, Sergeant Major."

Vega paused, eyes softening just a bit more. "Go home. Be with your kids. Be Jerry for a couple days, not Sergeant Duncan. That's an order."

He smiled tiredly, the warmth of her words breaking through his guarded posture. "Roger that."

She nodded once, then turned to leave, calling over her shoulder as she went, "Goodnight, Duncan."

"Night, Sergeant Major."

Once her footsteps disappeared around the corner, Jerry sagged into his chair, shoulders sinking as he turned his attention back to the screen with a resigned exhale.

Just five more minutes.

Jerry forced his eyes back to the screen, cursor blinking impatiently at the end of a half-typed sentence. He shook his head slightly, attempting to push through the fog of distraction Vega had left behind. His fingers hovered, ready to type.

But they refused to move.

He rubbed his face roughly, frustration bubbling up in a sigh.

His eyes wandered briefly across the desk before lifting a framed photo tucked among scattered files. The image was candid. Maggie sitting on the grass with Marty nestled in her lap, Emmett mid-laugh as he tackled them from behind, sunlight filtering through leaves, everyone caught in a moment of unguarded joy. The photo felt alive, warm, completely disconnected from the sterile fluorescent lights currently buzzing overhead.

Jerry's throat tightened, his pulse slowing.

It's not a combat op. Nobody's going to die if this waits till Monday.

Vega's voice echoed quietly in his thoughts, sharp in its gentle honesty.

He stared at the photo, seeing Marty's scrunched eyes, Emmett's mess of hair, Maggie's real, unposed smile.

The breath he let out was more than tired.

How had he let himself drift this far off-course?

Jerry lowered the photo carefully, his eyes lingering just long enough to notice the corner of something colorful peeking from beneath a thick stack of documents. He reached over, shifting the files aside and uncovering the Mingle at Sea flyer, slightly wrinkled, edges worn from Mac's repeated attempts.

He stared at it, reading the bold, cheerful letters and the inviting promise: Escape. Relax. Rediscover.

It had sounded absurd before. Now, in the quiet aftermath of Vega's blunt reminder, it didn't feel entirely impossible.

He glanced toward the doorway again, then back to the flyer. Slowly, hesitantly, he opened a fresh tab on his browser, fingers moving almost independently of thought as he typed out the web address printed neatly at the bottom of the flyer.

As the site loaded, Jerry leaned back in his chair, his tense shoulders finally dropping, eyes softening as images of sunlit decks, gentle waves, and smiling faces filled his screen.

The vibrant homepage greeted him with scenes that felt almost surreal after months of military gray and domestic beige. The first thing Jerry noticed was a stunning aerial shot of the Elysian Serenade, its sleek white hull cutting gracefully through the turquoise sea. His eyes lingered on the expansive deck, dotted with comfortable lounge chairs, colorful umbrellas, and smiling passengers sipping bright tropical drinks. He almost felt the gentle sway of the ship beneath his own tired feet.

The bold, welcoming headline beneath promised clearly:

"Mingle at Sea: Escape. Relax. Rediscover yourself."

Jerry scrolled slowly, absorbing each detail with cautious optimism. He skimmed past vibrant pictures showing luxurious staterooms with their spacious interiors, elegant nautical décor, and plush beds that looked impossibly inviting. He allowed himself to pause on the balcony rooms, imagining waking up to nothing but ocean, sunshine, and tranquility.

He shifted in his chair, hesitating only briefly before clicking the Onboard Experiences tab. His curiosity deepened as he scrolled past enticing images of gourmet restaurants where couples laughed warmly over candlelit dinners at Taste of Temptation and passengers gathered around sleek bars at The Social Butterfly Lounge, immersed in lively conversation. Another image captured the open-air dance floor, illuminated softly by strings of golden lights against a star-speckled sky. The whole scene looked impossibly carefree, and he felt the subtle pull of envy.

Further down, a vivid photograph showed the pool deck filled with passengers soaking up the sun. Next to it, another tagline confidently declared:

"Leave stress at the dock, and step into the adventure you deserve."

The message resonated deeply, drawing Jerry into an unfamiliar yet tempting idea of relaxation. For months, he'd pushed himself without pause, operating constantly at maximum capacity: deployed overseas for a year and a half, then straight back into full-time parenting, endless appointments, and a relentless workload. For nearly two years, since before he'd even left for Iraq, he hadn't truly stopped for himself. Every ounce of energy had gone into work or parenting, every waking moment focused outward, never inward.

The truth settled like a quiet revelation. He was running dangerously close to empty.

His thoughts drifted toward Marty and Emmett. They deserved more than a father whose patience was thinning and whose energy was perpetually depleted. They deserved the Jerry who could genuinely smile with them, laugh, and be fully present rather than the shadow he'd become over the last several months.

He glanced back at the website again, imagining, perhaps selfishly, what it might feel like to temporarily let go. What if, for once, he allowed himself permission to recharge? Not only would it benefit him, but more importantly, it would ultimately serve the boys as well.

Still cautious, but feeling lighter, Jerry decided he'd talk it over with Mac later that evening. Knowing Mac, he'd likely already started drafting a victory speech. Jerry shook his head slightly at the thought, smiling quietly. Before he could officially say yes, though, he needed to confirm that Maggie could watch the boys for the entire week. A quick call from the car would put that piece of the puzzle into place.

Decision now firm enough to give him some peace, he closed the browser tab, the vibrant images fading away. He powered down his computer, the office suddenly darker and quieter around him. He tucked the photo of Maggie and the boys carefully into his bag, gathered his belongings, and stood up, stretching tired muscles.

For once, he didn't feel like he was running from work, escaping only to face another overwhelming day tomorrow. Instead, Jerry felt strangely hopeful, as if stepping out that door tonight might lead him toward something brighter. Toward rest. Toward renewal.

This wasn't retreat. It was permission.

Four

The morning started like all the others. At least, that's what Jerry's body seemed to think.

His hand slapped the alarm before his eyes ever opened. That familiar buzzing sound, droning low and persistent, was silenced with the kind of mechanical precision that came from years of conditioning. He didn't even think about it. Just moved. Sit up. Rub eyes. Feet on the floor.

Everything was slow. Heavy. His legs protested the shift from bed to standing, and his shoulders rolled with the effort of staying upright. A sigh escaped him as he shuffled forward, his socked foot bumping the corner of the bed.

"Dammit," he muttered, fingers curling hard against the table, knuckles pale with tension.

The pain lingered longer than it should have. Sharp. Unexpected. The edge was wrong ... too square, too close. That wasn't where the bed was supposed to be.

He blinked against the dim light, trying to orient himself. The air smelled too clean. The sheets had been too white. The hum of the AC too loud. His usual kitchen light wasn't glowing faintly down the hall. And the faint swish of traffic outside didn't belong in his neighborhood.

He rubbed at his eyes, finally glancing at the unfamiliar furniture and generic framed artwork on the wall. A hotel.

Miami.

Right.

The fog didn't lift instantly. It never did. But something stirred within him, an itch of awareness, like a signal slowly climbing out of static. The clock glowed on the nightstand, but the numbers didn't register. Not yet.

He moved to the little countertop nook in the corner, fumbling for the hotel coffee kit. A packet tore open with a reluctant crinkle, the coffee grounds spilling too fast into the filter basket. He added water, hit brew, waited.

The coffee smelled like burnt cardboard and something stale. He poured anyway.

The first sip nearly turned his mouth inside out. Too bitter. Too hot. Too bland. And somehow, still the only thing holding him together.

He took another, made a face, and leaned against the counter, head tipped forward like gravity was suddenly stronger than it had been yesterday.

Behind him, something stirred.

The rhythm of Mac's snoring shifted. Less chainsaw, more congested bear. A half-muffled groan signaled awareness, though no commitment to full consciousness followed.

Jerry didn't turn. He didn't need to. He knew the routine: one arm over the eyes, foot peeking out from under the blanket like a thermometer for room temperature.

Jerry stared into his coffee like it might eventually taste better if he stared long enough.

He shuffled to the window, parting the curtains with two fingers. Morning light stabbed through the gap. He blinked, squinting. The street below was already busy, sunlight bouncing off windshields, glass buildings gleaming in the distance.

This wasn't his neighborhood.

Not Killeen. Not Fort Cavazos. Not beige, not quiet, not routine.

And there it was. Beyond the skyline, just where the water opened up wide and blue, the ship waited.

The Elysian Serenade.

Its white hull was impossibly clean, catching the light like a pearl, the decks alive with the tiniest hints of motion, even from this far away. Rows of balconies. Towering stacks. That distant hum of promise.

Jerry blinked again.

This wasn't just another Sunday.

Everything crashed into his awareness at once, his brain finally catching up to the day. The ache in his back, the awful coffee, the shift in environment. It was all buildup to this.

Today was embarkation day.

Behind him, a low groan broke the quiet.

"If you're gonna stand there breathing like a haunted man," Mac muttered from the bed, voice raspy with sleep, "at least bring me one of those burnt water specials."

Jerry reached for the second cup from the tray and walked it over, setting it gently on the nightstand beside Mac's phone. "One day," he said, voice still gravel-thick, "you're gonna wake up and realize how spoiled you are."

Mac cracked open one eye. "One day, you're gonna realize this is the best honeymoon you never asked for."

Jerry took another sip, face twisting slightly. "If this is your idea of a honeymoon, I'm filing for divorce before breakfast."

Mac stretched and grinned, blanket slipping halfway off his chest. "Fine. But I'm keeping the coffee maker in the settlement."

Jerry let out a quiet snort, turning back toward the window.

The ship was still there, waiting.

A glossy, impossible thing rising against the pale morning sky. It felt like something out of a brochure, not real life. But it was real. Docked, prepped, ready for passengers. Ready for *them*.

Jerry sipped his coffee again, mostly out of spite, and glanced down at his phone charging on the nightstand. That familiar, persistent feeling pulled at him again, the one he couldn't seem to shake. He reached for it without thinking.

"I need to call my mom," he muttered, already unplugging it.

Mac groaned and flopped onto his side. "Dude. We haven't even been gone twenty-four hours."

"I just want to check in."

"She's got everything under control, Jerry. She's *Maggie Duncan*. You think that woman can't handle a couple of wild boys and a daily med schedule? She ran your entire family during four deployments and a PCS move with a broken wrist."

Jerry tapped the phone screen, ignoring him. "Still. I need to hear it."

Mac let his head thump back against the pillow with a dramatic sigh. "At least put it on speaker so I can hear her call you out for being neurotic."

Jerry smirked, pressing the call button. The line rang once, twice …

"Good morning, sweetheart," came Maggie's voice, bright and smooth like fresh coffee and folded laundry. "Or should I say *bon voyage*?"

Jerry's shoulders softened at the sound. "Hey, Mom."

"You're on vacation. Why are you calling me?"

"I just wanted to check on things. The boys. Did Emmett remember his reading folder? Marty get his morning meds okay?"

"Jerry," Maggie said gently, the familiar warmth in her voice softening the edges of his nerves. "Everything's fine. We've got the folder, we've got the meds, and Emmett's already declared that I make better waffles than you."

Jerry winced. "Ouch."

"But I reminded him I don't have your secret weapon … peanut butter on everything. So your legacy lives on."

He let out a quiet laugh but didn't quite relax. "Okay. Good."

There was a pause on the line, just long enough for her to hear the hesitation he hadn't voiced yet.

"Talk to me, sweetheart," she prompted.

Jerry exhaled slowly. "It just feels weird. I've left them before, but that was for duty. Deployments, training, assignments. I didn't have a choice. This? This feels ... selfish."

"Taking care of yourself isn't selfish," Maggie replied, her voice soft but firm. "You're not running away from them. You're recharging so you can come back stronger. That's what good parents do."

"I still feel like I should be there," he admitted, eyes drifting toward the cruise flyer folded neatly on the table. "Helping with bedtime routines, cutting sandwiches into shapes, breaking up Emmett's dinosaur battles."

"And that's exactly why I know you're a good dad," she said. "Because even while you're trying to take a breath, your heart's still back home with them."

Behind him, Mac gave a dramatic silent *awww* and placed his hand over his heart.

Jerry waved him off without turning. "They just ... they've been through a lot. I don't want them to think I'm choosing to leave them."

"They won't," Maggie said gently. "You've shown them every single day how much you love them. A week of sunshine and sleep isn't going to undo that. If anything, it's going to bring more of *you* back to them."

Jerry rubbed the back of his neck, finally starting to feel some of the tension release. "Yeah. You're probably right."

"I *am* right," she said, playful and steady all at once. "And you better enjoy yourself, Jerry. That's an order."

He smiled. "Roger that."

"Love you, sweetheart."

"Love you too, Mom."

Jerry set his phone down on the nightstand, exhaling slowly. The call had helped. The guilt wasn't gone, but at least it had been properly mothered into submission.

Behind him, Mac stretched like a cat, arms overhead, joints popping in protest. "So," he said through a yawn, "does this mean I don't have to give you a motivational speech over continental breakfast, or are we still pretending you're on the fence?"

Jerry grabbed a clean T-shirt from the top of his open suitcase. "Don't tempt me. I'm still debating whether or not to crawl back under the covers and let you go without me."

Mac raised a single eyebrow. "You really think I'd let you back out now? I've got two words for you: non-refundable."

Jerry smirked and shook his head, tugging the shirt over his head. "You're relentless."

"That's why you love me," Mac said, rolling out of bed and stretching again with dramatic flair. "Now, chop chop, Duncan. We've got a ship to catch, drinks to drink, and at least one embarrassing activity to sign up for."

Jerry shot him a sidelong look. "I'm not doing karaoke."

"You *will* once you're three margaritas deep and surrounded by women who think you're broody and mysterious."

Jerry opened his mouth to argue but stopped himself. "... You're disgusting."

Mac winked. "I'm strategic."

They moved easily around the room now, that lazy hotel morning haze giving way to something brighter. Jerry shaved while Mac sorted through the shared suitcase of miscellaneous cruise-approved supplies: sunscreen, motion sickness pills, and a laminated cruise planner that Mac had color-coded like a field op.

"Found it," Mac announced, holding something up dramatically.

Jerry leaned out of the bathroom, towel around his neck. "Found what?"

"Your signed permission slip," Mac said, holding up the cruise flyer from weeks ago, now folded into quarters and scribbled across the top in Maggie's unmistakable handwriting: *Let him have some damn fun. Love, Mom.*

Jerry laughed. "She actually wrote that?"

"Oh yeah," Mac said proudly. "I asked her to. You didn't think I'd show up without documentation, did you?"

Jerry took it from him, eyes scanning the handwriting. "You're ridiculous."

"And yet, here you are," Mac replied, brushing lint off his shirt. "Now get your shoes on, Dad. We're going on vacation."

Jerry grabbed his sneakers, pulse quickening slightly. Not with anxiety this time, but something closer to excitement.

It was happening.

No turning back now.

The Florida heat hit them the second the hotel lobby doors slid open. Jerry blinked against the brightness, adjusting the strap of his duffel over his shoulder as he stepped outside.

He'd taken only a few instinctive steps toward the row of shuttles lined up near the curb when a hand gently tugged his arm in the opposite direction.

"Wrong way, Romeo," Mac said, steering him smoothly away from the hotel transport. "That's not your carriage."

Jerry blinked. Then stopped dead in his tracks.

"Mac," he said slowly, squinting at the polished black stretch vehicle parked with theatrical poise near the front of the hotel. "What the fuck is that?"

Mac grinned like a man who'd just revealed a magician's trick. "Our ride."

"That is a limo."

"Gold star, Sergeant. Want to try naming colors next?"

Jerry turned toward him, arms slack at his sides. "We agreed on a shuttle. Like, with other people."

"Yeah, and you also said you weren't doing karaoke," Mac replied, casually strolling toward the gleaming vehicle. "I had to make a few executive decisions."

The driver in a crisp suit stepped forward and opened the rear door with a practiced flourish.

Jerry just stared. "You seriously booked us a limo?"

Mac shrugged, not even remotely sheepish. "We're starting this trip with style, Duncan. Plus, if you think I was letting you show up to the *Elysian Serenade* in a sweaty van, you don't know me at all."

Jerry groaned as he climbed in after him. "You're lucky this isn't coming out of my bank account."

Inside, the limo was absurdly comfortable: cool air, leather seats, and tinted windows that dulled the morning glare. In the center console, a small bottle of champagne sat chilling in a silver ice bucket next to two flutes already gleaming in their holders.

Mac reached over without hesitation, popping the cork with a smooth twist and a muffled *pop*. He poured two glasses, handing one over with all the ceremony of a butler at a five-star resort.

Jerry took it reluctantly. "Isn't it a little early to start drinking?"

Mac lifted his glass with a grin. "Not when you're on vacation, my friend."

Jerry smirked and clinked his glass against Mac's. "This is going to be the most dramatic boys' trip ever, isn't it?"

"Only if you cry during karaoke."

They both took a sip of the light, bubbly cocktail that was just sharp enough to jolt Jerry's taste buds into awareness. He leaned back into the seat, letting the cool air and quiet luxury wash over him.

The drive through Miami began in easy silence, both men watching the city pass by in shades of coral and sun-bleached beige. The radio hummed in the background with some breezy Latin jazz, punctuated by the occasional cheerful voice of a DJ announcing the weather or a weekend event.

But then the limo crested the bridge and everything changed.

The Port of Miami stretched out before them like a high-end show-room, cruise ships docked side by side like glossy exhibits of modern marvels. Massive, towering floating skyscrapers of steel and glass, each one boasting its own version of excess and spectacle.

But only one ship *demanded* their attention without even trying.

There waited the *Elysian Serenade*, just off-center from the chaos, set apart as if she knew she was the one worth watching.

Jerry went still.

She wasn't the biggest ship in port. Not even close. But she didn't need to be.

Everything about her was deliberate and polished, tailored to perfection, utterly elite. Her hull shimmered a pristine pearl-white, catching the sun like a perfectly waxed sports car under showroom lights. Traces of rose-gold and coral traced her frame like luxury detailing, subtle enough to whisper class but bold enough to draw the eye. She didn't just float. She stalked the harbor like a panther in heels, her understated confidence carried in every line of a silhouette designed to make you stare.

Atop it all, like the final flourish to a designer ensemble, rose a vibrant red smokestack. Bold, striking, unapologetically vivid against the soft curves and shimmering finish of the ship's body. It sat like a perfectly curated accessory, one chosen for signature impact rather than mere utility. The kind of detail that made you remember her long after you'd looked away. Not gaudy or loud, just *right*. A splash of confidence that completed the look without stealing the spotlight.

She was elegance engineered, luxury in motion.

And she knew it.

Jerry leaned closer to the glass, eyebrows raised. "That's our ship?"

Mac smirked like he'd been waiting for this exact reaction. "That's her."

The *Elysian Serenade* looked like she belonged in a Bond movie. Not chasing action, but calmly sipping champagne while everyone else tried to catch up. Every deck swept back in clean layers, her windows tinted just enough to intrigue. She looked fast. Purpose-built. Almost *flirtatious* in her curves.

"Tell me she doesn't look like a damn concept yacht," Mac exclaimed. "Like if Aston Martin made cruise ships. Sleek, sexy, and probably smarter than both of us."

As if on cue, Mac reached forward and hit the sunroof button.

Jerry immediately turned. "Oh no. Mac, don't ..."

But Mac was already rising through the sunroof, champagne in one hand, the other thrown dramatically wide as the breeze tousled his hair. "Ladies and gentlemen," he announced to absolutely no one but the seagulls, "we have ARRIVED!"

Jerry groaned and slid lower in his seat. "I swear, I don't know this man."

Mac looked down through the sunroof. "Come on, get up here! What kind of co-star are you?"

Reluctantly, Jerry climbed up beside him, bracing against the roof as the ship came into full, commanding view. The breeze lifted his hair. The sea sparkled beyond the docks. It was like they'd stepped out of real life and into some kind of dream.

Mac leaned in with a smug grin. "Vacation mode: officially activated."

Jerry sipped the last of his champagne, a half-smile finally curling across his lips.

"Let's do this."

Five

O nce everything was checked and cleared, they were free to board.

Each step up the ramp felt like shedding an old version of himself. Jerry moved slowly, carried forward by disbelief and thrill, while Mac practically glided beside him, like he'd been waiting forever to arrive here.

Then they stepped inside.

Jerry froze.

Sure, he'd cruised before, but this? This was something out of fantasy. The Elysian Atrium didn't just welcome you. It enveloped you. His breath caught as his eyes followed the arching grandeur.

Marble staircases, sweeping like tides, reached up toward skylights that spilled golden light over everything. The chandelier sparkled midair, refracting color like a constellation of falling stars.

The scent of salt and blossoms lingered in the air, while palms waved softly, as if greeting him. Plush seating in ocean hues and sun-kissed rose lined the space, promising rest and wonder.

The breath Jerry pulled in felt thick with wonder, his heart pounding hard enough to echo in his ears. Every note of the piano, every soft chuckle or warm voice blended into a soundtrack of luxury he hadn't expected to feel so deeply.

Mac, meanwhile, was already in his element. He smiled with easy charm, nodding at strangers like old friends, fitting into the scene with practiced grace. Jerry couldn't help but watch, struck by how effortlessly his friend adapted.

Jerry felt the opposite, rigid, small. His fingers clutched his bag as if it might anchor him. The setting was beautiful, intoxicating, though he didn't quite know how to exist inside it. It felt borrowed.

Mac's voice broke through the haze. "Duncan, that brain of yours short-circuiting?" he asked with a wink.

Jerry laughed under his breath. "This is ... a lot to take in."

Mac's hand landed on his shoulder, solid and grounding. "Good. That means it's working."

And maybe it was. As Jerry took another breath, something began to shift. He didn't belong here, not yet anyway, but he was still willing to try.

Jerry hitched his bag higher, lagging a few steps behind Mac as they moved deeper into the glittering heart of the atrium. Light still scattered across surfaces, marble, velvet, glass, but the awe had started to twist into something heavier.

He wasn't in danger, he knew that.

But his body told a different story. Palm leaves rustled somewhere. A violin played a drifting melody. Laughter burst behind him. It wasn't loud, but it layered oddly. Each sound stacked in the wrong direction until it felt like pressure instead of ambiance.

Mac kept walking, tossing a flirtatious quip over his shoulder. Already in his element.

Jerry slowed, then stopped.

The crowd moved past him like a tide. Someone bumped into him and offered a distracted apology. The scent of a sweet drink mixed with perfume and ocean air. The marble under his feet looked too glossy, too sharp. His eyes tried to land on something, anything solid, but the whole room was in motion.

His grip tightened. *Breathe, just breathe.*

"Yo, Duncan. Did you see ..." Mac's voice drifted back.

A pause. "Jerry?"

No answer.

Mac turned back, took one look, and dropped the smile.

"Hey," he said, stepping in close. "You with me?"

Jerry blinked. His gaze slid sideways. Something had shifted.

Tucked behind the elegant curve of the staircase stood a woman with ember-red hair, vivid against the golden haze. She didn't move, didn't react. Just watched, steady as stone.

Their eyes met for a heartbeat.

That was all it took.

The storm inside him didn't vanish, but it slowed. Her gaze was grounding in its silent strength and stillness. Then she turned away.

Jerry exhaled, tension unspooling just enough to matter.

Mac raised a brow. "You good?"

Jerry nodded, his grip loosening. "Yeah. Just needed to hit the reset button."

Mac gave him a look, then flicked his fingers against Jerry's arm. "Cool. Bar's this way. I'm thinking frozen, fruity, and something you'll regret by midnight."

Jerry grinned. "That transparent?"

"Oh, please. I knew you when your idea of multitasking was drinking coffee while duct-taping a diaper bag to your backpack. You can't hide anything from me."

Jerry laughed quietly, falling into step beside Mac as the tension in his shoulders slowly unwound.

Mac reached into his back pocket like a magician mid-trick. "Navigation tool acquired."

He snapped open the map. "Let's chart a course to all points alcohol."

He scanned with mock seriousness.

"Deck Five. Bubbly Bar. Champagne, cocktails, and the vague sense someone named Vivienne frequents it."

Jerry gave him a look. "You're ridiculous."

"Deck Six. Topaz Lounge. Jazzy. Shady. Probably where the love triangles happen. Captain's Haven. Karaoke bar. You *will* sing."

Jerry groaned. "Over my dead lungs."

Mac grinned. "We'll see. Deck Seven: El Corazón. Latin cocktails. Rum. Regret. Probably a conga line."

Jerry snorted. "That sounds ... like a warning label."

"Exactly," Mac said, heading off toward the corridor.

Jerry started to follow but hesitated.

"Think I'll hit the room for a bit," he said.

Mac stopped, looked back. "You good?"

Jerry nodded. "Yeah. Just need to take five. Let it all settle."

Mac took it in, didn't push. "Fair enough. Catch up soon."

Jerry smiled. "Thanks."

He stepped into the elevator, the soft whoosh of the doors sealing him into a moment of peace. It was the first time since boarding that he wasn't surrounded by sound. He exhaled deeply, shoulders dropping.

As the elevator climbed, he adjusted his bag and tried to name the feeling. Not anxiety. Not exactly. But close. Everything had hit too fast. Flashes of movement, music, lights, voices. All of it incredible. All of it too much.

When the doors slid open, he stepped into a corridor bathed in soft light. Carpet muffled his steps. The quiet here felt different, more still than empty. Safe.

He reached the stateroom and slid his card. *Click.*

The door opened into peace. A compact, curated space. White linens. Coral tones. A little balcony filtering in soft light.

Jerry set down his bag.

Stood still.

No rush. No noise.

Just room to breathe.

This was the recalibration he needed, the quiet between the beats.

He crossed the room, sliding the balcony door open and stepping into a wash of golden air. The breeze wrapped around him with warmth, salt, and sunlight.

Far below, the port carried on: carts moving, voices rising, people weaving around each other in pre-departure chaos. But from up here, it was all soft edges and background hum.

Jerry leaned into the railing, resting his arms. Finally still.

You're here now, he reminded himself. *Let it happen.*

He pulled his phone from his pocket, holding it loose in one hand.

The lock screen lit up and showed a picture of Marty and Emmett. Caught in mid-laugh, sun in their hair, chaos in their smiles.

He stared. Just for a second too long.

Only a few hours had passed, but already the habit kicked in. That itch to check. To confirm. Even though he knew there was nothing to worry about.

It was early back home. The boys were probably watching cartoons. Maggie, as always, had everything under control.

Still, the guilt hummed with that quiet, familiar frequency.

He slid the phone into his pocket. Not ready to put it away completely.

Not gone yet, but not gripping it either. Small wins.

From behind him, the sound of the cabin door opening was followed by a familiar voice:

"You decent? Or am I about to traumatize myself?"

Jerry didn't turn. "I'm wearing more than you usually do around the house."

Mac chuckled and stepped out onto the balcony beside him, carrying two frozen drinks that were garnished with tiny umbrellas and far too much confidence.

"Then obviously," Mac said, pushing through the door, "this situation calls for frozen reinforcements."

He held out two drinks, umbrellas fluttering. "You're stuck with the mango-strawberry unless you want to tempt fate with the radioactive green one. Tastes like Coppertone and sugar crashes."

Jerry took the mango and gave it a suspicious sniff. "What the fuck is this? You trying to kill me with a smoothie?"

"Mango Bliss Swirl," Mac said. "Bliss being a loose term. Mostly sugar, a touch of alcohol, and probably something fluorescent."

Jerry lifted the sad-looking fruit slice off the rim. "Is this a peace offering or a subtle hit job?"

"For disappearing without a trace," Mac said. "And for overcomplicating what's supposed to be a damn vacation."

Jerry smirked. "Didn't know I was under surveillance."

Mac raised his glass. "Always. Now toast to taking a fucking breath."

Jerry clinked glasses with a reluctant smirk. "To frozen mistakes and better decisions."

They drank.

Jerry winced. "Jesus, that's sweet."

"Like your personality when you're not spiraling," Mac grinned. "Keep drinking. It grows on you. Or it kills your taste buds. Either way, it works."

Jerry took another sip, shaking his head. The drink was terrible in the best way. Cold, loud, unapologetic. It was hard to take anything too seriously while holding a slushy in a glass that looked like it belonged in a pool float.

"You know," Mac said, leaning his elbow on the balcony rail, "if I didn't know any better, I'd think this whole escape act was just a ploy to get first dibs on the drawer space."

Jerry chuckled, finally letting the tension slide off his shoulders. "Please. You packed like a high school sophomore on a field trip. I figured you'd just live out of your duffel the whole time."

"Wrong," Mac said proudly. "I'm evolving. There's a drawer-organizer system involved."

Jerry raised an eyebrow. "A what now?"

Mac ignored him. "Anyway, party's starting soon. Rumor has it there's dancing. Maybe even someone making balloon animals."

"I'm not dancing."

"Yet," Mac corrected. "Give it three drinks."

They stood in silence for a few more beats, the distant thrum of ship life just starting to build in the background. The breeze wrapped around them, warm and promising.

Then, Mac nudged Jerry's elbow. "C'mon. Let's go see what kind of bad decisions this boat has in store."

Jerry took one last sip, then pushed off the rail with a quiet nod. "Let's go."

Six

From the upper deck of the Elysian Serenade, Jerry watched the last sliver of Miami vanish into the glowing horizon. The city was nothing but a smudge now, its steel and glass fading into an amber haze. Above them, the sky flared in soft layers of peach and lavender, the kind of gradient no filter could improve.

Below, the ship's main pool deck throbbed with music and movement. The sail-away party had kicked into full swing, and a conga line twisted through the crowd like a cheerful sea serpent while the DJ called out instructions no one was actually following.

Jerry leaned against the railing, drink in hand, watching the scene unfold. Mac had shoved an unnaturally blue cocktail into his hand without warning or explanation. The thing glowed like radioactive antifreeze and tasted like melted snow cone and betrayal.

But still, he sipped. Because it was cold. Because he was here. Because it felt like something was beginning.

"You're smiling," Mac said beside him, nudging Jerry's ribs with a knowing elbow.

Jerry blinked. "What?"

"That," Mac said, gesturing broadly to Jerry's face. "Right there. That's a smile. I know it's been a while, so maybe it's unfamiliar."

Jerry fought it, but the smirk cracked wider. "It's not a smile. It's sunstroke."

"Oh, sure," Mac said with a nod. "The classic heat-induced facial twitch. Very rare. Very telling."

They stood together, shoulder to shoulder, gazing out over the party below. Someone launched a beach ball into the crowd. A guy in flamingo shorts caught it with his head, stumbled, then took a dramatic bow like he'd planned it all along.

Jerry exhaled. "It's chaos," he said. "But the good kind."

Mac grinned. "Told you. This isn't a mission. This is dessert. All-inclusive. No side quests. No villains. Just sun, salt, and strangers you might kiss."

Jerry took another sip of the syrupy drink. "Still feels weird being out here. Like ... untethered."

"Good," Mac said. "You were tied too tight for too long."

A long pause stretched between them, comfortable and unhurried. The sea wind rolled over the deck, lifting the edge of Jerry's shirt and carrying the thump of bass upward, like a heartbeat under glass.

Then, Mac checked his watch with a dramatic sigh. "Alright, enough reflection. Welcome mixer starts in ten, and I need time to find a woman who thinks I'm charming enough to buy me a drink."

Jerry snorted. "Smooth."

"I am smooth," Mac said, already turning toward the stairs. "Smooth as a fresh jar of peanut butter."

"You know all the drinks are free, right?"

"Yeah," Mac said over his shoulder, "but it's not about the price. It's about the principle."

Jerry shook his head, trailing Mac down the staircase toward the Topaz Lounge. As they stepped indoors, the vibrant energy of the sail-away party melted into something more refined. Cool air replaced the ocean breeze, plush carpet cushioned their steps, and the bass thump of music shifted into something smoother and jazz-tinged.

At the entrance to the lounge, a table draped in deep teal linen caught the light from golden sconces above. A polished acrylic sign beside it bore the signature wave-and-compass logo of *Mingle at Sea*, etched with the phrase: **Where solo journeys turn into shared memories**.

A hostess in a sleek navy dress greeted them with a practiced, cheerful smile. "Welcome aboard, gentlemen. Names?"

"MacIntyre and Duncan," Mac answered, already half-grinning.

She tapped briskly on her tablet and nodded. "Perfect. You're on our list. First, your official badge of honor."

From a small compartmentalized tray lined with colorful cords, she selected two matching bracelets: simple gold thread woven tight and clean, each one anchored by a polished silver helm charm. She set them on matching cardstock info cards, printed in soft sepia tones and cruise-blue accents.

Jerry picked his up, scanning the card.

This bracelet is more than just a token ... it's your key to the Mingle at Sea experience. It identifies you as one of our treasured Single Sailors, granting access to exclusive events, spaces, and surprises throughout your voyage. Chart your own course. Connect deeply. Make this journey yours.

"Wear them on your wrist at all times," the hostess instructed warmly, clearly having done this a dozen times already today but still making it feel personal. "They'll get you into mixers, cocktail tastings, workshops, you name it. Lose it and, well ... you'll have to sweet-talk Maude for a replacement. And she doesn't cave easily."

Jerry turned his over in his fingers. The helm charm was smooth and cool to the touch, gleaming faintly under the light. The gold cord shimmered subtly, the kind of sparkle that caught the eye without screaming for attention. He couldn't help but admire the quality. It was classier than he expected for what Mac had jokingly referred to as 'cruise camp.'

Mac slid his on without hesitation and flexed his wrist. "Come on, Duncan. It's not a blood oath. It's fancy adult friendship jewelry."

Jerry gave him a sideways look, smirk tugging at one corner of his mouth. "You say that like you don't still have your Cub Scout badges in a shadow box somewhere."

Mac gasped with faux offense. "That's called archival preservation, thank you very much."

Jerry snorted, but finally slid his bracelet on, the knot cinching neatly into place. It sat snug, the helm charm catching the light between movements. Simple, small, but undeniably significant. A quiet signal. A start.

Before Mac could retort, a cheerful voice called out behind them. "Scarlet! Glad you made it. Here's your bracelet, and have fun tonight."

Jerry turned at the name. His brain immediately short-circuited. There she was.

The woman from the atrium. Vivid red hair cascaded in fiery, tumbling curls, copper highlights catching the soft lights as they framed a face that shouldn't have belonged to real life. Hazel eyes flecked with gold, a confident half-smile, and a green wrap dress that swayed like it had its own soundtrack.

She looked like she owned the air around her.

She accepted the bracelet with an easy "thanks," then turned. She caught Jerry's stare head-on.

"You know," she said with a sly smile, "I thought I was being fashionably late. But I guess my timing's perfect."

Jerry's brain forgot how to brain.

"Oh. uh, yeah. You did. That. I mean, you're ... just in time. Or early. Not early. Definitely not too late."

He blinked. "Perfect timing. Is what I meant. That's ... what I was going to say."

Her smile widened, eyes lighting up with clear amusement. But it wasn't mocking. If anything, it softened, like she found his malfunction oddly endearing.

Mac didn't miss a beat. "MacIntyre. Just Mac. And this smooth talker here is Jerry Duncan, who usually has a vocabulary."

Scarlet laughed, rich and genuine. "Scarlet Bellari. But Scarlet's fine," she said, shaking Mac's hand before turning back to Jerry with an extra beat of eye contact.

He managed a shaky chuckle and tried again. "It's meet to nice you. Scarlet. You. I mean. Nice to meet *you*, Scarlet."

Scarlet tilted her head slightly and offered him a warm, amused smile. "It's nice to meet you too, Jerry." She slipped the bracelet onto her wrist with graceful ease, then gestured toward the lounge doors. "Shall we go in before you run out of sentence fragments?"

That earned a real laugh from Jerry, his cheeks warm but his smile finally settling. "Lead the way."

As they moved toward the entrance, Mac leaned in just enough to whisper, "Admit it ... you're glad you wore the good shirt."

Jerry just groaned. "Please stop talking."

Scarlet glanced back over her shoulder, clearly having caught the exchange. Her eyes sparkled with something between amusement and curiosity. "I think it's a great shirt, for the record."

Mac shot Jerry a smug look. "Told you."

Jerry gave a helpless shrug, his ears still slightly pink. He followed the two of them through the open double doors and into the Topaz Lounge.

The shift in ambiance was immediate.

Gone was the salty breeze and open sun of the upper deck. The Topaz Lounge wrapped around them like velvet. Deep navy walls were laced with golden inlay, casting warm reflections in the amber-toned lighting. Tiered crystal sconces sparkled along the perimeter, and the ceiling was inset with soft, glowing panels that gave the illusion of twilight above.

Plush armchairs in muted jewel tones formed intimate clusters around glass-topped cocktail tables that gleamed like polished obsidian. Fresh floral arrangements in coral and cream brightened the corners, while subtle piano jazz drifted from a stage at the far end. The air carried the faint scent of citrus and wood polish, layered with something sweeter that reminded him of vanilla.

Mac was already in motion, of course. Before Jerry could blink, he'd made his way to a group across the room, all wide smiles and open body language. He looked like he belonged there, like he'd been on this ship for weeks.

Scarlet watched him go, head tilted. "Your friend's a bit of a social butterfly, huh?"

Jerry snorted, still holding on to a bit of lingering awkwardness. "More like a party shark. Always moving. Always smiling. Usually circling the bar."

She laughed, her smile softening into something more relaxed. "Shall we circle the bar then?"

Jerry nodded, grateful for the lifeline. "Lead the way."

They slipped into two seats near the center of the crescent-shaped bar, the polished surface glowing subtly from the underlighting. Bartenders moved in practiced rhythm, the clink of ice and splash of spirits blending with the soft jazz floating from the stage across the lounge.

One approached with a towel over his shoulder and a bright, practiced smile.

Scarlet didn't hesitate. "I'll take a mojito, please. Extra lime. Real mint. None of that syrupy shortcut stuff."

The bartender gave her a nod of respect. "Fresh all the way. Coming right up."

Jerry glanced at the cocktail menu but barely scanned it. "Uh ... rum and Coke," he said, a touch sheepish. "Canned Coke's fine. Doesn't have to be fancy."

The bartender grinned. "Classic. You got it."

Jerry let out a low breath and leaned forward against the bar, his forearms resting on the polished surface. Scarlet swirled the ice in her drink once it arrived, the fresh mint leaves catching in the straw, her gold bracelet glinting in the light.

"Cami's probably going to find us in about ten seconds," she said with a knowing smile. "Just warning you. She's my best friend and unofficial cruise fairy godmother. Also the person who signed me up for this."

Jerry arched an eyebrow. "So, you got recruited, too?"

"Oh, full-on ambushed," Scarlet said. "Cami and one of our friends teamed up, insisted I needed a week of quote-unquote joyful debauchery." She took a long sip, the lime slice brushing her lips. "Still not sure what that means exactly."

Jerry laughed softly, taking a sip of his drink. It wasn't complex. It wasn't trendy. But it was cold, familiar, and hit the spot. He exhaled as the bubbles tickled the back of his throat. "Mac had his own intervention plan. Told me if I didn't get out of town soon, he was going to fake a medical emergency just to get me a leave form."

Scarlet tilted her glass toward him. "Sounds like our friends should never meet."

"Too late," Jerry said, glancing out toward the crowd. "They already have a ten-minute head start."

They raised their glasses.

"To pushy friends," Scarlet said.

Jerry smiled, the tension in his shoulders finally starting to slip away. "And slightly less pushy strangers."

They clinked and drank, and for the first time since boarding, Jerry felt like he might actually be where he needed to be.

Then, a voice chimed in from behind them.

"There you are, Scarlet. Hiding at the bar, huh?"

Scarlet turned just as a woman with a dazzling presence approached. She was striking. Tall, with radiant brown skin and shaved sides that framed long micro braids, each one gleaming like inky silk under the lounge lights. She wore wide-legged ivory trousers, a cropped halter top in bold coral, and oversized earrings shaped like abstract suns. Every step she took carried ease and confidence, like the room belonged to her and she was just letting the rest of them visit.

"Jerry," Scarlet said gesturing between them, "this is Cami Delgado, my co-conspirator. Cami, meet Jerry Duncan."

Cami looked him over, eyes sweeping slowly from his sneakers to his half-finished drink to the curve of his shoulders. Her lips curved into a smirk. "Well, damn. Who let this finely sculpted excuse for a man onto a singles cruise without a warning label?"

Jerry blinked, caught somewhere between flustered and flattered. "Uh ... hi?"

Cami laughed and extended a hand. "Relax, soldier. Your friend Mac told me to come over here and make you uncomfortable."

Jerry shot a glance across the room. Sure enough, Mac was leaning against the far wall, chatting up a group with a drink in one hand and a smug grin aimed squarely in their direction.

"Yeah, that checks out," Jerry muttered.

Scarlet sipped her mojito with obvious delight. "Told you this group was a full-contact sport."

Jerry raised his glass in surrender. "And here I thought I was easing into this cruise."

"Oh, honey, there's no easing. Just cannonballs," Cami responded feigning sympathy.

Before Jerry could come up with a clever response, the lights shifted across the lounge. A small platform near the center of the room brightened, and the low hum of conversation quieted almost instinctively.

A woman stepped up onto the stage. She was not flashy or loud, but commanded a presence that clicked the room into attention. She wasn't young, but she wasn't trying to be. Her long chestnut hair was streaked with silver and tied back with a colorful scarf. Her skin was sun-worn in the way that came from years outside, not just vacations. She wore a breezy sea-blue dress and a necklace made of little shells and silver charms that caught the light when she moved.

Jerry didn't know who she was, but the crowd clearly did.

She held her glass up with casual authority and gave a nod, like they were already all in on the same inside joke. "Good evening, sailors," she said. "Welcome aboard the Elysian Serenade."

Jerry sipped his drink, watching. She wasn't artificially polished. Instead, she was weathered in a way that felt earned. Comfortable in her own skin. She reminded him a little of the senior NCOs he'd served with, the ones who didn't yell to command respect. They didn't have to.

"You're here for different reasons," she went on. "Some of you came for something new. Some of you are looking for something you lost. And some of you ... don't even know why you're here yet. That's okay. This week isn't about having all the answers. It's about being open enough to ask the questions."

There were a few chuckles around the room, but mostly people just listened.

"You don't have to be charming. You don't have to be brave. You just have to show up."

She raised her glass a little higher, letting the pause land just long enough.

"To new beginnings."

The room echoed her. "To new beginnings."

Maude stepped down from the stage with the same easy grace she'd brought to it, her sea-blue dress swaying with each step. She didn't rush. Didn't linger. She moved through the lounge like someone who belonged there, not center stage but part of the deeper current that kept everything flowing.

Applause rippled gently, glasses clinked, and the mood of the room shifted. The energy didn't grow louder or rowdier, just more grounded. Like her words had nudged everyone an inch closer to where they were meant to be.

As she passed through the crowd, Maude glanced across the lounge and offered a small wave paired with a soft, knowing smile in their direction.

Jerry blinked, unsure. He glanced behind him, then back at her, brows pulling together slightly. Was that wave meant for Scarlet? For Cami? For him?

Beside him, Cami downed the last sip of her drink and stood with practiced flair. "Well, that's my cue."

"Your cue?" Jerry asked, still watching Maude.

Cami flashed a grin. "Captain Maude just called for her first mate." She hugged Scarlet and turned to Jerry, eyes gleaming. "Try not to fall in love while I'm gone. I'm still assessing your long-term viability."

And with that, she turned and strolled confidently across the lounge toward Maude. Their reunion was immediate, familiar and easy, like they'd done this dance before.

Jerry blinked after them. "Okay ... so she *really* knows the cruise director."

Scarlet smiled into her glass. "Maude's kind of a legend on these sailings. Cami's sailed with her before. I've known her a while too. She's not just the hostess ... she's like the emotional anchor of the whole thing."

Jerry gave a skeptical look. "An emotional anchor?"

"She's got a knack for saying exactly what you need to hear, exactly when you need to hear it." Scarlet shrugged, but there was something fond in her voice. "She's good people. A little ... nautical sage. But solid."

Jerry followed her gaze back to the center of the room, where Maude and Cami were already deep in conversation, smiles easy and bright.

Then, his eyes drifted further to focus on Mac. He was still holding court at the far end of the lounge, chatting animatedly, a drink in one hand and his other somehow already around someone's shoulders.

Jerry nodded toward him. "They're off to a strong start."

Scarlet grinned. "Fast-track to partner swaps by day three."

Jerry huffed. "Subtle foursome forming."

She lifted her glass again. "To conspirators and coincidental chemistry."

They clinked glasses. Jerry drank.

And something shifted.

Not drastically. Not loudly. But enough to make him pause.

Seven

It took Jerry a full minute to realize what was missing. No steel bedframe. No bunkmate snoring across the room. No call to muster echoing down concrete halls. Just the subtle rhythm of waves below and the unfamiliar quiet that came with peacetime.

The cruise ship. Right.

Sunlight streamed through a crack in the curtains, painting a warm stripe across the cabin wall. Jerry squinted at his watch and froze. 9:17 a.m. He couldn't remember the last time he'd slept past 5:00. Between Emmett's early rising, Marty's therapy schedule, and the Army's demands, sleep was a tactical operation: planned, executed, and usually insufficient.

The cabin's other bed was empty. A note sat on the desk in Mac's messy scrawl: *Gone for a run. Back soon.*

Jerry stretched, half expecting guilt to kick in. He should be up. Should be productive. Should be checking on a dozen different things. But there was nothing to check on. No schedule to maintain. His boys were safe with Maggie. His unit managed without him. For once, the only person demanding anything from him was himself.

And maybe, just maybe, he could give himself a goddamn break.

The notion seemed alien, uncomfortably close to self-care. But as Jerry rested in the gentle hush, allowing his muscles to surrender to the mattress, an unfamiliar sensation bloomed within him: peace. Not the fleeting quiet following accomplishment or the temporary lull of sleeping children, but something more essential. A loosening of a knot he'd forgotten was even there.

He thought about the woman from last night. Sharp, funny, with that flash of red hair and quick smile. The way conversation had flowed easily, without effort or pretense. How long had it been since he'd just talked to someone? Not about schedules or responsibilities or problems to solve, but just ... talked?

Jerry swung his legs over the side of the bed and padded to the small bathroom. The face in the mirror looked different somehow. Still tired around the eyes, but something had softened. One night of decent sleep didn't erase years of exhaustion, but it was a start.

After a quick shower, he dressed in casual jeans and a clean T-shirt, nothing with military insignia or superhero logos smeared with breakfast residue. Just a man on vacation.

Mac returned just as Jerry was lacing up his shoes, sweaty and grinning. "Well, look who decided to rejoin the land of the living! Sleep well, princess?"

Jerry rolled his eyes. "Yeah, yeah. You're one to talk. I thought we're supposed to be relaxing on this vacation? Since when is morning PT relaxing?"

"Since I met a cute redhead on the jogging track." Mac winked, grabbing a towel. "You've got competition, my friend. That girl, Scarlet, I saw you talking to her last night. She's here with her friend Cami, and I invited them both to brunch."

Jerry's head snapped up. "You what?"

"Relax, Staff Sergeant," Mac laughed. "She asked about you, you know. Wanted to know if you were still sleeping."

Jerry felt his neck warm. "She did?"

"Don't sound so surprised," Mac said, heading for the bathroom. "Some women actually like the strong, silent, emotionally constipated type."

"I am not ... what the fuck is emotionally constipated?" Jerry protested, but Mac just laughed, disappearing into the bathroom before Jerry could say more. The shower started, and Mac's voice carried over the sound of running water.

"We're meeting them in the main dining room in twenty," he called. "Try not to overthink it into oblivion before then!"

Jerry sat forward, elbows on his knees, a strange lightness dancing beneath the surface. The anticipation wasn't sharp, but felt like a current pulling him toward something just out of reach.

It had been years since he felt this kind of edge.

Scarlet had that effect.

He glanced at his phone, thumb hovering over Maggie's number. Too early to call, since the boys would still be getting ready for the day, but the urge to check in was strong. The longest he'd been away from them was during deployment, and even then, he'd had a mission, a purpose. This felt different. Indulgent.

"They're fine," he muttered to himself, putting the phone down. "Let them have their grandma time."

Mac emerged from the bathroom, toweling his hair. "So, you ready for your date?"

"It's not a date," Jerry said automatically. "It's brunch. With you and her friend there too."

"Yeah, because nothing says romance like me and Cami as chaperones." Mac grinned, pulling a fresh shirt over his head. "Come on, admit it. You like her."

Jerry busied himself with his wallet. "I met her yesterday."

"And?" Mac pressed. "You've talked to her for what, a couple hours total? And you've smiled more than you have in months."

Jerry shot him a warning look, but Mac just shrugged.

"Look, man, I'm not saying marry the girl. I'm saying it's nice to see you actually interested in something that isn't work or the boys for once." His voice softened. "You're allowed to have a life too, you know."

The words hit harder than Mac probably intended. Jerry swallowed against the sudden tightness in his throat. "I know that," he said, not entirely convincingly.

Mac clapped a hand on his shoulder. "Good. Then let's go eat some eggs and you can try not to stare at her the whole time."

"I hate you," Jerry muttered, but he was smiling as they headed out the door.

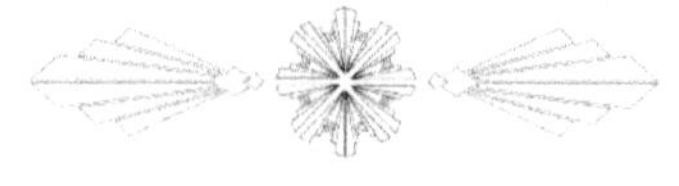

The main dining room was bustling with late-morning activity when they arrived. Sunlight poured through massive windows, illuminating tables draped in crisp white linen. The scent of coffee, bacon, and sweet pastries filled the air. Jerry and Mac secured a table by the windows overlooking the endless expanse of blue ocean.

"Not bad," Mac said, leaning back in his chair. "Better view than the DFAC, huh?"

Jerry had to agree. The stark contrast between the sterile military dining facility and this floating palace of luxury wasn't lost on him. "Definitely beats powdered eggs and mystery meat."

Mac was in the middle of a story about his last disastrous attempt at dating when Jerry spotted them. Scarlet and Cami were making their way through the dining room, Scarlet leading with purpose, Cami trailing with the careful steps of someone nursing a hangover. Jerry straightened reflexively, smoothing his shirt before catching himself.

"Hey there," Scarlet called as they approached. "Mind if we join you?"

Mac jumped up, pulling out chairs with exaggerated gallantry. "Of course, wouldn't want to enjoy this feast without some beautiful company."

Jerry met Scarlet's eyes and felt that same easy connection from the night before. She looked different in daylight, more relaxed, her hair pulled back, wearing a casual sundress rather than last night's cocktail attire. Somehow, he liked this version even better.

"Sleep well?" he asked as she took the seat next to him.

"Like a rock," she smiled. "First vacation in ages. You?"

"Best sleep I've had in years," he admitted. "Weird what happens when no one wakes you up at 5 a.m. demanding emergency drills."

Mac handed out mimosas like he was being judged on presentation, practically drowning Cami's glass for comedic effect.

The waiter slid in seamlessly, and everyone buried themselves in their menus.

Jerry stared at his, torn. He wasn't sure when the hunger crept in, but now it was loud and unhelpful.

"I think I'll go for the omelet with a side of pancakes," Scarlet announced, closing her menu. "Can't resist a bit of sweet and savory."

Jerry looked up. "Solid choice. I think I'll do the same thing. Can't beat the classics."

"How about you get the pancakes and I'll order the omelet, then we'll split them both to share?" she suggested. "I don't think I could eat all that food if I ordered it."

The casual offer caught him by surprise. It was such a simple thing, but something about the easy assumption of sharing, of collaboration rather than just parallel existence, struck Jerry deeply. This wasn't just mealtime coordination. This was different. This was a choice.

"I like that idea," he agreed, warmth spreading through his chest.

He caught Mac and Cami exchanging a look, and Mac's smirk told Jerry he'd never hear the end of this. But he couldn't bring himself to care.

Cami leaned over to Mac with theatrical formality. "What do you think, Mac? You get the steak and eggs while I get the French toast, and we, too, can split?"

Mac's eyes widened with mock horror, clutching his menu protectively to his chest. "And deny myself half my breakfast? Not a chance!" He grinned, patting his stomach. "I was already planning to order both of those for myself alone. I worked up quite an appetite with my morning workout today. But you can order whatever your heart desires, beautiful."

Cami rolled her eyes good-naturedly. "And they say chivalry is dead."

"Chivalry says nothing about sharing perfectly good steak," Mac countered with a wink.

As they waited for their food, the conversation flowed easily. Jerry couldn't remember the last time he'd just ... talked. Not about schedules or responsibilities, but about nothing important. Favorite foods. Worst vacation disasters. The ridiculous names of the ship's specialty cocktails.

Their food arrived, and with a simple, natural gesture, Jerry cut his stack of pancakes in half and slid them onto Scarlet's plate while she did the same with her omelet. Something about the exchange felt meaningful, like a small promise.

"So, any plans for the rest of the day?" Mac asked, draining his mimosa.

Scarlet shrugged, a mischievous glint in her eye. "Well, I heard there's a roundtable event happening this afternoon. Thought I might give it a try."

"Roundtable?" Jerry asked, trying to sound casual.

"It's not exactly speed dating," Cami explained, reaching for the carafe to refill her glass. "More like a casual way to meet people on the ship. You rotate every few minutes and chat with different folks."

"You should come too," Scarlet said, her eyes meeting Jerry's directly. "Both of you. Could be fun."

Jerry hesitated. Rotating through small talk with strangers wasn't exactly his idea of a good time. But Scarlet would be there ...

"Sure," he heard himself say. "Why not?"

Mac shot him a knowing look that Jerry studiously ignored.

The meal stretched lazily, champagne fizz giving way to caffeine as the energy softened.

Jerry felt himself settle, laughter slipping out more easily than he'd expected.

Time had slipped away without him noticing, and he didn't realize how long they'd been there until he glanced at his watch.

"We should probably head to that roundtable event if we're going," Mac said, finally pushing back from the table. "It starts in twenty minutes."

The event was set up in the Topaz Lounge, with its jewel-toned velvet seating and shimmering gold fixtures transformed into organized circles of chairs. Jerry noticed the Mingle at Sea banner hanging near the entrance, marking this as an exclusive event for their singles group.

An enthusiastic staff member named Mary explained the concept: "Today's speed meeting is all about connections, not just romantic ones, but friendships too. You'll have five minutes with each person before rotating."

Jerry drew a ticket placing him in the inner circle. Scarlet and Cami both ended up in the outer ring, seated next to each other. Mac was somewhere across the circle, already charming a blonde in a sundress.

As the rotations began, Jerry did his best to engage with each new person across from him. There was Harold, a retired professor with vivid travel stories. Then, Eliza, a pediatric nurse with a passion for photography. Ryan, a software developer who spent most of their five minutes explaining cryptocurrency.

As faces came and went, Jerry's gaze kept drifting across the room, landing on Scarlet.

She looked effortlessly magnetic, her laugh carrying even above the low hum of the crowd.

Every time he spotted her, something loosened inside him, a feeling that was pleasant and unsettling all at once.

Round four brought him to Stacy, who smiled wide and touched his arm with the casual confidence of someone used to getting what she wanted.

"So you're Army?" she asked, looking impressed. "My brother's a Marine. Staff Sergeant, stationed at Pendleton."

Jerry nodded, a flicker of genuine interest. "How long has he been in?"

"Eight years now," she said proudly. "Two deployments to Afghanistan. Our mom worries constantly, but he loves it."

"Marines are a different breed," Jerry said with a hint of the good-natured inter-service rivalry. "We Army guys actually like to have functioning knees past thirty."

Stacy laughed, louder than the joke deserved. "You military guys crack me up. My brother says the same kinds of things about you Army boys."

Jerry smiled politely, his gaze drifting past her shoulder to where Scarlet sat. For just a moment, their eyes met across the room. She quickly looked away, returning her attention to the man across from her. Had she been watching him?

Mary announced another rotation, and Jerry moved to the next seat. Two rotations later, he realized, with disappointment, that the event would end without him ever sitting across from Scarlet.

As Mary thanked everyone for participating, she made an announcement, "Don't forget about this afternoon's Battle of the Sexes event! It's a fun, fast-paced showdown of wits, skills, and maybe a little bit of sabotage. Ladies, you're riding a hot streak with thirty-nine straight sailings. The men are desperate to stop you from making it an even forty. No sign-ups needed, just show up and bring your A-game!"

Jerry stood, stretching. He had just decided to make his way over to Scarlet when Stacy appeared at his elbow.

"That was fun," she said brightly. "Are you going to the game show thing later? I'm definitely going to be there." She gave his arm another light touch. "Better watch out though, we ladies are going to crush you guys."

"We'll see about that," Jerry said with a polite smile, still watching as Scarlet and Cami headed for the exit, deep in conversation.

"See you there," Stacy said with a wink before sauntering away.

Jerry nodded vaguely, excusing himself as politely as possible. Outside in the corridor, Scarlet and Cami were already gone. He felt a twinge of disappointment, followed immediately by confusion at his own reaction. What was he doing? He barely knew this woman. A day and a half ago she hadn't existed in his life.

And yet he couldn't deny the pull he felt toward her, the easy comfort of their interactions that was so different from his usual guarded existence.

"Well, well, well," Mac appeared at his side, grinning. "Look at Bachelor Duncan, working the room! The brunette with the wandering hands, that blonde from the second rotation who couldn't stop giggling, and I'm pretty sure even the elderly gentleman's wife was checking you out."

Jerry rolled his eyes. "Shut up."

"Seriously though," Mac continued, waggling his eyebrows, "suddenly Mr. I-just-need-sleep has options. Who would've thought?" He elbowed Jerry playfully. "But I noticed a certain redhead kept looking your way. And you couldn't keep your eyes off her either."

Jerry didn't answer, but the heat in his face must have been answer enough.

"Thought so," Mac said triumphantly. "Battle of the Sexes at 1500. Your friend with the wandering hands will be there. And so will Scarlet." He grinned. "Let the games begin, lover boy."

As Mac disappeared around the corner, Jerry lingered in the hallway, caught between joining the group and escaping to their cabin's sanctuary to process these unexpected feelings. His military instincts cautioned against investing in a vacation connection with an expiration date. Yet something long-silent within him had awakened, whispering to explore where this unexpected spark might lead.

For once, he decided to listen to the second voice.

Eight

Jerry entered the piano bar with Mac, his eyes automatically scanning the space with practiced precision. Deployment had trained him to identify exits, assess potential bottlenecks, classify threats. Not that there were any real threats here, just the persistent discomfort that came with crowded spaces and too many strangers.

"You need a minute?" Mac asked quietly, positioning himself slightly between Jerry and the rest of the room. "We can hang back if you want."

Jerry forced his shoulders to relax. "I'm good. Thanks."

Mac nodded, not pressing further. "They've got seats near the back wall if you'd prefer."

The simple offer made Jerry grateful, not for the first time, that Mac understood without requiring explanations. Their years together in the service had taught Mac when to step in and when to let Jerry handle things himself.

"Let's grab them," Jerry agreed. As they made their way through the crowd, his eyes caught on Scarlet standing with Cami in the corner.

She was laughing, her red hair falling loose around her shoulders, looking more at ease than he'd seen her before.

Before Jerry could comment, he spotted Stacy approaching, the same brunette from the speed mingling event earlier. She wore an expectant smile, her eyes lingering on him appreciatively.

"Well, if it isn't the strong, silent type," she said, her voice dropping to a more intimate tone despite the noisy room. "Decided to join the fun after all?"

Her hand landed on his forearm, fingers tracing a slow path up toward his bicep where his tattoo peeked out from beneath his sleeve. She traced the outline through the fabric, her touch lingering as though committing it to memory without actually asking about its meaning.

"Just supporting the team," Jerry replied with a polite smile.

"I love a man who's ... supportive," she said, leaning closer than necessary. "Though I should warn you, I'm extremely competitive."

"So I've been told," Jerry said, taking a half-step back. "This is my friend Mac."

Mac stepped forward smoothly. "Jerry here is our team's dark horse. He's got skills you wouldn't expect."

Stacy's smile widened as her fingertips continued their path along his tattoo. "I bet he does. Looking forward to seeing them in action." Her retreat was deliberate, her glance over her shoulder sharper than words.

Jerry drew in air like it had just returned to the room, pulse catching up to everything else.

"You okay?" Mac asked once she was out of earshot.

"Fine," Jerry murmured, his eyes automatically finding Scarlet across the room. She was watching their interaction, a slight furrow between her brows. When their eyes met, she quickly looked away.

Before Mac could comment further, Maude took center stage, her flowing caftan glittering under the stage lights. As the host of the Mingle at Sea singles group, she commanded the room with practiced ease.

"Welcome aboard our nautical battle of wits, sailors!" she called out, her voice carrying effortlessly through the space. "Tonight, we'll see if the men can finally get their sea legs or if they'll continue to flounder! It's time to dive into the most wave-making competition on the seven seas ... Battle of the Sexes!"

Cheers rippled through the room as Maude walked them through the competition setup.

Jerry kept his focus on the rules, appreciating the sense of order amidst the energy.

He wouldn't have chosen this kind of night for himself, but now that he was in it, he wanted to see how it played out.

"Round one begins with Opposite Knowledge Trivia," Maude announced with a theatrical flourish. "Each team will navigate the choppy waters of topics typically associated with the other gender's expertise. Let's see which team will sink and which will swim!"

The first few questions were straightforward. The men's team fumbled through questions about fashion designers and romantic comedy plots while the women tackled sports statistics and car mechanics with surprising accuracy.

Jerry hung back, observing his team's dynamics. A pattern he recognized from his military days: assess before engaging, understand the terrain. When a question about women's health came up, the men around him exchanged blank looks.

"Does anyone know how often a typical menstrual cycle occurs?" Maude asked, clearly enjoying the men's discomfort.

Jerry hesitated, then raised his hand. "Twenty-eight days, on average."

His male teammates turned to stare at him in surprise.

"Correct!" Maude announced. "That's one point for the gentlemen, keeping them afloat for now!"

"Dude, how did you know that?" one of the guys whispered.

Jerry shrugged. "I pay attention."

Mac gave him an encouraging nod. "See? Told you we had an advantage."

He'd started the round with mild curiosity, but now he was all in, offering answers without overthinking, even grinning between turns.

Scarlet commanded the room with confidence, unflinching as her steady voice delivered fact after fact.

Jerry felt a quiet pride watching her work the room without even trying.

When Round two began, Maude explained that each participant would need to demonstrate or explain a task typically associated with the opposite gender.

"Time to test if you can navigate uncharted waters!" she declared. "Who's brave enough to be the first mate to volunteer for the men's team?"

The men shuffled their feet, no one eager to volunteer. One of Jerry's teammates was eventually pushed forward and given the task of explaining how to apply makeup. He stuttered through a painful explanation that had everyone cringing.

Scarlet moved into position, calm and focused.

Her explanation was clean and deliberate. No jokes. No stumbles … just confident instruction.

Jerry watched her, equal parts amused and in awe.

It was such a her moment: sharp, capable, completely in command

"Your turn again, gentlemen," Maude announced. "Don't be adrift without a paddle now!"

When no one moved, Mac gave Jerry a gentle nudge.

"You've got this," he said quietly.

Jerry stepped forward, and Maude's face lit up. "Our military man! Perfect. Your task is to demonstrate how to apply mascara."

A ripple of laughter went through the crowd. Jerry felt heat rise to his face, but he straightened his shoulders. Never show discomfort.

"Okay," he said, taking the mascara wand Maude offered. "First, you need to be steady." He demonstrated with his hand. "You hold the wand at the base of the lashes and gently wiggle it upward. You want to coat them evenly without clumping."

He pantomimed the motion with surprising accuracy, explaining the technique with the same focus he'd use describing field operations.

"I had a friend in high school who needed help before prom," he added, seeing the surprised looks. "Her arm was in a cast. You learn to be useful."

Scarlet was watching him intently, a small smile playing at the corners of her mouth. Something about her gaze made him want to keep talking, to explain more than was strictly necessary for the game.

"And you always do the bottom lashes more lightly," he continued. "Otherwise it gets messy."

"Ship-shape demonstration!" Maude declared, awarding the men five points. "Our military man knows how to navigate the treacherous waters of mascara application!"

From across the room, Stacy called out, "I'd let you do my makeup any day!" Her friends dissolved into giggles.

Jerry nodded politely but found his eyes drifting back to Scarlet, who was watching the exchange with an unreadable expression.

The Lightning Round came next, with each team selecting three representatives for the rapid-fire questions.

"Ladies, who will be your first champion to weather this storm of questions?" Maude asked.

"I'll do it!" Stacy's hand shot up immediately, her voice carrying across the room. She flashed a smile in Jerry's direction. "I've got this."

Before Maude could respond, Scarlet raised her hand as well. "I'd like to try too," she said, her voice quieter but no less determined.

The quick glance Scarlet threw Jerry's way carried a new intensity, a competitive gleam that hadn't been present earlier. A surprising rush of anticipation coursed through him at the notion she might be stepping forward partly to capture his attention.

"Wonderful! We have Stacy and Scarlet," Maude said. "And we need one more brave sailor."

Another woman from the group stepped forward, completing the women's team.

"And now for the men," Maude continued.

"Jerry," several teammates called out in unison.

"You've got this," Mac said simply, a steady hand on his shoulder as Jerry stepped forward.

Jerry took his spot, only to find both Stacy and Scarlet directly across from him.

Stacy's wink was almost theatrical. Scarlet, meanwhile, kept her posture sharp, eyes mostly elsewhere.

Except when they weren't.

He caught her looking at him with just enough intention to know it wasn't accidental.

The questions came rapidly, testing reflexes as much as knowledge. Jerry answered with the quick precision he'd developed during mission briefings: gather information, process, respond. His military training served him well here, allowing him to stay focused despite the noise and pressure.

When it was Stacy's turn, she handled her questions with enthusiastic confidence, making a show of each correct answer with a victorious fist pump. After her round, she caught Jerry's eye and mouthed, "Beat that."

Then came Scarlet's turn. Her approach was completely different. Measured and precise, almost surgical in her quick responses. No celebration, no flair, just a steady accumulation of points. But there was an intensity to her focus that Jerry found impossible to look away from.

When the Lightning Round ended, the scores remained tied. This was a first in the competition's recent history, according to Maude.

"All hands on deck!" Maude announced, drawing out each word like a drumroll. "We have reached uncharted waters with this tie. That means it is time for the ultimate tiebreaker."

A murmur rippled through the crowd as she lifted her chin with theatrical flair. "One champion from each team. Speed, precision, and very clean hands."

"The men's team will need to select their champion," she continued.

"Jerry," his teammates answered instantly, voices carrying above the din.

"And for the women?"

There was a pause as Stacy started to raise her hand, only for Scarlet to step forward with quiet certainty.

"Scarlet," her team echoed in agreement.

Jerry caught the flash of disappointment on Stacy's face before she smoothed it over with a supportive smile. The edge beneath it did not escape him.

And then he was standing across from Scarlet, the energy between them sharper than anything Maude could orchestrate. The crowd faded to a blur. Her focus locked on him, steady and unflinching.

"Alright, pretty boy, you're going down."

Her words came with playful ease, but the spark in her eyes hit him like a live current.

And before his brain could intervene, his mouth betrayed him. "Maybe down on you later."

The moment the words escaped, his stomach dropped. Heat rushed to his face. What the hell had he just said?

Scarlet leaned in before he could stammer an apology, her grin quick and daring. "Buy me a drink first, then we'll talk."

His laugh broke free, startled and alive, carrying relief and something deeper. She had not just let him off the hook. She had matched him step for step.

A drumroll began. Maude swept forward, hands raised high. With a grand flourish, the crew pulled a silk cover from two tables.

"Meet Ted and Beary Manilow," she announced. Two teddy bears appeared, both outfitted in innocent little diapers. "Your mission is clear. Change them and deliver those diapers to the bins at the far side of the room. Fastest, neatest team wins it all."

The crowd roared with anticipation as Jerry and Scarlet took their positions. From the corner of his eye, he could see Stacy watching intently from the sidelines, but his focus stayed locked on two things: the task ahead and Scarlet's determined expression beside him.

The whistle blew, and they lunged forward. Jerry reached for his bear's diaper, pulling it open with practiced efficiency. After all, he'd changed enough real diapers to handle a fake one with his eyes closed. What he found instead was a gooey brown surprise that was unmistakably chocolate pudding.

"What the!" he heard Scarlet exclaim beside him, followed by a shriek and eruption of laughter from the crowd.

Despite his shock, Jerry's hands moved methodically, containing the pudding mess with precise movements. He glanced over to see Scarlet covered in chocolate pudding, her diaper removal having gone spectacularly wrong. Despite the competitive pressure, he couldn't help but smile at the chaos.

He quickly cleaned his bear, wrapped on a fresh diaper, and headed for the disposal bin. His lead was substantial, thanks to years of diaper-changing experience that gave him a clear edge. Victory was within reach.

Until his foot hit a slick patch of pudding near the trash bin.

His military training kicked in as he caught himself before falling, but the recovery cost him precious seconds. From the corner of his eye, he saw Scarlet gaining ground, her face set with determination despite the chocolate smeared across her shirt.

They were going to reach the finish line at the same time.

In a split-second decision, Jerry did something he'd never normally do ... he played dirty. As Scarlet drew even with him, he gave her a playful, strategic bump with his hip. Not enough to knock her over, just enough to throw her slightly off balance.

"Sorry," he mouthed, not looking sorry at all, as he pressed the buzzer a split second before she recovered.

The men's team erupted in cheers, rushing forward to celebrate their victory.

"Man overboard! The streak is broken!" Maude announced, dramatically wiping away a fake tear. "After thirty-nine consecutive victories, the women's ship has finally sunk! The men's team takes the crown!"

As his teammates celebrated around him, Jerry looked for Scarlet in the chaos. She stood with her team, chocolate smeared across her shirt, hands on her hips, fixing him with a mock-accusatory stare. But she was genuinely laughing at the absurdity of it all.

Their eyes met across the room, and Jerry gave her an unapologetic shrug.

"Dirty tricks, Sergeant!" she called out, shaking her head.

"Nothing dirtier than a diaper cleanup," he replied with a grin.

It was only then, as the adrenaline of the competition began to ebb, that Jerry became aware of his surroundings again. The room suddenly felt smaller, more confined than it had during the game. The press of bodies, the overlapping conversations, the laughter. It all crashed into his consciousness at once. He hadn't noticed during the competition how the crowd had drawn closer, everyone packed together to watch the final showdown.

His breathing quickened slightly. The walls seemed to inch inward.

Stacy approached, catching Jerry by the arm, and he had to force himself not to flinch at the unexpected contact.

"That was impressive," she said, leaning closer than necessary, further invading his rapidly shrinking comfort zone. "We're having drinks in the Topaz Lounge to commiserate our loss. You should join us."

The thought of another crowded space made his chest tighten. That familiar pressure returned behind his sternum, the one he'd managed to forget existed during those blissful minutes of competition.

"Thanks," Jerry replied, carefully extracting himself from her grip, needing the space between them. "But I think I need to get cleaned up first."

"I can wait," she offered, clearly misreading his desire for distance as merely practical.

Mac stepped in the moment he noticed Jerry's telltale signs: the slightly rigid posture, the controlled breathing, the way his eyes had started scanning for exits again.

"Sorry, but we've got team plans already. Maybe another time," Mac said smoothly, positioning himself as a buffer between Jerry and the crowd.

Stacy looked disappointed but nodded. "I'll hold you to that," she said, squeezing Jerry's arm one last time before rejoining her friends.

"Thanks," Jerry murmured to Mac once she was out of earshot.

"Anytime," Mac replied simply, then added with practiced casualness, "You want to head out? Getting pretty crowded in here."

Jerry nodded, grateful again for Mac's intuition. "Yeah, I need some space." The walls felt even closer now, the air thicker.

"Go do your thing," Mac said, understanding exactly what Jerry needed without requiring explanation. "I've got a date with some blackjack anyway."

The two men parted ways, Mac heading for the casino while Jerry returned to their cabin to shower and change. The chocolate pudding had somehow found its way onto his shirt despite his careful technique.

As the hot water washed away the sticky residue, Jerry felt that familiar tension creeping between his shoulder blades. Post-social exhaustion was setting in. He had enjoyed himself tonight, which surprised him, but large groups always drained him, leaving him craving solitude to recharge.

What surprised him most was how completely he'd forgotten his anxiety during the competition. For those brief minutes, focused on the challenge and on Scarlet, his hypervigilance had temporarily deactivated. No scanning for threats, no monitoring exits, no controlled breathing. He'd just been ... present.

Towel in hand, Jerry headed for the top deck, drawn by the idea of sky and silence. Dinner hour had cleared the space, and he walked through warm air and sea breeze until the ceiling turned to stars.

Above him, the cosmos stretched wide and wild, untamed by city lights. The ocean whispered below, steady as a lullaby, the ship thrumming with its own low heart.

The hot tub was empty. Waiting. He sank into it, letting the heat reach places his tension had claimed.

His thoughts drifted to Scarlet's smile, her timing, that spark between them neither of them had quite named yet. And beneath it all, a strange kind of peace he hadn't known he'd missed.

He couldn't remember the last time he'd enjoyed himself this much in a social setting. Usually, he endured them out of duty. Work functions, unit events, command gatherings where he stood on the periphery, doing what was required but never fully engaging.

Tonight had been different. He'd actually participated, actually connected. With Mac, with the team, with ...

Footsteps approached, soft but certain, drawing Jerry back from his thoughts.

He opened his eyes to find Scarlet standing by the hot tub, damp hair curling against her shoulders, a towel hanging loosely over one arm.

The deck lights framed her in silhouette, every line of her form cast in gentle contrast against the night sky.

"Mind if I join you?" she asked.

Jerry jolted upright, water spilling over the tub's edge. "I. Uh ..."

Words tangled on his tongue, his brain momentarily short-circuiting.

He hadn't expected anyone. Least of all her.

"Yes. I mean, no. I don't mind. At all."

She raised an eyebrow, the hint of a smile playing at her lips.

"There's room," he clarified, gesturing awkwardly at the empty space beside him, then immediately wondering if he should have moved over more. "Plenty of it. Room, I mean."

Smooth, Duncan, he thought to himself. Real smooth.

She stepped in carefully, settling into the bubbling water with a contented sigh that did nothing to help his composure. "This feels amazing after all that chaos."

Jerry nodded, trying not to notice how the water beaded on her shoulders or how her hair caught the starlight. "Nothing like pudding warfare to make you appreciate hot water," he managed, surprised at how easily the joke came despite his internal floundering.

Scarlet laughed, the sound blending with the gentle splash of water. "I can't believe the mess I made. I'm usually more ... coordinated."

"The element of surprise will do that," Jerry said, finding his footing in the conversation as they shifted to the safer territory of the competition. "I've seen tougher people than you taken down by unexpected substances."

"Speaking from experience?"

He nodded, not elaborating further. Some stories weren't meant for casual conversation.

Scarlet seemed to sense his hesitation and smoothly changed the subject. "So, about that bump during the race," she said, her eyes sparkling with playful accusation. "Was that a tactical move, Sergeant?"

Jerry felt his face warm slightly. "Would you believe me if I said it was an accident?"

"Not a chance," she replied with a grin.

"Worth a shot." He smiled back, finding it surprisingly easy to banter with her despite his initial awkwardness. "Consider it payback for that comeback that nearly made me lose focus completely."

"Fair enough." She laughed again, leaning her head back against the tub to look up at the stars. "God, you can actually see them out here. In Miami, there's too much light pollution."

Jerry's attention drifted from the night sky to her profile, a peculiar sensation washing over him as he observed the rare, undefended quality of her expression.

"That's one of the things I miss most during deployment," he said without thinking. "The night sky in the desert is incredible, but you never get to just ... enjoy it."

Scarlet turned to look at him, her expression curious but not prying. "How long have you been in the military?"

"Twelve years," he replied. "Joined right out of high school."

"And you've been deployed?"

"Three times. Iraq, mostly." He shifted slightly, watching the water ripple around his movements. "Not my favorite topic."

Scarlet nodded, respecting the boundary. "So, what is your favorite topic?" she asked instead.

Jerry considered this. "Honestly? Other people," he said after a moment. "Their stories, what makes them tick. Used to play a lot of poker in the barracks, got pretty good at reading tells, the little things people do when they're bluffing or excited."

"That sounds dangerous," Scarlet said with interest. "Reading people like that."

"It can be," he admitted with a half-smile. "You learn things people don't always mean to share. But everyone's got a story worth hearing if you pay attention."

"So, you're studying me right now?" She raised an eyebrow, half joking.

"Hard not to notice things," Jerry said, his voice softening. "Like how you tap your thumb against your fingers when you're thinking about what to say next. Or how your eyes get sharper when someone challenges you, like during the competition."

Scarlet's eyes widened slightly. "I didn't realize I was so transparent."

"You're not," Jerry assured her. "Most people wouldn't catch it. I just ... notice."

"Sounds like a useful skill."

"Sometimes," he said. "Makes it easier to understand people, harder to misread situations. Comes in handy with ..." He caught himself before mentioning the boys. "Well, in a lot of contexts."

"What about you?" Jerry asked, shifting the focus. "What do you do when you're not crushing diaper-changing competitions?"

"I'm an accountant," she said. "Senior accounts specialist at a boutique firm in Miami."

Jerry reached up, thumb working at the knot in his neck. He'd heard her say that before, probably while his brain was still in fight-or-flight mode. He remembered how her calm, even voice had cut through the noise.

"That's right," he said, more to himself than her. "You told me that already." A pause, then quieter, "You enjoy it?"

Something flickered across her face. It was so brief he almost missed it. "It's challenging. Keeps me busy."

Jerry nodded, recognizing the deflection for what it was. Not an answer to the question he'd asked.

They settled into comfortable conversation, discussing everything from favorite movies to the best meals they'd had on the ship so far. The stars wheeled slowly overhead as the minutes stretched into an hour.

"We dock at Grand Turk tomorrow, right?" Scarlet asked eventually. "Any plans?"

"Actually, yeah," Jerry replied, feeling a small surge of enthusiasm. "I'm going paddleboarding. The water there is supposed to be incredible. Crystal clear and calm, perfect conditions."

"Paddleboarding?" She looked intrigued. "I've never tried that."

"It's easier than it looks," Jerry said. "You just stand on a board and use a paddle to move around. Great way to see the coastline, maybe spot some fish."

"Sounds fun," she said, a hint of wistfulness in her voice.

Jerry paused, hand drifting up to the back of his neck.

The idea had come out of nowhere. Invite her.

Now it sat there, waiting, tugging at his better judgment.

What if she turned him down?

Or worse ... what if she said yes and it went sideways?

"You could ... uh," he started, then stopped. "I mean, if you wanted to ... you know ..." He cleared his throat, annoyed at his own stumbling. "What I'm trying to say is, you should, you could join me. If you want."

The invitation hung in the water between them. Jerry immediately second-guessed himself. Too forward? Too presumptuous? They'd only known each other a few days, and here he was planning excursions together. What were they, anyway? Friends? Something else?

"Really?" Scarlet's face brightened, washing away his doubts. "I'd like that."

"You would?" The words slipped out before he could catch them, surprise evident in his voice. He quickly recovered. "I mean, great. That's ... great."

"Fair warning, I'm pretty good at it," he said with mock seriousness. "So don't expect to win this competition."

"Oh, it's a competition now?" She raised an eyebrow. "You're on, Sergeant. But I expect proper instruction before you start keeping score."

"Deal," Jerry said, surprised by the genuine anticipation he felt. "We can rent boards at the beach. I'll show you the basics."

"It's a date," she replied, then quickly added, "I mean, not a date-date, just a ..."

"Yeah, no ... I mean, yeah, I get what you meant," Jerry assured her, though part of him wondered if maybe it was a date after all. The thought didn't alarm him as much as it might have a few days ago.

They fell silent, the only sounds the bubbling of the hot tub and the distant hum of music from somewhere below deck.

"I should probably head back," Scarlet said eventually. "Early day tomorrow."

Jerry nodded. "Meet at the gangway around nine? The ship docks at eight."

"Perfect." She stood up, water cascading off her shoulders. "Thanks for the invite. And for not gloating too much."

Jerry replied with a smile. "I might still work it into conversation tomorrow."

Scarlet laughed as she stepped out of the hot tub, wrapping her towel around her waist. "Goodnight, Jerry."

"Goodnight, Scarlet."

He watched her walk away, her figure silhouetted against the deck lights. Only after she disappeared from view did Jerry realize he was still smiling.

Nine

Jerry had been awake for hours, watching darkness shift across the ceiling of their stateroom. Not even the gentle rocking of the ship could lull him back to sleep. Years of military routine and dawn therapy appointments had trained his body to function before the sun, but this restlessness was different. This was anticipation.

Mac's snoring rumbled from the other bed, a familiar soundtrack that usually faded into background noise. Tonight, each rasping breath seemed amplified, echoing against Jerry's thoughts.

Just a few hours until paddleboarding with Scarlet.

He turned onto his side, facing the glass balcony door. Through the thin crack in the curtains, the night sky was just beginning to surrender its hold, the faintest gray seeping into absolute black. Jerry checked his watch: 4:47 a.m. Dawn wouldn't fully arrive for another hour, but he could already make out the shadowy silhouette of Grand Turk in the distance, a promise on the horizon.

Sleep wasn't coming back. Not with his mind replaying fragments of her laugh from last night's mixer, the way she'd arched an eyebrow when challenging him during the Battle of the Sexes game. Not with his stomach doing that strange, forgotten flutter whenever he thought about today.

With a quiet sigh, Jerry slipped from beneath the sheets, careful not to let the bed creak. Dressed only in Army PT shorts, he padded across the cool floor and eased the balcony door open just enough to slide through.

The pre-dawn air hit his bare chest with a welcome chill. Out here, Mac's snoring was replaced by the gentle rush of the ship cutting through waves and the distant hum of engines far below. Jerry gripped the railing, his calloused palms rough against the smooth metal, and filled his lungs with salt air.

The silhouette of Grand Turk grew clearer with every mile, the sky behind it warming to day.

And Jerry realized this wasn't anxiety.

It was something brighter. Looser. Familiar, but distant.

Like joy trying to remember its way back in.

He ran a hand across the scruff on his jaw, suddenly wondering if he should have shaved last night. Soft skin for what, Duncan? A glorified boat ride with a woman who's just being friendly? But even as the thought formed, he knew it wasn't true. The way Scarlet looked at him wasn't just friendly. It was curious, attentive, as if she was trying to read something written beneath his skin.

The first blush of orange touched the horizon, sending gold rippling across the water. Jerry leaned forward, elbows on the railing, and allowed himself a rare moment of anticipation for something that was just for him.

A nervous energy surged through him. Before he could think twice, Jerry dropped to the deck and positioned himself for pushups. The balcony was narrow, but it beat the muddy fields back in Texas where he usually knocked these out before dawn. Twenty-five quick ones, just to burn off some of this jittery feeling.

One. Two. Three.

His muscles warmed quickly in the cool air. The metal deck was smooth against his palms, nothing like the gritty dirt he was used to. Below him, the Caribbean stretched out in watercolor splendor featuring deep navy fading to brilliant azure as the sun crept higher.

Fifteen. Sixteen. Seventeen.

"Seriously, dude?" Mac's sleepy voice came from the doorway. "You don't get enough PT at home?"

Jerry paused mid-pushup, suddenly aware of how absurd he must look. "Just ... maintaining readiness."

"Sure," Mac said, leaning against the door frame with a knowing grin. "Nothing to do with Red from Miami."

Jerry pushed back down, determined to finish what he'd started.

Twenty-one. Twenty-two. Twenty-three.

"What time is your date anyway?" Mac asked, scratching absently at his chest.

Twenty-four. Twenty-five.

"It's not a date," Jerry protested automatically, though the flutter in his stomach suggested otherwise. He pushed himself to standing, wiping a bead of sweat from his temple.

"Keep telling yourself that." Mac yawned, stretching his arms overhead against the balcony doorframe. "What time are you meeting her?"

"Nine," Jerry replied, leaning against the railing. "We're renting boards at the main beach. I was thinking maybe we could all meet up at that beach shack around one? For lunch?"

The horizon was on fire now, the water glittering like scattered diamonds. Maybe this morning routine wasn't so bad when you traded Army barracks for ocean views.

Mac's eyebrows shot up. "Whoa, inviting the ladies to lunch? This is serious."

Jerry rolled his eyes, though he couldn't quite suppress his smile. "Shut up. It's just lunch."

"Whatever you say, Romeo." Mac pushed off from the doorframe and shuffled back into the cabin, navigating around Jerry's bed to flop onto his own. "1300 works. I'm sure I'll find Cami around the ship later."

As Mac drifted back to sleep, Jerry showered and dressed, selecting his navy swim trunks and a lightweight gray T-shirt. He packed a small bag with essentials: towel, sunscreen, water bottle, and his phone in a waterproof case.

With careful consideration, he added the special zinc-based, waterproof sunscreen designed specifically for tattoos. It was expensive, but worth every penny to protect the symbols that kept Marty and Emmett close even when they were far apart.

Jerry arrived at the beach early, the morning sun warm against his back as he arranged the paddle board rental. The routine of preparation soothed his unexpected nervousness: securing equipment, checking conditions, establishing a plan. It reminded him of pre-mission protocols, the comfort of having everything in order before proceeding.

With the boards propped beside him, Jerry took a moment to apply the special sunscreen to his tattoo. His fingers moved methodically over the green wheelchair symbol for Marty and the rainbow infinity design for Emmett, the familiar ritual centering him despite their absence.

As he straightened, Jerry caught sight of Scarlet walking toward him along the beach. His breath caught, an involuntary response that surprised him with its intensity.

She moved with quiet confidence across the sand, her vibrant red hair catching the morning light. The red tankini she wore was simple yet striking, its ruched bodice and skirted hem drawing his eyes in spite of himself. Unlike the barely-there bikinis scattered across the beach, her choice was practical, steady, and still managed to make his throat tighten.

He stood a little straighter, suddenly aware of his own appearance. His throat worked as he swallowed, and he raised his hand in greeting, only to realize he was still holding the orange life vests. They flapped awkwardly in the breeze as he fumbled, nearly dropping one before catching it against his chest.

"Hey there!" she called, waving as she approached.

"Good morning!" he called back, feeling heat rise to his face as he regained control of the unwieldy vests. His eyes tracked her movement, noting her toned legs and the subtle sway of her hips before returning to her face. "You look ... wow. You look stunning."

The compliment left his mouth before he could filter it, honest and unpolished. To his relief, she smiled, a hint of color touching her cheeks.

"Thanks," she replied with a light chuckle. "What's with the kiddy vests?"

Jerry seized on the teasing question, grateful for the chance to recover his composure. He held up the bright orange life vests with exaggerated formality. "I thought these vests would be a perfect match for your bathing suit," he said, his voice steadier now. "I think they'll really enhance your overall outfit on the water."

Scarlet laughed, and something in Jerry's chest loosened at the sound. "Oh, is that so? I wasn't aware I needed to accessorize for paddleboarding. I'll take your word for it."

"Absolutely," he replied with a wink. "Nothing like being fashion-forward while you're balancing on a board."

With the initial awkwardness broken, Jerry motioned toward the boards staged near the shoreline. "Ready to give it a try?"

Jerry handed her a vest and started putting on his own. "It's pretty straightforward. I'll give you a quick rundown before we hit the water. And don't worry, I'll be right there with you."

The water was cool against their legs as they waded in together. Jerry glanced back at Scarlet, noting how the tropical print of her swimsuit created a vivid contrast against the clear turquoise water. Her red hair was pulled back in a practical bun, but a few loose strands caught the breeze around her face.

"Just a heads-up," he called over his shoulder with what he hoped was a reassuring smile. "Don't try to stand until we're a bit further from shore. It's a lot easier once we're out of the shallows." He demonstrated, mounting his board with practiced ease. "Start by lying on your stomach, then swing your legs over like you're getting on a horse, and finally, sit up."

"I've never ridden a horse either," Scarlet confessed, her expression a mix of determination and apprehension that reminded him powerfully of Emmett trying something new.

Jerry watched as she attempted to straddle the board. Before she could fully sit up, she wobbled and, with a surprised yelp, tumbled into the water.

She surfaced, sputtering, water streaming down her face, and Jerry bit back a laugh. Not at her but at the familiar scene of someone experiencing the learning curve of a new skill. How many times had he watched Emmett face the same process of try, fail, try again?

"That was quite the graceful dive!" he said, paddling closer.

"Guess I got a bit too eager," she replied, pushing wet hair from her eyes.

Without hesitation, Jerry hopped off his board and extended a hand toward her. "No worries at all," he said with a smile that he hoped conveyed understanding rather than pity. "It's all part of the learning curve. Let's give it another shot."

Her hand felt small in his as he helped her back onto the board. The fabric of her swimsuit clung to her curves, and Jerry forced himself to focus on stabilizing the board rather than noticing how the water droplets traced paths down her collarbone.

"Take your time," he encouraged. "Remember, the water's not going anywhere. We'll have you paddling like a pro in no time."

Jerry could read frustration in the set of her shoulders, the slight furrow between her brows. He recognized the look of someone used to mastering skills quickly, someone for whom competence was as natural as breathing. It was a feeling he understood well, that particular frustration of a capable person facing unfamiliar territory.

With his guidance, Scarlet managed to sit stably on the board. When Jerry suggested she try standing, however, he saw her hesitate.

"I don't know," she said, eyeing the water beneath her. "I'm just getting comfortable sitting."

"You don't have to," Jerry assured her, recalling how often he'd said those exact words to Emmett. He suddenly realized how similar his approach was now to the one he used with his son. Patient, encouraging, but never pushing. "But I think you can do it. Here ..." He paddled closer, positioning his board parallel to hers. "I'll help steady you."

With his hand on her board for support, Scarlet slowly shifted to her knees.

"I hate being a beginner," she admitted, frustration bleeding into her voice. "I'm not good at it."

"No one is," Jerry replied automatically, the words familiar from countless therapy sessions and learning moments with Emmett and Marty. "That's kind of the definition of 'beginner.' But you're doing great."

Her expression softened, and something in Jerry's chest tightened at the sight. With careful movements, she brought one foot forward, then the other, rising to a wobbly stand. For a terrifying moment, the board tilted precariously before steadying. She was standing.

"I did it!" Scarlet exclaimed, her face lighting up with an unguarded joy that transformed her features.

"You did," Jerry confirmed, unable to keep from smiling back. "Now, the real fun begins."

For the next hour, they paddled along the coast, keeping close to the shore. Scarlet fell twice more, but each time, she surfaced with increasing laughter rather than frustration. By the third dunking, she was accepting his hand without embarrassment, her competitive edge softening into genuine enjoyment.

As they rounded a bend in the shoreline, Jerry spotted a small cove ahead, protected from view by rocky outcroppings. The beach was empty, offering a rare moment of privacy.

"Check out that secluded spot up ahead," he said, pointing. "It looks perfect for a break."

Scarlet followed his gaze, nodding in agreement. "That looks perfect. And a break sounds wonderful. I could definitely use some time off the board."

Jerry navigated toward the shore, using the momentum to beach his board gently on the sand. He secured it before turning to assist Scarlet as she paddled in.

"Careful now, no more surprise splashes," he teased, offering a steadying hand.

Scarlet laughed, accepting his help. "Thanks. This place really is stunning."

With their boards secured on the sand, they stretched out side by side, the warmth of the sun seeping into tired muscles. Jerry closed his eyes briefly, savoring the moment. When was the last time he'd simply existed, without responsibilities or demands pulling at his attention? Even on deployment, there was always the next mission, the next task. At home, Emmett and Marty needed constant care. This moment of pure, unstructured peace felt almost decadent.

Opening his eyes, Jerry found Scarlet watching him, her gaze on his arm. He realized he was absently rubbing his tattoo, a habit he'd developed whenever his thoughts turned to Marty and Emmett.

"Does it have a meaning?" she asked, nodding toward the design. "Your tattoo, I mean."

The question caught him off guard, though he should have expected it. His hand stilled as a familiar tension crept into his shoulders. This was always the moment where a casual connection could turn complicated. In the past, he'd deflected or offered vague answers, wary of the change in expression that inevitably followed the full truth.

His back straightened almost imperceptibly, his posture shifting from relaxed to alert. His jaw tightened as he considered how to respond.

"Um, yeah," he said finally, his hands dropping to his sides and fingers digging slightly into the sand. "It does."

He fidgeted with a small pile of sand beside him, debating how much to share. His eyes met hers briefly, then darted away to scan the horizon. But the beach was deserted, and this wasn't a military secret. It was just his life.

After a moment, he took a breath and glanced down at the tattoo. His fingers traced the outline of a green wheelchair symbol intertwined with a rainbow infinity logo. His shoulders hunched forward slightly, an unconscious protective gesture.

"It's for my kids," he said simply, testing the words.

Scarlet blinked, clearly processing the unexpected information. "Your ... kids?"

Jerry nodded, his posture rigid despite his casual position on the sand. "Yeah, I've got two sons at home," he explained, his throat tightening even as pride warmed his voice. "Marty's eight, and Emmett's six. The green wheelchair is for Marty ... he has cerebral palsy. And the infinity symbol with the rainbow is for Emmett. It's the symbol for autism awareness."

"Marty and Emmett?" Scarlet's face broke into a grin, a light chuckle escaping her. "Like Back to the Future?"

Tension drained from Jerry's shoulders at her unexpected reaction. His whole body visibly relaxed, his hands unclenching from the sand. Instead of the pitying look or awkward pause he'd braced for, she'd found the humor, that personal connection that most people missed entirely.

"Yeah, exactly," he admitted with a sheepish grin. "I'm a big fan of the movies. Their mom wasn't thrilled about it, but she let me choose their names."

"I had no idea," Scarlet said softly. "You have children. You're a father."

Jerry nodded, his eyes focused on her face, carefully gauging her reaction. Her expression was thoughtful rather than alarmed. It was not the reaction he'd come to expect from women he met, especially in casual vacation settings.

"Yeah. They're staying with my mom while I'm away," he continued, sitting up straighter now, his voice growing more confident. "This is actually the first real break I've had in years. Mac practically forced me onto this cruise. He said I needed time to just be Jerry, not just Dad or Sergeant Duncan."

Scarlet studied his face, her gaze more analytical now, as if reassessing everything she'd learned about him in light of this new information.

"That explains a lot, actually," she said finally, adjusting the tie at the top of her swimsuit.

"Like what?" Jerry asked, genuinely curious about what she had seen in him.

"The way you helped me on the paddle board, so patient but never condescending. Your comfort with the diaper challenge." She smiled. "You've had practice."

Jerry laughed softly, his hands relaxing in his lap as his body shifted to a more open posture. "I guess I have. Though changing teddy bears is considerably easier than changing actual babies."

"Tell me about them," Scarlet said, her eyes warm with genuine interest. "Your kiddos; Marty and Emmett."

The invitation caught Jerry by surprise. His eyebrows raised slightly, and he leaned forward, his entire demeanor shifting. Most people, upon learning about his children's special needs, offered platitudes or quickly changed the subject. But Scarlet leaned forward slightly, her expression open and attentive, as if she truly wanted to hear more.

Something unfamiliar bloomed in Jerry's chest, a particular kind of joy that came from sharing what mattered most to him with someone who actually wanted to listen. The nervous energy that had made him fidget transformed into enthusiastic gestures as he began to speak.

"Marty's amazing. Despite the challenges with cerebral palsy, he's the happiest kid you'll ever meet. He can't communicate verbally, but his smile says everything he needs to say. He lights up any room and instantly makes everything seem a little bit brighter."

As he spoke, Jerry's hands moved animatedly, his face more expressive than Scarlet had yet seen it. His eyes crinkled at the corners, the usual vigilant alertness replaced by genuine warmth.

"And Emmett," he continued, "even though he's younger than Marty, he has this strong big brother quality about him. He takes his role seriously, always helping out and making sure Marty's okay. We spend a lot of time in the kitchen together. Cooking is one of our favorite things to do."

Jerry watched Scarlet's face as he spoke, alert for signs of the polite boredom or discomfort he'd grown accustomed to seeing. But her attention never wavered, her questions thoughtful and specific rather than generic. This wasn't distant politeness. This was the engaged curiosity of someone who genuinely cared about the answer.

"They sound wonderful," she said sincerely, adjusting the tie detail at the top of her swimsuit as she shifted to face him more directly. "Back to the Future boys who clearly hit the dad jackpot. You must miss them terribly."

"I do," Jerry admitted, his gestures settling as his tone grew more reflective. "But this break has been good for all of us. My mom loves having them, and it's given me a chance to ..." He paused, searching for the right words. "To reconnect with myself, I guess. To remember there's more to me than just being Dad."

Scarlet nodded, her expression reflecting understanding beyond what he expected. "It's easy to get lost in a role, isn't it? To become so defined by what you do that you forget who you are."

"Exactly," Jerry said, feeling a surge of gratitude for her insight. "Don't get me wrong, being their dad is the most important thing in my life. But sometimes I need to remember I'm still me, too."

The conversation flowed easily after that, until Scarlet hesitantly broached the subject he'd been anticipating since he first mentioned Marty and Emmett.

"If you don't mind my asking ..." she began tentatively, her fingers tracing circles in the sand. "What about their mother? Is she ... ?" The question hung in the air between them.

Jerry felt his expression close, the easy warmth fading as his jaw tightened. His shoulders squared, and he leaned back slightly. That familiar wall was rising reflexively. The failure, the guilt, the complicated history of this part of his story made it harder to share, even with someone whose company he genuinely enjoyed.

"I don't really want to get into it much," he replied, his voice more reserved. His fingers returned to that nervous fidgeting with the sand. "I'll just say that she's not really in the picture anymore."

"Oh, God, I'm sorry," Scarlet said quickly, color flooding her cheeks. "That was so inappropriate of me. I shouldn't have. I mean, we just met, and here I am asking personal questions about your ..." She shook her head, pressing her palm into the sand. "Just forget I asked. Seriously."

Her embarrassment tugged at him, making him regret his abrupt response. "No, no, it's okay," he assured her, though the tension in his shoulders contradicted his words. "You didn't know. I just ... prefer to talk about some happier subjects." He shifted slightly, eager to move the conversation away from territory that still held too much pain. "So, tell me about your story."

The redirection worked. Scarlet took a deep breath, her gaze turning toward the horizon. Jerry watched as she traced patterns in the sand with her finger, a careful organization that seemed to mimic her thought process.

"Well, I guess you could say I'm on this cruise for a mental break," she began slowly. "Cami practically had to drag me here. She thought I needed to … reconnect with actual humans, I guess."

"As opposed to?" Jerry prompted, relieved to be on safer conversational ground. His posture gradually relaxed again as the conversation moved away from his past.

Scarlet laughed softly. "As opposed to my Netflix account and take-out delivery guys. Dating in Miami is …" She shook her head, searching for the right words. "It's a wasteland. Seriously. It's like there are only two types of guys left: the finance bros who never outgrew their frat phase, or thirty-five-year-olds who still live with their parents and work 'flexible hours.'"

Jerry chuckled, enjoying her candid assessment. "Sounds rough."

"You have no idea," Scarlet continued, smoothing the fabric of her swimsuit. "The last guy I went out with spent the entire dinner talking about his cryptocurrency investments and then suggested we 'split the check down to the penny.' Another one showed up thirty minutes late and then spent the whole date texting someone else."

She sighed, a hint of vulnerability in the sound. "It just feels like all the decent ones got snatched up years ago, you know? By thirty-one, the dating pool is basically a puddle, and it's not even a clean puddle. It's one of those gross ones with cigarette butts floating in it."

Jerry laughed, the metaphor striking him as both funny and sad. How many people felt that way? How many gave up hope of finding someone who truly saw them?

"I needed a break from the constant disappointment," she admitted. "I wasn't looking to meet anyone on this cruise. I just wanted to float in a pool with a drink in my hand without having to fend off pickup lines about my 'vibe' or whatever." She glanced at Jerry, a small smile softening her features. "But meeting you has been nice. Different."

The simple admission made something warm unfurl in Jerry's chest. "I get it," he said, recognizing the exhaustion in her voice. "Sometimes it's just ... too much. Too many bad dates, too many disappointments. You need to reset."

Scarlet nodded, drawing her knees up to her chest and wrapping her arms around them. "Exactly. I just needed a chance to breathe, to remember what it feels like to enjoy the moment without analyzing whether it's going anywhere."

Her words resonated with Jerry in a way he hadn't expected. How long had it been since he'd allowed himself to simply be present in a moment, without the constant calculations of logistics and responsibilities? Ever since gaining full custody of Marty and Emmett, his life had become an endless series of carefully managed minutes, each one allocated to necessary tasks or brief, stolen moments of rest.

"This," Scarlet gestured around them at the tranquil beach, "this has been a good reminder of what it means to just be present."

Jerry smiled, feeling a connection deepen between them. "Well, for what it's worth, I'm glad we both ended up on this ridiculous singles cruise. Seems like we needed it for completely different reasons."

"Yeah, me too," she said softly. "It's been nice to just ... talk. No expectations, no pressure."

Jerry glanced at his watch and sighed, reluctant to break the moment but aware of their plans. "Speaking of which, we should probably start heading back to the main port area. Mac will never let me hear the end of it if we're late."

"Right," Scarlet laughed, getting to her feet and brushing sand from her swimsuit. "Cami's probably wondering where I am, too. Or she's still passed out by the pool."

As they retrieved their paddle boards and headed back into the water, Jerry felt something shifting inside him. He'd perfected a careful compartmentalization over the years, keeping Dad in one box and Sergeant in another. It had served him well. But now those lines were blurring, and surprisingly, it felt right.

"Ready?" he called to Scarlet, steadying her board as she mounted it.

Her smile in response sent a current of warmth through him that had nothing to do with the Caribbean sun. He watched her find her balance, admiring the determination that made her push through frustration to master something new.

For once, thinking about Emmett and Marty didn't tug at his conscience.

Instead, Jerry imagined how they'd react to Scarlet. Emmett would bombard her with endless questions about her city, her job, her favorite superhero. Marty, though, would just smile that soft, heart-melting smile that said everything without needing words.

As they paddled back toward the shore, Jerry's thoughts shifted from tactical awareness to something more personal. Practicalities that suddenly felt pressing: how far Texas really was from Miami. How often he could call. How much they could bend time to make something real work.

"You're quiet," Scarlet observed, paddling alongside him. "Penny for your thoughts?"

Jerry smiled, caught in his strategic planning. "Just thinking about how much has changed in a few days."

"Good change?" she asked, a hint of vulnerability in her voice.

"Definitely good," he replied without hesitation.

The main beach came into view, crowded now with cruise passengers enjoying the sun. Soon, they'd rejoin Mac and Cami, return to the ship, and eventually step back into the world of schedules and expectations. But something fundamental had altered in Jerry's understanding of his life's parameters.

He'd been living as if joy and duty couldn't coexist, as if enjoying himself automatically meant failing his responsibilities. But what if they could coexist? What if connection wasn't a distraction from duty but a source of strength for it?

The thought was as exhilarating as it was terrifying.

"Race you to shore?" Scarlet challenged with a playful grin.

Jerry laughed, all calculation temporarily suspended. "You're on."

As they raced toward shore, Jerry felt something he hadn't experienced in years, a pure, uncomplicated happiness that he'd forgotten was possible, one that was awakened by a red-haired accountant who'd stumbled into his carefully ordered life.

Mac

"Whatever you say, Romeo." Mac pushed off from the doorframe and shuffled back into the cabin, navigating around Jerry's bed to flop onto his own. "1300 works. I'm sure I'll find Cami around the ship later."

As the door clicked shut behind Jerry, Mac couldn't help but chuckle at his friend's excitement. Jerry's excitement was a welcome sight after everything he'd been through these past few years. Between the deployments, the divorce, and gaining full custody of the boys, Jerry had been running on fumes for as long as Mac could remember.

But now? The man was doing pre-date pushups, for God's sake.

After dozing for another hour, Mac forced himself out of bed. A quick shower and change later, he made his way up to the Lido deck. The sun cast a warm glow over the ship as he headed toward the breakfast buffet. The smell of fresh coffee and sizzling bacon wafted through the air, making his stomach growl in anticipation.

As he passed by the pool, someone caught his eye. Cami was already up, sitting near the water with a steaming cup of coffee in one hand

and a book in the other. Her focus was intense as she seemed absorbed in whatever she was reading. Mac smirked, thinking this would be a good opportunity to follow through on Jerry's lunch suggestion.

He continued to the buffet, piling his plate with eggs, bacon, fresh fruit, and a donut—for balance, of course. As he approached Cami, he considered his opening line. Nothing too flirty; she'd shut that down immediately based on their previous interactions. Something light, maybe a little teasing.

"Well, look who's up early," Mac said as he walked up to her, balancing his plate in one hand and coffee in the other. "I didn't know bookworms liked to sunbathe."

Cami looked up from her book, her expression flat and unimpressed. "That's original. Did you come up with that all by yourself?"

"Ouch. Harsh this early in the morning, don't you think?" Mac responded, not deterred by her coolness. "Mind if I join you, or is that against bookworm protocol?"

After an audible sigh, Cami closed her book and motioned toward an open chair at her table. "Go ahead. I suppose I can tolerate your presence for a little while."

Mac sat across the table and then took an oversized bite out of his donut. "So, what's on your agenda for the day?" he asked, still attempting to chew his massive bite of food. "Planning on reading by the pool until lunch?"

"You know, you could chew first," Cami replied, pointing out his lack of manners. "I haven't decided yet. What about you?"

Mac swallowed before answering, oddly concerned with impressing her despite her apparent immunity to his charm. "Well, Jerry and I were talking earlier, before he left to meet Scarlet for their paddle boarding thing, and we talked about meeting for lunch on the beach. There's a snack shack that's supposed to have some good local food. What do you think?"

Cami raised an eyebrow, hinting toward some skepticism. "A double date? Really?"

"No, not a date," Mac quickly clarified, recognizing the trap. "Just a casual hangout." The last thing he needed was to spook her with romantic implications. Cami reminded him of women he'd known before: fiercely independent, sharp as a tack, and absolutely allergic to anything that smacked of being tied down.

"Alright, fine," she conceded. "But, just so we're clear, I'm not into the whole double date thing. You and I, this is not a thing."

Mac chuckled, impressed by her directness. "Oh, I am very aware. I'd need a silver spear if I wanted any chance to pierce that hardened heart of yours. However, Jerry agreed to buying the first round, so, you know, at least there's that."

"Okay, fine. We'll see how it goes. But if this turns into some cheesy couples' thing, I'm out."

"Deal," Mac agreed, raising his coffee mug as if to toast to the day ahead. "To a drama-free lunch with good food and decent company."

Cami clinked her mug against his to participate in his toast. "I'll drink to that."

With the plans set, the conversation smoothed into something more natural.

Mac realized he wasn't just tossing out jokes anymore, he actually wanted to know her. Not out of politeness, but genuine interest.

"So, what did you do before the military?" Cami asked.

Mac hesitated, but only briefly. Usually, he'd deflect with a joke, but something about Cami's directness inspired honesty.

"College baseball scholarship that went nowhere," he admitted. "Turns out I wasn't as good as my high school coach thought." He shrugged, the old disappointment long faded. "What about you?"

"Public relations for a record label. Too many late nights and entitled rock stars," she replied. "Now I run social media for a boutique hotel chain. Less glamorous, way more sane."

Mac whistled appreciatively. "I can see you handling entitled rock stars. You've got that don't-mess-with-me vibe down pat."

"You should see me with entitled hotel guests," Cami replied. "I'm even scarier."

"I don't doubt it," Mac said, his eyes lingering a moment too long. Before he could stop himself, he added, "That confidence looks good on you, by the way."

Cami's expression cooled instantly. "Don't even try, playboy. Your charm might work on the ship's dance instructor, but I'm immune."

Mac raised his hands in surrender, though his smile remained. "Just stating facts. No ulterior motives."

"Mmhmm," Cami hummed skeptically.

He understood her wariness. The image he projected wasn't exactly built for trust: charming, detached, disposable.

That persona had always worked in his favor. Until now.

Because, as Cami turned back to her book, the dismissal hit somewhere he hadn't prepared for.

They spent a few hours by the pool, Mac chatting with various passengers while Cami read, before it was time to head ashore. Mac returned to the cabin to change, taking a moment to prepare for the afternoon ahead.

Pristine white sand stretched beneath their feet as Mac and Cami walked the shoreline at Grand Turk. Turquoise water lapped at the beach, so clear they could see fish darting just offshore, while palm trees swayed overhead in the gentle breeze. They bypassed the crowded bars near the cruise terminal, preferring the quieter stretch of paradise.

"Jack's Shack should be just up ahead," Mac said, pointing to a weathered tiki structure in the distance. Jerry had mentioned it that morning, saying he'd read about it in the port guide.

"Try to keep up," Cami replied, quickening her pace as her sandals dangled from her fingers.

Mac watched her move through the sand with quiet confidence, each step natural and unforced. In a place full of posturing, her complete lack of performance stood out. There was no effort to impress, just an ease that felt earned.

As they approached the beach bar, Mac spotted Jerry and Scarlet at a weathered wooden table, colorful drinks catching the sunlight between them. Mac blinked twice at what he saw. Jerry sat completely relaxed, his usual rigid posture replaced by something loose and natural as he leaned toward Scarlet, hanging on whatever story she was telling. In all their years of friendship, Mac had never seen Jerry look so genuinely at ease with anyone outside their unit.

"Well, well, the lovebirds found their nest," Cami announced as they approached.

Jerry straightened slightly at the interruption, but his smile remained genuine. "We just got here a few minutes ago," he said. "The paddle boarding was amazing."

A golden retriever trotted over to their table and Mac immediately dropped to a knee to greet him. Dogs were safer territory than analyzing Jerry's obvious interest in Scarlet. "Who's this guy?"

"That's Topher," Jerry explained. "The unofficial mascot."

Mac gave the dog a good scratch behind the ears before settling into a chair. He noticed Jerry didn't move away from Scarlet, even with their friends now present. *Interesting.*

A server in a faded Jack's Shack T-shirt approached. "What can I get you folks? Ready to order?"

"Jerk chicken spring rolls and conch fritters to start," Jerry said. "And I'll have the jerk chicken plate with a Turk's Head lager."

"Make it two on the beer," Mac chimed in. "And I'll take the loaded burger." Nothing beat a good beach burger, especially one topped with bacon and a fried egg, according to the menu description.

As the server departed, Cami leaned forward. "So, details. How was paddle boarding?"

While Scarlet described the crystal-clear water and colorful fish, Mac observed his friend's reactions. Jerry was keeping his distance physically, but his eyes never left Scarlet as she spoke. His usual hyper-vigilance was completely absent. Instead, he was fully present, smiling at her enthusiasm.

"I need to use the restroom," Cami announced after they'd been chatting for a few minutes. "Scarlet, come with me?"

"I'm fine, actually—" Scarlet began.

"Now," Cami insisted, already standing.

Mac watched them go, then turned to Jerry with a knowing grin. "Classic bathroom pow-wow. Ten bucks says she's grilling Scarlet about your date."

"It wasn't a date," Jerry insisted, though the color in his cheeks betrayed him.

The appetizers arrived, and Mac immediately reached for a spring roll. "Alright, dude, you've got about three minutes of privacy. Fill me in on all the details."

"It was nice," Jerry responded before taking a sip of his beer, maddeningly vague.

"Nice?!" Mac retorted, incredulous. "I'm gonna need more than that, brother."

"Yes, it was nice. We went out on the boards. We explored the water for a bit. We took a break on the beach to chat for a bit. It was a nice time," Jerry conceded, offering the bare minimum in additional details.

Mac wasn't about to give up. Not when Jerry had that look.

"Nah, dude, I need the PG-13 version, not the fairy tale princess cliff notes."

"We had a good time," Jerry responded, this time with a hint of annoyance. "There are no juicy details to be had. No tea to spill. Just two people enjoying each other's company in a tropical paradise. Now, can we move on and enjoy some lunch on this beautiful beach?"

Mac studied his friend, noting the slight defensive posture. "I know you better than that, man. Your face says everything. I've seen you through two deployments, a divorce, and countless 3 a.m. fevers with the boys. I know when you're into someone. You haven't taken your eyes off her since we sat down. Your shoulders are relaxed for the first time in years. And you're smiling. Like, actually smiling, not that polite grimace you use at mandatory unit functions."

Jerry sighed, grabbing a conch fritter. "Fine. Yeah, being with Scarlet is ... fun. Refreshing. She's smart, she's funny in this dry way that catches me off guard. And she didn't flinch when I told her about the boys."

Mac nearly choked on his beer. "You told her about Emmett and Marty? Already?"

"It came up," Jerry said with a shrug that failed to be casual. "She asked about my tattoo."

"And?"

"And she was cool about it. Genuinely interested, not doing that pity thing people do." Jerry's expression softened at the memory, then quickly clouded. "But it doesn't matter, you know? We live in different states, different worlds. I've got the boys, the Army, my whole life structured around their needs. And she's got this big career in Miami."

Jerry took a long sip of his beer, then continued, his voice lower. "Can you imagine trying to maintain a long-distance relationship with my schedule? Between Marty's physical therapy three times a week, Emmett's occupational therapy, their school schedules, and my unpredictable Army duties, I barely have time to breathe. Let alone foster a relationship across state lines. And what about the boys? They've already been abandoned by one mother figure. I can't introduce them to someone who might not stick around."

He ran a hand through his hair, a gesture Mac recognized as a sign of his internal struggle. "And let's be realistic ... why would someone like Scarlet want to take on all that baggage? Two special needs kids, and a job that could ship me off to a combat zone with minimal notice. She deserves someone who can take her to fancy restaurants and weekend getaways, not someone whose idea of a romantic evening is successfully getting both kids to bed by 8:30 without a meltdown."

Mac reached for a second spring roll, considering his friend's words. "These are amazing," he said after taking a bite. "You should definitely serve them at your wedding."

Jerry kicked him under the table.

"Look, all I'm saying is don't write the story before it ends," Mac continued. "You don't know what she wants or what she's willing to accept. Maybe complicated isn't a dealbreaker for everyone."

"It's not fair to drop all that on someone," Jerry insisted. "Besides, we've known each other for what, three days? It's crazy to even be having this conversation. After this cruise, that's it. We go back to our real lives."

"You're an idiot." Mac could see the women making their way back from the bathroom. "But sure, keep telling yourself that, buddy. I haven't seen you look at anyone like this in ... well, ever."

"Everything okay?" Jerry asked as the women sat back down.

"Just girl talk," Cami replied smoothly.

Their main courses arrived, and conversation resumed. Mac watched Jerry and Scarlet carefully, noting how Jerry's fingers brushed hers when passing the salt, how he leaned in when she spoke, how his usual habit of scanning public spaces had disappeared entirely. For all his talk of vacation flings and incompatible lives, Jerry's body language told a completely different story.

As they finished their meal, Topher returned to their table, flopping dramatically at Jerry's feet.

"I think he's adopted you," Scarlet observed, smiling.

"Story of my life," Jerry replied with a soft laugh. "I seem to collect strays."

The afternoon sun was beginning its descent as they paid their bill and gathered their belongings. Jerry and Scarlet walked slightly ahead on the beach, their conversation too quiet for Mac to hear.

"So," Cami said, falling into step beside him, "mission accomplished? Your friend seems happy."

Mac watched Jerry's face light up at something Scarlet said, his laughter warm and unguarded in a way Mac rarely heard in social situations. "Yeah, he does. But this is only day three of the cruise. A lot can happen."

"True," Cami agreed. "But I haven't seen Scarlet this relaxed in … well, maybe ever."

"You know what this means, right?" Mac said, a mischievous glint in his eye.

"That we're going to be stuck as third and fourth wheels for the rest of this cruise?"

"Worse," Mac replied solemnly. "We're the comedic side characters in their romantic comedy. You know, the sassy best friend and the goofy sidekick who exist solely to push the main characters together while offering witty commentary."

Cami snorted despite herself. "Oh God, you're right. Quick, we need a subplot of our own before we're reduced to nothing but one-liners and knowing glances."

"Too late," Mac grinned, gesturing ahead where Scarlet and Jerry had paused, silhouetted against the setting sun. "Look at that framing. Pure rom-com gold. I bet there's even inspirational music playing somewhere."

"Kill me now," Cami groaned, though she couldn't help smiling as she watched her best friend lean slightly into Jerry's space, happy and unguarded in a way that made Mac feel both hopeful and concerned for his friend's heart.

Ten

Morning light washed over the balcony as Jerry watched Tortola's harbor coming alive. The ship had docked before dawn, and already the port hummed with movement. Water taxis cut through the harbor, ferrying early passengers to shore while vendors below arranged colorful displays at their stalls. He checked his watch: 10:17 a.m. ship's time, 9:17 a.m. back in Texas. The boys would be at school by now.

Jerry sipped his coffee, savoring the rare quiet. The shower ran inside the cabin, punctuated by Mac's off-key singing.

He pulled out his phone and tapped FaceTime. Two rings, then Maggie appeared on screen, her silver-streaked hair in a messy bun, wearing a faded Utah Jazz T-shirt that had once belonged to his dad.

"There's my boy," she said warmly. "Ship still floating?"

"So far," Jerry replied with a half-smile. "Though Mac might go overboard if he uses all the hot water."

"Emmett was excited this morning," she continued, adjusting her reading glasses. "His class is starting a volcano project."

Jerry felt the familiar tug of absence. "That would be right up his alley. How was therapy yesterday?"

"Marty had a breakthrough in music therapy. The instructor tried drums, and he couldn't get enough. Pure joy, Jerry." She paused. "And Emmett's been watching that cooking competition show religiously. Made me promise we'd try fresh pasta this weekend."

"Fresh pasta? That's ambitious."

"Says the man who wouldn't even boil water two years ago."

The bathroom door opened with a cloud of steam, and Mac emerged, a towel wrapped around his waist, hair dripping.

"Is that Mrs. D?" he called, crossing to the balcony door. "Let me say hi!"

Before Jerry could protest, Mac leaned into frame, grinning widely.

"Morning, Mrs. Duncan! Don't worry, I'm keeping Gilmore out of trouble."

Maggie laughed. "I'm more concerned about him keeping you out of trouble, Jude. Last time you two were on leave together, there was that business with the karaoke bar and the—"

"Whoa, whoa," Mac interrupted, hands raised. "Ancient history. I'm a mature adult now, leading cultural excursions and everything."

"Mmmhmm." Maggie's tone was playful but skeptical. "Well, don't let my son sit around being serious the whole time."

"Yes, ma'am. Primary mission."

Mac saluted dramatically and disappeared back into the cabin.

"How's the trip, really?" Maggie asked once they were alone. "Made any friends?" The careful neutrality in her voice wasn't fooling anyone.

Jerry studied the horizon. "It's been ... nice. Different." He thought of Scarlet's laugh, the way her eyes crinkled at the corners. "Met some interesting people."

Maggie studied him with that uncanny maternal perception. "You sound ... lighter."

Jerry didn't answer. The observation hit closer than he cared to admit.

"I'm just getting some actual sleep for once," he deflected. "No one waking me up at 2 a.m. because Marty's escaped his bed again and rolled his toy basket across the living room floor."

"Mmm-hmm." Maggie wasn't buying it. "Speaking of which, I found him halfway down the hallway last night. That boy can army crawl faster than most kids can run."

Their conversation drifted to safer topics: the leaky faucet in the guest bathroom, the neighbor's overhanging tree, Hannah's messy breakup with that 'investment banker who wasn't good enough for her anyway.'

When they hung up, Jerry sat with the silence, turning over his mother's observation. *Lighter.* Was that true?

Mac emerged, fully dressed, in board shorts and a tropical shirt that somehow managed to be even louder than yesterday's.

"Virgin Gorda awaits," he announced, slinging a small backpack over his shoulder. "Last chance to join the fun, Cap'n."

Jerry shook his head. "Think I'll stay aboard today."

"Your loss." Mac paused, giving him an unusually direct look. "Your mom's right, you know. You do sound different."

Before Jerry could respond, Mac was already heading for the door. "Don't wait up, honey!" he called over his shoulder, and then he was gone.

Jerry stared at his phone, then deliberately set it on the table beside his empty coffee mug. Today, just for a few hours, he would disconnect.

He collected his notebook and pen, leaving his phone behind.

The Aphrodite's Pool area was practically deserted when Jerry arrived just before noon. With almost everyone on shore excursions, he had his pick of loungers. He settled near the infinity edge, where the pool water seemed to merge with the ocean beyond, and opened his weathered leather notebook across his lap.

It had been months since he'd written anything beyond lists and reminders. The notebook had traveled with him through his last two deployments, but these days he rarely found time for reflection. Today felt different, though. The quiet morning, the unscheduled space stretching ahead of him, stirred something he'd almost forgotten. Made him want to try.

His pen hovered over the blank page. If he was going to tell Scarlet how he felt, he needed to find the right words.

I've been thinking about you ...

He scratched it out. Too generic.

The way you laugh makes me forget to ...

Another scratch-out. Too sentimental.

Jerry sighed. He could draft a perfect speech for Sergeant Major Vega in under an hour, but his own feelings left him fumbling. He tried again.

I didn't expect to meet someone like ...

Scratch.

These past few days with you have been ...

"Well, look who decided to play hooky from the island adventure."

Jerry's head snapped up. He fumbled to close his notebook, nearly dropping his pen in the process.

Stacy stood before him, her curves barely contained by a tiny, bright yellow bikini. A hot pink sheer coverup hung loosely around her waist, the transparent fabric serving more as invitation than modesty. Gold bangles adorned her wrists, and oversized sunglasses pushed back her dark hair. Everything about her seemed calculated to attract notice, a stark contrast to Scarlet's natural ease yesterday in her simple one-piece on the paddle board.

"Not much for crowds today," he replied, discreetly sliding his notebook beneath his towel.

"Mind some company?" Without waiting for an answer, she settled into the lounger beside his, adjusting her top in a way that seemed deliberately designed to draw his eye.

"Be my guest." Jerry's tone remained neutral, polite without encouragement.

Stacy stretched languidly, very aware of the picture she made. "Smart move staying onboard. Those excursions are always overrated." She gestured toward his partially hidden notebook. "Ooh, what are you writing there, soldier? Secret plans or private thoughts?"

Jerry shifted uncomfortably. "Just notes."

"I bet that's not true." She leaned closer, and the heavy tropical scent of her perfume invaded the space between them. "You know what they say about the quiet ones ... always the most interesting beneath the surface."

She trailed a finger along the edge of his lounger. "I bet you've got plenty of ... depth to you."

Jerry cleared his throat. "Just collecting thoughts."

"So mysterious." Stacy smiled, lowering her voice. "I like a man who keeps me guessing. Though I can be very ... persuasive when I want to know something."

The innuendo hung in the air, making Jerry acutely aware of how alone they were by the pool.

Trying to steer the conversation away from her advances, Jerry cleared his throat. "You're from Cincinnati, right? You mentioned that at the mixer."

"Good memory, soldier." She adjusted her sunglasses. "Born and raised. Though it wasn't exactly the Brady Bunch growing up."

"No?"

Something shifted briefly in her expression. "Dad was in sales. International accounts. He was never around when I was a kid. We'd see him maybe two weekends a month if we were lucky." She shrugged, the vulnerability disappearing as quickly as it had appeared. "Mom made up for it by buying us whatever we wanted, though."

He nodded, and the moment struck deeper than he let on. The pattern: disappear, return, try to rebuild. It was one he knew too well.

"That must have been tough," he offered.

"Ancient history." Stacy waved it away with a flick of her wrist. "So," she continued, trailing a painted fingernail up her own thigh, "there's karaoke tonight at the Captain's Haven. Want to be my duet partner, sweetie? I've been told my performance is ... unforgettable."

Before Jerry could formulate an answer, a familiar voice cut through the poolside ambiance.

"Jerry, just the person I was looking for."

Cami stood just beyond their chairs, shades propped on her head, arms folded across her chest. Her expression was unreadable, but her presence hummed with the kind of purposeful energy that never waited for permission to speak.

"Cami," Jerry acknowledged, caught between relief and wariness. "Thought you were on the excursion."

"Changed my mind." Her eyes flicked to Stacy, then back to him. "Mind joining me at the bar for a sec? Ship business."

Stacy's smile tightened. "Sure. We were just warming up anyway." She stood, adjusting her bikini top. "Think about karaoke, stud. Offer stands."

She sauntered away, leaving Jerry facing Cami's arched eyebrow.

"Ship business?" he asked.

"Bar. Now."

Jerry followed Cami to the nearly empty poolside bar, where a lone bartender was polishing glasses. He slid onto a stool beside her, curious and wary.

The moment they were settled, Cami reached over and smacked him across the back of the head. Not hard, but definitely not gentle either.

"Ow!" Jerry rubbed the spot. "What was that for?"

"What the fuck are you doing?" Cami's voice was low but intense, her eyes flashing.

Jerry frowned. "Having a conversation?"

"With Stacy. Who, in case you haven't noticed, is trying to wedge herself between you and Scarlet."

"We were just talking."

"Uh-huh." Cami's skepticism could have cut glass. "And you were, what? Just being polite?"

The accusation lurking beneath her casual question sparked something defensive in him, a flare of irritation at her tone. "Not that it's any of your business, but yes. I wasn't encouraging anything."

"You weren't exactly discouraging it either." She studied him. "So, what's your deal with Scarlet, then? Just keeping your options open?"

The question hit like a bucket of ice water. Jerry went still.

"There's no 'deal.' We've been hanging out. Getting to know each other."

"Right. And that paddle boarding date? The way you look at her when you think no one's watching? The fact that Mac can't shut up about how different you've been this week?"

Jerry ran a hand over his face, suddenly aware of how exposed he felt having this conversation. "It's complicated."

"Try me," Cami challenged.

The words jammed in his throat. He'd barely admitted them to himself, let alone spoken them aloud. He opened his mouth, closed it again, searched for the right words.

"I ... it's not ... I mean, we're ..." He exhaled sharply, frustrated with himself. Then the words escaped before he could stop them. "Ah, hell. I'm falling for her."

The admission seemed to surprise them both. Jerry blinked, as if hearing the words for the first time himself.

Cami's eyebrows shot up, clearly not expecting such raw honesty.

"But. I mean ... it doesn't matter anyway," Jerry continued hastily, the words tumbling out. "What am I supposed to do? Uproot my whole life for someone I've known for all of three days? Or worse, ask her to join my complicated world of deployments and ... everything else?" He shook his head. "This is a cruise. It's not real life."

Understanding flickered across Cami's face, softening her posture slightly.

"So, you're, what? Preemptively bailing because it might be difficult?"

"I'm being realistic," Jerry countered. "Long distance is hard enough without ... complications. And Scarlet's got her whole life figured out. I doubt my situation factors into her five-year plan."

"You're a soldier. You've faced actual bombs. But you're running scared from a woman who makes you smile. Make it make sense, Jerry."

Cami laughed with genuine amusement. "You think Scarlet has her life figured out? That woman is as lost as the rest of us, just better at faking it."

She paused, her tone dipping just slightly. "Something happened with her ex, Alex. She won't tell me what, and believe me, I've tried getting it out of her more than once. But whatever it was broke something in her. Quietly. She didn't go nuclear or anything dramatic like burning down his apartment or slashing his tires, though I would've helped with that. Instead, she just buried it. Threw herself into work and didn't come up for air for years."

She leaned in a little, voice softer but still edged with her usual sass. "That woman lived off spreadsheets and iced coffee for two full calendar years. It was like watching a heartbreak power a Wall Street algorithm. I'm not saying she's fragile ... she's not. She's steel when she needs to be. But she's also ... rebuilding. You get me?"

Cami leveled him with a look that left no room for confusion. "Look. If she's showing up for you, even just a little, that's a big fucking deal. Don't screw with it. Or I swear to God, I'll track you down in whatever dusty deployment tent you end up in and make you cry in front of your entire unit."

She moved closer, her voice lowering. "Look, I'm not saying you need to propose. But if you're feeling something real for her, then have the decency to see it through, not hedge your bets with Bikini Barbie."

"I wasn't ..." Jerry started to protest, then stopped, honesty winning out. "You're right. I shouldn't have let that conversation go on as long as it did."

Cami's expression softened further. "What are you really afraid of, Jerry?"

The question hung between them, deceptively simple yet impossibly complex. Jerry stared at his untouched water glass, watching condensation bead on the outside.

"Scarlet deserves someone whole," he finally said. "Not someone held together with duct tape and stubbornness."

"That's bullshit and you know it." Cami's voice was gentle despite the words. "You think any of us aren't broken in some way? You think Scarlet's looking for perfect?"

When Jerry didn't answer, she pressed on.

"She's brave enough to stay. You better be brave enough to show up."

The comment stayed with him.

Scarlet hadn't reacted with pity or forced sympathy when he mentioned the boys. She had simply paid attention, her focus steady and real. "I'm sorry about—" he gestured vaguely toward where Stacy had been.

"I'm not the one you should apologize to." Cami's tone gentled. "Just … figure your shit out, Jerry. Scarlet doesn't deserve to get hurt because you're scared."

With that parting shot, she headed back toward the main pool area, leaving Jerry alone with thoughts too big for the bright afternoon.

Jerry leaned against the railing of an empty deck, watching the sunlight dance across the harbor water. The island beyond was lush and inviting, but he remained aboard, his body anchored to the ship while his thoughts drifted elsewhere.

She's brave enough to stay. You better be brave enough to show up.

Cami's words echoed, challenging and true. He'd been treading water, not just on this cruise, but for years. Maintaining, surviving, but never really moving forward. Every decision calculated around minimizing damage, protecting what mattered, staying afloat.

The realization dawned on him, not overwhelming, just unmistakable. For the first time in years, he craved something beyond his current life. And that prospect unnerved him more than any deployment ever had.

When he finally returned to his cabin, Jerry stood before the small closet, fingers running over the hanging garments. Mac had insisted he pack a few 'real shirts,' not just his usual collection of T-shirts and hoodies. He pulled out a blue Hawaiian shirt patterned with subtle white flowers, the kind of thing he would never have chosen for himself.

Karaoke tonight. The thought of singing in public made his stomach clench, but the thought of seeing Scarlet again ... that was another feeling entirely.

Jerry laid the shirt across his bed. Maybe it was time to stop treading water and start swimming toward something.

Eleven

The Captain's Haven was quiet in its pre-karaoke transformation, caught between nautical day lounge and evening venue. Crew members adjusted stage lights and sound equipment while Maude supervised from the center of the room, clipboard in hand, looking less like a cruise director and more like a general preparing for battle.

Jerry sat back in a booth, watching the preparations with mild amusement. He'd chosen a spot with good sightlines to both exits. He resisted the urge to fidget with the collar of his blue Hawaiian shirt, already second-guessing his decision to step outside his comfort zone.

"My, my," Maude approached their table, eyebrows raised. "The early birds catch the best seats, I see. You gentlemen are quite prompt."

"In the military, you're either early or late," Jerry replied with a half-smile. "There's no such thing as on time."

Maude's eyes sparkled with something knowing. "The tide doesn't arrive on schedule either, darling. It simply comes when it's meant to, and it can be gentle or arrive with force enough to change the shoreline forever." She patted his shoulder. "And we never know which tide might change everything, do we?"

Mac snorted. "Is she always this cryptic?"

"Only when she senses reluctant hearts," Maude winked, drifting away to intercept a crew member struggling with a microphone stand.

"She's definitely ... something," Jerry said, watching her go.

"Speaking of reluctant hearts," Mac leaned forward, lowering his voice. "You gonna tell me why you're wearing that Hawaiian shirt? Because I'm pretty sure it has something to do with a certain redhead."

Jerry's jaw tightened. "You're the one who packed it for me."

"Yeah, but I didn't force you to wear it," Mac's grin was unbearable. "Come on, man. You've been checking your watch every two minutes since we sat down."

Jerry exhaled slowly, surrendering to the inevitable. "I don't know what I'm doing here, Mac."

"Sitting in a bar waiting for karaoke to start?"

"With Scarlet," Jerry clarified, keeping his voice low despite the empty tables surrounding them. "She's not ... this isn't just a cruise thing. At least, it doesn't feel that way."

Mac's teasing expression softened. "That's a good thing, isn't it?"

"Is it?" Jerry stared down at his hands. "What happens when we dock? She goes back to her accounting firm and fancy Miami apartment, and I go back to 4 a.m. alarms, therapy appointments, and deployments?" He shook his head. "It's not fair to drag someone into that life."

"First of all," Mac held up a finger, "you're not dragging anyone anywhere. Scarlet's a grown woman who makes her own choices. And second," he added another finger, "she asked about you today."

Jerry's head snapped up. "What?"

"During the excursion. She was all casual about it at first, asking things like 'So, how long have you known Jerry?' and 'What's he like when he's not on vacation?' But trust me, she's just as tangled up as you are."

A dangerous warmth kindled in Jerry's chest. "She asked about me?"

"Mmhmm. And about the boys. Wanted to know what they're like, their ages." Mac shrugged, as if this weren't significant information. "She even asked what kind of father you are."

"What did you tell her?" The question came out rougher than intended.

"The truth. That you're the best damn dad I know." Mac's tone was light, but his eyes were serious. "And that the boys are lucky to have you."

Jerry swallowed against the sudden tightness in his throat.

"Look," Mac continued, "I get it. You've been in Dad Mode and Sergeant Mode for so long you forgot there's a Jerry Mode. But that guy deserves to exist too." He nodded toward the bar. "I'm gonna grab us some liquid courage before this place fills up. Don't overthink while I'm gone, okay?"

Before Jerry could respond, Mac slid out of the booth and made his way toward the bar. Jerry watched as his friend's path—coincidentally—intercepted Maude, their heads bending together in a suspiciously conspiratorial manner. Jerry was certain he wouldn't like whatever they were plotting, but knowing that Scarlet had been asking about him, about his boys, made it impossible to focus on Mac's mischief.

By the time Mac returned, the lounge had begun to fill with cruise guests ready for an evening of entertainment. Jerry spotted Scarlet and Cami the moment they appeared in the doorway. Scarlet was scanning the room, her hair falling in loose waves around her shoulders, wearing a simple green top that made her eyes seem even brighter across the distance. When she spotted them, a small smile that was tentative but real curved her lips.

"Don't say I never did anything for you," Mac muttered, raising his arm in an exaggerated wave.

As the women approached, Jerry stood without thinking, a reflex of military courtesy that felt suddenly, awkwardly formal in the casual setting. Mac snickered beside him, but Jerry ignored him, too focused on the way Scarlet moved through the crowd with easy confidence, the subtle scent of her perfume reaching him as she drew closer.

"Well, look who finally made it," Mac called out.

"Sorry we're late," Cami replied, sliding into the booth. "Someone had to try on three different outfits."

"It was two, not three," Scarlet corrected with an arch of her brow, settling into the booth next to Jerry, their shoulders nearly touching in the small space. "And worth it. Unlike some people, I don't have a uniform to fall back on." Her eyes flickered over Jerry's Hawaiian shirt with approval that made his chest tighten.

"Ladies, your timing couldn't be better," Mac grinned as a waitress arrived with a tray laden with drinks. The four cocktail glasses held different shades of green—from pale mint to deep emerald—garnished with fresh lime wedges and salt-crusted rims that caught the dim lighting of the lounge. Beside them, four shot glasses of clear tequila waited like small liquid challenges.

Mac distributed glasses around the table. "First round of liquid courage, coming right up."

"Nice," Cami grabbed her margarita. "I was gonna need at least two drinks before I got up there anyway."

"Much appreciated," Scarlet added, examining her glass with the critical eye of someone who knows the difference between top-shelf and well liquor. "Though, I should warn you, I've been known to hijack entire karaoke nights after sufficient tequila."

Jerry leaned closer to her. "Sorry about the head start. Mac was getting antsy."

"Yeah, they almost dragged me into hosting this thing," Mac said, passing shot glasses around. "Which I would've killed at, by the way."

"But Maude wasn't having it?" Cami guessed.

"Nope. Said something about 'maintaining the delicate ambiance' or whatever."

Scarlet sipped her margarita. "So that's why you ordered tequila? Drowning your disappointment?"

"More like preparing for disaster," Jerry said with a half-smile. "Some of us need it more than others."

"Wait," Scarlet turned to him, one perfectly shaped eyebrow arching upward. "You're not telling me Mr. Army Strong is scared of a little karaoke?"

"Petrified," Jerry admitted with a laugh. "Give me a combat zone over a microphone any day."

"Then why'd you come?" she asked, genuine curiosity softening her teasing tone.

Jerry's eyes met hers. "Mac said it'd be fun." He shrugged, voice softening. "And it seemed like a good way to spend the night."

The way he looked at her made it clear: *with you.*

"Alright, enough flirting," Mac interrupted, raising his shot glass. "A toast!"

"To new friends," Cami joined in.

"And unexpected adventures," Mac finished.

"And totally embarrassing ourselves," Cami added with a wink.

They raised their shots in brief salute before tipping them back. The liquor seared Jerry's throat, offering no relief from the strange combination of anxiety and eagerness pulsing through him. When their eyes connected again, Scarlet was observing him intently, her expression carrying a fresh, questioning quality.

On stage, Maude had taken command of the mic, resplendent in an over-the-top bedazzled blazer that caught every beam of light in the room. She'd transformed from elegant cruise host to her version of a rock star, complete with dramatic hand gestures and an exaggerated swagger.

"Welcome, darlings, to our Mingle at Sea karaoke extravaganza!" Maude's voice carried through the room. "Remember, what happens on the Elysian Serenade stays on the Elysian Serenade ... unless someone catches it on Instagram, in which case, make sure you tag us!"

"She's something else," Jerry murmured, a hint of amusement in his voice.

"So," Scarlet asked, turning toward Jerry, "what's your go-to karaoke song? Everyone has one, even if they deny it."

"I plead the Fifth," he replied, but his eyes crinkled at the corners, inviting her to press further.

"Oh no, that's not how this works," she insisted, leaning slightly closer. "Mac, help me out here."

"Let it Go," Mac announced without a hint of apology. "From *Frozen*. It's Marty's favorite song."

Jerry felt heat rush to his face as he covered it with his hand. "Jesus, Mac. Really?" He shot his friend a look that promised retribution later. Of all the things Mac could have shared about him, he had to pick the one that stripped away every ounce of his carefully maintained military persona. Princess songs were not exactly compatible with Staff Sergeant Duncan's image.

Her laugh surprised him. It was real, full of warmth, and not the ridicule he'd half-expected.

Just hearing it took the edge off, a quiet relief settling in its place.

"Marty lights up whenever he hears that song," Jerry admitted reluctantly, torn between mortification and the instinctive pride that always surfaced when he talked about his sons. "I mean, he can't speak, but you can see it in his whole body. His eyes get wide, and he starts rocking with the music. By the time Elsa belts the chorus, he's making these little joy sounds and his whole face just ..." Jerry gestured expansively, unable to adequately describe the pure happiness that transformed his son's face.

"And Jerry knows every word by heart," Mac added with a mischievous grin. "Meanwhile, Emmett's always giving stage directions. 'Dad, do the hand thing! You're not doing it right!'"

"I'm going to kill you in your sleep," Jerry muttered through a forced smile, feeling completely exposed. The fact that he sang Disney songs to make his sons happy wasn't something he typically advertised—especially not to a beautiful woman he was trying to impress.

As if on cue, Maude's voice rang out over the speakers. "Next up, we have ... Jerry! Come on up, soldier boy!"

Jerry's head snapped toward Mac, who was failing miserably at looking innocent. "You didn't."

"I absolutely did," Mac confirmed, raising his glass in salute. "Consider it payback for the time you signed me up for that talent show in Baghdad."

"That was three years ago!" Jerry protested, but Maude was already scanning the crowd.

"Jerry? Where's my Jerry? Don't be shy, darling!"

Panic clawed at his chest, raw and immediate. Jerry glanced at Scarlet, who looked surprised but not mocking. Still, the thought of making a fool of himself in front of her sent cold dread through his veins.

"You don't have to—" she began.

"No backing out now," Mac interrupted, nudging Jerry's shoulder. "The princess awaits."

Jerry shot Scarlet one last desperate look before grabbing his margarita and downing the rest in one swift motion. "If I don't make it back, tell my boys I died with dignity."

"Not likely," Cami quipped, but her tone was kind.

Drawing on every ounce of discipline from his years of service, Jerry pushed himself to his feet and made his way to the stage. The crowd parted before him, expectant faces turning to watch. Maude handed him the microphone with a wink that confirmed his suspicion that she and Mac had planned this ambush together.

"Break a leg, darling," she whispered before sweeping off stage.

The opening piano notes hit, and Jerry immediately recognized his fate. Mac was a dead man. The lyrics appeared on screen, he found his gaze drawn back to Scarlet at their table, watching him with open curiosity and the beginnings of a smile.

His military training hadn't prepared him for this particular battlefield.

The first verse began, and Jerry surrendered to the inevitable. There was no tactical retreat available.

His mind flashed to Marty at home, the way his son's entire face would light up whenever he heard this song. His eyes would widen, his body swaying with the music, his hands making small, excited motions. He thought of Emmett, who would provide running commentary: *Dad, you need to look sad now. No, sadder! Now you need to do the magic hands!* The countless bedtimes spent with this soundtrack. The words were burned into his memory now, as familiar as his service number or the disassembly sequence for his M4.

So Jerry sang. Terribly. God, so terribly. But with the same commitment he gave to everything that mattered to his sons.

He hit the first high note and his voice cracked spectacularly. Someone whooped. Rather than duck away from the embarrassment, Jerry leaned into it. Every awful note became a tribute to Marty, honoring the joy his son found in this ice queen's anthem and the childhood magic Jerry had fought to preserve despite everything else that had been taken from him.

Halfway through, something shifted inside him. The embarrassment dissolved, replaced by an unexpected lightness. What had started as enduring torture transformed into genuine enjoyment of the absurdity: belting out a snow queen's power ballad to a room full of buzzed solo travelers.

He caught Scarlet's eye again. She wasn't mocking him. She was laughing with genuine delight, her hand pressed to her heart.

Screw it. If he was doing this, he was committing fully.

With the famous chorus, Jerry channeled his inner Disney princess. He swept his arm dramatically, mimicking the iconic moves that Emmett had coached him through hundreds of times. *Do it like Elsa, Dad! You need to be POWERFUL!*

Inspiration struck. Jerry grabbed a stack of cocktail napkins from a nearby table and flung them into the air, watching them flutter down like snow. The crowd roared with approval.

Military bearing be damned. Jerry Duncan was a snow queen now.

By the final verse, he'd abandoned all pretense of dignity. He was gesturing wildly, hitting the emotional beats with exaggerated facial expressions that would have made Emmett shout corrections and Marty wiggle with uncontained joy.

As he delivered the final dismissive line with a theatrical hair flip that would haunt his military reputation forever, the crowd erupted in thunderous applause.

With his face burning and heart hammering, Jerry returned to find Scarlet watching him with an expression that went beyond simple amusement. Her look held genuine appreciation, the kind that suggested she'd seen past his usual guardedness to something real underneath. Something she wanted to explore further.

Maybe karaoke wasn't the tactical disaster he'd initially calculated.

"That," Cami declared as he slid back into the booth, "was the best thing I've seen all cruise."

"I hate you," Jerry told Mac, but there was no heat in it.

"You crushed it," Mac replied, offering a high five that Jerry reluctantly returned.

Scarlet turned to him, her face bright with genuine amusement. "That was …"

"Humiliating?" Jerry suggested, though the word didn't match what he was feeling.

"Amazing," she corrected, still smiling. "I didn't know you had that in you."

"Most people don't." Jerry took a deep breath, feeling strangely like he'd just run a tactical drill. "The things we do for our kids, right?"

"I wouldn't know," Scarlet replied, a flicker of something unreadable crossing her face before she reset to her usual sharp-witted self. "But if that performance is any indicator, I'd say your boys are pretty lucky."

Something about her expression made him brave. "There's a lot you don't know about me yet."

"Yet?" she asked quietly.

The question hung in the air between them, loaded with possibility. Jerry smiled, suddenly certain that whatever this was between them, it was something he wanted to explore.

From the corner of his eye, Jerry noticed a familiar figure at the bar. Stacy. She had been pursuing him not-so-subtly since the welcome mixer, and now she was watching their table with barely concealed intensity. Her eyes narrowed slightly as they met his, then flicked dismissively to Scarlet before she turned away. The message was clear: *this isn't over.*

Mac gave "Sweet Caroline" everything he had, hamming it up until Jerry's cheeks ached from laughing.

But between songs, Jerry noticed the small things: the warmth of Scarlet's arm brushing his, the curve of her grin when she cracked up, the quiet signature of her perfume floating just close enough to feel intentional.

"So, tell me more about your boys," Scarlet said during a lull between performances. "Marty's the older one?"

Jerry nodded, surprised by his eagerness to share. "He's eight. Has cerebral palsy. Non-verbal, but communicates just fine if you know how to listen." He smiled, thinking of his son's expressive face. "And Emmett's six. On the autism spectrum, but high-functioning. Talks enough for both of them, honestly."

"They sound amazing," Scarlet said, her voice softening. "You must miss them terribly."

"Every second," Jerry admitted. "But Mac was right, I needed this." His eyes met hers. "More than I realized."

Scarlet held his gaze for a long moment before looking away, a faint color rising in her cheeks. "Well, I'm glad you came," she said, her voice carrying the slight huskiness he was coming to recognize as genuine emotion. "Even if it meant public humiliation."

"Highlight of the cruise so far," he replied with a grin.

Cami checked her phone and abruptly stood. "Mac, didn't you say you wanted to check out that late-night jazz thing in the Celestial View?"

""Not really, I was having a good time here," Mac replied, confusion written across his face until something connected with his shin under the table. Jerry strongly suspected Cami's foot. "Oh! Right. That thing. At that place. We should definitely go now."

Jerry frowned. "I thought you wanted to—"

"Next time," Mac cut him off, already sliding out of the booth. "You two stay, though. Have fun. Don't wait up."

The others melted into the crowd, their departure quiet but intentional.

And just like that, Jerry was alone with Scarlet, the table between them shrinking by the second. The hum of the room faded slightly, replaced by something far more focused.

"That wasn't subtle," he said, unable to keep the amusement from his voice.

"Cami doesn't do subtle," Scarlet replied, a hint of color rising in her cheeks. "Though I can't say I mind the result." She slid her eyes toward him, then back to her drink, the gesture carrying a hint of vulnerability beneath her usual confidence.

They sat in comfortable silence, watching a young couple stumble through "Islands in the Stream." Jerry was hyperaware of Scarlet beside him, of the few inches separating their hands on the bench between them. He thought of Maude's words about tides changing shorelines forever, and wondered if this night might be his tide.

"So," he asked quietly, "what's your karaoke song?"

Scarlet smiled without looking at him. "You've covered it for both of us tonight."

He chuckled, the sound rough, even to his own ears. "Thanks for not recording it. Some things are better left at sea."

"Some things," she agreed, meeting his gaze with something new and unguarded in her eyes, "are worth remembering, though."

Jerry made a decision then, one that was simple and deliberate yet terrifying in its implications. Under the table, he slid his hand toward hers, giving her every chance to move away. When she didn't, he took her hand in his, their fingers interlacing with a rightness that took his breath away.

A group of college students attacked "Don't Stop Believin'" with more enthusiasm than talent, their off-key wailing filling the room. Jerry grimaced, his thumb tracing small patterns against Scarlet's skin.

"Another drink?" he asked, not wanting to break the spell between them but needing some small action to help navigate the unexpected depth of feeling that had surfaced without warning.

She nodded and he flagged down a server without letting go of her hand. "So," she said after a moment, "you're a single dad with two kids who sings Disney songs and works as … what exactly? You never actually told me what you do in the Army."

"Staff Sergeant," he replied, grateful for the simple question. "Primarily, I'm a squad leader. By training, I'm a combat photographer."

"Photographer?" Scarlet looked genuinely surprised. "That's … unexpected."

"Most people think that." He smiled slightly. "But I've always had a thing for capturing moments. Started as a hobby, became part of my service."

"I'd love to see your work sometime," she said, her tone casual but her eyes intent.

"Maybe someday," he replied, the promise in his voice unmistakable.

Their joined hands stayed hidden, a quiet promise neither had to voice.

Jerry lost track of time, the usual urgency to move on replaced by a desire to stay in this moment a little longer.

His body leaned before his mind could justify it, inching closer.

And when Scarlet settled slightly against him, the contact went deeper than skin. This was the kind of closeness that whispered safe, not just wanted.

The lights dimmed for a slow song, and without thinking, Jerry lifted his arm to rest along the back of the booth behind her. He wasn't quite touching, but he was close enough to feel the warmth of her against his skin.

When Maude called for the final round of performers, Jerry realized with a start that hours had passed in what felt like minutes. He couldn't remember the last time he'd lost track of time like this. It had been years, since before the boys, before deployments, before responsibility had wrapped around him like armor.

Sitting here with Scarlet, his hand in hers, Jerry felt something he'd almost forgotten: presence. Not escaping his life or running toward a new one, but simply existing in this moment, with this woman, feeling more like himself than he had in years.

Twelve

Jerry squinted against the Caribbean sun as he and Mac approached the party bus parked at the pier. The converted school bus was a riot of color. Its neon yellow base was covered with splashes of hot pink, electric blue, and lime green painted in wild patterns across its sides. A painted tragedy-comedy mask hung from the front grille, and "DA PARTY BUS" was emblazoned in bold orange letters across the top. Flags from different Caribbean nations fluttered in the breeze, and the front bumper proudly proclaimed "THE FUN STARTS HERE!!!"

Reggae bass thumped so hard it vibrated Jerry's chest before he even reached the bus. The air smelled of coconut sunscreen, sea salt, and the promise of rum.

"This is what I'm talking about!" Mac shouted over the music, practically skipping toward the entrance. "No thinking allowed today, brother. Just feeling!"

Jerry spotted Scarlet's vibrant red hair immediately. She and Cami were already aboard, dancing in their seats with plastic cups raised high. When Scarlet saw him, she whistled and waved wildly, her usual polish replaced by unfiltered joy.

A barrel-chested man with sun-bleached dreadlocks and a tie-dyed tank top bounded down the bus steps. A massive gold medallion bounced against his chest, and his smile was as bright as the Caribbean noon.

"Welcome, welcome! I be Captain Coconut, your guide to paradise and mischief!" He draped plastic leis around their necks and pressed rum punches into their hands. "First rule of Da Party Bus: no one stays thirsty! Second rule: no one stays serious!"

Sweet and deceptively smooth, the rum punch hit Jerry's tongue like liquid sunshine with a strength that snuck up on him. Mac drained his in one go, slamming the cup down with a whoop.

Inside, the bus was a sensory explosion. Rainbow streamers hung from the ceiling, catching the breeze from open windows. The seats were upholstered in mismatched fabrics: leopard print, neon stripes, tropical flowers. A gleaming stripper pole stood in the center aisle like an invitation to bad decisions, and portable speakers blasted Bob Marley at volumes that made conversation an athletic event.

Jerry slid into the seat beside Scarlet, who immediately grabbed his face and planted a rum-flavored kiss on his cheek.

"You're late!" she shouted over the music, her eyes sparkling with mischief. "We're already on drink number two!"

"Guess I'd better catch up," Jerry replied, emptying his cup. The rum delivered a pleasant burn, swiftly unwinding the knots he typically carried in his shoulders.

Captain Coconut bounded back aboard, shaking maracas above his head to get everyone's attention. "Beautiful people! We gonna make one quick stop for more provisions, then straight to the most beautiful, most free beach on the island!" He cranked a dial on the sound system, and the music somehow got even louder. "But first ... ROAD DRINKS!"

He began passing out more cups as the bus lurched into motion, its horn playing the first notes of "Hot Hot Hot." Passengers cheered and swayed with the rhythm of the moving bus.

Jerry couldn't stop laughing as gusts of wind turned Scarlet's hair into a curtain across his face.

"Looking good, Red!" Mac called out to Scarlet, giving her a thumbs up before shimmying past.

Across the aisle, Jerry spotted Stacy grinding playfully against a tall guy in board shorts. She caught Jerry's eye and raised her cup in a friendly toast before turning her full attention back to her new companion.

Twenty minutes and two more rum punches later, Captain Coconut pulled the bus over at a roadside shack painted in Jamaican flag colors.

"Quick rum restock, my friends! Not that we running low, but Captain Coconut never lets the party run dry! Keep the vibes flowing. I'll be right back!"

As the captain hopped off, passengers cranked the music even louder. Someone started a limbo competition using a beach towel as the bar, while others drummed on the bus seats. The coolers at the back of the bus were still well-stocked with bottles and cups, ensuring the party wouldn't pause even for a moment.

Scarlet pulled Jerry to his feet. "Dance with me!"

Before he could respond, she was guiding his hands to her hips, swaying to the reggaeton beat. Her body moved with a freedom he'd never seen in her before, completely unselfconscious. Her vibrant red hair whipped around as she spun, catching the sunlight like flames.

"You're different today," he said into her ear.

"So are you," she responded, her eyes bright with something that looked like happiness. "I like it."

Captain Coconut returned with a crate of additional bottles, setting off a fresh round of cheers. "Next stop, Orient Beach! Where the only rule is there are no rules!"

The bus roared back to life, now equipped with enough alcohol to sustain their revelry well into the night. As the journey continued, Captain Coconut's enthusiastic top-ups transformed the rum punch from mildly potent to dangerously strong, each refill containing significantly more rum than juice. By the time they neared the beach, what had started as fruit punch with a kick was essentially just rum with a hint of color.

Someone started a sing-along to "Red Red Wine," with Mac conducting the chorus from atop his seat. Scarlet sat half on Jerry's lap, feeding him slices of mango from a plastic container that materialized from Cami's beach bag.

"I can't remember the last time I had this much fun," Jerry admitted, the confession slipping out easier than it would have twenty-four hours ago.

"The day's just getting started," Scarlet replied with a grin that promised trouble of the best kind.

Orient Beach emerged from behind a bend in the road like a postcard come to life. The sand was impossibly white, the water a gradient of turquoise so vivid it looked digitally enhanced. Palm trees swayed in the breeze, their fronds casting dancing shadows on the shoreline.

The group tumbled out of the bus in a tangle of beach bags, towels, and half-filled drink cups. Captain Coconut led them to a spot on the beach, but Jerry caught Mac's eye, nodding toward a more secluded area beneath a cluster of palm trees.

The foursome broke away from the main group, claiming a perfect patch of sand with just the right balance of sun and shade. They dropped their bags, and Jerry spread out towels while Cami produced a portable speaker from her bag, instantly creating their own private sound bubble.

Mac was already stripping down to his swim trunks, spinning Cami around in an impromptu dance that nearly sent them both tumbling into the sand.

Without warning, Cami hooked her thumbs into her bikini bottoms and dropped them right there on the beach.

"Last one in the water buys drinks tonight!" she shouted, looking directly at Mac as she untied her bikini top while already sprinting toward the waves. The top fell abandoned on the sand, marking her path like a breadcrumb.

Mac's eyes bulged comically. "Challenge accepted!" He lunged after her while trying to strip off his swim trunks mid-run, an ambitious multitasking attempt that sent him face-planting spectacularly into the sand when his feet tangled in the fabric.

"Ten out of ten on the dismount!" Jerry called out, doubled over with laughter.

Mac recovered with the resilience of the truly intoxicated, kicking free of his trunks and charging naked into the water with a rebel yell that turned every head on the beach.

Jerry stood there grinning, the sun warm on his shoulders, feeling lighter than he had in years. In a moment of perfect clarity, he decided to stop thinking altogether.

With one fluid motion, he stripped off his swim trunks and stepped free of them, feeling the Caribbean breeze against parts of him that hadn't seen the sun since ... well, ever. The wildly liberating sensation went deeper than physical freedom, as if he was shedding layers of himself along with the fabric.

He ran into the waves without looking back, letting out a whoop of pure, uncomplicated joy that surprised even himself with its freedom. The water embraced him, warm and crystal clear. Jerry dove under a wave, emerging to find Mac and Cami splashing each other and cackling like children discovering water for the first time.

When he turned toward shore, the world seemed to exhale.

Time loosened its grip, stretching thin around the edges as if to make room for the moment.

Scarlet stood with her back to him, bare from the waist up, framed by sun and sea.

With slow, deliberate grace, she bent to peel the bikini bottoms from her hips, sliding them down her legs like the sea itself had asked for them back.

Then, she rose, her hair flaring out in a fiery arc of red that shimmered in the light.

She gathered the flowing strands, twisting them into a high ponytail that revealed the elegant slope of her neck and the long line of her spine, all quiet strength and grace.

He didn't move. Barely dared to blink.

Inside him, a hush fell that carried both wonder and longing.

Then, she turned, bathed in gold, and her gaze caught his with a smile that curled with mischief and something more tender beneath it.

She ran toward the waves, limbs sure and free, and launched herself into his arms with the full force of joy.

They plunged beneath the surface, the sea swallowing them whole.

When they rose again, laughing and breathless, she was right there waiting. Her eyes shone bright, lashes jeweled with seawater, her smile unguarded and real.

He didn't hesitate.

He kissed her, tasting salt and heat and the wild sweetness of her.

And just like that, he was swept away, caught and dragged under by the scarlet wave.

Her mouth on his, her body warm against his chest, and the world narrowing to this single, perfect moment of yes.

When they broke apart, her eyes were wide and bright.

"What was that for?" she whispered.

"Being you," he answered simply. "Being here."

"Hey, Red! Jerry! Get a room already!" Mac hollered, sending a splash their way.

Jerry responded by splashing a tidal wave in his direction, starting a water war that quickly pulled in Cami too. Soon, all four of them were engaged in an all-out splash battle, shrieking and laughing like they were teenagers again.

"Wait, wait!" Mac shouted suddenly, raising his hands in surrender. "I have an idea. Water jousting!"

"What are you talking about?" Cami asked, but she was already grinning.

"I'll get on your shoulders," Mac declared, moving toward her with a gleam in his eye.

Cami burst out laughing. "You're kidding, right?"

"Dead serious," Mac said, eyebrows wagging. "Me and you against Jerry and Red."

Jerry looked at Scarlet, who was already moving toward him with a competitive glint in her eye. "You game?"

"Oh, I'm going to destroy them," she said, wading closer.

With a laugh, Jerry ducked underwater, positioning himself between her legs. He felt her thighs tighten around his neck as he stood, lifting her clear of the water. She let out a squeal of surprise that dissolved into laughter.

"Oh my God!" she shouted, wobbling before finding her balance with her hands on top of his head. "This is insane!"

Across from them, an absurd scene was unfolding. Cami was at least five inches taller than Mac and significantly more solid, yet she was attempting to balance the shorter man on her shoulders. Mac flailed wildly, nearly toppling sideways before somehow finding his balance. The sight of the muscular, petite Mac perched precariously on the statuesque Cami's shoulders had Jerry laughing so hard he nearly dropped Scarlet.

"Tremble before us!" Mac shouted from his wobbly perch, pointing dramatically at Jerry and Scarlet despite nearly capsizing. "The water warriors have arrived!"

"Shut up and hold on, short stack," Cami growled, gripping his ankles as she stabilized herself. "Or I'm dunking you."

What followed was the most absurd jousting match in the history of the Caribbean. Scarlet, completely nude and laughing hysterically, grappled with Mac, who was equally naked and even more unstable. Jerry could feel Scarlet's thighs tightening around his neck as she leaned forward to push at Mac, could hear her breathless laughter above him.

"You're going down, Red!" Mac shouted, grabbing for Scarlet's arms.

"In your dreams, pipsqueak!" Scarlet shot back, managing to land a solid push to Mac's chest.

Mac windmilled his arms dramatically, throwing Cami off balance. With a cry of "Timber!" they went down in spectacularly uncoordinated fashion, creating a massive splash as they collapsed into the water.

"Victory!" Scarlet crowed from her perch on Jerry's shoulders, arms raised in triumph.

Jerry, caught up in the moment and feeling playful, called out, "Oh no, we're going down too!" He twisted slightly and then fell backward deliberately, sending both of them crashing into the water with a giant splash.

Scarlet came up sputtering and laughing, her red hair plastered to her face. "Traitor!" she accused, launching herself at him.

Jerry caught her easily, spinning her around in the water before pulling her close. "Couldn't let you get too cocky," he murmured against her ear.

"Rematch!" Mac demanded, already trying to climb back onto Cami's shoulders despite her protests. "Best two out of three!"

The next hour dissolved into a sun-drenched dream of water fights, swimming races, and increasingly ridiculous challenges. At some point, Captain Coconut appeared with a floating cooler of rum punch that was essentially just rum with a splash of grenadine for color. They passed the plastic cups back and forth, the alcohol and sun creating a perfect bubble of joy and abandon.

When they finally decided to head back to shore, Mac made a startling discovery.

"Guys?" he called out, scanning the beach with increasing panic. "Where are my shorts?"

They combed the area where they'd left their things, but Mac's swim trunks had vanished, probably carried off by the tide or buried beneath the sand during their chaotic beach day.

"Well, this is awkward," Mac said, hands on his hips, standing naked as the day he was born.

Cami rolled her eyes. "Oh, for God's sake." She rummaged through her bag and pulled out her bikini bottoms. "Here. These should fit your tiny ass."

"My ass is perfectly proportional to my body, thank you very much," Mac protested, but he took the offered bikini bottoms and examined them doubtfully.

"My coverup is long enough," Cami shrugged, wrapping herself in a flowing beach dress that hit mid-thigh. "Just don't bend over too much on the bus."

Mac wiggled into the bright teal bikini bottoms, which stretched across his hips in a way that was both horrifying and hilarious. Jerry nearly collapsed with laughter at the sight.

"I think you've started a new fashion trend," Scarlet managed through her giggles.

"I make these look good," Mac insisted, doing an exaggerated catwalk strut and posing with his hands on his hips. "I should've been wearing women's swimwear all along."

Jerry couldn't remember the last time he'd felt so completely present, so utterly free from the constant low-level anxiety that had become his baseline. In this moment, there were no deployments, no therapy appointments, no logistic puzzles to solve. Only sky, water, laughter, and the warm press of Scarlet's body against his whenever she drifted close.

The rum flowed even more freely on the return journey, everyone sun-flushed and riding the high of shared abandon. Jerry sat with his arm wrapped around Scarlet, who was practically in his lap, her head resting in the crook of his neck. Her vibrant red ponytail tickled his skin, still damp from the ocean.

Across the aisle, Mac was holding court, regaling the group with increasingly outrageous stories about their military adventures, each tale more embellished than the last. He'd wrapped a beach towel around his waist to maintain some semblance of dignity over Cami's borrowed bikini bottoms.

"So, there we were, surrounded by camels," he proclaimed, gesturing so wildly he sloshed rum punch onto his chest, "and the biggest one, I swear he was the size of a Humvee ... locks eyes with the colonel and just ..." Mac paused for dramatic effect, "... PFFT! Right in his face! Full camel spit! Like a Super Soaker filled with camel loogies!"

The bus erupted in laughter, and Jerry couldn't even bring himself to correct the story, which had actually involved a very small, very old camel and a near-miss that barely grazed the lieutenant's boot.

"You're completely full of shit," Jerry called out instead, grinning ear to ear.

"I swear on the sacred stripper pole!" Mac declared, swaying to his feet and grabbing the center pole for stability. He gave it an experimental spin, nearly toppling into someone's lap. "Hey, Captain! This thing is sturdy, right?"

Captain Coconut glanced back from the driver's seat. "Built to withstand professionals, my friend, but I wouldn't recommend ..."

Mac was already swinging around the pole, to the delight of the entire bus. "Ladies and gentlemen, for your viewing pleasure ... Magic Mac: The Uncensored Edition!"

What followed was perhaps the most gloriously terrible pole dance ever performed on the island of St. Maarten. Mac had boundless enthusiasm but the coordination of a newborn giraffe, especially after a day of continuous drinking. He attempted a spin that turned into an awkward slide, tried to climb the pole using only arm strength, and ended up hanging upside down by his knees with a terrified expression.

In the midst of a particularly ambitious move, Mac's beach towel finally gave up its valiant struggle and slid off entirely, revealing Cami's teal bikini bottoms stretched to their absolute limit. The bus erupted in fresh howls of laughter and applause.

"Work it, Mac!" someone shouted from the back.

"The teal really brings out your eyes!" called another.

Mac, never one to be embarrassed, took a dramatic bow as he finished his routine, making a show of adjusting the bikini bottoms. "And that, ladies and gentlemen, is how you rock beachwear."

He staggered back toward his seat. Instead of sitting down, however, he paused in front of Cami, who was wiping tears of laughter from her eyes.

Without warning, Mac grabbed her face in both hands and planted a kiss directly on her lips. The bus erupted in wolf whistles and applause.

Jerry's eyebrows shot up, and he exchanged a surprised look with Scarlet. When Mac finally pulled away, Cami looked momentarily stunned before a slow, wicked smile spread across her face.

"I'd give the dance a three," she said, voice carrying over the music, "but the kiss was at least an eight."

"I'll take it!" Mac crowed, flopping down beside her and immediately launching into an animated conversation that involved a lot of hand gestures and leaning into her personal space.

Jerry made a mental note to interrogate Mac about this development later. For now, though, he was content with Scarlet curled against him, her fingers tracing lazy patterns on his thigh.

"You seem happy," she murmured, lips close to his ear.

"I am," he replied, surprising himself with how true it was. "Happier than I've been in ... hell, I don't even know how long."

She smiled, the expression reaching all the way to her eyes. "It looks good on you."

As they approached the pier, Jerry spotted a welcoming committee waiting at the dock, consisting of Maude with the head of security and the ship's captain, all looking like parents ready to corral a group of wayward teenagers.

"Uh-oh," Jerry muttered to Scarlet. "Looks like we've made an impression."

She followed his gaze and let out a groan. "Nothing says 'responsible adult' like being escorted back to the ship by security."

"Worth it, though?" he asked, squeezing her hand.

"Every single second," she replied, squeezing back.

Captain Coconut stood at the front of the bus as they pulled to a stop. "Beautiful people! I hope you enjoyed the real St. Maarten experience! Remember, what happens on Da Party Bus ..."

"Stays on everyone's Instagram forever!" someone called out, setting off a final round of laughter.

As they disembarked on wobbly legs, Jerry watched Maude embrace Scarlet warmly, whispering something in her ear. Whatever she said made Scarlet's expression shift to something soft and thoughtful.

Jerry started toward them, curious, when Mac practically tackled him from behind, throwing a heavy arm across his shoulders.

"Dude!" Mac exclaimed, still in his borrowed teal bikini bottoms, beach towel long forgotten. "We're totally hitting the club tonight, right?"

Jerry shoved him away with a grimace. "Keep your distance until you're wearing actual pants. I've seen enough of you today."

"Oh please," Mac snorted, attempting to drape himself over Jerry again. "Like we weren't all completely naked an hour ago. Don't get shy on me now, Staff Sergeant!"

Jerry dodged Mac's second attempt at a bear hug, laughing despite himself. "There's a difference between nude at a beach and you grinding on me in women's swimwear."

Scarlet and Cami had already started up the gangway, heads together in animated conversation, occasionally glancing back with amused smiles at the boys' antics.

"You love it," Mac insisted, sashaying after the women with an exaggerated wiggle. He turned back with a grin that promised more chaos to come. "Come on brother, the night is still young!"

Jerry followed behind, watching as Scarlet paused at the top of the gangway and looked back. When she caught his eye, her whole face lit up with a smile he'd never seen before. It was open, unguarded, and full of promise.

Thirteen

T he cabin lights pierced through Jerry's eyelids like daggers. He groaned, immediately regretting the rum-soaked beach excursion from earlier. His mouth felt like sandpaper, his head throbbed, and something was poking his face. That something turned out to be Mac's finger.

"Rise and shine, Sleeping Beauty," Mac chirped, standing over him, fully dressed in a light beige linen suit that somehow managed to look both perfectly tailored and carelessly thrown on. The crisp white button-down beneath it was open at the collar, no tie in sight.

Jerry blinked, struggling to focus on the digital clock. The numbers swam in his vision. "What time is it?"

"Quarter to six," Mac replied. "The mingle thing starts at 6:30."

Jerry squinted at his watch to confirm. 5:45 p.m. The "Glam & Champagne" themed Mingle at Sea Pre-Gala Mixer started at 6:30. Usually, forty-five minutes would be child's play for a man who could be ready for morning PT in under ten, but the lingering fog of

Caribbean rum made everything feel like it was happening underwater.

"You could've woken me sooner," Jerry muttered, hauling himself upright.

Mac was examining his reflection, adjusting his collar with practiced nonchalance. "And miss the little snoring symphony you had going? Besides, I figured you earned the rest after drinking half your body weight in rum punch." He turned, flashing a grin. "Though I suspect a certain redhead might've factored into those calculations."

Jerry ignored the comment and ducked into the bathroom.

By the time he stepped out of the shower, the steam was thick enough to write his thoughts in. He wiped the mirror and frowned at the man behind the glass. Not angry. Just ... off.

He worked his fingers through damp hair, trying to wrangle it into something presentable. Not that a buzz cut left many options. Still, he lingered. Adjusted. Checked again.

Maybe she'd notice. Maybe that meant something.

By the time he emerged in a towel, Mac was examining his watch with theatrical concern.

"Ten minutes," he said with a smirk. "Think you can beat the clock?"

The best formal attire Jerry had brought on this trip lay waiting on the bed. A blue and white gingham check button-down, slim-fitting navy dress pants, and a narrow black tie with a simple silver clip. Nothing fancy, nothing that screamed cruise ship formal night, but it was neat, clean, and pressed within an inch of its life.

He dressed mechanically, the routine familiar even as his fingers fumbled with the tie. Military life had ingrained the movements, even if the outcome tonight felt strangely significant. Mac lounged against the cabin wall, scrolling through his phone with one hand, the other tucked casually in his pocket.

"Not bad," Mac said as Jerry stepped back for a final check in the mirror. "You clean up decent."

Jerry snorted, but secretly felt a flush of relief. He'd polished his dress shoes to a military shine, tucked in his shirt with parade-ground precision, and adjusted his tie clip until it sat perfectly horizontal. The whole effect was ... acceptable. Not the tuxedo-level elegance that was probably parading around the ship tonight, but it would do.

"We're officially late," Mac announced, pushing off the wall. "Hopefully the champagne hasn't run dry."

They left the cabin at 6:40, and as they walked down the corridor, Jerry decided to finally ask what he'd been wondering since the night before.

"So, what happened with you and Cami last night? You two conveniently disappeared after karaoke."

Mac's casual stride faltered for half a second. "Nothing happened."

Jerry raised an eyebrow.

"Fine," Mac conceded. "Something happened. But it was just a one-time thing, you know? We got talking after you and Red had your moment in the spotlight, and then—"

"You abandoned us to go hook up," Jerry finished.

"I prefer to think of it as giving you two privacy while pursuing my own diplomatic relations. Besides, it worked out for everyone, didn't it? And honestly, we didn't plan for anything to happen, it just—"

SLAM!

The sound detonated through the air like an IED.

Somewhere behind them, a cabin door slammed shut, sending a booming, violent crack reverberating down the narrow hallway.

The world compressed around Jerry in an instant. The tasteful corridor became a narrow alley in Fallujah. The plush carpet beneath his dress shoes transformed into packed dirt. The sound echoed, not as a simple door, but as an explosive device detonating just behind him.

His body reacted before his mind could process what was happening. Jerry dropped instantly to the floor, knees striking the carpet as he instinctively shielded his head, curling forward, lungs frozen mid-breath.

"Hunter! Get down!" he called out sharply, reaching blindly for a battle buddy who wasn't there.

The walls seemed to vibrate with the aftermath of the sound, phantom echoes ringing in his ears. "Incoming," he whispered, the word barely audible, even to himself.

Mac was beside him in an instant, not touching, just present. "Hey man, everything alright?" His voice was casual, but his eyes were watchful as he positioned himself between Jerry and the curious stares of an elderly couple who'd emerged from their stateroom.

"Just heading to dinner," Mac explained to them with a casual wave. "Had a bit too much sun today."

They moved on after a moment's hesitation, and Mac turned his attention back to Jerry.

"Just breathe, man," Mac said quietly. "In through the nose, out through the mouth. Think about those clear blue waters from today. Remember how Emmett laughed in that video your mom sent? Focus on that."

Jerry's fingers fumbled with his tie, loosening the knot as he struggled to catch his breath. His hands moved to his collar, unbuttoning the top two buttons as the fabric suddenly felt like it was constricting his airway. Sweat beaded at his temples despite the chill of the air-conditioned hallway.

"I'm good," he managed after a minute, beginning to pull himself upright.

"No, you're not okay," Mac said firmly, his usual joking manner gone. "You need to breathe. Take your time. There's no rush."

Jerry shook his head, shame burning hot behind his eyes. His carefully arranged outfit now felt like a costume, the tie constricting around his throat, the polished shoes pinching and foreign.

"I ... I ... I need to ..." he started.

"Head back," Mac finished for him. "No problem. I'll run blocker with the girls. They're bound to ask questions."

"Tell Scarlet ..." Jerry tried again, unable to find the words.

Mac nodded. "I got it. Go do what you need to do."

Jerry's steps faltered the moment the hallway ended.

Inside the cabin, he pulled at his tie like it was choking him, unfastened a few buttons, and forgot about one shoe entirely.

He landed on the bed with a thud, the tension still coiled in his shoulders.

His thumb hovered for a beat before swiping to the album of his boys, frozen in moments where everything still felt right.

There was Emmett at his fifth birthday, chocolate cake smeared across his serious little face. Marty in his adaptive swing, head thrown back in silent laughter. Both boys asleep in the backseat of the car after a rare day at the water park.

His breathing slowed as he scrolled, his other hand unconsciously finding the tattoo on his right bicep. His anchors. His reasons.

Time slipped away as he sat there, moving between photos of his boys and deep breathing exercises. The ship's movement beneath him gradually became a comfort rather than a distraction. The hum of the engines a white noise that helped slow his racing heart.

Nearly an hour had passed when a knock at the door jarred him from his reverie.

"No room service tonight, thanks," he called out, voice still rougher than he'd like. "Just forgot to put up the sign."

"It's me," came Scarlet's reply, and Jerry froze.

Jerry glanced down at his rumpled clothes, the ghost of the panic attack still humming faintly under his skin. He wasn't ready for anyone.

But her voice was gentle and sure, and something in it pulled him to the door.

Scarlet stood there, robe belted over a red swimsuit that peeked out at the collar. Her hair still gleamed from formal night, every wave pinned and shaped to perfection. Every trace of makeup remained perfect, bold eyes and red lips untouched, like she hadn't stopped moving since she left the ballroom.

She could've stayed in that world. Instead, she came here.

"Mac said you weren't feeling well," she said, her eyes taking in his unbuttoned shirt, a single shoe. No judgment, just quiet observation.

"I'm just—" he started, then stopped, unsure how to explain.

"Not feeling the formal night vibe?" she supplied, her lips quirking into a small smile. "Me neither, as it turns out."

"I was thinking," she continued, "the hot tubs on the aft deck are usually empty during formal night. Everyone's too busy showing off their fancy clothes." She tilted her head. "Care to join me for something a little less ... formal?"

The suggestion suspended in the air between them, and Jerry felt long-held barriers starting to crumble. Her gaze offered not pity, but authentic invitation. Not rescue, but a path forward together.

"Give me two minutes," he said, and meant it.

Heat rushed up Jerry's neck. "Come on in," he said, stepping aside with a nervous laugh. "But no peeking," he added, grabbing his swim trunks and heading to the bathroom.

In the small bathroom, Jerry changed quickly, his hands still unsteady from the earlier episode in the hallway. He splashed cold water on his face, studying his reflection in the mirror. The man staring back looked tired around the eyes. Vulnerable. He took a deep breath, belted the white terry robe around his waist, and opened the door.

The moment stopped him cold.

Scarlet sat on his bed, fingers brushing over the single photo he kept close, one of Emmett guiding Marty down a sidewalk, his backpack nearly swallowing him whole.

That shot held more than memory. It held purpose.

Scarlet looked up, placing the photo carefully back in its place. Something in her expression made his throat tighten.

"Ready?" she asked, standing and adjusting her robe as if she hadn't just glimpsed the most precious part of his life.

"Yeah," he managed to respond. He held the door open for her, trying to decode what had just happened. She hadn't asked questions. Hadn't made it a thing. And somehow, that felt right.

They walked together toward the elevators, both in identical white robes, moving against the flow of formally dressed passengers heading to dinner.

The aft deck was blissfully quiet, the hot tubs steaming invitingly in the night air. Stars were scattered across the inky sky, and the moon cast a silver path across the water behind the ship. The deck was lit by soft spotlights, creating pools of golden light amid the shadows.

"Why don't you get comfortable?" Scarlet suggested, nodding toward the nearest hot tub. "I'll grab us something to drink."

Jerry slipped off his robe, draped it over a nearby deck chair, and eased himself into the hot tub. The warm water immediately began working magic on his tense muscles. He leaned back, tilting his head to look at the stars overhead, letting himself simply exist in the moment.

When Scarlet returned a few minutes later, she was carrying two frozen piña coladas. She set them carefully at the edge of the hot tub before untying her robe and letting it fall onto the chair beside Jerry's. As she descended the steps into the water, drinks in hand, Jerry's breath caught.

She wore the same vibrant red tankini from their paddle boarding excursion and it looked just as good tonight.

"That's from our paddle boarding date," he said without thinking, then froze when he realized what he'd called it.

A slow smile spread across Scarlet's face. "So it was a date?" she asked, her eyes glinting with mischief in the low light.

Jerry couldn't help the answering smile that tugged at his lips. "I guess it was."

She handed him one of the drinks before settling to his left, nestling against his ribs as naturally as if they'd been doing this for years. Jerry tentatively draped his left arm around her shoulders, and she leaned into his touch without hesitation, her right hand coming to rest lightly on his thigh. He held his piña colada in his right hand while she held hers in her left.

"How'd you know this was exactly what I needed?" he asked, taking a sip of the icy drink.

She shrugged. "Just a hunch that you might prefer this to champagne and small talk."

The only sound was the water's quiet swirl, punctuated by the occasional creak of the ship as it rocked gently in its course. Neither of them felt the need to fill the space between them.

Jerry's mind wandered to places he usually avoided. That sharp, breath-stealing moment in the hallway. The ghosts that clung to him in the shape of old commands and unspoken failures. Most terrifying of all was the fear of letting everyone down, especially the people who mattered most.

Scarlet didn't press. She just stayed there, steady and silent, as if she understood that silence sometimes said enough.

Around fifteen minutes in, another pair joined them. The man wore plain navy trunks, the woman a modest black one-piece that spoke more to comfort than style.

"Mind if we join?" the woman asked. "We couldn't face another minute in formal wear."

Jerry and Scarlet welcomed them, making room in the circular tub. The newcomers introduced themselves as Dave and Lynn from Cleveland, celebrating their tenth anniversary.

"And how about you two?" Lynn asked, settling into the bubbling water. "How many years have you been together?"

The question caught Jerry off guard, but Scarlet didn't miss a beat.

"We're still counting in days, not years," she said with a laugh that somehow managed to be both honest and evasive.

"Awe ... Newly-weds?" Dave guessed, raising his eyebrows.

"No, no ... just ... new," Jerry said, surprising himself with his steadiness.

"We actually just met on this cruise, a couple days ago." Scarlet chimed in but couldn't help but toss in a casual joke. "But you know, we had just hit it off so well since Sunday, we had the captain read us our vows yesterday after dinner."

Jerry felt his lips twitch as Lynn's eyes widened for a split second before she caught the joke.

"You really had me going there!" Lynn laughed, shaking her head. "I would have believed it. You two seem like you've known each other forever."

The conversation drifted around them like soft waves. Jerry let himself sink into what they were creating together, no longer feeling like pretense. Scarlet leaned in close, her red hair brushing past him now and again, as natural as the tide.

They chatted about ports, excursions, and onboard meals in the easy, undemanding way that asked little of Jerry. It gave his mind room to uncoil, to settle into something resembling ease.

Then, he felt Scarlet's hand, still resting on his thigh, begin to move. The touch started subtle, just a shift in pressure, the faintest trace of intent. Then the motion deepened, slow circles that crept upward with deliberate calm.

He kept talking with Dave about Gulf fishing, kept his voice steady, even as her fingers slipped beneath the hem of his swim trunks and found bare skin, triggering an immediate, unmistakable response.

The moment her fingertips brushed over the head of his growing erection, Jerry's world tilted. His drink lurched from suddenly unsteady fingers, icy piña colada shocking his heated skin as it spilled across his torso. A guttural sound caught in his throat as tremors raced through him, his thighs tensing so hard they ached. Vision went white-hot. Breathing fractured into desperate gasps. His entire existence contracted to that single, electric point of contact beneath the water.

"You okay there, buddy?" Dave asked.

"Fine." Jerry's voice cracked with tension as he turned to face Scarlet. She held his gaze with practiced poise, but he caught the flicker of mischief tugging at the corner of her lips.

"Just went down the wrong pipe."

Her hand never faltered. Beneath the cover of bubbles, she continued her quiet torment, all while chatting with Lynn about St. Maarten's best shopping. The disconnect between her words and her touch unraveled him by the second.

After what felt like an eternity of exquisite torture, Jerry set his empty glass on the deck with deliberate care.

"You know," he said, interrupting a discussion about Caribbean cuisine, "I ... I think we might call it a night. It's been a long day of excursions."

"So nice meeting you both," Scarlet added, withdrawing her hand with one final, deliberate stroke that made Jerry's breath catch.

"Enjoy the rest of your cruise," Lynn called as they climbed out.

Jerry angled himself away from the couple as he exited the hot tub, nervously adjusting his trunks to try to hide his obvious arousal. He quickly grabbed his robe, holding it strategically in front of himself before slipping it on. He held Scarlet's robe for her, a gentlemanly gesture that also provided him a moment to compose himself. The night air cooled his flushed skin, but did little to calm the fire she'd stoked.

As they walked toward the door leading inside, Jerry's hand found the small of her back, guiding her with a sureness that belied the tremor in his fingers.

"Your room or mine?" he asked quietly, no pretense left between them.

Scarlet's smile was slow and certain in the dim light. "Yours is closer."

Fourteen

J erry patted his pockets with increasing desperation, the cold realization settling in his gut. He tried his swim trunks pocket again,
though he knew it was empty. Scarlet watched him with raised eyebrows, amusement playing at the corners of her mouth.

"I don't believe this," he muttered, checking every possible hiding
place a third time. "I must have ... when I changed earlier ..."

"Locked yourself out?" Scarlet finished for him, a smile tugging at
her lips.

Heat crept up his neck. In his rush to meet her, he'd broken one of
his cardinal rules: always have a backup plan. Staff Sergeant Duncan
didn't forget keys. He didn't misplace vital items. He definitely didn't
strand himself without access to his own quarters.

Yet, here he was, standing in a cruise ship hallway in nothing but
swim trunks and a bathrobe, completely locked out.

"I'm sorry," he said, running a hand through his damp hair. "I was
rushing to get changed and must have left the key inside. I can go to
guest services, but it might ..."

Scarlet stepped closer, eliminating the space between them. She rose on her tiptoes, her lips brushing against his ear as she whispered, "Don't worry, Soldier, you're still getting laid tonight."

Her breath tickled his ear, hot against his skin. Jerry bit his lower lip, his pulse jumping like he was about to leap from a transport. She followed her promise with a quick bite to his earlobe, then a wet kiss behind his ear. His hands found her waist through the terry cloth robe, fingers digging in slightly as his body responded.

"Your place?" he asked, voice rough.

"Follow me," she replied, taking his hand.

He followed a step behind, watching the swing of her hips beneath the white robe. The hallway stretched forever, the few other passengers they passed barely registering. He caught himself staring at the curve where her neck met her shoulder, nearly walking past her door entirely.

When she let him in, the first thing he noticed was the red dress lying across the bed.

It was formal-night attire designed for champagne and small talk.

And yet, she'd walked away from it. From all of it.

For him.

"Sorry about the mess," she said, grabbing the satin dress and tossing it onto the sofa.

The careless way she handled what was clearly expensive surprised him. Scarlet always seemed put-together, precise. Something about that casual toss felt significant, suggesting her priorities had shifted.

"Is it okay if I hang my trunks in the shower to dry?" he asked, desperate for an excuse to compose himself.

"Of course," she replied.

The bathroom hadn't shrunk. He knew that. It was no smaller than his own.

But the space felt too small for Jerry now, his nerves too wired, his energy too keyed up.

He shut the door and hit his elbow anyway.

Hands braced on the sink, he tried to find his rhythm, but the mirror offered back a man whose pupils swallowed the color from his eyes.

Under the robe, his trunks stuck like glue. He pulled them off in one quick move and caught the toilet with his shin.

He winced.

Water to the face. Breathe. Move.

The chain around his neck tugged free with a jerk, dog tags sliding into his palm, warm from adrenaline.

When he set them down, they clipped a row of her carefully arranged toiletries. Bottles skittered into the sink in a clatter that seemed far louder than it was.

"Shit," he muttered, hastily rearranging the scattered items. Fancy perfume, moisturizer, hair products covered the counter, all far nicer than anything he owned, though he couldn't tell if they belonged to Scarlet or Cami.

His hands trembled slightly as he hung his trunks over the shower rod, which was unusual for a man who could field-strip a rifle blindfolded. His reflection showed a man he hardly recognized: flushed, disheveled, eyes bright with anticipation rather than vigilance.

For one moment, he just breathed. Tonight, he wouldn't be Staff Sergeant Duncan or Emmett and Marty's dad. Just Jerry. A man with a beautiful woman who, for reasons he couldn't fully understand, seemed to want him as much as he wanted her.

When he emerged, Scarlet stood near the bed, her posture calm and assured. Jerry paused in the doorway, unable to stop the quiet swell of admiration that rose at the sight of her.

"Hi," he said, feeling strangely awkward despite everything they'd done in the hot tub.

"Hi yourself," she replied.

He crossed to her in two strides, hands finding her waist with more confidence than he felt. Their lips met, and what started as gentle quickly turned hungry. He bumped his nose against hers, muttered a quick "sorry" that she silenced with another kiss.

"I've been thinking about this all day," she confessed between kisses.

"Me too," he admitted, fingers tangling in her hair. "Oh my God, I want you so bad."

Scarlet stepped back, holding his gaze as she untied her robe belt. With a roll of her shoulders, the white terry cloth dropped to the floor.

"Fuck." The word punched out of him at the sight of her in red lace lingerie.

She hit him like a revelation in red, a living flame walking straight out of his imagination. The fabric barely counted as clothing, its cling designed to torment, to tease, to brand itself in his mind.

Jerry's brain short-circuited. He stepped back blindly until the bed caught him, hard and sudden.

She smiled, pushing her tongue against her teeth in a way that made his heart pound. She walked toward him with deliberate steps, then straddled his lap in one smooth motion. The pressure of her against his hardness nearly made his eyes cross.

"You're so beautiful," he managed, hands resting on her hips. "I can't believe this is happening."

She pushed his robe off his shoulders, the fabric pooling at his waist and pinning his arms.

"Believe it," she said, claiming his mouth again.

He'd never been good at surrendering control. Military life demanded constant vigilance; parenting required endless responsibility. But here, with Scarlet setting the pace, he found unexpected freedom in following rather than leading.

He wrestled his arms free, hands exploring her back, feeling the delicate straps crossing her skin. His calloused palms caught slightly against her softness. When he touched behind her ear, the side of her neck, the small of her back, the small sounds she made felt like victories.

His hand slipped beneath the lace, cupping the warmth and softness he found there.

When he looked up, her steady, inviting eyes met his. She nodded.

He lowered his mouth, lips closing around her nipple, tasting her skin tinged with salt and heat.

She inhaled sharply, and the sound undid him, every nerve suddenly tuned to her.

She reached behind her neck, untying something that made the top part of her lingerie fall to her waist. Both breasts now bare to his eyes and hands, he felt something beyond lust surge through him. Was it gratitude? Awe? Maybe both.

"God, you're perfect," he murmured.

After minutes of increasingly heated exploration, Jerry grabbed her ass and stood in one urgent motion, lifting her with him. Her legs wrapped around his waist, a surprised sound escaping her lips. Three quick steps to the head of the bed, and he laid her down, following her with his body. They lined up perfectly, his need pressed against the damp lace between her legs.

His robe fell away completely during their shifting and repositioning, leaving him naked above her. She ran her hands over his chest and shoulders, nails lightly scratching paths of fire across his skin.

His mouth traveled lower, from her throat to her breasts, the slight scratch of his evening stubble making her squirm beneath him. His hand moved down her side to her hip, then inward. Even through the lace, he could feel how wet she was, the fabric damp against his fingers. The knowledge that she wanted him this much made his cock throb painfully.

"You're so wet," he said, voice rough with want.

"Just for you," she replied, breathless and strained.

He slipped beneath the delicate material, the hot slickness he found making him groan. He explored her with the same focused attention he'd give to learning new terrain, watching her reactions to discover what brought the strongest response. When his fingers curled forward inside her, she gasped.

"There," she said, nails digging into his shoulders. "Right there."

He kept at it, adding a second finger while his thumb worked in circles above. The way her inner muscles tightened around his fingers told him she was close.

"Wait," she gasped suddenly. "I want you inside me when I come."

He nodded, pulse hammering in his ears. "Do you have ... ?"

"Condom," she finished. "Nightstand. Cami's side."

He raised an eyebrow, momentarily distracted.

"Thank God she's always prepared," Scarlet added with a breathless laugh.

Jerry retrieved the condom, fumbling with it as urgency throbbed through his veins like wildfire. His fingers slipped and he nearly dropped the packet, scrambling to catch it before it hit the floor. So much for calm under pressure. He let out a rough breath, trying to steady himself, but the ache in his gut and the sharp pull of desire in his groin made it almost impossible.

Behind him, Scarlet shed the last of her lingerie with unselfconscious grace, revealing herself in full. Her skin glowed in the low cabin light, kissed bronze and stretched smooth over curves that made his hands twitch with the need to touch. Her breasts rose and fell with each breath, nipples flushed, hair a wild red halo against the pillows. When she opened her arms, the gesture went beyond invitation to become something deeper: a claiming. And Jerry felt utterly *claimed*.

He moved between her legs, arms trembling as he braced himself above her, drinking in the sight of her flushed and open beneath him. The heat radiating from her core was intoxicating, humid and warm as it wrapped around the head of his cock like an invitation he could barely resist. He slid against her lips, her arousal slicking his path as he rubbed along her entrance, coating himself in liquid desire. The intimacy of it, the trust in her eyes, nearly shattered him. His hips bucked involuntarily, and he had to close his eyes and steady his breathing, overwhelmed by how desperately he wanted to worship every inch of her

"Please," she whispered, hips lifting in a fluid offering.

He entered her in one slow, controlled thrust, and they both gasped, the sound low and startled and utterly reverent. She enveloped him, gripped him, drew him deeper until he was fully seated inside her velvet embrace. The sensation was *devastating*. He pressed his forehead to hers, their chests touching, breath mingling in shallow, desperate exhales as they savored this moment of perfect connection.

"You feel amazing," he rasped, voice almost guttural.

She tightened her legs around him, adjusting her hips just enough to draw a low, unguarded groan from his throat.

"Move," she breathed, voice shaky with need, hands grasping his ass, urging him deeper.

He obeyed.

His first movements were slow, deliberate. He withdrew until just the tip of him remained inside, then thrust forward again, hips meeting hers with a soft, wet sound that echoed between the walls. Each glide in and out was a stroke of pleasure so intense it bordered on pain, but Jerry held himself back, unwilling to rush. He didn't want friction. He wanted *connection*.

And Scarlet gave it freely.

Her body rose to meet his again and again, rhythm building between them in a shared, wordless language. Her fingers wove into his hair and tugged him closer. Her lips brushed his jaw, his shoulder, her teeth catching slightly on the curve of his neck. Her moans were open, real. They weren't pretty noises for his benefit, but unfiltered responses to how he touched her, how he filled her.

He angled his hips, adjusting until her breath hitched sharply. *There*. The right spot. He held it steady, pushing deeper, and her nails raked down his back in approval.

Then, his hand slipped between them, almost shy at first. His fingers found her clit, swollen and slick, and he circled it with gentle, deliberate strokes. Not too hard. Not too fast. Just enough. The response was immediate and electric. Her hips bucked against him, her breath stuttered, and a strangled moan vibrated against his skin.

He adjusted his rhythm, letting her reactions guide him like sonar. Faster when her hands clenched. Slower when her breath caught. He kissed her jaw, her collarbone, her shoulder, lavishing attention on every inch of skin he could reach without ever breaking that deep, steady connection between their bodies.

"I'm close," she gasped, voice taut with tension, every muscle drawn tight beneath him.

"Me too," he managed, his own control unraveling, thrusts turning erratic as the pressure coiled low in his spine.

"Don't stop," she cried, legs locking around him, dragging him even deeper.

And he didn't.

He drove into her once, twice, and on the third thrust she shattered completely. Her body clamped around him, inner walls pulsing, her cry caught somewhere between pleasure and surrender. The sheer force of her climax undid him entirely. His own release crashed through him like a wave against rock, blinding in its intensity. His body convulsed with it, hips jerking as he spilled into the condom, her name falling from his lips like a prayer.

For a long moment, they were just breath and skin, slick and tangled in each other.

Jerry didn't move. Didn't want to.

It wasn't until the latex started to feel uncomfortable as he softened that Jerry remembered the condom. He reluctantly shifted to take care of it, then immediately pulled her back against his chest.

"That was …" He trailed off, the rest caught somewhere between his heart and his tongue.

"Yeah," she agreed, understanding.

They shared an easy silence, her fingertips wandering from his chest to the tattoo on his bicep representing Marty and Emmett, side by side, permanent and proud.

"Tell me more about them," she said softly, fingertip outlining the infinity symbol. "What are they like as people, not just diagnoses?"

The question caught him off guard with how perfectly it landed. Not because it was unwelcome, but because it was exactly right. Not questions about therapies or schools or challenges. Just about his boys as individuals.

Jerry smiled instantly. "Emmett talks enough for both of them. He's constantly asking questions I don't know how to answer. 'Why is the sky sometimes pink?' 'How do planes stay up?' 'Do fish get thirsty?'"

Scarlet laughed softly. "Smart kid."

"Too smart sometimes. And Marty …" His expression softened. "Marty feels everything deeply. He can't speak, but his eyes say more than words. He has this laugh that's like …" He paused, searching for the right description. "Like sunshine breaking through clouds."

Talking about his sons came easier than expected. Usually, he measured his words carefully, prepared for polite interest that barely masked discomfort. But Scarlet's questions felt genuine rather than obligatory.

"Before the cruise—" he began, wanting to tell her how compartmentalized his life had become, but exhaustion suddenly claimed him. The words slowed, then stopped as his eyelids grew heavy.

As consciousness faded, he thought he heard her whisper, "This doesn't have to be just a cruise thing, you know."

The words might have been a dream, but they wrapped around him like a promise. His lips curved slightly as sleep pulled him under, half-formed hopes following him into darkness.

For the first time in years, Jerry slept deeply without checking the time, without listening for distress calls, without planning tomorrow's logistics. Just sleep. Just peace. Just surrender.

Fifteen

Jerry watched the sunlight filter through the sheer curtains of Scarlet's balcony door. He'd been awake for a while, content to lie still and listen to the shower running in the bathroom. His body felt pleasantly worn out, muscles relaxed in a way that had nothing to do with PT.

He stretched, feeling the clean ship sheets against his skin. No reveille this morning. No crying child. No list of appointments and chores waiting for his attention. Just this moment, quiet and unscheduled and unexpectedly perfect.

"Hey," he called toward the partially closed bathroom door. "What do you think about ordering room service instead of fighting the breakfast crowd?"

"Yes," Scarlet called back immediately. Then, with more emphasis, "God, yes."

He chuckled, reaching for the room phone. The breakfast menu sat on the nightstand, and he scanned it quickly before dialing. When the line connected, he ordered with practiced efficiency. Pancakes for himself, a veggie omelet for her, coffee for both, a fruit plate to share. He added orange juice and specified extra syrup, remembering how she'd drizzled it liberally over her French toast yesterday morning.

"Twenty minutes, sir," the cheerful voice confirmed.

"Perfect. Thank you." He hung up and settled back against the headboard, adjusting the sheet across his hips.

Steam escaped as Scarlet opened the bathroom door, her hair darkened with moisture, her skin glowing from the warmth. The sight of her struck him with how effortlessly confident she appeared, as if their connection spanned years rather than a single night.

"Hi," she said, a hint of shyness in her voice that hadn't been there last night.

"Hi yourself." His mouth curved into a smile.

She crossed to the bed, dropping her towel carelessly as she slipped beneath the covers next to him. His arm found its way around her shoulders like it belonged there.

"We should probably get dressed before room service arrives," she murmured against his chest.

"Probably," he agreed, pressing his lips to her temple. His fingers traced lazy patterns across her shoulder. "But I'm not sure I can. Pretty sure you broke something essential last night."

She laughed, the sound vibrating against his skin. "Funny. I was about to say the same thing."

They fell into gentle stillness, the kind he rarely experienced with anyone. Usually, silence meant something needed fixing, whether a problem to solve or a crisis to manage. This silence asked nothing of him. It just was.

Her fingers traced along his collarbone, following the ridge of muscle and bone with gentle curiosity. Nothing demanding in the touch. Just appreciation.

"I like this," she said softly.

"This?" The question emerged as a deep, resonant murmur.

"This," she confirmed, gesturing vaguely between them. "Not rushing. Not ... performing."

His hand paused momentarily on her skin, struck by the honesty of it. "Yeah," he said simply. "Me too."

The peaceful moment shattered when the door flew open without warning.

Jerry tensed instinctively, years of training kicking in before his brain caught up to confirm they weren't under attack. Just Cami, bursting in without knocking, wearing what looked suspiciously like men's clothes, carrying what appeared to be a dress from the night before.

"Well, good morning, lovebirds!" she announced, kicking the door shut behind her.

Beside him, Scarlet froze. Jerry tightened his arm around her slightly, a protective reflex.

Without missing a beat, Cami strode across the room and flopped down on the foot of the bed, grinning triumphantly. Her eyes landed on something on the floor. "Well, well, well. That lingerie was worth every penny, wasn't it?" She waggled her eyebrows suggestively.

"Cami!" Scarlet hissed, clutching the sheet higher. "We're still naked under here!"

Cami waved this off, unconcerned. "Oh please, after yesterday's beach adventure, we've all seen everyone's everything. Nothing to be shy about now."

Something between a snort and a chuckle rose within Jerry, surprise and amusement fighting for dominance. He clamped his jaw tight, trying to maintain composure as a telltale warmth spread to his temples.

"Oh my God," Scarlet groaned, burying her face against his shoulder.

Cami stood, stretching casually. "Relax. I just need to grab some clean clothes." She sauntered toward the bathroom, pulling off her shirt mid-stride and tossing it carelessly to the floor. Jerry averted his eyes quickly, catching only the silhouette of her bare back before she disappeared into the bathroom.

"I'm so sorry," Scarlet whispered, looking up at him with mortified eyes.

His shoulders shook with suppressed laughter. "No, no. This is ... educational."

"Is that what we're calling it?"

The bathroom door opened again, and Cami emerged in casual resort wear, looking refreshed and entirely unrepentant.

"So," she said, applying lip gloss in the mirror by the door, "did you make her squeal? It's been forever for her."

"Oh my God, Cami!" Scarlet threw a pillow, which Cami dodged with practiced ease.

Jerry cleared his throat, a sudden glint in his eye. "Actually, I think the whole floor knows the answer to that. The neighbors sent a thank you note."

Cami's mouth dropped open for a split second before she cackled with delight. "I knew I liked this one." She pointed her lip gloss tube at Scarlet. "This one's a keeper, babe."

Jerry felt a ridiculous surge of pride at making Cami laugh. It was like passing some unspoken test.

Cami checked her phone, sliding it into her pocket. "I'm heading to the casino. Are you guys gonna join the living by lunchtime?"

"Yes, fine, please leave now," Scarlet begged, torn between laughter and horror.

"Later, lovers!" Cami called, blowing a kiss before closing the door behind her.

In the silence that followed, Jerry glanced at Scarlet, finding her eyes already on him. He couldn't hold back his grin.

"She's something else," he said finally.

"That's putting it mildly."

"I can see why you keep her around, though."

"When I'm not plotting her murder, you mean."

A knock at the door announced the arrival of room service. Jerry quickly scooped up his robe from the floor while Scarlet grabbed hers from the bathroom. The server wheeled in their breakfast with practiced indifference, likely having seen far worse on a singles cruise.

When they were alone again, Scarlet lifted the silver domes covering their plates. The aroma of fresh coffee and warm food filled the small space.

"Balcony?" Jerry suggested, already lifting the tray.

Scarlet nodded, grabbing the coffee carafe and following him through the sliding door. The morning air was warm and salty, the endless ocean stretching blue and calm around them. They settled into the chairs on either side of the small table, breakfast laid out between them.

For several minutes, they ate in quiet ease. Jerry cut into his pancakes slowly, savoring each bite instead of rushing like he would at home. It felt strange to actually taste his food rather than inhale it between one demand and the next.

"Who knew eggs and coffee could feel like a luxury?" Scarlet said, her tone carrying equal parts humor and wonder.

He looked up, catching the curve of her smile, and something in him loosened.

"Not the food," she added quickly, gesturing with her fork. "The quiet. The ease."

Jerry's mouth tugged into a smile, one that felt unguarded in a way he had not managed since stepping aboard. For a moment he let himself simply sit with it, the ocean, the morning light, and the woman across from him who made everything feel lighter.

He pushed some extra pineapple toward her plate, having noticed her preference for it. The gesture was automatic, the same way he anticipated his sons' needs and noticed their preferences. But this felt different. Not duty or obligation. Just ... care.

"I should probably head back to my cabin after this," he said eventually. "Get some actual clothes on for the day."

"I don't know, I'm not complaining about the current view." She wiggled her eyebrows suggestively, her lips stretching into an appreciative grin.

Jerry glanced down and suddenly froze. The sea breeze had been providing a pleasant sensation he hadn't thought much about until now. His robe had completely fallen open, leaving his half-flaccid cock fully exposed beneath the table. His eyes widened in horror. "How long has that been happening?"

Scarlet snickered into her coffee. "The whole time."

"And you weren't going to say anything?" His face burned as he frantically readjusted his robe, glancing around trying to clock if any of the adjoining balconies had a direct line of sight into their private bubble.

"Like I said …" She took another slow sip, eyes dancing with mischief. "Not complaining."

"Oh, God." He sank lower in his chair. "I just flashed half the Atlantic. There's probably a dolphin out there right now bragging about the free show."

Scarlet burst out laughing. "If it helps, I think we're too high up for dolphins to see."

"Yeah, just the entire ship above us and possibly a passing cruise liner." He shook his head, but a reluctant smile tugged at his lips.

"So we're still on for lunch with the chaos twins?" He asked desperately, in order to change the subject and take the focus off of himself.

"I guess we probably should," she replied, echoing his earlier nonchalance.

Jerry reluctantly put on his still slightly damp swim trunks under his robe. Last night's unexpected detour to Scarlet's cabin had left him without any other clothing options.

"See you at lunch," he said finally, pressing a kiss to her temple.

"See you then."

The hallway was mercifully empty as Jerry made his way back toward his cabin. He'd known since last night that he'd be locked out. Still, he tried the door handle out of stubborn hope.

Locked. Of course.

He knocked firmly. "Mac? You in there?"

Silence.

"Dammit, Mac." He sighed, leaning his forehead against the door. He'd have to go down to guest services for a new key card. Perfect.

The journey through the ship's public areas was an exercise in maintaining dignity. Jerry kept his head high, his pace brisk, his expression neutral. It was the same face he used during uniform inspections. A family with young children passed him, nobody batting an eye at his attire. A group of older ladies definitely looked him up and down, one of them giving an approving nod that made his ears burn.

At guest services, the staff member's professional demeanor cracked only slightly, evident in a twitch of her lips as she said, "Locked out, sir?"

"Yes, ma'am." He cleared his throat. "Cabin 9124."

"May I see some ID?"

"That would also be in my cabin."

Her smile widened marginally. "Name on the reservation?"

"Gilmore Duncan."

She tapped at her computer. "And your birthday?"

"January 16."

A few more keystrokes, and she produced a new card. "There you go, Mr. Duncan. Enjoy the rest of your cruise."

"Thank you." He took the key with as much dignity as a man in a bathrobe could muster.

When he returned to his cabin, he found Mac face down in his bed, one bare leg hanging off the side, the rest of him thankfully covered by sheets up to his waist. The room smelled like tequila and casino smoke.

Jerry kicked the dangling foot. "Wake up, princess."

Mac groaned, burying his face deeper into the pillow. "Go 'way."

"You could've answered when I knocked earlier." Jerry tossed the robe over a chair. "Had to do the walk of shame to guest services."

Mac rolled over, squinting at him. "Why didn't you just hang out in Scarlet's room? That's where you spent the night, right?"

"How'd you know that?"

"Dude." Mac pushed himself up on his elbows, hair sticking up at odd angles. "The whole ship knows. You two weren't exactly quiet."

Heat crept up Jerry's neck. "Speaking of not being quiet, Cami stopped by Scarlet's cabin this morning. Wearing your PT gear, I believe."

Mac's eyes widened momentarily before a lazy grin spread across his face. "Yeah, she borrowed it."

"I figured that part out."

"She was supposed to meet me at the casino." Mac frowned, suddenly looking more alert. "What time is it?"

"Almost noon."

"Shit!" Mac scrambled up, keeping the sheet around his waist. "I fell back asleep after she left. She's gonna kill me."

Jerry laughed, pulling clean clothes from his suitcase. "Better hurry then. We're all meeting for lunch at one."

Mac disappeared into the bathroom, the shower starting seconds later. Jerry shook his head, amused despite himself. Their last full day on the ship, and both he and Mac had ended up with women who could probably kick their asses.

He dressed in silence, already feeling the shift. Tomorrow meant the end of drifting, meaning a return to Texas, back to schedules and obligations. Strange how solid earth could feel more confining than open water.

What would happen when they stepped off this ship? When the expanse of the Gulf of Mexico stretched between them, when duty and responsibility reclaimed their rightful places in his life? When Scarlet returned to her career and her world?

The questions had no easy answers, but for the first time in years, Jerry wasn't trying to map out every contingency. For once, he was willing to let something unfold without a meticulous plan of attack.

The rest of the day slipped past in bright, boozy ease. They claimed poolside chairs, shared jokes, swapped stories. Mac exaggerated his way through old Army escapades. Scarlet and Cami built cocktail brackets like sports commentators. Jerry let himself laugh. Let himself forget.

Later, when Scarlet's hand slid into his between their chairs, he didn't flinch. He just held on.

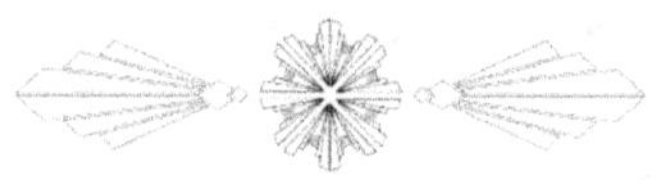

The Topaz Lounge glowed with golden light as sunset painted the horizon. Jerry had arrived early, securing their usual table near the windows. Tonight he'd taken extra care with his appearance, choosing khaki shorts and a navy button-down with the sleeves rolled up, his hair still damp from a recent shower.

The moment Scarlet entered, something inside him quieted, his attention drawn completely to her simple blue sundress and her hair cascading around her shoulders. A week ago, she'd been a stranger. Now, she was ... what exactly?

She looked up, catching his gaze across the room. The smile that spread across her face answered the question before he could fully form it.

"Hey, you," he said when she reached him.

"Hey, yourself."

His hand found the small of her back naturally, as if they'd been doing this for years instead of days.

Mac and Cami arrived together, still bickering good-naturedly about something that had happened in the casino. Despite their obvious chemistry, Jerry noticed how they maintained a careful distance, treating their night together as clearly just a vacation fling, no strings or expectations. He wondered if that's what Scarlet assumed they were too.

They claimed their seats, Cami immediately signaling for drinks.

"Last night, people!" she announced. "Let's make it count."

The farewell toast was Maude's domain. She took the small stage as she had on their first night, elegant in flowing turquoise, her silver-streaked hair swept up. But where her welcome speech had been bright and buoyant, tonight she carried a quieter energy.

"My dear voyagers," she began, voice carrying effortlessly across the hushed lounge. "Our journey together reaches its final evening. Tomorrow, we return to the lives we temporarily left behind."

Jerry felt Scarlet's hand find his beneath the table, warm and certain. He intertwined their fingers, hoping she couldn't feel his pulse quickening at the simple contact.

"But remember," Maude continued, "endings are often disguised beginnings. The sea has a way of revealing truths we carry back to shore … if we're brave enough to honor them."

She raised her glass. "To discoveries made. To connections forged. To the courage that awaits us beyond the horizon."

"To courage," Jerry echoed softly, turning to meet Scarlet's gaze as they sipped their champagne.

The ocean stretched to the horizon, sky and sea blending into one quiet promise.

Beyond that line ... home. Responsibility. The relentless rhythm of needs and expectations. And the scaffolding he'd built, piece by piece, to hold it all together.

He knew what made this impossible. He also knew how it felt to have her hand in his, steady and sure, and to see her light up with laughter.

And suddenly, impossibility didn't feel like such a barrier.

He didn't need guarantees. He just needed the courage to try.

Sixteen

The El Corazón lounge felt different in the morning light. Jerry sat with his duffel wedged under the small table, watching Mac tap rapidly through his phone messages. Last night, this space had been filled with salsa music and laughter. Now, it was just another holding pen for tired passengers waiting to reclaim their real lives.

"Your mom wants to know if I kept you out of trouble," Mac said without looking up. "Should I tell her about the nude beach?"

Jerry shot him a warning look. "I wasn't even—"

"Relax," Mac grinned. "I'm not suicidal. Maggie would have my head."

Jerry's phone buzzed with another photo from his mother. Emmett had constructed an elaborate blanket fort that now consumed most of the living room. His small, serious face peeked from behind a pillow barricade, his expression a miniature version of Jerry's own focused stare.

"Apparently, this is my 'welcome home surprise,'" Jerry said, showing Mac the photo.

"Impressive engineering," Mac nodded. "Kid's gonna be building bridges someday."

Scarlet was studying her phone with narrowed eyes, face tightening in thought. Jerry couldn't help tracking the details, noticing the stillness of her shoulders, the focused silence that filled the space between them.

"Everything okay?" he asked.

She looked up, surprised. "Just work. My boss is offloading someone else's project onto me the minute I get back."

Jerry nodded, understanding the universal language of being volunteered for things you never asked for. He offered his phone to her. "Emmett built a fort."

As she looked at the photo, an unexpected softness crossed her face, making his breath catch.

"He's got your serious face," she said, and the observation caught him off guard. Most people didn't notice things like that about his kids.

"Yeah," he managed, feeling strangely exposed. "Too much sometimes."

The overhead speaker crackled. "Now calling group seven for disembarkation. Group seven passengers, please proceed to Deck 4."

"That's us," Cami said, standing and stretching. "Back to reality."

Scarlet gathered her bag, then hesitated. "What time is your flight again?"

"Not until 9:15," Jerry answered, hope flickering unexpectedly.

"So, my parents are hosting a Memorial Day barbecue today." She bit her lower lip. "You guys should come by before your flight. If you want."

She watched Jerry's face, her heartbeat suddenly loud in her ears.

"Yeah?" A slow smile spread across his face. "I'd like that."

"Free food? I'm in," Mac declared.

Scarlet couldn't hold back a smile, her tongue pressing briefly against the small gap in her front teeth when Jerry accepted. "I'll text you the address."

"Come on, Romeo," Mac said, tugging at Jerry's arm. "Let the ladies escape before they miss their exit call."

Their eyes held. One week ago, she'd been a stranger. Now, letting her walk away felt wrong somehow.

After Scarlet and Cami disappeared into the crowd, Jerry slumped back in his chair. His phone buzzed with Scarlet's text. It was her address in Coral Gables.

"Wow," Mac said, peering over his shoulder. "That's a nice neighborhood. We're definitely gonna be underdressed."

"We don't have to go," Jerry said, though, even as the words left his mouth, he knew they weren't true.

"Nice try. You're going."

Around them, passengers shuffled impatiently, anxious to reclaim their luggage and leave the floating world behind. A couple across the lounge argued in hushed voices about taxi arrangements. A child wailed about leaving the "fun boat." The cruise director's voice announced more group numbers in forced cheerful tones.

"Weird, isn't it?" Mac said, watching a woman try to reorganize her overstuffed carry-on. "Week ago, none of these people existed for us."

Jerry nodded, understanding what Mac meant. The strange intimacy of ship life—strangers becoming familiar, then suddenly strangers again. Except Scarlet. Somehow, she had become more than just a ship passing in the night.

"Now calling group nine for disembarkation. Group nine passengers, please proceed to Deck 4."

"That's us," Mac said, standing and stretching. "Ready for the real world, Duncan?"

Jerry wasn't sure how to answer that. The real world was boys with therapy appointments and duty rosters and budgets. But maybe, now, it could include something more.

"So, what exactly is your plan here?" Mac asked as their cab pulled into traffic, Miami's heat shimmering off the road. "You know you live in Texas, right? With two kids?"

Jerry stared out the window, watching palm trees blur past. "I know where I live, Mac."

"Just checking. Because meeting the parents is usually a pretty serious step. Not exactly cruise fling protocol." Mac's voice had lost its usual edge of humor.

"It's just a barbecue." Even to his own ears, it sounded hollow.

"Uh-huh. When's the last time you did the 'meet the parents' dance anyway? Her?"

Jerry tensed at the deliberate avoidance of his ex-wife's name. Even after all these years, Mac knew better than to say it. "Yeah. And she was already pregnant with Marty."

Mac whistled low. "So, what ... seven years? eight?"

"Something like that." Jerry watched the city flash by, remembering the awkward dinner with his ex's parents. They'd been cordial but cold, eyeing his uniform with barely concealed disapproval. The shotgun wedding that followed had been equally frigid.

"I'm just saying," Mac continued, "this isn't like you. The Jerry Duncan I know needs a strategic plan, contingencies, and an exit strategy before agreeing to coffee, let alone family barbecues."

"Maybe I'm tired of planning everything to death," Jerry said quietly.

Mac's expression softened. "Hey. I'm not criticizing. It's good to see you ... I don't know, taking a chance."

Jerry nodded, tension still knotting his shoulders. "I've got no idea what I'm doing here, Mac."

"Join the club," Mac laughed. "But if it helps, she's into you. Like, really into you."

"How would you know?"

"Because I have functioning eyeballs?" Mac rolled his eyes. "And because Cami told me."

Jerry frowned. "You and Cami talked about us?"

"Buddy, everyone in the Mingle group talked about you two. Half of them had a betting pool going on whether you'd figure it out before we hit port."

"Great," Jerry muttered, embarrassment heating his neck.

"Relax," Mac punched his shoulder lightly. "It's a good thing. Now, let me impart some bachelor wisdom for meeting the parents."

"You've met parents exactly twice," Jerry reminded him.

"Which makes me an expert on what not to do." Mac ticked off points on his fingers. "No politics, no religion, compliment the food even if it tastes like cardboard, and if her dad asks about your intentions, lie your ass off."

Jerry snorted. "Stellar advice."

"You got better?"

He didn't. It had been so long since he'd navigated this particular social minefield that all his instincts felt rusty. He considered texting Scarlet to back out. It would be simpler. Cleaner.

But as the cab turned onto a tree-lined street in what must be Coral Gables, he realized he didn't want simpler. For once, he wanted to see where this went, complications and all.

The cab pulled up to a modest two-story house with white trim and potted bougainvillea flanking the entrance. Jerry paid the driver while Mac wrestled their luggage onto the curb.

"Not too late to run," Mac joked, but his eyes were serious.

Jerry squared his shoulders similar to the same automatic posture adjustment he'd made a thousand times before troop inspections and commanding officer meetings. "Not running."

As the cab pulled away, the front door opened. Scarlet stood framed in the doorway, tension visible in the set of her shoulders. Behind her, a young woman who had to be her sister peered over her shoulder, not even attempting to hide her curiosity.

Jerry felt suddenly, absurdly self-conscious in his faded jeans and untucked button-down. He should have changed. Or bought flowers. Or both.

"Hey. You made it," Scarlet said, relief evident in her voice.

"Yeah." He cleared his throat, aware of his baggage, both literal and figurative cluttering the scene. "Thanks for inviting us."

Mac appeared beside him, ever the social buffer. "Nice neighborhood. Very ... palm tree-y."

Scarlet blinked. "Palm tree-y?"

"You know, Fresh Prince ... Welcome to Miami ... lots of palm trees."

Jerry shot Mac a look that clearly communicated *not helping*.

"Come in," Scarlet stepped back, gesturing toward the living room. She began introductions, pointing toward a kitchen where amazing smells were emanating and then to an older man coming in from what looked like a backyard.

"And that's my dad, Leo, coming in from the back."

Jerry straightened automatically as Leo approached. First impressions mattered, and fathers mattered most of all. The man had Scarlet's eyes and an easy, assessing gaze that missed nothing.

"Nice to meet you all," Jerry said, extending his hand to Leo first. "Jerry. Thank you for having us."

His voice sounded too formal, even to his own ears, but the training was ingrained: respect, deference, clarity. He noticed his own pulse quickening, the slight dampness of his palms.

Mac, naturally, stepped in with his most disarming grin. "And I'm Mac. Thanks for having us on such short notice."

"Any friend of Scarlet's," Leo said with a nod that seemed to contain layers of evaluation. He looked between them. "You boys want a beer? Got some cold ones in the fridge out back. I've got Peroni, Corona ... take your pick."

Jerry's first instinct was caution. "Water would be fine, thank you."

Scarlet leaned close, her breath warm against his ear. "You might want that beer. Trust me."

The proximity of her sent a current through him. Jerry glanced at her, surprised by the playful warning, then back to Leo. "Actually, a beer sounds great. Thank you."

"Absolutely!" Mac chimed in, already moving toward the back of the house. "Hell, I'm not drivin'!"

Jerry caught Scarlet's eye briefly. She gave him a small shrug that somehow communicated both apology and solidarity. It struck him that she was nervous too, and somehow, that steadied him. They were in this together ... whatever "this" was.

The Bellari backyard looked like something from a lifestyle magazine, complete with terracotta tiles, flowering plants, and a kidney-shaped pool that reflected the cloudless Miami sky. Jerry accepted a Corona from Leo, hyperaware of his posture, his expressions, everything he might be silently communicating.

Mac, of course, had already charmed Scarlet's mother and was now gesturing animatedly about something in her herb garden, as if he'd been cultivating rosemary all his life instead of living off base cafeteria food.

Jerry hung back, bottle sweating in his hand, trying to look casual while surveying for conversational landmines.

Leo approached with the comfortable confidence of a man who knew his territory. "You a steak guy or more of a burger man?"

"Burgers, usually," Jerry answered, standing a little straighter.

"Good. You're on flipping duty. Come keep me company."

It wasn't a request. Jerry followed Leo to a massive grill setup by the pool, recognizing the time-honored tradition of male bonding through meat and fire. His father had taught him the same ritual when he was twelve. It was a way to talk without the pressure of direct conversation.

"Scarlet says you're military," Leo said, arranging coals with methodical precision.

"Yes, sir. Army. Staff Sergeant," Jerry replied, careful not to overexplain.

"Combat experience?"

"Some. Everyone's a soldier first, but my specialty is public affairs."

Leo nodded, seemingly approving of the answer. "You shoot?"

"Yes, sir. Expert marksman three years running."

"Call me Leo," he said, handing Jerry a pair of tongs. "Meat goes on when the coals turn white. Chicken first, five minutes each side."

As Jerry arranged the seasoned chicken on the grill, Leo glanced at him with a more measured expression.

"Memorial Day weekend," Leo said, his tone shifting subtly. "Means something different to you than most folks, I imagine."

The words caught Jerry off guard. He'd been so immersed in the whirlwind of the cruise and Scarlet that he'd lost track of dates. Memorial Day. Which meant June was approaching. June 18th. The knot in his stomach tightened instantly.

"Yes," he managed, his voice rougher than he intended. "It does."

Leo watched him carefully, the way men do when they're measuring another man's boundaries. "Lost anyone close?"

Jerry fixed his gaze on the coals, their orange glow hypnotic. He rarely spoke of Hunter to anyone, not to therapists, not to Mac, not even to his own family. But something about Leo's direct approach, free of pity or awkward sympathy, made the truth easier to voice.

"A buddy. Afghanistan. James Hunter." The name felt heavy on his tongue, sacred somehow. "Almost six years ago now. Anniversary's coming up next month."

Jerry kept his focus on the grill, but he could feel his composure thinning at the edges. "He was a hell of a photographer. Better soldier." He paused, swallowing hard. "Best friend anyone could ask for."

He wasn't sure why he added that last part. It wasn't like him to volunteer emotional details. But something about this moment, standing in the sunshine of a family backyard instead of the sterile confines of a therapy office, loosened the words from his chest.

Leo didn't push, just nodded with the gravity of someone who understood loss on a personal level. "To absent friends," he said, raising his beer bottle in a simple, dignified toast.

Jerry met his eyes, raising his own bottle. "And to never forgetting the impact they had on the world while they were here."

Something passed between them in that moment: a connection that transcended the newness of their acquaintance. Leo gave a single, firm nod, as if sealing a pact.

They shared the silence like a pact, neither rushing to break it.

Then, Leo returned to the grill, giving Jerry a moment to breathe, to gather himself without eyes on the unraveling.

It was the kind of respect that didn't need declaring.

The solemnity dispersed as Mac appeared with a fresh beer, already in storytelling mode. "So there we are, full tactical gear, 110 degrees, and this camel just decides our Humvee is his new girlfriend. Started making these ungodly sounds—"

Jerry couldn't help but laugh, recognizing the heavily censored version of a deployment story that was significantly less amusing in its original form. But Mac had always been good at turning the grit of military life into something palatable for civilians.

Even Leo cracked a smile, shaking his head.

Across the yard, Jerry caught sight of Scarlet arranging napkins on a patio table. She was watching him, a small smile playing at the corners of her mouth. His heart did that strange kick again, the one he'd been feeling all week whenever she looked at him.

Scarlet's sister sidled up with a glass of what looked like sangria. *Jade*, Jerry reminded himself of her name. "So, Jerry," she said, drawing out his name. "Army, huh? You don't look like G.I. Joe."

"Jade," Scarlet warned from across the patio.

"What? It's a compliment." Jade's smile was sharp but not unkind. "I just meant he doesn't have that meathead military look."

Jerry couldn't help but smile. He knew that expression well, the way a protective sibling sized up someone dating their family member. "Sorry to disappoint. I left my fatigues and thousand-yard stare in my other luggage."

Jade laughed, appearing genuinely surprised. "He has a sense of humor! Scarlet didn't mention that."

"What did she mention?" Jerry asked before he could stop himself.

"Not nearly enough," Jade said with a meaningful look that made Jerry's neck warm.

Before the inquisition could continue, Leo handed him a platter of seasoned chicken. "Showtime, soldier."

Jerry was grateful for the interruption, even if it meant he was now responsible for not ruining lunch.

As food and laughter filled the yard, a familiar rhythm took hold with the rise and fall of voices, the quiet choreography of people who knew each other well. Jerry walked the edge of it, not quite an outsider, not fully one of them either. But the Bellaris reminded him of his own family, their warmth understated, their closeness measured in subtle glances and half-finished sentences.

They arranged themselves in the shade of a flowering tree, plates balanced on laps. Midway through the meal, Lucas arrived. Jade's fiancé greeted everyone with the casual confidence of someone already accepted into the fold.

"So, Jerry," Lucas said, spearing a grilled pepper, "What do you do when you're not cruising the Caribbean with my future sister-in-law?"

"I'm active duty Army. Based in Texas. I work in public affairs—media coordination, photography, documentation."

Leo nodded from across the yard. "Good skill set. Not just muscle."

"Sometimes I get to use both," Jerry replied, surprised by his own ease. The laughter that followed felt genuine.

By the time they'd made it to second helpings, Jerry was laughing freely. Mac was in full storytelling mode, Elisa grilled him about life in Texas, and Leo let out an unexpected laugh at one of his jokes. And then there was Scarlet, watching him when she thought he wasn't looking, her expression a mix of shyness and something softer, something that lingered.

After helping clear plates, Jerry sought a moment of quiet by the garden. Lucas appeared beside him, Corona in hand, his casual designer outfit making Jerry's discount-store button-down feel suddenly inadequate.

"So," Lucas said, voice lowered conspiratorially. "You and Scarlet, huh?"

"Friends," Jerry's guard went up immediately. "We just met a week ago. I wouldn't necessarily classify us as a thing yet."

"Hey, I get it. I remember when I first met the Bellaris." Lucas took a swig of his beer. "Let me give you some advice: these women, they're a handful. Strong personalities run in the family. Best thing you can do is just nod and agree until you're officially 'in.'"

Jerry blinked, taken aback by both the advice and the casual way Lucas lumped Scarlet in with some stereotype. "I don't mind strong personalities."

"Trust me, it's easier this way," Lucas continued, oblivious to Jerry's cooling expression. "I started with trying to make points with Leo, but it's really Elisa you need to impress. She runs this show."

"Good to know," Jerry said neutrally, though, internally, he was re-assessing the man beside him. There was something off about Lucas's advice. There seemed to be a hint of calculation that didn't fit with what Jerry had observed of the family dynamics.

"And don't worry about the whole military thing," Lucas added with a dismissive wave. "They're pretty liberal, but they'll overlook it."

Jerry stiffened. "Overlook it?"

Lucas seemed to realize his misstep. "I just meant, with the moving around and all that. It's complicated, right? But look, you're both adults. I'm sure you'll figure it out."

Before Jerry could respond, Jade called Lucas over to help with something. He clapped Jerry on the shoulder with attempted man-ufactured camaraderie before walking away.

Jerry stood still, processing the exchange. The dismissive attitude about his service rankled, but more concerning was how Lucas spoke about Scarlet's family ... like they were obstacles to manage rather than people to know.

Jade appeared beside him a few minutes later, startling him from his thoughts. She had the same dark eyes as Scarlet, but they were sharper, more direct.

"So," she said, rearranging a bowl of chips on the nearby table. "Military life. That must be fascinating."

Jerry could tell the casual tone was an opening gambit. "It has its moments."

"Must be hard to maintain relationships, with all the moving around."

And there it was, the real question beneath the small talk. Jerry considered deflecting but decided honesty might be the better approach. "It can be challenging."

"Mmm." Jade stirred her sangria with a straw. "Do you move around a lot?"

"I've been in Texas for about four years now."

"And how long are you planning to stay in?"

The question wasn't subtle, but Jerry respected her directness. "I'm hoping to retire, which could be as early as eight years or so. But who knows."

"Scarlet's entire life is here," Jade said, her gaze direct.

"I have zero intention of trying to take her life away from her," Jerry replied evenly. "I've known her a week, we're friends, and Scarlet's old enough to make her own decisions about her life."

Jade's eyebrows rose slightly, clearly not expecting such a direct response. "I'm just curious," she said, her stance casual but her eyes watchful. "She doesn't do this, you know. Not since Alex. Five years."

The name registered. Cami had mentioned him briefly on the ship. "I know it's a lot to bring someone home."

"It's monumental. So either you're just a casual fling she's feeling reckless about, or—"

"A friend," Jerry said quietly, in an attempt to complete her sentence. "She invited me over as a friend. We're not dating, engaged or having a baby together … just friends."

Something in Jade's expression shifted. "And do you always move this fast? Or just on cruise ships?"

Jerry's smile was patient. "I don't really know what all is going to happen between your sister and I, and I'm not trying to push anything. But, in general, I don't tend to move fast in anything."

"Because of the military?"

"Because of a lot of things." Like two kids with special needs, and a marriage that imploded, and the particular kind of loneliness that comes from being surrounded by people who only see the uniform.

"Look … you seem like a nice guy, but I should mention that Scarlet values honesty above almost everything else. And if you ever lie, cheat, or break her heart … I will kill you."

Before he could respond, Jade continued. "Oh, also, I should warn you, our parents are already planning your wedding in their heads. They're pathologically romantic, especially with Scarlet."

Jerry blinked at the abrupt change of topic. "We just met."

"Doesn't matter. They married after three months of dating, and they've been trying to recreate that magic for their daughters ever since." Jade rolled her eyes, but there was affection beneath the exasperation.

Jade had a way of smiling while cornering you. Her questions weren't aggressive, but they landed with precision. Texas. Scarlet. His plans.

Jerry held his ground. He was used to scrutiny. But her loyalty had an edge that left no room for carelessness. And he respected the hell out of that.

Still, the social gears kept turning, and by late afternoon, he needed to step out of their rotation. The weight of Scarlet's gaze, the noise, the roles they were all playing pressed in on him.

He wandered to the pool's far side, away from clinking glasses and easy laughter. Sitting down, he slipped his feet into the water. It was sharp, bracing.

Finally, a pause.

Jerry closed his eyes briefly, listening to the distant conversation and laughter. This wasn't at all where he'd expected to find himself a week ago when Mac forced him onto that cruise. Meeting parents, navigating family dynamics, feeling things he'd locked away since before Marty was born.

"Mind some company?"

Scarlet's voice brought him back. He looked up, the tension he'd been carrying slipping away at the sight of her. "I was hoping you'd find me."

She settled beside him, passing him a fresh beer before slipping off her sandals. The water lapped gently as her feet broke the surface. Their shoulders brushed, and he noticed neither of them moved away from the contact.

"So," she said, "on a scale of interrogation to inquisition, how bad was it?"

Jerry laughed softly. "Somewhere between friendly questioning and enhanced interview technique."

"I'm sorry about Jade. She's in extreme protective sister mode."

"Don't be," he said, meaning it. "She loves you. I get it." He paused, then added with a hint of amusement, "Though she did inform me your mother is allegedly already planning a double wedding."

Scarlet nearly choked on her beer. "Oh, my God. She's just trying to get under your skin. My parents got married after three months of dating, so they think everyone should follow suit."

"It worked," Jerry admitted. "For about ten seconds I considered jumping the fence and making a run for it."

They both laughed, and the tension between them softened. They sat in comfortable silence, watching light dance across the rippling water. A citrus tree nearby released its scent into the air, mixing with the chlorine from the pool.

"Your family's nice," Jerry said finally, meaning it despite the subtle interrogations. "I see where you get it from."

Scarlet snorted. "The cross-examination skills or the inability to stay out of each other's business?"

"The warmth," Jerry said, turning to face her. "The way you listen like you're collecting every word."

She looked genuinely surprised by the observation, which only confirmed for Jerry how little she realized about her own best qualities. He hesitated, then decided to voice something that had been nagging at him.

"Though, I did get a strange vibe from Lucas," he admitted carefully, studying her reaction. "Something felt ... off about how he talked about your family."

Scarlet's expression shifted, not quite defensive but dismissive. "Lucas? He's still trying to fit in. We've all only known him for about two months, since Jade finally introduced him."

"Of course," Jerry nodded, backing off. "It just seemed—"

"Not everyone can waltz in and charm the Bellaris in one afternoon like the great Jerry Duncan," she teased, bumping his shoulder playfully. Her tone was light, but there was an edge beneath it that suggested this wasn't a topic she wanted to pursue.

Jerry let it drop immediately, recognizing the subtle boundary she'd drawn. "Fair enough. I've just had years of practice reading people. Occupational hazard."

"Well, save your people-reading skills for your own family," she said, her smile softening the words. "Trust me, Lucas is harmless. Just nervous about the wedding."

Jerry nodded, filing away his impression without pushing further. It wasn't his place to question her sister's relationship, especially not after knowing these people for all of a few hours.

"It's been nice seeing you here," he added, his voice lower, shifting back to safer ground. "Outside of vacation mode. In your real life."

Scarlet studied him, her eyes catching the late afternoon sun. "And? Verdict?"

"I like Scarlet-in-her-element even more than Scarlet-on-vacation," he said simply.

Her breath caught audibly. "That's ... not what most people say after meeting my family."

"I'm not most people."

"No," she agreed. "You're definitely not."

The silence between them shifted, charged with something new. Jerry traced slow circles in the water with his toe, gathering courage for what needed to be said.

"So," he said finally. "What happens when I get on that plane tonight?"

The question hung between them, deceptively simple but loaded with implication.

Scarlet looked down at their reflection in the water. "Logically? You go back to your life in Texas. I stay here with mine. We text for a while until it fades."

Jerry nodded slowly, their shoulders still pressed together. That was the practical outcome, the one his rational mind had sketched out a dozen times. "That's what logic says."

"But?"

"But I don't know if I want to put up walls just because there's distance," he said, his voice steady. "It feels like ... closing a door before we've even looked inside."

Scarlet turned to face him fully. "I've spent so much time being practical. Always thinking ten steps ahead."

"And now?"

"Now I'm wondering what happens if I don't overthink it for once," she said, the corner of her mouth lifting. "If we just ... see where it goes. No promises, no pressure."

Jerry's hand found hers between them, fingers interlacing. The simple contact sent warmth through him that had nothing to do with the Miami heat.

"I'd like that," he said. "Not closing doors just because the path looks complicated."

"It's going to be complicated," she acknowledged. "Your boys, my job, the distance—"

"One day at a time," he suggested. "Phone calls. Maybe visits when we can manage it."

"One step at a time," she agreed, squeezing his hand.

"You know, for two people who just met a week ago, this is either very romantic or completely insane," Jerry said, letting a touch of humor back into his voice.

Scarlet laughed softly. "Let's go with romantic. It sounds better on paper."

He shifted closer, his free hand moving to brush a strand of hair from her face. The warmth of her beside him made all his usual caution feel distant and unnecessary.

"I'm really glad you invited us today," Jerry murmured, his eyes dropping briefly to her lips. "I wasn't ready to say goodbye."

"Me either," Scarlet whispered.

The moment stretched between them, fragile and perfect. Then, Jerry leaned forward, closing the distance between them. The kiss was gentle. Her lips were warm against his, and he felt her hand come up to rest against his chest, directly above his quickening heartbeat.

When they pulled apart, Jerry kept his eyes closed for a heartbeat longer, committing the moment to memory.

Mac's voice shattered the bubble. "Yo, Duncan! Cab's on its way. T-minus ten!"

Jerry sighed, resting his forehead briefly against hers. "Timing was never my strong suit."

Scarlet laughed softly. "To be continued?"

"Definitely," he said, brushing his thumb across her knuckles. "That's a promise I can make." They slipped their feet from the water and stood together, both reluctant to break contact. As they walked back toward the house, their hands remained loosely linked until the last possible moment.

Ten minutes later, Mac was already waiting beside the taxi, their luggage loaded. Jerry hung back, caught in the strange ritual of saying goodbye to people he'd only just met but somehow already mattered.

"I swear," Mac called from the car, "if TSA confiscates my leftover chimichurri, I'm writing to Congress. This is cultural discrimination."

Elisa gave Jerry a tight hug that caught him off guard. "You're welcome back anytime. Preferably with more notice so I can plan a proper meal."

"Thank you, ma'am," he managed. "Everything was delicious."

Leo shook his hand firmly. "Good man. Don't be a stranger."

"Thank you, sir. For everything."

The simple approval in Leo's words meant more than Jerry expected. He'd forgotten how it felt to be evaluated as a man rather than a soldier or a father.

Scarlet walked him to the car. The driveway felt longer now, the breeze cooler as the late afternoon shadows stretched.

"I'm glad you came," she said, tucking a piece of hair behind her ear.

"So am I," he said, inadequate words for the tangle of emotions. "It meant more than I think I can explain. This whole week did."

They stood for a beat longer than necessary, both searching for the right words.

"I'll text you when we land," he said finally.

"I'd like that."

His lips brushed her cheek, more question than farewell.

There was so much he wanted to name: the risk, the hope, the ache of almost.

But nothing belonged in this brief hush between greeting and goodbye.

As the cab pulled away, he watched her through the back window until she disappeared from view. Mac, for once, remained silent beside him, allowing Jerry the space to process.

"So," Mac said finally as they turned onto the main road. "We're really doing this long-distance thing?"

Jerry kept his eyes on the receding neighborhood. "Looks like it."

Mac nodded, surprisingly serious. "She seems worth it."

He thought of her laugh, the way she'd tilted her head as she studied the photo of his boys, how she hadn't flinched when things got heavy. There was something steady about her.

"She is," he said softly.

Outside, Miami blurred by in streaks of motion and light. Jerry sat back, and for once, his mind didn't dart toward the next appointment or what he'd have to fix next.

Instead, he wondered what it might feel like to have a future again.

It was a fragile thought. But it fit.

Seventeen

The stuffy conference room made Jerry's uniform collar feel too tight. Maps and operation schedules lined the walls, remnants of morning briefs that now seemed distant under the fluorescent lights of late Friday afternoon. Around the table, soldiers shifted in their seats, eyes occasionally darting to watches or phones. The universal end-of-duty-day restlessness was something even the most disciplined couldn't fully suppress.

First Sergeant Parker tapped his pen against his notepad. "Duncan, what's the status on the photos from Tuesday's ceremony?"

Jerry straightened. "Submitted to HQ yesterday afternoon, First Sergeant. Lieutenant Colonel Davis already signed off on them."

"Good." Parker made a checkmark. "Anything else media-related on your radar?"

"No, First Sergeant. All quiet until the community open house next month."

Parker nodded, attention already shifting. "MacIntyre, equipment status for next week's field exercise?"

As Mac launched into his report, Jerry's mind drifted. One week since the cruise. Seven days since sitting poolside with Scarlet at her parents' house, her shoulder pressed against his, that unspoken question hanging between them: what happens next?

The past week had slipped into familiar rhythms of wake-ups with Emmett bouncing on his bed, Marty's physical therapy on Tuesday, paperwork and meetings filling the spaces between. But something had shifted. He caught himself reaching for his phone during downtimes, disappointed when no messages awaited him.

"Duncan? You with us?" Parker's voice cut through his thoughts.

"Yes, First Sergeant."

"Then I suggest you start packing up like everyone else. Unless you wanted to stay for additional duty?" The hint of amusement in Parker's voice drew chuckles from around the table.

Jerry glanced up to find the room already clearing out, Mac standing by the door with an exaggerated expression of impatience.

"No, First Sergeant. Just ... reviewing mental notes."

"Save it for Monday. Dismissed."

Outside, the Texas sun hit like a physical force after the air-conditioned building. Mac loosened his collar with an exaggerated gasp.

"Man, I thought he'd never finish. You were a million miles away in there."

"Just thinking."

"About a certain redhead?" Mac grinned, nudging Jerry's shoulder. "You've been checking your phone like a teenager waiting for prom results."

Jerry didn't deny it. "Mom's got the boys. Need to drive her to the airport tonight."

"Then back to just us men," Mac said, climbing into Jerry's truck. "Though, I gotta say, your mom's cooking almost makes me wish she'd stay."

The drive home was quiet, Mac scrolling through his phone while Jerry's mind drifted back to Miami. He thought of Scarlet's laugh, the way she'd listened when he talked about the boys, how her fingers had felt intertwined with his.

Jerry's neighborhood was a maze of identical beige houses with matching lawns. The kind of cookie-cutter development that sprouted around military bases like mushrooms after rain. Nothing distinguished his from any other, except perhaps the specialized ramp he'd installed for Marty's wheelchair and the brightly colored wind spinner Emmett had insisted on planting in the front garden.

Inside, the house smelled of tomato sauce and garlic. Maggie stood at the kitchen counter in an apron, her silver-streaked hair pulled back in a loose bun. The sound of cartoons drifted from the living room.

"There they are," she called, looking up from where she was carefully cutting lasagna into small, manageable squares. "How was the last day of the work week?"

"Same old," Jerry said, setting his keys in the bowl by the door. "Where are the boys?"

"Emmett's watching that dinosaur show he likes. Marty's in the living room with that mirror toy he loves."

Jerry followed the sounds to find Emmett sprawled on the floor in front of the TV. Marty was nearby on his play mat, lying on his stomach and giggling at his reflection in a plastic mirror toy. When they spotted Jerry, Emmett launched himself across the room.

"Dad! Grandma made lasagna and I helped! I stirred the sauce and everything!"

Jerry caught him mid-leap, swinging him up. "That so? Did you wear more sauce than you stirred?"

"No!" Emmett giggled, then lowered his voice conspiratorially. "But Marty made a big mess with his basket again. He dumped everything."

Jerry set Emmett down and crossed to kneel beside Marty, who had pushed himself up slightly on his forearms when he heard his father's voice. Marty's face lit up with a radiant smile, arms reaching out.

"Hey, buddy," Jerry said softly, gathering him up. Though Marty's muscles often resisted coordination, his desire for a bear hug was unmistakable as he threw his arms around Jerry's neck with surprising strength, his whole body vibrating with happiness.

"Missed you too," Jerry murmured, holding him close and breathing in the baby shampoo scent of his hair. Jerry treasured these moments most of all, when Marty's physical limitations seemed to vanish in the pure joy of connection.

"Mac!" Emmett had spotted Mac attempting to sneak past toward his room. "Wanna see my new dinosaur drawing? It's a T-Rex eating a building!"

"Absolutely," Mac said with exaggerated seriousness. "That's exactly what I need after a long day of boring adult stuff."

Dinner was organized chaos. Maggie had placed a plastic mat under Marty's chair, anticipating the inevitable mess. Emmett's conversation jumped around: dinosaurs, his friend Jake's new skateboard, the fort they'd built in the backyard that afternoon. Mac matched his energy, spinning wild tales about dinosaurs that made Emmett giggle uncontrollably.

Jerry watched his mother carefully feed Marty small bites of lasagna between the ones Marty managed himself. Her patience was infinite, wiping his face after each messy handful and encouraging his attempts at self-feeding. Tomato sauce smeared across his cheeks and chin, but Marty's delight in the meal was evident in his wide smile.

"So," Maggie said during a rare lull when Emmett paused for breath, "have you heard from Scarlet since Sunday?"

Jerry paused, fork halfway to his mouth. "Some. Just texts."

Mac snorted. "He means he checks his phone every five minutes to see if she's messaged."

"I do not," Jerry protested, but the heat in his face betrayed him.

"It's sweet," Maggie said, her eyes soft. "Mac's been filling me in on some details this week."

Jerry shot Mac a look that promised retribution. "Has he now?"

"Oh, don't blame him. I was curious about the woman who seems to have captured my son's attention." She turned to help Marty with another bite. "She sounds lovely."

"She is," Jerry admitted, surprising himself with the simple honesty.

Emmett perked up. "Who's lovely?"

"A friend of Dad's," Mac supplied.

"Like a girlfriend?" Emmett pressed, suddenly very interested.

"Like a friend," Jerry corrected.

"But a pretty one," Mac added with a grin.

"I wanna meet her!" Emmett declared.

Jerry felt his pulse quicken. The idea of Scarlet meeting his boys, of these separate worlds colliding, was both exhilarating and terrifying.

"Maybe someday," he said carefully.

After dinner, Jerry checked his watch. "Mom, we should head out if you're going to make your flight."

Maggie nodded, wiping Marty's face one last time. "All packed and ready. Mac, would you mind keeping an eye on the boys?"

"Like they were my own," Mac promised. "Emmett, want to show me that fort you were talking about?"

"Yeah!" Emmett jumped up. "Marty can come too. We made it so his chair fits through the door!"

He tossed Maggie's suitcase into the back of the truck, grateful more than anything.

This week, she'd kept things running while he caught his footing again.

Her ability to step in so seamlessly still amazed him.

The air was thick with summer heat as they drove off.

She rolled down the window, her hair lifting in the wind, already talking about when she'd be back.

Then, as the silence settled between them, she shot him a look that was all motherly mischief. "You seem different," she said, her tone casual but not careless.

"Different how?"

"Lighter. Even with all the chaos this week, you seem different. Emmett's summer energy, Marty's therapy sessions, all of it. But you seem ... I don't know. More present."

Jerry considered this as he navigated through the neighborhood streets. "The cruise was good. Getting away."

"I don't think it was just the cruise," Maggie said gently. "Mac told me how you were around her. Scarlet."

Traffic thickened as they approached the highway. Jerry focused on changing lanes, buying time to collect his thoughts.

"She's different," he finally said. "Easy to talk to. Smart. Funny in this dry way that catches you off guard."

"And beautiful, according to Mac."

Jerry couldn't help smiling. "Yeah. That too."

"He also mentioned she's in Florida. With a career."

The implied question was clear. Jerry sighed. "I know it's complicated, Mom."

"Life is complicated, sweetheart. That doesn't mean you shouldn't reach for good things when they come along."

His phone chimed with a text notification. At the next red light, Jerry glanced down to see Scarlet's name on the screen.

Scarlet

> What would you think about me visiting sometime soon? Maybe next weekend?

His heart jumped, a physical sensation so strong he actually pressed a hand to his chest. Maggie noticed both the text and his reaction.

"Good news?" she asked.

"She wants to visit. Next weekend."

Maggie's face lit up. "That's wonderful! The boys will be so excited to meet her."

The light turned green. Jerry hesitated, then typed quickly.

Jerry

> I'm already on my way to the airport to pick you up.

Technically, it wasn't a lie since he was going to the airport, just not for Scarlet. The response felt right in its spontaneity, something he rarely allowed himself.

"Is she the first girl you've brought home since—" Maggie began.

"Don't." The word came out of Jerry like shattered glass as his entire body tensed, knuckles white on the steering wheel. The truck swerved slightly before he corrected it with a jerk.

His jaw clamped shut, muscles working visibly along his temples. "Please, don't say that name."

The familiar chill washed over him. The same ice that formed whenever he was forced to think about his ex-wife. Five years since the divorce. Three years since he'd won full custody after a battle that had nearly broken him. The courtroom flashed in his mind: her voice dripping with boredom as she listed Marty's diagnoses like inconveniences, her visible relief when surrendering her parental rights. *Never again*, he'd promised himself. *Never let anyone like that near the boys again.*

Jerry realized he'd missed a turn. He blinked hard, forcing himself back to the present, aware of his shallow breathing.

"I'm sorry, sweetheart," Maggie said softly.

Jerry just nodded, unable to form words yet. His right hand released the steering wheel long enough to rub at his sternum, trying to ease the phantom pressure there. The reflexive check of his rearview mirror was an old habit from when custody exchanges meant hours of tension, always watching for her car to appear.

"Yes," he finally managed, voice rougher than before. "She's the first."

They drove in silence for nearly a mile, the hum of the road filling the space between them. Jerry's shoulders remained rigid, his fingers still gripping the wheel too tightly.

"Scarlet is nothing like her," he said eventually, the words emerging like he was pushing them through a narrow space. "Nothing."

"I can see that already," Maggie said, careful to keep her tone neutral. "I haven't seen you light up like this in so long, Jerry. The boys notice it too."

He took a deliberate breath, forcing his shoulders to lower, though the tightness in his neck remained. "The boys need that version of me."

Jerry nodded again, eyes fixed on the road. The familiar signs for the airport appeared, but the peaceful anticipation he'd felt earlier had been replaced by a lingering unease that clung to him like smoke.

As they pulled into the departure lane, Jerry's hands still trembled slightly as he put the truck in park. The ghost of his past had a way of ambushing him, even in moments of joy.

"She seems like a good one, Jerry. I can hear it in your voice when you talk about her," Maggie said, reaching for the door.

"You haven't even met her," he said, helping his mother with her suitcase, his movements more deliberate than before.

"I've seen what the idea of her does to you." Maggie's smile was gentle but knowing. "Besides, my grandmotherly instincts are never wrong."

Jerry laughed despite himself, the sound releasing some of the lingering tension. "That a fact?"

"Absolutely." She cradled his face between her palms, the way she'd done since he was small. "I knew the moment I saw Emmett that he'd have your serious nature. I knew Marty would have your resilience. And I know you're overthinking this."

"It's what I do best."

Maggie kissed his cheek. "I'll see you soon."

Jerry watched her disappear into the terminal, feeling simultaneously lighter and heavier. Having Scarlet visit and meet his children filled him with a strange mixture of anticipation and terror.

The truck hummed through twilight, the land bathed in a hush that matched the mood inside.

Jerry's mind wandered.

Scarlet, standing in his kitchen. Scarlet, watching the boys from the old fort. Scarlet, curled on the couch as he read aloud.

The images came easily. The answers didn't.

By the time he pulled into the driveway, the yard was dark except for the porch light. Through the window, he could see Mac sitting on the floor between the boys, apparently acting out some elaborate dinosaur scenario with Emmett's toys. Marty was giggling in his adaptive seat, hands flapping with delight.

Jerry sat in the truck a moment longer, taking in the scene. His home, his life, his boys. All the complications and joys that came with them. Soon, Scarlet would witness the full picture, not just the glimpses he'd shared through stories on the ship, but the beautiful, messy reality.

He was terrified. And, for the first time in years, hopeful.

Eighteen

Morning crept into the room slowly, slipping between the blinds in faint silver ribbons.

Jerry's eyes opened without effort.

Even before the light registered, he felt her curled against him, her steady breath warming his chest.

Scarlet.

Here, not in memory or a screen, but real and sleeping beside him.

He shifted slightly, careful not to wake her, and let the memory of last night surface in quiet waves.

Jerry's body stirred at the memory, but he fought the urge to wake her. She'd flown in late after a full workday; she deserved to rest. More importantly, there was a morning routine to manage before she faced the beautiful chaos of his real life.

With practiced stealth, Jerry slipped from the bed. He found sweatpants and a T-shirt, dressing quietly in the dim light. At the door, he paused for one more look at Scarlet, allowing himself a moment of pure optimism before the day's reality set in.

The hallway was quiet, but not for long. His first stop was Emmett's room, where his younger son was already half-awake, stuffed orange cat clutched to his chest.

"Morning, buddy," Jerry whispered, sitting on the bed. "Ready for pancakes?"

Emmett's eyes flew open fully. "It's Saturday! Pancake day!" He bolted upright, then froze. "Is she here? Your friend?"

"Yes," Jerry confirmed, smoothing down a cowlick in Emmett's hair. "Miss Scarlet is still sleeping, so we need to use our inside voices, okay?"

Emmett nodded solemnly, then stage-whispered, "Is she pretty? Mac said she was pretty."

"She is," Jerry said, feeling his ears warm. "Now go brush your teeth while I get Marty up."

Marty's room was adapted to his needs, with a specialized bed with safety rails, accessible storage, and walls painted a calming blue. Jerry's heart swelled as it always did when his eldest son's eyes opened, recognition and pure love shining through despite the physical limitations Marty lived with daily.

"Good morning, soldier," Jerry murmured, gently lifting Marty from his bed. The boy's arms wrapped around his neck, his face burrowing into Jerry's shoulder. "Ready to meet someone special today?"

Marty made a soft humming sound that Jerry recognized as excitement. He carried his son to the other room for their morning routine, which was a practiced dance of care and efficiency he'd perfected over years. Even on weekends, the routine didn't change. Structure was safety for both of them.

Once both boys were dressed and ready, Jerry fell into the comforting rhythm of Saturday morning. Marty settled in his adaptive chair at the kitchen table while Emmett helped arrange plates. Coffee brewing, pancake batter mixed, Marty's specialized utensils laid out. Everything needed to be just right this morning. Perfect, even.

Mac shuffled in, hair sticking up at odd angles. "Morning, Duncans," he yawned, making a beeline for the coffee pot. "Our guest still sleeping?"

"Don't wake her," Jerry warned, pouring batter onto the griddle with precision. "And remember—"

"I know, I know. Best behavior. No embarrassing stories," Mac recited dutifully. "Relax, man. You're going to strain something if you keep tensing like that."

Jerry realized his shoulders were indeed knotted with tension. He consciously tried to relax, but his mind kept racing through potential problems like what if Emmett had a meltdown? What if Marty didn't respond well to a new person? What if the chaos of their morning overwhelmed Scarlet?

"Is she going to like my pancakes?" Emmett asked, carefully placing blueberries on each circle of batter as Jerry had taught him. "What if she doesn't like blueberries? What if she's allergic? Will she have to go to the hospital?"

"She likes blueberries," Jerry assured him, though he realized with a jolt that he wasn't entirely certain. There were still so many small details about Scarlet he didn't know, like her allergies, her morning habits, how she likes her coffee. The thought both unsettled and excited him.

"She's here!" Emmett suddenly hissed, eyes wide, staring at something behind Jerry.

When Jerry turned around, there was Scarlet in the kitchen doorway. She looked sweetly uncertain, wearing his oversized blue T-shirt and gym shorts that she'd tightened around her narrow waist. Sleep had left her hair mussed and her face makeup-free, creating an intimacy that caught him off guard. Jerry felt his breath catch at how right she looked standing there in his clothes, in his kitchen, part of his morning.

"The sleeping beauty arises!" Mac announced, breaking the moment.

"Hey," Jerry managed, suddenly aware of how his kitchen must look to her. Slightly battered cupboards, Marty's adaptive equipment tucked in a corner, the refrigerator plastered with Emmett's artwork and therapy schedules. He'd meant to tidy up more last night, but then Scarlet had arrived and all his good intentions had vanished.

Emmett, predictably, launched into rapid-fire questions, barely pausing for breath. Jerry watched Scarlet's face, trying to gauge her reaction to the sensory overload that was his younger son at full morning energy.

"Yes, I'm Scarlet," she replied, and Jerry felt a wave of relief at the genuine warmth in her voice. "You must be Emmett."

"That's me! I'm six but I'll be seven in forty-three days. That's Marty over there. He's my brother. He's eight but he doesn't talk like I do. He makes sounds though! And Dad says he understands everything, just like I do, only different."

Jerry stepped forward, placing a calming hand on Emmett's shoulder. "Buddy, let's give Scarlet a chance to get some coffee before the interrogation, okay?"

"Is this an interrogation?" Emmett's eyes somehow grew wider. "Like the police shows Mac watches after I go to bed?"

Jerry caught Scarlet's eye over Emmett's head, silently apologizing for the morning intensity. To his surprise, she seemed more amused than overwhelmed.

"A figure of speech," Jerry clarified, shooting a pointed look at Mac. "Why don't you finish setting the table while I get Scarlet some coffee?"

He leaned in to kiss her cheek as he moved past, noticing how her hair smelled faintly of his shampoo. "Sorry," he murmured. "Morning volume control isn't his strong suit."

"It's fine," she whispered back. "I like his energy."

Jerry poured her coffee and set out cream and sugar on the side, his movements careful and deliberate. He straightened the handle of the cream pitcher twice, adjusted the sugar bowl until it sat just so. Everything needed to be perfect. He was acutely aware of how this morning might set the tone for everything to follow.

"I stole your clothes," she admitted quietly. "I didn't exactly pack appropriate pajamas for meeting kids."

Heat flickered through him as he imagined what she might have packed instead. "I noticed. Looks better on you anyway."

At the table, Jerry focused on managing breakfast while watching Scarlet navigate her first interactions with his sons. She approached Marty's chair with a gentleness that made his throat tight, speaking directly to him rather than around him as so many adults did. And the

smile that transformed his son's face told him everything he needed to know.

"He likes you," Emmett announced with characteristic blunt-
ness. "I can tell because his eyes got all crinkly. That means he's
happy."

Jerry caught Scarlet's eyes across the table, hoping she could
read the gratitude in his. The simple validation of his son's approval meant more than he could possibly explain.

Breakfast progressed with the usual Emmett narrative, this
time peppered with questions for Scarlet. Jerry tensed when Emmett blurted out that she was the first "friend" to visit, hyperaware
of what that revelation might sound like. But Scarlet took it in
stride, smoothly answering Emmett's questions about Miami and
her gray cat named Storm.

Then came the Orange Cat incident. Jerry watched in silent
alarm as Scarlet innocently reached for Emmett's beloved stuffed
animal, knowing what would follow.

"NO!" Emmett's shout cracked through the kitchen. "You
can't just TAKE him! You have to ASK first!"

Jerry's anxiety spiked. This was exactly the kind of moment
he'd been dreading: the unpredictable nature of life with Emmett, the delicate balance that could so easily tip into chaos. He
kept his voice deliberate and calm. "Emmett, Scarlet didn't know.
Remember how we talked about using our words calmly when
someone doesn't know our rules?"

Emmett clutched Orange Cat protectively, but nodded. "I'm
sorry I yelled," he said, his voice small. "But Orange Cat doesn't
like strangers touching him without permission."

"That makes perfect sense," Scarlet replied with such genuine understanding that Jerry felt a rush of admiration. "I should have asked first. I promise I'll always ask from now on."

What happened next astonished him. Emmett studied Scarlet, then extended Orange Cat toward her. "You can hold him now if you want. I give permission."

Jerry's breath caught. He met Scarlet's eyes across the table, trying to convey the significance of what had just happened. Orange Cat represented far more than a simple stuffed toy to Emmett, functioning as his emotional barometer, constant companion, and security object all rolled into one. Permission to hold him was something Emmett granted to almost no one outside immediate family.

After breakfast, Jerry announced bath time for Marty, guiding his son through their weekend routine while keeping one ear tuned to the kitchen where Mac was regaling Scarlet with stories from their deployment days. He worked with focused precision, maintaining the exact water temperature Marty preferred, using the specific soap that didn't irritate his sensitive skin, following each step in the familiar sequence. It was easier to focus on these details than to wonder what Scarlet was thinking, whether she was overwhelmed by the reality of his life.

Later, the four of them gathered in the living room. Jerry helped Marty with a stacking toy, explaining softly how to grasp each piece, celebrating small victories with gentle high-fives. Across the room, Emmett sprawled on the floor drawing, periodically asking Scarlet if she thought his dinosaurs were "scientifically accurate."

Then, Marty did something unexpected. He abandoned his toy and crawled across the floor with determined focus until he reached

Scarlet's legs. Without hesitation, he pulled himself up and wrapped his arms around her calves, gazing up with that radiant smile that never failed to melt Jerry's heart.

"He wants up," Jerry explained, watching carefully for Scarlet's reaction.

She lifted Marty onto the couch beside her, but he immediately climbed into her lap, settling against her chest with the comfortable ease he usually reserved for family. Jerry's breath caught at the sight.

"Around his middle is good," he guided softly. "He likes the pressure."

As Scarlet embraced his son, something broke free in Jerry's heart, a guard he hadn't known was there dropping all at once.

"He doesn't usually take to new people this quickly," Jerry said, barely recognizing his own voice for the emotion it carried.

"Must be my natural charm," Scarlet joked, but he could hear the touched uncertainty beneath.

"Must be," he agreed simply, unable to articulate the complex emotions swirling through him.

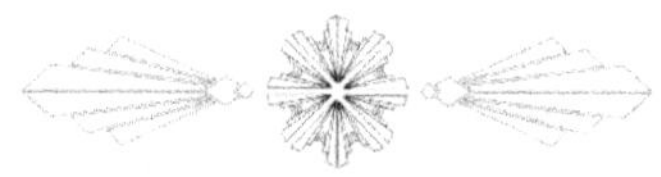

The sprinkler sent arcs of water spinning through the air, and Mac, ever the clown, turned the yard into a splash zone of shrieking, giggling chaos.

Jerry hung back, towel in hand, more observer than participant. But he couldn't look away from Scarlet.

She crouched beside Marty, showing him how to catch the spray on his toes, her face soft with laughter. When Emmett latched onto her with another elaborate story, she leaned in without flinching, nodding at every twist and turn. Rather than simply enduring the chaos, she *joined* it completely, instinctively syncing with the pace of two very different little boys.

He hadn't expected her to fit so easily.

But she did.

At one point, Mac joined him on the back porch, handing him a cold water bottle.

"You know, you can stop hovering," Mac observed. "She's doing fine."

Jerry hadn't realized how tense he'd been, how watchfully he'd been monitoring every interaction. "Is it that obvious?"

"Only to someone who's known you for a decade," Mac replied. "But seriously, man, you don't need to orchestrate everything. They like her. She likes them. It's working."

Jerry watched as Scarlet helped Emmett adjust the sprinkler pattern. "I just want everything to go well."

"Sometimes perfect is the enemy of good," Mac said, with uncharacteristic insight. "This isn't a military operation. It's a Saturday with someone who cares about you. Let it breathe a little."

Jerry considered this, recognizing how exhausting it had been to chase the impossible goal of controlling the uncontrollable by anticipating every problem, smoothing every rough edge, and maintaining the facade of having everything perfectly in hand.

His attention was drawn back to the yard as Emmett ran toward Scarlet, thrusting Orange Cat into her hands before racing back to the sprinkler. Jerry felt the profound weight of that simple gesture as Emmett entrusted his most precious possession to Scarlet's care.

"He gave her Orange Cat," Jerry said, voice hushed with disbelief.

Mac whistled low. "Damn. Not even your mom gets Orange Cat duty."

"I know." The implications weren't lost on him.

"So what are you afraid of?" Mac asked bluntly.

Jerry kept his eyes on Scarlet, now cradling the stuffed animal with exaggerated care. "That this feels too right, too fast."

"Or maybe," Mac countered, "you've been doing everything the hard way for so long that you've forgotten it's allowed to feel right."

The words stayed with Jerry through the afternoon and into evening. He gradually felt the tension in his shoulders ease, the hypervigilance fading as he allowed himself to simply experience rather than manage the day.

Dinner unfolded as an unspoken collaboration. Scarlet joined him at the counter, slicing vegetables while he browned the meat. Without any direction or assigned tasks, they simply moved together in natural alignment.

Jerry caught himself smiling more than usual, chuckling at Emmett's wild, half-true stories. Across the table, Scarlet met his gaze now and then, quiet smiles passing between them like secrets they hadn't spoken yet.

After dinner, Mac made a suspiciously hasty exit, mentioning plans with friends that Jerry strongly suspected were invented on the spot.

"Subtle," Jerry muttered as Mac winked on his way out the door.

"Like a freight train," Mac agreed cheerfully. "You can thank me later."

Bath time and bedtime routines followed with their familiar rhythm, but now with Scarlet naturally integrated into the flow. When Emmett asked her to read his bedtime story, Jerry leaned against the doorframe, watching her settle beside his son with Orange Cat carefully tucked between them. The scene felt like a glimpse into a possible future. Her voice shifted for each character while Emmett listened with rapt attention, the soft lamplight casting them both in a gentle glow.

"Will you be here tomorrow?" Emmett asked, his voice small and hopeful.

"Yes. I'm here until tomorrow afternoon," Scarlet assured him.

"Good." Emmett yawned enormously. "I like you being here. Dad smiles more."

The simple observation, so characteristically blunt, hit Jerry with unexpected force. Did he smile more with Scarlet around? Was his happiness that visible to his six-year-old?

In Marty's room, Jerry sang the familiar lullaby that had become their nightly ritual, unchanged through deployments and hospital stays, the same song he'd sung every night since his son was born. Scarlet stood in the doorway, watching silently, and Jerry felt rather than saw her understanding of the sacred space she'd been invited into.

"Be right out," Jerry mouthed to Scarlet as she lingered in Marty's doorway. She nodded and backed away, leaving him to finish the lullaby.

As he sang, Jerry kept his hand on Marty's shoulder, maintaining the same steady rhythm that had worked since his son was small. Marty's eyes grew heavy, his breathing slowing into the familiar pattern of approaching sleep.

Jerry tucked the blanket around Marty's shoulders, checked the night light, and headed into the hallway, carefully avoiding the squeaky floorboard near the door.

When he reached the living room, Jerry paused, watching Scarlet before she noticed him. She stood at his entertainment center, studying the photograph of Emmett behind Marty's wheelchair. During deployments, Jerry clung to exactly what that photo captured: Emmett stretching to see around the wheelchair, insisting 'I'm really strong today. I ate two bowls of cereal,' Orange Cat's ear peeking from his backpack, Marty turning slightly to smile at his brother. The perfect moment of brotherly connection that got Jerry through his darkest nights overseas.

Scarlet moved on to the football display taking notice of a football signed by the entire 2008 undefeated Utah team. Jerry stepped forward.

"That's the 2008 squad," he said, moving closer. "Best team Utah ever fielded. Went undefeated that year."

Scarlet turned, seeming genuinely interested. "You're from Utah?"

"Born and raised," he nodded, crossing the room. "My dad and I never missed a game if we could help it. He took me to meet the team after their Sugar Bowl win ... hence all those signatures."

That day remained vivid in his memory: fifteen years old, standing in line with his dad for hours in Salt Lake City, the January chill making their breath visible as they waited. How his father had put his arm around Jerry's shoulders when he'd nervously approached the players for signatures, some of them already NFL-bound. The pride in his dad's eyes when Jerry had managed to ask Kyle Whittingham for his autograph without stammering. One of those perfect teenage moments that felt significant even while it was happening.

"Feel like some wine?" he offered, changing the subject. "Fair warning ... my wine expertise stops at 'red' and 'white,' but Mac left a bottle of merlot he swears isn't terrible."

Her laugh loosened the tension in his shoulders. "Coming from Mac, that's high praise. I'd love some."

Jerry searched the kitchen drawer for the corkscrew, his mind wandering to the last movie debate he and Mac had over beers. Mac insisted that *Die Hard* was the greatest Christmas movie ever made while Jerry had defended *It's a Wonderful Life*. They'd known each other less than a year when they'd been assigned to the same unit on this deployment, but Mac had quickly become the brother Jerry never had, going far deeper than just military connection, helping with the boys whenever Jerry needed a hand.

He caught Scarlet studying his DVD collection, her head tilted as she scanned the titles. He knew exactly when she found his romantic comedies as her posture shifted slightly in surprise.

"Before you comment," he started, bringing over the glasses, "Mac claims those are his."

"And they're not?" she asked, accepting the wine.

"Not even close." Jerry felt oddly exposed by this minor confession. "Though I'll deny it if you tell him I said so."

"So, which one's your favorite?"

"*Fools Gold*, hands down," he answered honestly. "Treasure hunting, second chances, McConaughey being ridiculous ..." He shrugged, feeling self-conscious. "Sometimes you need something lighter to balance out the rest."

"No judgment here," she said. "I've seen *The Proposal* at least twelve times."

Jerry laughed with genuine warmth, the kind of response Mac could usually draw out of him after a few beers and bad jokes.

His attention shifted as Scarlet noticed the small bronze Battlefield Cross. Her hand reached toward it but stopped, showing unexpected respect for something she likely didn't fully understand.

"It's called a Battlefield Cross," he explained, moving beside her. "Traditional memorial when a soldier falls in combat."

She nodded, recognition immediate. "Is it for someone specific?"

Hunter's name stirred the usual pressure.

There were things Jerry had never voiced, even to people who'd lived through it with him.

But now wasn't the moment to open that door.

"For all the brothers and sisters we've lost," Jerry said, his voice measured. "But particularly for Hunter."

"Hunter," she repeated softly.

Jerry waited for the usual responses: awkward questions, forced sympathy, or the quick subject change. Instead, Scarlet simply met his gaze, offering presence without demands.

"The reverence in your voice tells me enough," she said quietly. "I understand the love behind it."

The unexpected response hit Jerry square in the chest. She hadn't pushed for war stories or details. She'd simply acknowledged what Hunter had meant to him.

"Thanks," he managed, taking her hand and squeezing gently.

They moved to the couch, Jerry settling into his usual position. The air conditioner hummed steadily, accompanied by the familiar settling sounds of the house.

Scarlet curled her legs beneath her, the borrowed T-shirt riding up to reveal more thigh than she'd intended. Jerry felt the day's vigilance shifting into a different kind of awareness.

"Been wanting to do this all day," he murmured, setting aside his wine to pull her closer.

Their kiss was different from the urgent ones they'd shared the night before. It was deeper, richer, and infused with everything they'd witnessed about each other throughout the day. Jerry's hand slid up her back, beneath the borrowed T-shirt, feeling the warmth of her skin against his palm. Scarlet's fingers traced the line of his jaw, then moved to the nape of his neck, drawing him closer.

"Bedroom?" she whispered against his lips.

He nodded, standing and pulling her with him. The short walk down the hallway felt charged with anticipation, his fingertips never leaving her skin, as if breaking contact might shatter the moment.

Inside, he closed the door with deliberate care, turning the lock with a soft click. The room was bathed in silver moonlight streaming through half-drawn blinds, casting shadows across Scarlet's face as she stood before him. She reached for the hem of her borrowed shirt, pulling it slowly over her head to reveal the pale curve of her breasts in the dim light.

Jerry's breath caught. Last night had been frantic, driven by weeks of separation and pent-up desire. This was different, slower, more deliberate. He stepped forward, hands sliding around her waist, marveling at the softness of her skin beneath his calloused fingers.

"You're beautiful," he murmured, bending to press his lips to the hollow of her throat.

She sighed, head tilting back, hands moving to his shoulders as he traced a path of kisses along her collarbone. Her fingers slipped beneath his shirt, tugging it upward until he helped her remove it entirely. The press of skin against skin drew a low sound from his throat as they moved toward the bed.

They fell into the bed in quiet tandem, Jerry gently lowering her beneath him, steady on his forearms.

His lips met hers again, this time with more heat, more certainty.

Her hands explored his back, gliding over each contour and the ghosted marks of a life worn into his skin.

"I've been thinking about this all day," he confessed against her skin, trailing kisses down her neck to the curve of her breast.

"Me too," she breathed, arching slightly as his tongue traced a sensitive path.

Everything distilled down to breath, skin, the soft rhythm of touch.

Jerry moved with intention, every stroke a silent vow, every sound she made etched into the space between them.

Her gasp beneath his mouth. The subtle pull of her fingers when he hovered near her edge.

But it wasn't just her response, it was her trust, raw and unshielded, that unraveled him most.

This wasn't just intimacy. It was a reminder of what it felt like to be safe. To be trusted.

He moved back up, bracing on one elbow, drawn to her like gravity.

She looked back at him. Moonlight flickered in her eyes, her breath slow and steady.

And in that moment, the feeling that rose inside him wasn't just overwhelming. It was absolute.

"I'm falling for you, Scarlet," he murmured, the words escaping before he could consider the impact.

The momentary stillness beneath him was subtle. It was just a fraction of a second where her breathing paused, but he felt it like a physical blow. Her eyes widened slightly, a flash of something that looked too much like panic crossing her features.

Jerry's body reacted before his mind could intervene, muscles tensing as he pulled back reflexively. A cold wave washed through him as unwanted memories flooded back: another woman's face, cruel laughter, words like 'too much' and 'suffocating.' The familiar feeling of being too invested, too emotional, too vulnerable.

He rolled away, sitting up at the edge of the bed, his back to her as he sucked in a ragged breath. "I'm sorry," he said, voice rough. "That was ... I, I didn't mean to push. Too soon. I know."

"Jerry," Scarlet's voice was soft behind him, followed by the warm press of her palm against his bare back. She moved beside him, not forcing him to face her, simply offering presence. "Look at me."

He turned, bracing for pity or discomfort in her expression. Instead, he found only warmth and understanding.

"Don't apologize," she said firmly, her hand coming up to cup his cheek. "I'm just ... processing. This is all so new, and there's so much at stake." Her eyes flickered briefly toward the door.

She hadn't backed off. She was still right there, steady and sure, looking at him like he wasn't too much.

"I know," he said, gradually steadying his breathing. "We don't have to race to some finish line." He leaned his forehead against hers, needing the contact. "I just wanted you to know."

"I'm here," she whispered, the simple declaration more powerful than any promise could have been. Her thumb traced the line of his cheekbone, gentle and grounding. "I'm not running. But I want to do this right."

The word 'right' hung between them, rich with meaning. Not just for them, but for the boys, for the life he'd so carefully constructed. For everything that mattered.

Jerry nodded as her arms wrapped around him, the tightness in his shoulders slowly releasing.

She eased him back onto the bed, her body curving to his with quiet certainty, as if she could root him there with nothing but touch.

Her kiss was soft but resolute. It felt like a silent vow of presence.

She wasn't backing away. Even after seeing him at his lowest, she chose to stay.

Their pace was gentle now, shaped by tenderness instead of urgency.

Their touch became its own language, speaking hope and healing through each motion.

Jerry met her in it fully, strength and vulnerability no longer at odds.

And when feeling surged too fast, too full, she simply held him, allowing her body to become both refuge and reassurance.

Later, they settled into sleep, Scarlet's back pressed against his chest, her curves fitting perfectly against him. Jerry draped his arm over her side, his hand finding hers in the darkness. Their fingers intertwined naturally, resting near her heart. Something about the simple intimacy of the moment, both protective and equal, felt like everything they couldn't yet put into words.

He'd invited Scarlet to Texas hoping to discover if their connection could survive reality. What he'd discovered was the impossible: someone who saw his whole life, his boys, his struggles, and chose to stay anyway.

Nineteen

The public affairs office hummed with post-lunch energy, key-boards clicking as everyone settled back into their afternoon routines. Jerry scrolled through a draft press release about the upcoming community open house, red pen poised to mark corrections on the printed copy beside his keyboard. The September afternoon sun slanted through the blinds, casting bars of light across his desk that highlighted the small framed photo of Emmett and Marty that hadn't moved in years, alongside a newer one featuring all three of them with Scarlet at the local park near his house, her red hair blazing in the sunlight as she helped Marty feed ducks.

"So," Mac's voice broke through his concentration, "want to explain the one-man boy band routine I witnessed at the intersection of Tank Destroyer and Mills Blvd?"

Jerry looked up, pen freezing midair. "What?"

Mac leaned against the doorframe of Jerry's office, arms crossed, grin threatening to split his face. "Don't play innocent with me, Duncan. I caught you singing and drumming on your dashboard at that red light coming back from lunch. And was that ... were those actual dance moves happening in the driver's seat?"

Heat crawled up Jerry's neck. "I have no idea what you're talking about."

"Dude, you were jamming so hard you didn't even see me pull up next to you." Mac's eyes gleamed with mischief. "I haven't seen you that happy in, well, ever. What was it? Please tell me it was something embarrassing. Backstreet Boys? Spice Girls?"

Jerry refused to admit it had been something from Taylor Swift which Scarlet had added to a playlist she'd made for him before her last visit. His phone had been playing through the car speakers when her text brightened his afternoon with a simple selfie featuring Storm, her gray cat, and a message about missing him.

"I was just ... it was nothing."

"Nothing looks good on you, man." Mac's teasing softened into something more genuine. "Whatever's happening with Red, it's working."

Jerry couldn't argue with that. Weekend visits when possible, late-night phone calls when not. Emmett had started counting down days between "Scarlet time," while Marty kept a small blanket she'd given him close at all times. As for Jerry himself ... he'd started singing in the car again. That said enough.

Before he could respond, Corporal Barrett appeared in the doorway, her usually composed expression tense. "Staff Sergeant Duncan, Sergeant MacIntyre ... Sergeant Major Vega has called an urgent meeting for all senior NCOs. Conference room, ten minutes."

The atmosphere in the office instantly shifted. Mac straightened, teasing forgotten. "Any idea what it's about?"

Barrett shook her head. "All I know is the command team was behind closed doors with Division staff most of the morning. Rumors are flying."

"What kind of rumors?" Jerry asked, already saving his work and standing.

"Hard to say. Some think there's trouble brewing somewhere. Others are betting Command Sergeant Major Vega's putting in for retirement." Barrett lowered her voice. "All I know is Colonel Sharp looked grim when he came through earlier."

Jerry exchanged a glance with Mac. Unscheduled meetings rarely brought good news.

"Thanks for the heads-up," Jerry said. "We'll be there."

As Barrett left, Mac closed the office door. "What do you think?"

Jerry shrugged, but an uneasy feeling had settled in his gut. "Only one way to find out."

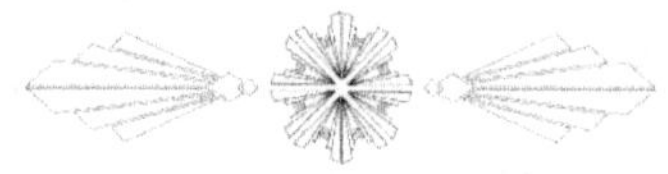

The corridors of the Brigade Headquarters bustled with more activity than usual for a Thursday afternoon. Small clusters of NCOs moved toward the conference room, voices pitched low in speculation. Jerry nodded to colleagues from other sections, noting the same tension he felt mirrored in their expressions.

The conference room was already half-full when they arrived. Jerry took his assigned seat at the large oval table between the legal team's NCO and the chaplain's assistant. Mac positioned himself against the back wall with the other NCOs who didn't have a primary seat at the table. The low murmur of conversation filled the room, theories bouncing between the participants.

"Heard CID was in the building earlier," muttered Sergeant First Class Lin from Intelligence.

"Nah, this is about the budget cuts," countered someone else.

Jerry said nothing, preferring to observe. Whatever was coming, speculation wouldn't change it. Years in the military had taught him to wait for confirmed information before reacting.

The room fell silent when Vega entered, her boots striking the tile with precise rhythm. Colonel Sharp, the brigade commander, was noticeably absent, which only heightened Jerry's sense that something significant was about to happen.

"At ease," Vega called out, preemptively preventing the room full of noncommissioned officers to jump to their feet. She took her position at the head of the table, her expression professionally neutral, but Jerry had worked with her long enough to note the slight tension around her eyes.

"Thank you all for adjusting your schedules on short notice. I'll get straight to the point." She paused, scanning the faces around the table. "Division has confirmed deployment orders for our brigade. Nine months in Kuwait, beginning right after Christmas."

The room remained silent, but Jerry felt the collective tension rise. Deployment wasn't unexpected in their line of work, but the timing was a surprise. Their unit had only returned from rotation eighteen months ago.

"At least there'll be less chance of being shot this time," quipped Sergeant First Class Diaz from the Motor Pool, breaking the tension with nervous laughter.

Vega acknowledged this with a nod. "Different mission set, different challenges. We'll be supporting Operation Spartan Shield. It's primarily training exercises and regional stability operations."

She continued outlining preliminary details, but Jerry's mind had already leapt ahead, calculating implications. Nine months beginning after Christmas. Home by next September, maybe October. Emmett would be in second grade by then. Marty would have his next major assessment at the children's hospital in Austin. And Scarlet ...

His chest tightened. They'd only just found their rhythm, bridging the distance between Texas and Florida with calls and visits. Now, they'd be adding seven time zones and a combat deployment to that equation.

"Colonel Sharp is meeting with the staff officers later this afternoon once he returns from Division HQ," Vega was saying. "Feel free to give your bosses a heads-up about the coming announcement, but please refrain from sharing with junior enlisted at this time. Colonel Sharp would like to address the entire unit before we break for the evening."

She paused, her eyes softening almost imperceptibly. "And I should mention, the Colonel is planning to give the entire unit tomorrow off for an impromptu three-day weekend so everyone can spend some time with their families."

The irony wasn't lost on Jerry. A three-day reprieve before the long countdown to a nine-month separation.

As the meeting concluded with instructions about readiness timelines and follow-up briefings, Jerry remained in his seat, still processing. This wasn't his first deployment—not even his second or third—but it was his first since Scarlet had entered their lives.

The room gradually emptied, NCOs breaking into small groups to discuss logistics. Mac materialized beside Jerry's chair, his usual humor replaced by quiet concern.

"You okay?"

Jerry nodded automatically. "Just thinking through the timeline."

"I meant about Scarlet."

Jerry's jaw tightened. Of course that's what Mac meant. "I'll figure it out."

"Phone call? Video chat? Or you planning to fly down there?"

"This isn't something I can do over the phone." Jerry gathered his notebook, movements precise. "She deserves to hear it face to face."

Mac nodded, then glanced around before asking softly, "What about the boys?"

"Same drill as last time. Mom will relocate the boys temporarily." The words came out clipped, efficient. It was easier to focus on logistics than emotions.

Before Mac could respond, Vega approached, most of the room now empty.

"Duncan," she said, her tone less formal now that they were relatively alone. "Got a minute?"

"Of course, Sergeant Major."

Mac took the hint and moved away, giving them privacy.

Vega studied him with the shrewd assessment that had earned her respect throughout the Brigade. "I know your situation is more complicated than most. If you need any specific support with your boys' arrangements, the Family Readiness Group is already mobilizing resources."

"Thank you, Sergeant Major. We've got a system in place from previous deployments."

She nodded, then added more quietly, "And your ... personal situation? MacIntyre mentioned you've been seeing someone."

"I might need to kill him before we deploy." Jerry's eyes flickered briefly to where Mac stood across the room, pretending not to eavesdrop. Of course he'd mentioned Scarlet to Vega. The three of them had served together too long for such details to remain private.

"Well, don't tell me that, I don't want to testify that it was premeditated and I did nothing to stop you," she joked back.

"It's still relatively new, but yes," he admitted.

Vega's expression remained neutral, but her voice carried understanding. "The Colonel's three-day weekend isn't just for show. If you need to make arrangements, make them. That's an order."

"Roger that, Sergeant Major."

The rest of the afternoon passed in a blur of activity. Jerry briefed his direct supervisor, Maj. Wainwright, who received the news with the resigned acceptance of a career officer. He processed paperwork, participated in the unit-wide announcement where Colonel Sharp officially broke the news, and kept up the facade of the steady, reliable Staff Sergeant Duncan everyone expected him to be.

Inside, his mind raced through scenarios and complications. Nine months away while the boys stayed with his mother. Nine months of missed bedtimes and school projects. Nine months of trying to maintain a still-developing relationship across thousands of miles and multiple time zones.

Jerry drove home in silence, the truck's stereo off, no impromptu singing this time. He'd done this before ... the pre-deployment ritual of reorganizing life, preparing the boys, arranging logistics. It should feel routine by now. Instead, it felt heavier than ever before.

At home, he watched the boys with a new intensity, acutely aware of the time slipping away. Emmett chattered about his school's fall festival as Jerry prepared dinner, unaware of how each casual mention of future plans now carried additional implications his father couldn't ignore.

"My class is doing a booth about dinosaurs," Emmett explained, carefully arranging silverware on the table. "Ms. Wilson says I have the most dinosaur knowledge in the whole class so I'm going to be the expert advisor."

"That's great, buddy." Jerry managed a smile, mentally adding it to the growing list of moments he might miss.

Marty was quieter than usual during dinner, his eyes frequently finding Jerry's face, as if sensing the shift in his father's mood. When Jerry helped him with his bath later, Marty clung to him a little longer than normal, small arms wrapped tightly around Jerry's neck.

"It's okay, buddy," Jerry murmured, though he wasn't sure which of them he was reassuring.

After both boys were finally asleep, Jerry sat at the kitchen table with his phone. The house was uncommonly quiet with Mac out for the evening. Jerry stared at his mother's contact information for a long moment before pressing call.

She answered on the second ring. "Jerry? Everything okay? It's a bit late for your usual call."

"Hey, Mom." He drew a breath, steadying himself. "I got some news today. Brigade's deploying to Kuwait after Christmas. Nine months."

The brief silence that followed carried the weight of nearly a decade worth of similar conversations, each one marking another deployment, another goodbye.

"I see," Maggie said finally, her voice shifting into the practical tone she always adopted at such news. "So the boys will come up to Utah like before?"

"If you're able to have them. I know it's a lot to ask—"

"Jerry." Her tone softened. "They're my grandsons. The whole family helps when you're deployed. You know that."

They spent the next twenty minutes discussing logistics with the efficiency of people who had done this dance before. School records, therapy needs, medication schedules. Jerry took notes, though most of these details were already memorized from previous deployments.

"And what about Scarlet?" Maggie asked, once the practical matters were handled.

Jerry's pen stilled. "I haven't told her yet."

"Will you call her tonight?"

"No." He pinched the bridge of his nose, fighting a headache. "I need to tell her in person."

Maggie paused. "That's probably best."

"Mom, I know it's a lot, but … could you check your calendar? See when you might be able to come down for a weekend? I need to fly to Miami, and—"

"Of course," she interrupted. "Let me look at what I've got going on. I'll call you tomorrow with some dates that might work."

Relief coursed through him. "Thank you."

"Jerry," Maggie said, her voice gentle but firm, "this girl … she makes you happy. I've seen it, the boys have seen it. Trust that to be enough."

After they hung up, Jerry sat in the quiet kitchen, rolling an empty glass between his palms. He would need to tell Scarlet face to face. Some news couldn't be delivered through a screen. Would she understand? Would she be willing to wait nine months for a relationship still in its early stages?

But Scarlet wasn't like others who had left. She'd already shown more genuine interest in his children than their own mother ever had. Her last visit, she'd spent an entire afternoon helping Emmett with a science project, then sat through Marty's physical therapy session, paying careful attention to the techniques so she could help with his exercises.

Jerry pulled out his phone and opened the photo gallery. There she was, red hair wild in the Texas wind, holding Marty on her hip while helping Emmett fly a kite. Another showed her asleep on the couch, Emmett tucked against her side with a book, Marty curled at her feet. Small moments of a life they'd only just begun building together.

Nine months was a long time. Long enough for feelings to fade, for lives to drift apart. Long enough for someone to realize that a single father with special needs children and a demanding military career might not be worth the complications.

Jerry set the empty glass down with a quiet thud. Whatever happened, Scarlet deserved to hear it from him directly, to see his face when he told her. He owed her that much, and so much more.

Twenty

Instinct had Jerry awake before the sun, just as it always had. But today, there was no need to rise. No orders. No noise. Just her.

Scarlet's hair was a tousled flame against the pillow, a few tendrils falling across her mouth as she breathed slow and deep. The early light traced the lines of her. Soft freckles, the subtle curve of her body beneath the blanket, the old scar he'd once kissed without asking.

He didn't want to disturb her. Just hold onto the sight of her, framed in quiet.

Seven time zones away, he would remember this. In a desert cot, surrounded by sand and soldiers, he would close his eyes and summon this exact moment.

The purpose behind his visit hadn't faded. It sat just beneath the surface, dense and unspoken.

But in this quiet stretch of time, none of it mattered.

Scarlet slept beside him, her breathing slow and even. When it shifted ever so slightly, he knew she was beginning to wake. Jerry leaned in and kissed her shoulder, the contact gentle, instinctual.

Her scent clung to him. Citrus and cocoa. He'd caught it before, lingering in the air after she left, clinging to his shirt hours later. He couldn't help searching for it now.

She stirred beneath him, murmuring, "Good morning to you too."

The sleep-roughened quality of her voice sent heat coursing through him. Jerry slid his hand up her side, memorizing the texture of her skin, the slight give of flesh over ribs, before cupping her breast. He circled her nipple with his thumb, feeling it harden beneath his touch. The responsive gasp she gave burned itself into his memory, filed away for lonely nights to come.

His other hand moved lower, tracing the flare of her hip before slipping between her thighs. Finding her already slick and ready for him made his shaft throb with anticipation.

"Already?" he murmured against her ear, the evidence of her desire coating his fingers.

"It's been three weeks," she breathed, reaching behind to thread her fingers through his hair.

When she turned to face him, Jerry lost himself in the hazel depths of her eyes, gold flecks catching the morning light. Her hand trailed down his chest, fingers tracing the ridges of muscle earned through countless pre-dawn PT sessions, following the line of hair downward. Her touch was knowing now, confident in a way it hadn't been during those first tentative explorations on the cruise.

At her first stroke, he nearly lost control. Three weeks of distance. Three weeks of late-night phone calls that always ended with him aching for her touch. Three weeks imagining this reunion while simultaneously dreading what would follow.

He rolled over her slowly, supporting his weight on his forearms as he studied her face.

She met his eyes with a kind of hunger that went beyond physical.

And in that breathless quiet, he knew.

Nine months couldn't touch this.

Not this closeness. Not what they'd just begun.She pulled him down, their mouths meeting with an urgency that belied their four months together. Her lips parted beneath his, tongue seeking entrance, hands roaming across his shoulders with growing insistence.

When he finally pushed into her, the sensation was overwhelming. Wet heat enveloped him, her body yielding and then tightening around him. Jerry held still, fighting for control, forehead pressed against hers as their ragged breathing synchronized.

"God, I've missed you," he groaned, the words escaping without his permission.

"Show me how much," she challenged, wrapping her legs around his waist, drawing him deeper.

Jerry began to move with deliberate strokes, angling his hips to hit the spot he'd learned made her gasp. She met his rhythm perfectly, her body arching up to take him deeper. Her fingers dug into his shoulders, then traced down his back, nails leaving light scratches that sent shivers down his spine.

This wasn't the desperate coupling of their reunion the night before. This was something more profound, serving as a claiming, a promise, a connection he needed to sustain him through what was coming.

He slipped a hand between them, finding the sensitive nub at her center and stroking with practiced tenderness. Her reaction crashed through him like a wave: sharp intake of breath that hitched into a moan, thighs tightening around him with desperate need, inner walls clenching in pulses that nearly destroyed his restraint. Jerry drank in every sensation, every sound she made, cataloging the way her body responded to his touch, desperate to carry these moments through the long months ahead.

"Look at me," he said softly, needing to see her face, to watch her come apart in his arms.

Her eyes met his, the vulnerability in her gaze striking him like a physical blow. The intimacy of being inside her while holding her gaze amplified everything. In that moment, there was nothing else: no deployment looming, no difficult conversation ahead, only Scarlet, only this connection.

"I'm close," she gasped, fingers gripping his biceps with bruising pressure.

"I know," he replied, his voice strained as he maintained the rhythm that was pushing her toward the edge. "Let go, Scarlet. I've got you."

Her climax broke over her like a wave, eyes widening, mouth forming a perfect 'O', body arching beneath him as she cried out his name. The sight of her release, the feeling of her pulsing around him, the sound of his name on her lips, all of it was too much. Jerry buried his face in her neck, thrusting deeply once, twice more before his own orgasm overtook him, emptying himself inside her with a guttural groan he couldn't suppress.

For several moments, they remained joined, hearts thundering against each other's chest. Jerry fought to catch his breath, his face still pressed into the curve of her neck, inhaling her scent, tasting the salt of her skin.

Eventually, he rolled to his side, taking her with him so they remained face to face, legs still intertwined. He brushed a strand of vibrant red hair from her cheek, tucking it behind her ear. The simple intimacy of the gesture nearly broke him. Nine months without this. Nine months.

"Now it's a good morning," she murmured, eyes crinkling at the corners.

"The best," he agreed, pressing a kiss to her forehead before pulling her closer.

Jerry watched as she traced the lines of his tattoo. The boys. Always the boys. The thought of them strengthened his resolve. This conversation had to happen, no matter how much he dreaded it.

"Coffee?" she offered, sitting up, completely at ease in her nakedness.

Jerry folded his arms behind his head, allowing himself to appreciate the view. "Please."

He watched as she moved around the bed, the morning light casting her silhouette in gold. She paused to consider her robe before deciding against it, padding naked toward the kitchen. The way she moved with such casual intimacy, comfortable in her own skin and space with him there, felt like a gift he hadn't earned.

The sound of the coffee maker humming to life drifted in from the kitchen. Jerry sat up, sheet pooled around his waist, watching through the doorway as Scarlet moved with graceful efficiency. This was her territory and yet she'd made space for him in it. The thought knotted his stomach with what was coming.

When she returned, carrying two mugs, Jerry accepted his with a murmured thanks. Black, no sugar ... she remembered. Of course she did. Scarlet slipped back under the sheets beside him, and he automatically adjusted to make room, his arm coming around her shoulders as she nestled against him.

They sipped their coffee in comfortable silence, Jerry savoring the moment, knowing it was about to end. He'd rehearsed this conversation a dozen times on the flight, but now that the moment had arrived, all his practiced words seemed inadequate.

"I was talking with Jade last week about the wedding," Scarlet said, breaking the silence. "She wants the boys to be part of it."

Jerry's chest tightened. Here was the opening he'd been both waiting for and dreading. "In the wedding party?"

"Mmhmm," Scarlet nodded, curling her feet beneath her. "She's already found matching mini-tuxes online. She thinks Emmett would be perfect as a ring bearer, and Marty could either join him or be an honorary usher with one of the groomsmen." She smiled, clearly pleased. "She said, and I quote, 'We need to balance the child cuteness quotient since Lucas has his niece as flower girl.'"

Under normal circumstances, seeing his sons welcomed so fully into her family would have filled Jerry with gratitude.

Today, it only made what he needed to say feel heavier.

He set his coffee down, his shoulders tightening with the effort to stay composed.

"That's really nice of her," he said carefully, measuring his words. "But I'm not sure we'll be able to make it to the wedding."

Scarlet's expression shifted, confusion replacing her smile. "What? Why not? It's not until spring, so we have plenty of—"

"I won't be around then," Jerry interrupted, the words feeling like gravel in his throat.

The moment the sentence left his lips, panic flashed across Scarlet's face in a quick succession of emotions: confusion, hurt, fear. Her body went rigid beside him, coffee mug suspended midair as her breathing visibly changed.

"Not … make it?" she repeated, her voice suddenly small and uncertain. "Is this … are you …?"

Jerry's heart slammed against his ribs as he recognized the conclusion she'd jumped to. Horror surged through him at the realization she thought he was ending things. He quickly reached for her hand, desperate to correct the misunderstanding.

"No, Scarlet, I'm not breaking up with you," he said firmly, squeezing her fingers. "That's not what this is about at all."

Relief flooded her features, quickly replaced by confusion. "Then what—"

"I'm being deployed to Kuwait," he explained, forcing his voice to remain steady despite the storm of emotions behind it. "The orders came down a week and a half ago. Nine months, starting right after Christmas."

"Nine months?" Scarlet set her mug down with unsteady hands. "But that's … that's almost a year."

Jerry nodded, watching her closely for signs of retreat. He'd seen it before, when the subtle distancing began, the quick mental calculations about whether a relationship was worth sustaining across such time and distance. His jaw tightened against the memory of another woman deciding it wasn't.

"I wanted to tell you in person. That's why I came down this weekend."

Scarlet pulled the sheet higher around herself, a protective gesture he recognized from his boys when they felt vulnerable. "What does this mean for … us?" she asked.

"That depends on what you want it to mean." Jerry held his breath, waiting.

"I don't understand."

"Scarlet," Jerry said gently, choosing his words with military precision, "military relationships are hard. When I'm deployed, communication will be limited. Sometimes there will be blackout periods where you can't reach me at all. I'll be seven time zones away, working long hours in a different world."

She nodded slowly, processing. "And the boys?"

"They'll stay with my mom in Utah for the entire deployment. We have doctors and specialists already lined up from last time. They have a whole support system there. It's just a matter of getting them settled before I leave."

Scarlet stood abruptly, visibly needing distance to process. "We should get dressed," she said, gathering his clothes from the floor. "This feels like a conversation we should have with clothes on."

Jerry nodded, accepting the shift. As she disappeared into the bathroom, he dressed quickly, mind racing through scenarios. Was this it? Would she back away now? He wouldn't blame her if she did. His life was complicated enough without adding a deployment to the mix.

When she came back, he was already waiting with elbows on knees, mouth set in a hard line, gaze fixed on the floor.

He'd been through combat zones. Cleared buildings under fire.

None of it rattled him like this did.

"Let's go sit in the living room," she suggested, reaching for his hand.

Her physical connection caught him off guard when he'd expected her to create distance. He took her hand and followed her to the couch, where sunlight streamed through the balcony doors.

"When did you find out?" she asked, tucking her feet beneath her.

"Last week. Thursday. Command called an unexpected meeting." Jerry sat beside her, deliberately leaving space between them. "Division confirmed the orders. The whole brigade is going."

"And Mac?"

"He'll be there too." Jerry felt his mouth quirk slightly, despite everything. "Someone has to keep me out of trouble."

The ghost of a smile touched Scarlet's lips, a brief respite from the tension.

"So, what happens now?" she asked, more directly.

Jerry carefully studied her face, looking for clues to what she was really asking. "For deployments? There's a preparation phase … lots of paperwork, medical checks, training. I'll need to get the boys settled with my mom, prepare the house. There's usually a farewell ceremony just before we leave."

"No," Scarlet shook her head. "I mean with us. What happens with us, Jerry?"

He took a deep breath, steeling himself. This was the moment of truth. "That's up to you. I would never ask you to put your life on hold for nine months, especially when we've only been together for four. I know that's a lot to ask of anyone."

"Don't do that," she said sharply.

"Do what?"

"Give me the easy out. Tell me what this is really like. What will it mean if we stay together?"

Jerry chose his next words carefully. "It means a lot of waiting. Letters that arrive late. Video calls at odd hours because of the time difference. Care packages that take weeks to arrive. It means I won't be there for birthdays or anniversaries or if something goes wrong. It means trusting that things will still be there when I get back."

Scarlet seemed to absorb this, her expression thoughtful. "Have you done this before? The relationship-during-deployment thing?"

A shadow passed through him, memories surfacing that he'd spent years trying to bury. The betrayal. The humiliation. The slow-motion collapse of his marriage during his third deployment, culminating in divorce papers waiting for him when he returned stateside. The custody battle that followed when she decided the boys were too difficult, special needs too demanding. Jerry pushed the memories down, locking them away.

"Yes," he managed. "It doesn't always work out."

"I'm not them," Scarlet said simply.

The statement caught him completely off guard. "What?"

"Whoever they were. The ones who couldn't wait. I'm not them." Scarlet moved closer, taking his hand between both of hers. "This isn't what I expected, and I won't pretend it doesn't scare me. But I'm not walking away just because it got complicated."

Relief flooded through Jerry with such force that he nearly gasped. He hadn't realized how tightly he'd been bracing for rejection until that moment.

"It will be hard," he warned, though his fingers tightened around hers. "There will be days when you don't hear from me, when you have no idea what's happening. Days when the boys are struggling, and I can't help."

"Jerry," Scarlet said firmly, "I care about you. I care about your boys. That doesn't stop because there's distance between us."

He studied her face, searching for hesitation or uncertainty. Finding none, he felt himself begin to outline the practical details that would make this possible. "We can figure out a communication schedule that works with the time difference. I'll have limited internet access, but enough for video calls most of the time, barring operations or blackouts."

Scarlet nodded, seeming to grasp onto the concrete aspects. "And I can write letters. Real ones, on paper. Emmett can send drawings for you to put up."

"You'd do that? Keep in touch with the boys too?" It wasn't just about the question. It was about trust, about the shape of what they were building. And Jerry could tell she heard all of it in his voice.

"Of course I would," she said softly. "They're part of you. And they're ..." she paused briefly, "they're important to me too."

Jerry exhaled slowly, releasing a breath he'd been holding since receiving the deployment orders. "I've been terrified of having this conversation."

"Why?"

"Because I know what I'm asking. I know how selfish it sounds to say 'wait for me' when we're still figuring out what this is." Jerry attempted to raise the same defensive barrier he'd built countless times before, designed to keep people at a safe distance from his complicated life. "Because deployment changes people. Because it's not fair—"

"FUCK YOU!"

The words slammed into Jerry like a blast wave, stunning him more than any firefight ever had. He didn't move, he couldn't, as Scarlet surged forward and grabbed his face between her palms, eyes blazing.

"You don't get to tell me what's fair," she hissed, her grip sure, anchoring him in place. "You don't get to decide what I can handle."

He stared at her, heart racing, unable to catch a full breath.

He had run through every possible outcome in his head.

Tears. Silence. A slow fade-out.

What he hadn't seen coming was this kind of fire.

It didn't push him away. It pulled him in.

"I know exactly what I'm choosing, Jerry." Her voice cracked with emotion, but her gaze never wavered. "Don't you dare try to protect me from my own decisions."

Then, her mouth was on his, fierce, hot and unrelenting. It wasn't tenderness. It was a declaration. And he couldn't breathe through it, couldn't think past it. This wasn't her begging for space in his life. She was *taking it.*

When she pulled away, her breathing was ragged. Her eyes searched his face like she was trying to locate solid ground in a storm.

"I need to tell you something," she said, her voice barely above a whisper. "And I don't know how."

Jerry froze at the unmistakable tone in her voice, understanding instinctively that this wasn't small. This wasn't casual. He kept his touch steady, thumb brushing over her knuckles.

"Okay."

She swallowed, like she was forcing the words past something jagged in her throat.

"Eight years ago ... I was pregnant."

His breath caught. Just for a second. He didn't speak. Didn't move. Just stayed quiet.

"I didn't tell anyone. Not Jade. Not Cami. Not even him." Her voice cracked on that last word, splintering.

Jerry's grip on her hand tightened reflexively.

She pressed on, her eyes flashing, her face impossibly vulnerable. "It ended before I ever really understood what it meant. Just a couple months in. I went to the ER alone. Bled alone. Went to work the next day like nothing had happened." Another crack in her voice. "And I never talked about it. Not once. I buried it so deep I thought maybe I'd imagined it."

Something hollow opened in Jerry's core. Not pity. Not shock. Something closer to reverence for the strength it took just to say the words aloud.

But still, he said nothing. This wasn't a moment to talk. This was a moment to hold space.

"But I didn't imagine it. I feel it every time I'm with your boys. Not in a way that replaces anything. Not like that. But there's a version of me that still wonders who they would've been. Who I would've been."

His heart clenched. He didn't need to say a damn thing. His whole body was listening.

"I didn't mean to keep this from you. I just ... didn't know where to put it until now."

Jerry reached up and cupped her face, his thumb brushing away a tear she hadn't even noticed. Her skin was warm and damp and human in his hands.

"Scarlet ..."

"I'm not broken," she said quickly, like she needed to get it out before he offered sympathy she didn't want. "This isn't me asking for your pity. I'm telling you because if I'm going to walk through this deployment with you, if I'm going to love your boys like they're already becoming part of me, you deserve all of me. Not just the shiny parts."

His hands slid around her, pulling her to his chest. She came willingly, her breath shuddering against his collarbone.

He didn't speak. He just pulled her in, arms tight across her back.

And then, against her hair, he whispered the only words that mattered.

"Thank you for trusting me. And I'm so fucking sorry you went through that alone."

Her body softened into him, just slightly. And he could feel her exhale. That release of something she'd carried far too long.

For the first time since she'd started talking, she let herself rest.

"Okay," she said after a long beat, breath steadying. "So tell me the plan. When exactly do you leave? Will you be somewhere safe? What can I send in packages?"

Jerry sat there, wrecked and wanting, and suddenly ... not afraid.

She had just handed him something sacred and shattered and said, *Here, this is part of me too.* And somehow, it didn't scare him. It humbled him.

Every doubt he'd nursed about her readiness faded, one by one.

Scarlet didn't just endure the hard things, she absorbed them, re-shaped them, and stood taller.

There was strength in her that had nothing to prove and everything to give.

He didn't know what to say that would honor it. So he just held her, because that was something he *could* do. Something he *would* do, again and again.

And now she was sitting beside him, talking about care packages and logistics like they hadn't just cracked each other open.

Jerry had seen the worst of the world in worn boots and flak vests. He knew how quickly things could fall apart, how temporary *everything* really was. But this? This was one of those rare, quiet moments that felt permanent. Like something had shifted between them and couldn't be undone.

He didn't just want her with him through the deployment, he wanted her in his world for the long haul. Not just as the woman who had his heart, but as someone who already lived in his kids' drawings and his mother's questions and the little future scenarios he was afraid to name out loud.

That morning he'd steeled himself for letting her go, convinced himself he was capable of it.

But she hadn't walked away. She'd met fear with fire, and her own history with unflinching truth.

And she was still here. Not despite the scars. Because of them.

So when he said, "I want you to come to Texas for Christmas," it wasn't just about December.

It was about inviting her into the rooms that had long stayed closed.

And when she said yes, something deep within him finally let go.

They sat in the stillness that followed, city noise weaving in at the edges, their coffee forgotten.

The months ahead stretched like an endless highway, flat, hot, and uncertain.

But for the first time in years, Jerry didn't dread the drive.

Twenty-One

Jerry knelt beside Marty on the bedroom floor, where his eldest son lay on his play mat, giggling at his own reflection in a small mirrored toy. The familiar sound washed over Jerry like a physical comfort as he tried to mentally record each precious detail: the pitch of Marty's laugh, the way his eyes crinkled at the corners, the pure joy that radiated from him despite his physical limitations.

"Time to get dressed, buddy," Jerry said, gently rolling Marty onto his back. "Christmas Eve dinner waits for no man, not even handsome devils like us."

Marty fixated on his own reflection, ignoring the bright red sweater Jerry had picked out for him.

That was fine. Jerry had the process down to a science: pants first, always, while Marty was occupied. Then the top.

He slipped the pants up one leg, then the other, gently lifting Marty's hips and tying the drawstring, careful to leave a little slack on the right.

As he worked, his hands moved without thinking. But his mind kept circling the same question: Would his mother catch that nuance while he was gone?

"Hold still, champ," Jerry murmured as Marty twisted, reaching for his mirror with his more cooperative left hand. The right arm remained stiff, requiring gentle manipulation as Jerry worked the sleeve over it. He counted silent breaths as he eased the arm through the fabric, careful not to force the movement when Marty's muscles tensed against him.

The simple, familiar act of dressing his son suddenly felt precious, knowing he'd miss nine months of these moments he'd performed thousands of times. Nine months of growth, of subtle changes in muscle tone, of new expressions and sounds. Jerry swallowed against the tightness in his throat, focusing on securing the last sleeve over Marty's left arm.

"There we go," he said, voice deliberately steady as he lifted Marty to a sitting position. "Looking sharp, soldier."

Marty grinned and held the mirror tightly, his good hand pressed over it like a shield.

Jerry scooped him up, feeling the small body shift and settle, one arm wrapped snug around his neck.

His son smelled like shampoo and sleep, and the way he clung without hesitation stayed with Jerry more than he could explain.

Boxes lined the hallway, each one a reminder of what needed to be left behind.

The home they'd built had begun to feel like a checklist.

Only the Christmas tree remained whole, its lights still twinkling in the corner, untouched by the process of leaving.

In the kitchen, the scent of ginger and molasses hung in the air as his mother expertly rolled dough between her palms. The familiar scene of his mother making Christmas cookies, a tradition he could remember from childhood, was now overlaid with the knowledge that he wouldn't taste them again for nearly a year.

"I smell cookies," Jerry announced, adjusting Marty on his hip. His son immediately perked up, recognizing the familiar aroma that meant sweet treats were imminent.

His mother swatted away his approaching hand with practiced precision. "Gilmore Paul Duncan, don't you dare," she warned, the childhood reprimand so familiar it almost made him smile. "You'll spoil your dinner."

"Come on, Mom," Jerry pleaded, setting Marty in his adaptive chair. "They're best when they're still warm and gooey. Just one."

This was part of the tradition too: his plea, her refusal, the inevitable theft that followed. The dance they'd performed for decades.

"Better listen to your mom," Mac advised from behind him. "I hear she knows karate."

"I do not know karate, Jude MacIntyre, and you know it," his mother replied, turning to deal with Mac's teasing.

The momentary distraction was all Jerry needed. With the stealth born from years of practice, he snatched four cookies from the cooling rack, the warmth seeping through his fingertips. He popped one in his mouth first, closing his eyes briefly at the perfect balance of sweet and spice, before distributing the contraband.

One to Scarlet with a conspiratorial wink, another to Emmett whose eyes widened with delight at being included in the cookie heist. The fourth cookie he broke into smaller pieces, carefully depositing them into Marty's open mouth. His son's tongue extended eagerly for each bite, reminding Jerry of a baby bird awaiting feeding, his eyes closing in bliss with each successful morsel.

"I saw that!" his mother called without turning around.

Jerry grinned, unrepentant. "Worth it," he murmured, meeting Scarlet's eye across the kitchen. The simple moment of shared rebellion, the inclusion of Scarlet in this small family tradition, felt significant in ways he couldn't fully articulate.

As he waited by the door, Jerry glanced around the room and saw it all with new eyes.

The stockings hung as if they could anchor the season, even on a bare mantle. Boxes loomed in the periphery, half-forgotten, half-denied. The coffee mugs and toiletries, scattered signs of daily life stayed where they were, as if packing them away would make everything too final.

The house was in limbo.

So was he.

"Everyone ready?" he called, helping Marty with his sweater one last time. "It's a bit chilly tonight."

They sorted out who would ride with whom, Mac volunteering to take Maggie in his car since Jerry's truck couldn't comfortably accommodate everyone with Marty's specialized seat.

"Three Duncan men, one Duncan lady in training," Mac said with a wink at Scarlet as they headed toward the vehicles. "See you there!"

Jerry watched Scarlet's reaction to the casual inclusion, the way her cheeks colored slightly at the implication. Lately he'd found himself constantly watching her, gauging her responses to family dynamics, searching for signs of overwhelm or retreat. So far, she'd exceeded every expectation, slotting into their chaotic routine with surprising ease. Still, he couldn't quite silence the voice that whispered, *But will she stay? Nine months is a long time to wait.*

The restaurant's exterior was adorned with twinkling white lights and plastic garlands, holiday music drifting faintly from inside. As they approached the entrance, Jerry spotted the sign propped on an easel: "Christmas Eve Karaoke! 6-9 p.m."

"Shit," he muttered under his breath, reflexively tightening his grip on Marty's carrier. The combination of crowds, noise, and unpredictable performances was exactly the kind of sensory overload that could trigger Emmett's anxiety.

"Everything okay?" Scarlet asked, noticing his hesitation.

Jerry nodded toward the sign. "Karaoke night. Probably means it'll be louder than expected."

He watched Emmett's reaction carefully, already calculating alternatives. "Maybe we should try somewhere else," he suggested. "The noise might be too much."

Through the glass doors, he could see the restaurant was busy but not packed, with a small stage set up near the bar where a man in a Santa hat adjusted a microphone stand. The host approached to greet them, but Jerry held up a hand, unwilling to commit before ensuring his son's comfort.

"What do you think, buddy?" Scarlet asked Emmett. "Will the singing bother you?"

Jerry felt a rush of gratitude at her consideration. Most people wouldn't think to ask Emmett directly, assuming Jerry would make the decision.

Emmett's face scrunched in thought. "Will it be very loud?"

"Probably," Jerry admitted, ready to turn back toward the parking lot. "And there might be some bad singers."

Emmett considered this, looking up at Scarlet with complete trust. "I'll be okay if I can sit next to Mom. She can help if it gets too noisy."

The word hit Jerry hard.

His breath halted briefly, eyes locking on Scarlet's.

Then, her expression shifted, seemingly fragile.

She had told him, not long ago, about the miscarriage.

A truth she'd held in silence for years.

Now, here was Emmett, naming her with the kind of certainty that came from love, not biology.

And Jerry suddenly worried it might hurt more than heal.

What if this moment reopened old wounds?

What if the title she hadn't dared claim now came too soon?

"Um," Scarlet began, clearly thrown off balance.

"Sure thing, buddy," Jerry intervened smoothly, giving her a small nod of reassurance. "Scarlet can sit right next to you."

He guided them inside, hyperaware of Scarlet's stunned silence. The host seated them at a center table that wasn't ideal but provided enough space for Marty's wheelchair to roll right up to the edge.

Mac and his mother joined them moments later, and Jerry felt Maggie's questioning glance as they arranged themselves, with Scarlet beside Emmett as promised. He gave her a subtle head shake, a silent promise to explain later.

A server appeared to take drink orders, temporarily diffusing the tension. But Jerry's mind remained fixed on Emmett's casual use of 'mom,' not as a slip or a question, but as a simple statement of fact. He couldn't decide if it was concerning or comforting that his son had so readily accepted Scarlet in that role.

Mac steered the conversation toward deployment logistics, cutting through the emotional undercurrent with his typical directness.

"Maggie, are your husband and daughter still coming for the deployment ceremony?" he asked.

Jerry listened as his mother explained that Thomas and Hannah were staying in Utah to prepare for the boys' arrival. The practical discussion of arrangements helped ground him, providing structure amid the emotional turbulence.

"What about your parents?" Maggie asked launching Mac into another of his animated stories.

"Last deployment, his mom brought enough cookies to feed the entire battalion," Jerry told Scarlet, grateful for the shift to lighter topics. "Mac had to fight off sugar-crazed infantrymen."

"That sounds like Sarah MacIntyre," his mother laughed. "Still trying to fatten you up after all these years."

"That's a mother's prerogative," Mac said with a grin. "Isn't that right, Scarlet?"

Jerry tensed at the teasing reference to Emmett's earlier comment, but Scarlet surprised him with her composed response.

"I wouldn't know yet, but I'm learning fast."

The graceful acknowledgment, neither embracing nor rejecting the title, eased some of the tightness in Jerry's chest. She wasn't running. At least, not yet.

As the appetizers arrived, Jerry shifted into auto pilot, cutting up Marty's food, coaxing him into a few bites. But his eyes kept drifting.

Scarlet had excused herself with a smile and a vague nod toward the restrooms, but she veered off-course, heading, instead, toward the karaoke corner.

He raised an eyebrow, but said nothing.

The meal progressed amid laughter and storytelling, punctuated by occasional carols from aspiring singers. Jerry helped cut Marty's chicken into manageable bites, listening as Mac recounted the infamous Christmas tree disaster from Emmett's toddler years.

"So there he is," Mac continued, gesturing with a french fry, "covered in pine sap, ornaments scattered everywhere, and Emmett, this tiny little three-year-old, just looks up and says, 'I think we need a plastic one, Daddy.'"

"Which is exactly what we've had ever since," Jerry confirmed, forcing a smile through the ache.

The tree was still up at home, lights twinkling bravely amid the clutter of boxes and taped lids.

It would come down soon, like everything else. It was just part of the countdown he couldn't stop.

As they finished their main courses, the DJ's voice cut through the ambient noise: "Next up, we've got Scarlet performing "Stacy's Mom"! Come on up!"

Jerry's head whipped toward her, eyebrows raised in surprise. "You signed up?"

"Surprise?" Scarlet replied with a nervous laugh, already standing.

Emmett cheered enthusiastically, drawing attention from nearby tables. Even Marty joined in, hands flapping with excitement.

"You don't have to," he said instead, though he couldn't deny the anticipation building inside him.

"It's Christmas Eve," Scarlet replied, squeezing his shoulder as she passed. "Might as well make it memorable."

As Scarlet stepped onto the stage, Jerry felt a flicker of awe. Not for the song, or the setup, but for her.

For the quiet boldness it took to stand in front of a room full of strangers and let herself be seen.

Guitar riffs rolled out like an invitation.

She raised the microphone, and the world seemed to still.

"This is for the Duncan men," she announced, "who have made this the most unexpected Christmas ever. I'm improvising a bit, so bear with me!"

When she began to sing, her eyes locked with his, Jerry felt the world narrow to just the two of them despite the crowded restaurant. "Marty's dad has got it goin' on ..." she sang, and he felt heat rise to his face at the playful lyrics.

Emmett hovered by the stage, clapping with pure childhood energy, unfiltered and unbothered by tempo.

Marty rocked gently, lost in the joy of the music.

Scarlet's voice rose, sure and steady, each line spoken like a promise she was finally letting herself believe.

The song started cheeky and fun, featuring references to juice boxes and sunscreen that made Mac howl with laughter, but when she reached the bridge, everything shifted. Scarlet slowed the tempo, her expression softening as the playfulness gave way to something more vulnerable.

"And soon you'll lace up boots again," she sang, her voice dropping lower, more intimate, "chasing shadows with your steady hands ..."

Unexpected force hit Jerry through the lyrics and their simple acknowledgment of what was coming, the reality of his departure so often skirted in casual conversation.

"But I'll be here, a beat behind ... your girl, your crew, your peace of mind ..."

Something tightened in Jerry's chest, a pressure both painful and exquisite. He'd spent weeks managing everyone else's emotions about the deployment by reassuring the boys, coordinating with his mother, and giving Mac space to process in his own way. He'd compartmentalized his own feelings, focused on logistics instead of loss. But Scarlet's lyrics slipped past those careful barriers, speaking directly to the fears he'd pushed aside.

"No rings, no rush, just what is real, this slow and steady kind of feel ..."

Jerry blinked against the sudden warmth in his eyes, aware of his mother watching him with knowing sympathy. The lyrics carried a promise that wasn't about forever, not yet, but about something intentional and worth waiting for, and it settled around him like a physical comfort.

As Scarlet powered into the final chorus, Jerry rose to his feet with fierce, unexpected pride.

She wrapped the song with a playful wink and a dramatic bow, breaking the tension like popping a bubble.

Jerry let out a sharp whistle, clapping harder than anyone else in the room. Maybe too hard.

But he didn't care.

"That was AWESOME!" Emmett declared when Scarlet returned, throwing his arms around her waist. "You're the best mom EVER!"

The title came again, spoken with such natural confidence that Jerry felt his throat tighten. He reached out as Scarlet returned, unable to find adequate words for what her performance had meant.

"That was something else, Bellari," he managed, pulling her into a hug that lasted longer than was probably appropriate for a family restaurant. "Thank you."

"I just wanted to give you something to remember," she murmured against his chest.

"Mission accomplished," he replied, lowering his voice to ensure only she would hear. "That's going to get me through a lot of lonely nights."

The rest of dinner passed in a blur of dessert and more karaoke performances, but Jerry found his attention continually drawn back to Scarlet. Not just with desire, though that was certainly present, but with a deeper appreciation for how completely she'd embraced his complicated life. His past relationships had faltered under far less strain than a deployment with two special needs children. Yet here she was, creating memories they could carry with them through the separation ahead.

Twenty-Two

During the drive home, Jerry caught snippets of conversation from the back seat as Emmett insisted Scarlet should audition for a talent show and Scarlet gracefully deflected the suggestion. In the rearview mirror, he could see Marty fighting sleep, head nodding only to jerk upright again, determined not to miss a moment of the Christmas Eve magic.

Back at the house, bedtime routines took precedence, a familiar choreography of teeth-brushing, pajamas, and stories. As Scarlet helped Marty with his evening routine, Jerry took the opportunity to have a private moment with Emmett, something that had been on his mind since the restaurant.

"Hey buddy," Jerry said, sitting on the edge of Emmett's dinosaur-printed sheets. "I wanted to talk to you about something."

Emmett looked up from his stuffed dinosaur. "About Santa?"

"No, about what you called Scarlet at dinner. You called her mom."

Emmett's expression grew serious. "Was that wrong?"

Jerry chose his words carefully. "It's not wrong, but it's a pretty important title. When you call someone mom, that's a really special thing. It's the kind of thing you should probably ask about first, instead of just saying it."

"But she does mom stuff," Emmett reasoned.

"She does," Jerry agreed, smoothing the blanket. "And I think she cares about you a lot. But using that word might have surprised her. It surprised me too."

Emmett considered this with the intense concentration only a seven-year-old could muster. "So I should ask her if it's okay?"

"That would be the respectful thing to do," Jerry nodded. "Some things are important enough to ask about first."

Emmett nodded solemnly, accepting this wisdom. Before they could continue, Scarlet appeared in the doorway, and Jerry excused himself to assist with Marty's needs.

With both boys settled, they joined Mac and Maggie in the living room, where whispered conversations about Santa duties immediately ceased.

"All tucked in?" his mother asked, sipping from a mug of hot chocolate.

"Excellent," Mac said, producing a small flask from his pocket. "Operation Christmas Cheer continues at 0900 tomorrow. But first," he offered the flask, "a toast, to surviving karaoke night with our dignity mostly intact."

The warmth of whiskey spread through Jerry's chest, complementing the emotional warmth that had been building all evening. They shared quiet conversation for a while, carefully avoiding direct mention of the deployment looming just three days away. Eventually, his mother announced she was turning in, followed shortly by Mac, who winked unsubtly before disappearing down the hall.

"Subtle," Jerry muttered.

Once they were alone, he reached under the couch and retrieved a bag of wrapped presents. "Santa duty," he explained. "Care to help?"

Together, they filled the space under the tree, their movements seamless, their silence full of everything left unsaid.

The room felt gentler in the low light. Even the boxes and bare walls felt less harsh now, suggesting a pause rather than an ending.

But Jerry knew it wouldn't last. This was Christmas borrowed from a future that would soon separate them.

Scarlet knelt to adjust a ribbon, and he stared longer than he should have. He memorized every curve of her smile, every flicker of light in her hair, storing them away like a man counting down.

Because he was.

"So," he said casually as they finished, "about that karaoke performance ..."

"I can't believe I actually did that," Scarlet replied, a flush rising to her cheeks.

"I can't believe you came up with those lyrics on the spot," Jerry said, moving closer. "You planned that, didn't you?"

"Maybe," she admitted. "I had about fifteen minutes between signing up and performing to figure out what I was going to sing. The bridge was the most important part to get right."

Jerry's expression softened at the confession. "It was perfect. All of it." He paused, then added, "Emmett called you mom again during bedtime. We talked about it while you were with Marty. I told him he should have asked first."

"He did," Scarlet confirmed. "Asked if it was okay, I mean. I told him I was honored."

"Are you? Really?" The question emerged from a place of genuine uncertainty. "It's a lot. Too much, maybe, too soon."

Jerry watched her face as she considered this, aware of how much he was placing on her. The boys had already lost one mother. He couldn't bear for them to lose another, especially with his deployment approaching.

"I think," she said slowly, "that titles matter less than actions. I care about them. I want to be part of their lives, however that looks. If mom works for Emmett right now, I'm okay with that."

Relief swept through Jerry, his arms tightening around her. "You're remarkable, you know that?"

"I'm just doing what feels right," she replied simply. "One day at a time."

Jerry kissed her then, trying to convey through touch what words seemed inadequate to express. When they broke apart, he asked, "Santa's work is done. Ready to turn in?"

"Almost," Scarlet said, a mischievous smile playing at her lips. "I've got one more gift for you that didn't make it under the tree."

"Oh?" Jerry raised an eyebrow, a pleasant anticipation building. "And where might this mystery gift be?"

"Bedroom," Scarlet said, taking his hand and backing slowly toward the hallway. "Very private. Unwrapping required."

Understanding dawned immediately, desire flaring hot beneath his skin. "Well, we shouldn't leave any presents undelivered on Christmas Eve. That would be irresponsible."

As she led him down the hallway, Jerry cast one last glance at the tree, at the carefully arranged presents, at the remnants of their home amid boxes.

The bedroom door closed behind them with a soft click. Jerry pulled Scarlet close, his hands finding her waist as he backed her gently against the door. Their lips met in a kiss that started tender but quickly deepened, his body responding to the press of her against him.

"Mmm, best Christmas Eve ever," he murmured against her neck, savoring the way she shivered at his touch.

"It's not over yet," Scarlet promised, her fingers threading through his short hair.

They moved toward the bed, lips still connected, hands exploring with increasing urgency. When she broke away, both of them breathing heavily, Jerry looked down at her with naked adoration.

"This is the best gift you could give me, you know that?" he said softly. "Just being here."

"Hold that thought for a second," Scarlet replied, pressing a finger to his lips. "Don't move."

Jerry sat, brows still lifted, listening to the faint sounds behind the door.

He thought of the months ahead: lonely nights, spotty calls, and too many hours spent pretending distance didn't matter.

But that was later. This was now. And now deserved his full attention.

When the bathroom door opened, Jerry's thoughts scattered like smoke. Against the doorframe, Scarlet posed in a bright red lingerie set trimmed with soft white fur, every inch a Christmas fantasy made flesh. His mind went completely blank, breath catching in his throat as he took in the sight of her.

"Merry Christmas," she said softly.

"Holy ..." Jerry couldn't finish the thought, his brain short-circuiting as she crossed the room slowly. He memorized every detail: the red fabric against her tan skin, the curve of her breasts above the fur trim, the long lines of her legs, an image he would carry with him through desert nights and lonely mornings.

When she reached him, his hands found her hips instinctively, fingers tracing the edge where fabric met fur. "Like your present?" she asked, standing between his knees.

Jerry pulled her closer, pressing his lips to her stomach just above the waistband. "You are ..." he murmured against her skin, "absolutely incredible."

His hands moved up her sides, thumbs brushing the undersides of her breasts, memorizing the texture of the silky material. When Scarlet straddled his lap, knees on either side of his hips, Jerry's hands slid down to cup her backside, steadying her as she settled against him.

"The lingerie isn't the actual gift, you know," she said, rocking slightly.

Jerry's thumbs traced circles on her hips, his attention divided between the sensation of her body against his and the playful mystery in her expression. "No, I get it," he replied with a smirk. "It's the sex that's about to follow shortly."

"No," Scarlet laughed, then reconsidered. "Well, yes, you are absolutely getting sex ... but, no, I actually have something for you."

Jerry watched, intrigued, as Scarlet reached into the fur-lined edge of her bra and pulled out a small item. His breath caught as she revealed a simple gold-threaded bracelet with a small silver helm charm.

"Is that ...?" he began, recognition dawning.

"My Mingle at Sea bracelet," Scarlet confirmed, holding it out to him. "I want you to wear it while you're away. To always remember me."

Jerry took the bracelet, turning it carefully between his fingers. He was struck deeply by the significance of the gesture, this tangible connection to the day they'd met, to the beginning of everything that followed.

"You've kept this all this time?" he asked quietly.

Scarlet nodded, her expression open and vulnerable. "Since the day we met. It seemed right that you should have it now."

Jerry examined the woven gold thread, running his thumb over the small helm charm. It wasn't standard military attire by any means, but in that moment, he would have challenged anyone who questioned it.

"It's not really standard uniform attire," he said with a small smile, "but I'll wear it anyway."

He slipped it onto his wrist, then cupped her face in his hands, bringing her down for a kiss meant to convey his gratitude, his promise, the depth of feeling that had grown between them in just six months.

"Thank you," he whispered against her lips. "For this. For tonight. For being here."

She nudged him onto the mattress, then climbed over him with a slow, deliberate grace. The look in her eyes left no room for misinterpretation. "Now," she said, eyes dark with intention, "about that other gift I mentioned ..."

Jerry's hands slid up her thighs to her hips, holding her firmly as she leaned down to kiss him. "Merry Christmas to me," he murmured, and Scarlet laughed against his lips before settling into his embrace.

Her fingers traced fire over his skin, slow and sure, like she had all night to wreck him.

When she settled between his legs, Jerry rose onto his elbows, already breathless.

He didn't want to miss a second.

Scarlet's hair spilled forward, catching the light in wild, copper waves. Her smile curled like a secret she intended to keep.

She pressed her lips to his stomach in a series of kisses, one, then another, each one lower than the last.

By the time her mouth finally wrapped around his girth, Jerry wasn't ready.

He groaned, loud and helpless, as his body arched toward her.

God, she was devastating.

Nine months. The thought sliced through him.

But he dragged it back, forced himself into presence.

His head dropped back, vision blurred, and still he held on.

Because this wasn't just desire.

It was a memory being made.

A story he'd replay when the nights stretched too long and too quiet.

Her mouth worked him like a promise, her hands anchoring him, her rhythm devastating.

He wanted to stay here forever, in this moment where nothing hurt and everything made sense.

Twenty-Three

This wasn't new. He had stood in line before, listened as the words echoed through the air, and felt farewell settle over him like a second skin.

But never like this.

Not with Scarlet's eyes locked on his.

Not with his sons tucked against her, as if they already knew how much time they were about to lose.

The woman he'd been falling for since their first real conversation, though he'd been careful not to say those exact words aloud.

His gaze flickered to her face, composed but tense as she listened to Colonel Sharp. He'd told her once, after a particularly perfect weekend together, that he was falling for her, the words slipping out before he could stop them. Her response had been cautious: appreciation and warmth, but not quite reciprocation, teaching him patience. Military life had taught him timing.

Beside him, Mac maintained perfect posture, but Jerry felt his friend's subtle glance. The familiar ritual played out around them:

the ceremony, the speeches, the tightly choreographed farewell before boarding buses that would take them away from everything soft and real in their lives.

"... and now, families, you have fifteen minutes to say your goodbyes before the buses depart."

At the commander's dismissal, the formation dissolved. Jerry moved through the crowd with purpose, his eyes fixed on his family. Scarlet was standing now, Marty on her hip, following Emmett who pulled her forward with urgent steps. When they met in the center of the gym, Jerry dropped to one knee, meeting Emmett at eye level.

"Remember what we talked about, soldier?" he asked, fighting to keep his voice steady.

Emmett nodded solemnly. "Take care of Marty and be brave."

"That's right. And I'll call whenever I can," Jerry promised, pulling his son close. Jerry focused intently on absorbing every sensation: the press of Emmett's body, the cling of his small arms, the unmistakable scent of that ridiculous dinosaur shampoo.

He didn't just want to remember. He needed to.

These were the things that would keep him anchored when everything else felt too far away. "I love you, buddy. To the moon."

"... and back and to the moon again," Emmett finished.

Jerry rose, reaching for Marty, who transferred willingly from Scarlet's arms. His eldest son's body felt both familiar and suddenly precious as Jerry held him close, pressing his face into Marty's neck.

"I'll be back, buddy," he whispered, words meant only for Marty. "Keep practicing those exercises, okay? And take care of Grandma for me."

Marty's small hands patted Jerry's cheeks, a gesture of pure trust that nearly broke his composure. Four deployments, and this part never got easier.

"I've got them," his mother said, appearing with the quiet efficiency born from decades of military life. She gathered both boys, leaving Jerry and Scarlet standing in their own small island amid the chaos of other goodbyes.

"So," Scarlet began, then stopped, uncharacteristically at a loss for words.

"Scarlet, I ..." Jerry started, wanting to tell her everything he'd been holding back, everything he feared might sound like too much, too soon.

"I love you," she said suddenly, the words clear and certain, cutting through his hesitation.

Jerry froze, the words hitting him with physical force. Months of careful restraint, of not pushing too hard or moving too fast, of swallowing those exact words during late-night phone calls and quiet moments in his truck, only to have her say them first, in the middle of a crowded gymnasium with fifteen minutes left before he deployed.

The tension unraveled in a rush of joy so sharp it almost hurt.

He smiled, wide and instinctive, with no hope of reining it in.

"I love you too," he replied, the words falling easily now that she'd opened the door. He'd been holding them back for what felt like forever, waiting for the right moment, afraid of overwhelming her. Instead, she'd simply claimed them, offered them freely when he least expected it.

She stepped into his arms, and Jerry held her tight, the familiar curves of her body contrasting with the stiff fabric of his uniform.

Her familiar scent filled his senses while he memorized each layer: the bright citrus of her shampoo, the delicate perfume reserved for meaningful moments, and beneath it all, the essence that was uniquely Scarlet.

"Nine months," she whispered against his chest.

"I'll be counting every day," he promised, feeling her heartbeat against his, syncing with his own.

"Me too. I'll fly out to see the boys in Utah as often as I can," she added softly.

Jerry nodded, throat tight with all the future plans he wanted to make, all the promises he wanted to offer. But time was running out. Around them, soldiers were shouldering duffels, families stepping back with tear-stained faces.

"Duncan," Mac's voice cut through their moment. "Time to move out, battle."

Reality crashed back. Jerry kept his eyes on Scarlet, memorizing every freckle, every fleck of gold in her hazel eyes. His hands framed her face, thumbs brushing her cheekbones. "Wait for me," he said softly, suddenly vulnerable despite his uniform.

"Always," she promised.

The kiss they shared was fleeting yet flawless, holding within it a promise, a lifeline, a memory to sustain him through desert nights. Then, Jerry forced himself to step back, the physical act of separation like tearing open a wound. The rucksack at his feet suddenly weighed a thousand pounds as he hoisted it onto his shoulder.

His mother appeared beside Scarlet, one arm around her waist, steady as always. Emmett stood between them, holding Scarlet's hand.

Marty reached toward Jerry from his grandmother's arms, understanding in his own way what was happening.

"I love you," Jerry mouthed again to Scarlet, the words new enough that he needed to say them once more.

She nodded, her smile brave despite the brightness in her eyes. "I love you too," she mouthed back.

Jerry turned away, each step requiring deliberate effort as he followed Mac toward the idling buses. He found his assigned seat mechanically, muscle memory taking over where emotion threatened to paralyze him.

Through the window, he could see the group still standing together, watching him leave. Scarlet, his mother, and his sons formed a family constellation missing its center point. As the bus engine rumbled to life, Jerry's fingers found the bracelet Scarlet had given him at Christmas, the small helm charm cool against his skin. He rotated it once around his wrist, a silent promise to navigate his way back to her, to all of them.

The bus pulled away from the gymnasium, and Jerry watched his family shrink in the distance until they were no longer visible. Mac remained unusually quiet beside him, offering silent understanding in the way only a brother-in-arms could.

Nine months until he'd hear those three words in person again. But she'd said them. She loved him. And somehow, that made everything both easier and infinitely harder all at once.

Twenty-Four

J erry's eyes snapped open at 0430, wide awake despite the darkness still blanketing the container housing unit. Six weeks in-country had been enough for his body to adapt to the new rhythm: sleepless nights, early rises, the constant low-frequency hum of generators that powered the camp.

Beside him, Mac's rhythmic snoring filled their shared space within the shipping container they called home.

"For fuck's sake, Duncan," Mac's sleep-roughened voice cut through the darkness. "The sun's not even thinking about rising yet. Go back to sleep like a normal human being."

"Can't," Jerry replied simply, swinging his legs over his bunk.

"We're not getting shot at, so there's no need to run for the bunkers at 0500," Mac grumbled, pulling his pillow over his head. "Just once, I'd like to wake up to my alarm instead of your goddamn morning ritual."

Jerry ignored him, reaching for his phone. The screen illuminated his small corner of the CHU: 0432. Another night of broken sleep. He absently rubbed his forearm where his tattoo lived. The gesture had become reflexive, a way to feel connected to his boys across continents and time zones.

His eyes drifted to the small collection of photos taped above his bunk. Emmett grinning with a missing front tooth. Marty beaming from his adaptive chair. Scarlet with both boys during Christmas. His fingers ghosted over their faces, another ritual he'd never admit to performing each morning.

Jerry reached for his gym shorts and a faded Army T-shirt, the movement causing the bracelet on his wrist to catch the dim light from his phone. The small silver helm charm of Scarlet's Mingle at Sea bracelet glinted back at him. Against regulations, technically, but he hadn't taken it off since the deployment ceremony.

"I'm heading to the gym," Jerry said quietly, lacing up his running shoes.

"Black. Two sugars. And an apology note for ruining my beauty sleep," Mac mumbled, already drifting back under.

A crisp February wind slipped through Camp Arifjan, sharper than it had any right to be.

Jerry walked the gravel path between the container units, each step sending pebbles scattering.

The sameness of the buildings stretched in both directions, giving the place a strange, hushed rhythm.

The guilt crept in again as he walked, bringing the unwelcome realization that part of him appreciated the simplicity of deployment. Here, his schedule was his own. No IEP meetings. No late-night therapy exercises with Marty. No carefully negotiated breakfast rituals with Emmett. Just wake up, work out, do the job, repeat. The thought made his stomach turn. What kind of father felt relief at being separated from his children?

The gym was nearly empty at this hour, with just a few dedicated souls scattered across the equipment. Jerry made his way to the treadmills, settling into a steady pace that would quiet his mind for a while.

He'd barely completed a mile when Corporal Barrett entered, her petite frame sharp in the standard Army PT uniform. She spotted him immediately, her expression shifting from surprise to recognition.

"Duncan," she nodded, stepping onto the treadmill beside his. "Still can't sleep past dawn, I see."

Jerry managed a small smile. "Some habits stick, Simone. Kuwait or Iraq, doesn't matter."

"At least no one's shooting at us this time," she replied, falling into an easy jog. "How's the trailer park treating you?"

"Like a five-star resort. If the stars were made of dust and broken air conditioning units."

Simone laughed, the sound genuine despite the early hour. They'd served together in Iraq, had seen things they rarely discussed outside their unit. That created a shorthand, an ease that transcended rank when they were alone.

"Ally asked about the boys," Simone said, adjusting her speed. "She saw the photos you posted on the unit page before we left."

Jerry nodded, the mention of his sons bringing both warmth and a sharp twinge. "They're good. With my parents in Utah. Structured. Safe. They have everything they need."

"And your girlfriend?" Simone asked carefully. "Scarlet, right?"

"She's good too," Jerry replied automatically, his pace quickening slightly. "She actually just got back from Utah. Finally met my dad and sister."

"That's a big step," Simone observed. "Meeting the extended family."

Jerry didn't respond immediately, focusing on his breathing instead. After a moment, he said, "She's been great with the boys. Even with the distance."

"Not always easy," Simone agreed. "When I first deployed, Ally and I had been married less than a year. Those first few months, I nearly convinced myself she'd realize she'd made a mistake and want out."

Jerry glanced sideways at her, suddenly more interested. "What happened?"

"I started pulling away," Simone admitted, wiping sweat from her brow. "Shorter calls. Basic texts. I figured if she was going to leave, better to make it easy for her."

The description hit uncomfortably close to home. Jerry increased his speed again, as if he could outrun the recognition.

"What changed?" he finally asked.

"Ally called me on my bullshit," Simone laughed. "Told me I didn't get to decide for her what was too hard. Said if I was going to leave her, I should do it honestly, not by slowly disappearing."

Jerry's rhythm faltered slightly. "Sounds like something Scarlet would say."

"Smart women usually recognize the same patterns," Simone replied. "You doing okay with the distance? For real?"

Jerry rubbed his thumb over Scarlet's bracelet, a gesture Simone didn't miss. "It's fine. We have a system. Scheduled calls, updates on the boys." Even to his own ears, the description sounded clinical, lacking the warmth that had defined their early relationship.

"Right," Simone said, unconvinced. "Very efficient."

They ran in silence for several minutes, only the mechanical whir of the treadmills and their steady breathing filling the space between them.

"She's different," Jerry finally said, the words emerging reluctantly. "Not like …" He cut himself off, unwilling to complete the comparison to his ex-wife.

"I know," Simone said simply. "I saw you two at the deployment ceremony. Anyone with eyes could see it."

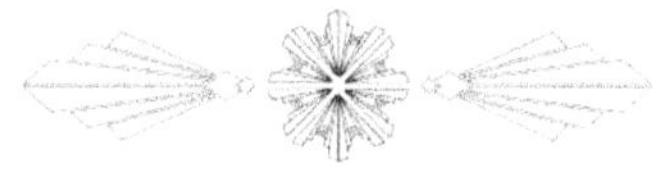

By midday, Jerry had immersed himself in work, grateful for the distraction. His current assignment involved photographing equipment for inventory purposes, tedious work that was nonetheless necessary and required just enough focus to quiet his thoughts.

He checked his phone between shots, seeing a message from Scarlet.

Scarlet

Just got the package you sent! Your mom's going to take pictures of the boys opening their presents this weekend and send them. Can't believe you found that dinosaur book Emmett wanted. Love you. Can't wait for our call later.

Jerry read it twice, searching for a way to meet her tone. But when he replied, the words that came out were cold, clinical.

Jerry

Great. Looking forward to our lunchtime chat, your time. Signal's been spotty today.

He frowned at his own message, sensing its inadequacy but unable to access the emotional language he needed. His thumb hovered over the screen, considering an addition, but he set the phone aside instead, returning to the task at hand.

Throughout the afternoon, Jerry moved through his duties with practiced efficiency. Deployment's routine had become a second skin, comfortable in its familiarity yet simultaneously creating distance from the life he'd left behind. Here, he was Sergeant Duncan, not Jerry, the single dad juggling therapy appointments and school schedules.

By late afternoon, Kuwait's winter sun had begun its descent, casting long shadows across the base. Jerry finished his final task and headed back to the CHU, his steps quickening as the time for his call with Scarlet approached. Seven his time, noon hers, and somehow they'd managed to synchronize the rhythm of their days across thousands of miles.

Mac was absent when Jerry returned. Jerry found rare privacy in the empty container as he arranged his laptop on his improvised desk of a wooden footlocker balanced on concrete blocks.

At exactly 1900, Jerry initiated the video call. The connection spun, buffered, then failed. He tried again, tension building in his shoulders. The third attempt connected, Scarlet's face appearing on screen, slightly pixelated but unmistakably hers. From the background, he could tell she was sitting in her car, which was her lunchtime sanctuary for their calls.

"Hey," he said, relief washing through him at the sight of her.

"There you are," Scarlet smiled, the connection lagging slightly. "I was getting worried."

"Internet's being temperamental," Jerry explained, adjusting his position so the small desk lamp cast better light on his face. "How's your day going?"

"Busy. Eric's being a pain about the Henderson account, and Maya keeps asking for help with stuff she should already know." Scarlet paused, her expression softening. "But better now. I miss you."

"Miss you too," Jerry replied, the words automatic but sincere. "Got your text about the package. Glad it finally arrived."

"It was perfect. How did you manage to find that dinosaur encyclopedia? Emmett's going to lose his mind."

Jerry allowed himself a small smile. "Amazon delivers, even to war zones. Well, to the APO address, anyway."

The familiar quiet returned, settling between them. Not comforting, not hostile, just *there* like an uninvited presence.

Jerry checked the time, noting the slow crawl of minutes. He'd have to leave soon.

But that wasn't really why he'd looked.

"So," Scarlet said, breaking the silence. "I was thinking. Maybe for my next visit to Utah, I could stay longer? Like two weeks instead of just the weekend?"

A complex emotion washed over Jerry: hope mixed with fear, longing tangled with doubt. "That would be ..." He searched for the right word. "Great. The boys would love that."

"And you?" Scarlet asked, her eyes searching his through the digital distance.

"Of course," Jerry said quickly. "I just don't want you to put your life on hold too much."

Scarlet's expression shifted subtly. "It's not putting my life on hold. It's being part of yours."

Jerry rubbed his forearm where his tattoo lay hidden beneath his sleeve. "I know. I just—" He stopped, struggling to articulate the conflict within him. "I worry sometimes that it's too much. The deployment. The boys' needs. All of it."

"Jerry," Scarlet started, but he was saved from her response by a sharp knock on his door.

"Duncan!" a voice called. "Lieutenant needs that equipment report ASAP!"

"I've got to go," Jerry said, tension uncoiling from his shoulders at the interruption. "Duty calls."

"Oh," Scarlet's disappointment was palpable even through the pixelated connection. "Will you call tomorrow?"

"I'll try," Jerry said, avoiding a firm commitment. "Things are busy here."

"Okay," Scarlet replied, visibly regrouping. "I love you."

"Love you too," Jerry said, ending the call before the emotions those words stirred could reach his face.

He sat motionless, staring at the blank screen. The conversation replayed in his mind, and he recognized, with uncomfortable clarity, his own retreat. Two weeks in Utah. Being part of his life. Scarlet was reaching out, building bridges across the distance, while he was constructing walls she couldn't see.

The door to the CHU swung open, and Mac strode in, balancing two takeout containers from the DFAC.

"Saved you from the mystery meat tonight," he announced, setting one container on Jerry's footlocker. "You can thank me with undying loyalty and your next weekend pass."

"Just talk to Scarlet?" Mac asked, unwrapping his sandwich.

"Yeah."

"How is Red doing? Still putting up with your emotionally constipated ass?"

Jerry shot him a look. "She's fine."

"Really convincing, Captain Communication," Mac replied. "Let me guess. She said something meaningful, and you gave her the deployment equivalent of 'k'?"

"Fuck off, Mac."

"That's a yes," Mac said, taking a bite of his sandwich. "You know, for someone who claims to be crazy about this woman, you sure have a weird way of showing it."

Jerry stared at his untouched food. "It's not that simple."

"Never said it was," Mac shrugged. "But pretending everything's fine while you build a wall between you isn't exactly the path to happily ever after."

"Since when are you the relationship guru?" Jerry asked, irritation rising.

"Look, I get it. This whole thing ... it's fucking terrifying. You've got the boys to think about. You've got history. But Scarlet isn't going to wait around forever while you decide if you're brave enough to let her all the way in."

Jerry stood abruptly, appetite gone. "I'm going to the MWR."

"Running away from this conversation won't help either," Mac called after him, but Jerry was already out the door.

Night had settled fully over Camp Arifjan by the time Jerry made his way back to the CHU. He'd spent hours at the Morale, Welfare, and Recreation center, mindlessly playing video games and avoiding both Mac and his own thoughts. Now, approaching midnight, the container village had quieted, most soldiers either asleep or settled into their evening routines.

The room was dim and still when Jerry stepped in.

Mac lay sprawled across his bunk, earbuds tucked in, a thin blanket pulled up like he was trying to disappear.

Jerry didn't bother with the light. He'd done this routine enough times to manage by touch.

The bunk groaned under his weight, the sound sharp in the stillness of the room.

Sleep hovered out of reach, just like it had every night since arrival.

He stared at the ceiling, then at his phone. 0023.

In another world, Scarlet was probably buried in meetings, glancing at her screen between tasks, maybe wondering why he had cut their call short.

The distance wasn't just measured in hours or ocean.

It pulsed in everything unsaid.

He had tried to shield her from the worst of it, the broken edges he'd long since stopped trying to fix.

But what if she saw them?

Really saw them.

And decided that whatever future they were building couldn't survive the wreckage of his past?

Jerry rubbed his thumb over the small helm charm on Scarlet's bracelet, the metal warm from constantly being against his skin. The gesture brought back Christmas Eve; Scarlet in red lingerie, slipping this bracelet from her bra and placing it on his wrist. "To always remember me," she'd said.

He'd promised to wear it, regulations be damned. It was the one promise he'd kept without hesitation.

His phone glowed in the darkness as he opened their text thread, reading her earlier message again. The warmth and easy love in her words deserved so much better than the sterile response he'd sent. Without fully thinking it through, Jerry began typing.

His thumb hovered over the send button, the message more vulnerable than anything he'd written in weeks. Something in him resisted, warned against lowering the drawbridge. But the part of him that ached with missing her pushed through the hesitation.

He sent the message, then placed the phone face down beside him, exhaling slowly. The confession felt both freeing and frightening, opening a door he'd been systematically closing.

Jerry leaned back against his pillow, eyes fixed on the blank ceiling above. His hand drifted back to his forearm, tracing the outline of his tattoo through his T-shirt. Somewhere in Utah, his boys were sleeping, safe under his mother's watchful care.

They had been so excited during their video call last week. Emmett chattering about his new school, Marty beaming at the sound of Jerry's voice. Scarlet had visited them the weekend before, had finally met his father and sister. "They loved her," his mother had reported. "Thomas couldn't stop talking about how good she is with the boys."

The knowledge should have comforted him. Instead, it amplified his constant fear since deployment that Scarlet would realize what she was missing while he was gone, that the life he offered was too complicated, too broken to fit into her organized, successful world.

Jerry reached for his phone again, checking if Scarlet had responded to his uncharacteristically emotional message. No reply yet, but he hadn't really expected one. It was the middle of her workday; she'd likely see it later.

He opened his photo album instead, finding the Christmas photos where Scarlet and the boys all smiled at the camera together. Her arm wrapped protectively around Emmett, her other hand resting gently on Marty's shoulder. The ease in their posture, the natural connection evident even in a still image.

Jerry let the truth land. Mac's words from earlier echoed in his mind. *Scarlet isn't going to wait around forever while you decide if you're brave enough to let her all the way in.*

He knew exactly what he was doing by creating distance before she could, protecting himself from the pain of another abandonment. The pattern was familiar, almost comfortable in its certainty. Except Scarlet wasn't ... her. She hadn't walked away when things got hard. She'd stepped closer, had embraced the complexity of his life with surprising grace.

Yet here he was, manufacturing the very distance he feared.

Jerry set his phone aside and rolled onto his back, the bracelet on his wrist catching the faint light that filtered through the thin curtains. Seven more months. Seven months until he could hold his boys again, until he could look Scarlet in the eyes and see if what they'd built could survive the strain of separation. Seven months to decide if he was brave enough to risk his heart again.

His last thought before exhaustion finally claimed him was of Scarlet's face during their call, how it had been searching and concerned yet still so loving despite his walls. Tomorrow, he promised himself hazily. Tomorrow, he'd try to bridge the gap he'd been widening. Tomorrow, he'd be braver.

But even as sleep pulled him under, a part of him knew that tomorrow would likely bring the same pattern of retreat, the same protective distance that had become his deployed rhythm.

Twenty-Five

Jerry's eyes burned from staring at his laptop screen in the darkness of the CHU. The clock in the corner read 0002. Midnight. Another day officially begun in the endless march of deployment. The only illumination came from his computer and the small desk lamp angled to prevent disturbing Mac, who appeared to be asleep in the bunk across the narrow container.

He squinted at the image on his screen, studying the staff sergeant who knelt beside a Kuwaiti child during a community relations event earlier that day. The composition was decent, but the lighting needed adjustment. Kuwait's harsh midday sun cast unflattering shadows across the soldier's face. Jerry tweaked the exposure levels, enhancing the connection between the American servicemember and the smiling local child. Public affairs was all about the narrative, the story the Army wanted to project to the world.

Not unlike the story I'm projecting back home, he thought, the bitter comparison unexpected and unwelcome.

Jerry rotated his shoulders, trying to release the tension that had taken up permanent residence there. April in Kuwait brought slightly cooler night temperatures, but the CHU's air conditioning struggled against the accumulated heat of the day. Sweat prickled at his hairline as he added a caption to the image.

U.S. Army Staff Sgt. Melissa Chen distributes school supplies during a community outreach event with local children in Kuwait City, April 15. (U.S. Army photo by Staff Sgt. Gilmore Duncan)

His phone vibrated beside the laptop, the screen illuminating with a notification that briefly drew his attention from his work. Scarlet's name appeared with a message preview.

Scarlet

> Hey stranger, just checking if we're still on for our call tomorrow at …

Jerry's eyes slid away from the notification, returning to his work without opening the message. He'd respond later. The command had requested these images for a press release going out tomorrow, and he needed to finish editing the entire set. At least, that's what he told himself as he closed out the notification with a swipe.

He opened the next image in the folder, a wide shot of American and Kuwaiti soldiers in a planning session. His fingers worked automatically, adjusting shadows and highlights, sharpening focus points, while his mind wandered.

The distance he'd created between himself and Scarlet had grown steadily over the past two months. What had started as slight emotional withdrawal had evolved into calculated avoidance. Shorter calls became the norm, messages stayed strictly practical, and video chats were missed with increasing frequency, all explained away by "operational tempo." He'd become an expert at maintaining just enough connection to prevent alarm while keeping a protective barrier in place.

It was better this way, he told himself as he cropped the image to improve composition. The longer he spent in Kuwait, the clearer it became that his life was fundamentally incompatible with Scarlet's. She deserved someone whole, someone without the baggage he carried. Someone whose children didn't need specialized care, whose career didn't include deployments to faraway deserts.

His phone vibrated again. Not Scarlet this time, but a message from his mother that expanded automatically on the screen.

Mom

Are you awake, honey? Need to discuss something about the cruise.

Jerry glanced at Mac's still form before quietly closing his laptop. He slid off his bunk and grabbed his phone, slipping outside to avoid disturbing his roommate. The night air hit him with its relative coolness as he settled on the metal step outside their CHU, the gravel beneath his boots shifting slightly.

He dialed his mother's number, calculating the time difference automatically. It would be early afternoon in Utah. Around 3 p.m. The connection clicked through after two rings.

"Jerry?" His mother's voice carried surprise. "What time is it over there?"

"Just after midnight," he replied, rubbing his eyes with his free hand. "Saw your message. What's up with the cruise?"

"Midnight? Sweetheart, why are you still awake? Is everything okay?"

"Fine, Mom. Just finishing some work. Public affairs deadlines." He leaned against the metal railing, staring out at the rows of identical container units that housed hundreds of deployed soldiers. "What about the cruise?"

"Well, I wanted to run something by you before we finalize plans," Maggie began, her voice taking on the excited tone she reserved for family events. "The cruise leaves Miami on Mother's Day but your dad and I were thinking of flying in on Friday instead of Sunday morning. That way we could spend some time with Scarlet before we board."

Jerry's attention sharpened at the mention of Scarlet's name. "Oh?"

"Yes, she suggested meeting at South Beach for the day. The boys are beyond excited. Emmett's been talking about building sandcastles with her all week."

Something uncomfortable shifted in Jerry's chest. "Sounds nice."

"We found the perfect Mother's Day gift, too," Maggie continued, either missing or choosing to ignore his flat response. "The boys picked out this beautiful charm bracelet. It has a little green wheelchair charm for Marty and a rainbow dinosaur for Emmett. Emmett said it's to match your tattoo, but better because it's a dinosaur. Isn't that sweet? Emmett says she's 'officially their mom now,' so she should have the symbols too."

Jerry's throat tightened unexpectedly. "He said that? About her being their mom?"

"Oh, yes. Emmett's been calling her mom for months now. I thought you knew? He says she does 'mom stuff' like helping with homework and making dinosaur-shaped pancakes when she visits."

He went still, pulse hitching before he could stop it.

Emmett's use of the word had once felt like a hopeful guess.

Now it was routine, unthinking.

Scarlet had filled a space in their lives he hadn't realized was so open.

And now that she was there, the fear of what might happen next began to creep in.

"Jerry? Are you still there?"

"Yeah, sorry," he said, forcing his voice to remain neutral. "Just tired. The bracelet sounds … thoughtful."

"It's more than thoughtful," his mother replied, her tone shifting to something more pointed. "That woman has been a godsend for these boys. She flies out every other weekend, helps with therapy exercises, and remembers all of Emmett's dinosaur facts. She even figured out that trick with the weighted blanket that helps Marty sleep through the night."

Jerry nodded, though his mother couldn't see him. "I know," he said quietly. "She's amazing with them."

"She's amazing, period," Maggie corrected. "And between you and me, I'm a little worried. She called last week about the cruise plans, and she sounded … I don't know. Distant. Sad, maybe."

"What do you mean?"

"I asked how things were between you two, and she got very vague. Said everything was 'fine' … you know, the kind of 'fine' that means it's not fine at all."

Jerry closed his eyes, guilt washing through him. He'd been telling himself his withdrawal was gradual enough that Scarlet wouldn't notice, that she'd be too busy with her career and life in Miami to track the subtle changes in their communication.

"It's just deployment," he managed. "Everything's harder with distance."

"Gilmore Paul Duncan," his mother said, using his full name in the way that had made him snap to attention since childhood. "I've been a military wife and mother for over thirty years. I know what deployment communication sounds like. And I know when my son is pulling away."

"Mom, it's not—"

"No, you listen to me," she interrupted firmly. "That woman loves you. She loves your children. She is going above and beyond anything I've ever seen, and if you're pushing her away because you're scared or guilty or whatever nonsense is going through your head, you need to stop it right now."

The door creaked open behind Jerry, but he barely registered the sound, too caught in his mother's unexpected confrontation.

"It's complicated," he said finally.

"Love always is," Maggie replied, her voice softening. "But that doesn't mean you run from it. Those boys have already lost one mother. Don't make them lose another because you're too stubborn to let yourself be happy."

Jerry had no response, her words landing like physical blows against his carefully constructed defenses.

"Just think about it," she continued. "We'll see Scarlet at the beach in a few weeks, and I expect you to have sorted yourself out by then. Call her. Really talk to her. Don't throw away something precious because you're afraid it might break."

"I'll try," he said quietly.

"Good. I love you, sweetheart. Get some sleep."

"Love you too, Mom."

The call ended, leaving Jerry sitting alone in the darkness, his mother's words echoing uncomfortably in his mind. He remained motionless on the step, staring out at the dimly lit container village, the distant hum of generators providing a mechanical soundtrack to his thoughts.

The door opened wider behind him, and Mac emerged, dressed in PT shorts and a faded Army T-shirt. Without invitation, he dropped onto the step beside Jerry, his presence both familiar and intrusive.

They sat in silence for several moments, the quiet between them loaded with unspoken thoughts. Finally, Mac turned toward him.

"You're being a nitshit, you know that?" he said, smacking the back of Jerry's head with casual precision.

Jerry jerked away, scowling. "Were you eavesdropping on my call?"

"Hard not to hear half a conversation in a tin can the size of a walk-in closet," Mac replied unapologetically. "Besides, someone needs to witness the spectacular way you're sabotaging your life."

"I'm not sabotaging anything," Jerry insisted, though the defense felt hollow even to his own ears. "I'm just—"

"Being a coward?" Mac supplied helpfully. "Pushing away the best thing that's happened to you in years? Setting new records for emotional constipation?"

Jerry's jaw tightened. "You don't understand."

"Actually, I understand perfectly," Mac countered, his usual joking tone replaced by something more serious. "You're terrified that Scarlet's going to realize what Marisa did. That your life is too complicated, that the boys are too much work, that you're damaged goods."

"Don't bring Marisa into this," Jerry warned, a flash of genuine anger cutting through his exhaustion. The one relationship he'd attempted after his divorce had crashed and burned when she'd decided his life was too messy.

"Why not? She's the ghost haunting every decision you make." Mac shifted to face him more directly. "Scarlet isn't her, man. And she's absolutely not your fuck-shit ex-wife. She's not running. She's flying to Utah every other weekend. She's being a mom to your kids while you're gone. She's waiting for you to let her in."

"I know that," Jerry said, the admission emerging with reluctance.

"Then why are you ghosting her?"

"I'm not—"

"You are," Mac interrupted firmly. "For at least two months now. Short calls. One-word texts. Conveniently being 'in the field' during scheduled video chats. I've watched you do it, and it's painful. You haven't really talked to that woman in weeks."

Jerry fell silent, unable to refute what they both knew was true.

"Look," Mac continued more gently, "I get it. It's fucking terrifying to let someone matter that much, especially when you've got the boys to think about. But pushing her away before she can leave doesn't protect you, it just guarantees you end up alone."

"What if she's better off without all this?" Jerry asked, the question revealing more vulnerability than he'd intended. "My career, the boys' needs, deployment after deployment—"

"That's not your decision to make," Mac said simply. "It's hers. And from where I'm sitting, she's already made it. She chose you, all of you, complications included."

He sat and rubbed both hands over his face as if trying to stay grounded. The silence pressed in, thick with everything they weren't saying. "It's not that simple," he said finally, voice more fragile than firm.

"It never is," Mac agreed, reaching for Jerry's phone where it lay between them on the step. "But this part can be."

Before Jerry could react, Mac had unlocked his phone and was scrolling through his contacts. The traitor knew his passcode.

"What are you doing?" Jerry demanded, reaching for the device.

Mac held it out of reach. "It's midnight here which means it's 5 p.m. in Miami. Perfect time to call your girlfriend, like a grown-ass adult."

"Mac, don't—"

Too late. Mac had already hit the call button and was holding the phone toward Jerry with a stubborn expression that said clearly, *Take it or I'm doing this for you.*

Jerry grabbed the phone, heart suddenly pounding as the connection rang through. He considered ending the call, but Mac's unwavering stare promised consequences if he did.

The call connected, and Scarlet's voice came through, a mixture of surprise and caution in her tone. "Jerry? Is everything okay?"

He hadn't called unexpectedly in weeks. Of course she'd assume something was wrong.

"Hey," he said, trying to keep his voice casual. "Everything's fine. Just finished work and thought I'd call."

"At midnight your time?" The disbelief was evident in her voice.

"Mac's being a meddling pain in the ass," Jerry admitted, shooting a glare at his friend, who merely grinned and pantomimed a chef's kiss.

A pause followed, filled with all the things neither of them was saying. When Scarlet spoke again, her voice was softer, more tentative. "Are you sure everything's okay? You've seemed … distant lately."

The direct approach caught Jerry off guard. He'd expected her to maintain the polite fiction that nothing had changed, that their increasingly superficial communication was just a normal part of deployment.

"I'm fine," he assured her automatically. "Just tired. Work's been demanding."

"You've been saying that for weeks," Scarlet observed, the gentleness of her tone making the observation more painful, not less. "I'm worried about you."

Jerry's chest tightened. He didn't deserve her concern, not when he'd been deliberately creating the distance between them. "Don't be. I'm just pulling long hours. Public affairs never sleeps during deployment."

Mac rolled his eyes dramatically from beside him, clearly unimpressed with Jerry's deflection.

"Your mom called about the cruise," Scarlet continued, changing tactics. "We're going to spend the day at the beach before they board. The boys are excited."

"She just told me," Jerry said, some of the tension easing from his shoulders at the safer topic. "Sounds like they'll have a great time."

"I wish you could be there," Scarlet said, the simple honesty in her words making it harder to maintain his emotional walls.

"Me too," he replied, and meant it.

Another pause stretched between them, heavy with unspoken words.

"Jerry," Scarlet began carefully, "talk to me. Please. If something's wrong, if I've done something—"

"You haven't done anything," he interrupted quickly, hating that she would blame herself for his retreat. "You're perfect. It's just …" He trailed off, unable to articulate the complicated tangle of fear and unworthiness that had driven his behavior.

Mac poked him hard in the ribs, mouthing silently, *Tell her.*

Jerry took a deep breath. "I'm sorry I've been distant. It's not you. It's just hard sometimes, being away from everyone. From you."

It wasn't the whole truth, but it was more honesty than he'd offered in weeks.

"I understand," Scarlet said, though something in her voice suggested she knew he wasn't telling her everything. "I miss you too. More than I expected to."

The simple confession hit him with unexpected force. "I miss you," he echoed, the words emerging before he could filter them.

Mac nodded approvingly, then stood and quietly retreated into the CHU, leaving Jerry alone on the step.

"The boys miss you too," Scarlet continued. "Emmett keeps asking how many days until you come home. He's made a countdown calendar with dinosaur stickers."

Jerry smiled despite himself, imagining his son's meticulous approach to tracking days. "Tell him I miss him too. Both of them."

"I will," Scarlet promised. "I'm going to visit them this weekend. Any special messages I should deliver?"

"Just …" Jerry hesitated, the words catching in his throat. "Just tell them I love them. And that I'm proud of how brave they're being."

"What about me?" Scarlet asked, a hint of her usual playfulness breaking through. "Any special messages there?"

The question hung between them, an opportunity to bridge the distance he'd created. Jerry's thumb brushed absently over the helm charm on her bracelet, still faithfully worn, despite regulations.

"I love you too," he said softly, the words both true and insufficient. "More than I know how to say."

"Then stop trying to pull away," Scarlet replied, her voice suddenly raw with emotion. "Because it feels like you're slipping away from me, and I don't know how to hold on."

The directness of her observation struck him like a physical blow. She had noticed. Of course she had. He'd been foolish to think otherwise.

"I'm not going anywhere," he assured her, the promise feeling hollow against the reality of his recent behavior.

"Good," Scarlet said, sounding unconvinced but willing to accept the assurance for now. "Because neither am I."

They talked for a few minutes more, discussing her work, the boys' latest achievements, and the mundane details of daily life separated by seven time zones. It wasn't the deep reconnection they needed, but it was more than they'd shared in weeks.

He didn't go back inside right away. Instead, he stood beneath the stars, the desert air cool on his skin.

The pressure was still there, lingering in his chest like a bruise, but it no longer stole his breath. It had softened, made room for other things.

He returned to the CHU to find Mac sprawled on his bunk, flipping through a well-worn paperback. "Well?" his friend prompted without looking up.

"She says I'm pulling away," Jerry admitted, sinking onto his own bunk.

"No shit," Mac replied, turning a page. "What are you going to do about it?"

Jerry's eyes fell on his footlocker, where Scarlet's most recent letter lay unopened beneath a stack of operational reports. He'd received it three days ago and hadn't found the courage to read it yet, afraid of the emotion it might contain.

"I don't know," he said honestly.

Mac finally looked up from his book, his expression uncharacteristically serious. "Figure it out fast, man. Women like Scarlet don't wait around forever for guys to get their shit together."

Jerry nodded, reaching for his footlocker. His hand hovered over the latch before he pulled back, not yet ready to face whatever truths Scarlet had committed to paper.

Tomorrow, he told himself. Tomorrow he would read her letter. Tomorrow he would try to bridge the distance he'd created.

But as he stretched out on his bunk, staring at the corrugated metal ceiling above him, Jerry knew that tomorrow would likely bring the same pattern of retreat, the same protective distance that had become his deployed rhythm. Because the alternative, which meant letting himself be fully seen, fully known, fully loved, was far more terrifying than any battlefield he'd ever faced.

Twenty-Six

The hum of the base never stopped: machines, murmurs, the distant thud of training drills. Jerry stared at the half-written report on his screen, not reading, just existing. Five months down, and the sameness was starting to feel like erosion.

His phone vibrated against the metal desk, briefly illuminating with a notification. Jerry glanced at it, expecting another logistics update or schedule change. Instead, his mother's name appeared with a video attachment and a simple message.

Mom

> Thought you might want to see this. Beach day with the boys and Scarlet. They miss you.

Jerry hesitated, his thumb hovering over the screen. He'd been careful about exposure to home life, limiting himself to scheduled calls and practical updates. It was easier when he maintained distance, when he controlled the emotional toll. But something about this unexpected glimpse pulled at him.

He glanced around the empty office. Mac was off handling logistics for an upcoming mission, and most of the unit was at afternoon chow. Alone for the moment, Jerry plugged in his earbuds and tapped the video.

His mother's slightly unsteady camera work captured South Beach's white sand and turquoise waters first, then panned to reveal the scene that knocked the air from his lungs: Scarlet kneeling beside Marty in a small beach tent, carefully applying sunscreen to his son's shoulders. Her hair was pulled back in a messy bun, loose strands catching the sunlight like copper wire.

The camera shifted to Emmett, who was meticulously arranging plastic dinosaurs around an elaborate sand structure. "Mom!" he called out, and Jerry's heart stuttered at the casual use of the title. "Can you help me with the moat? It keeps caving in."

"On my way, buddy," Scarlet replied, finishing with Marty before moving toward Emmett.

The video stretched on for nearly five minutes, each frame showing Jerry what his family looked like without him. Scarlet helped Emmett dig his moat while Thomas carried Marty to the water's edge so he could feel the waves on his feet. His mother's voice drifted from behind the camera, commenting on the simple moments that felt anything but ordinary to Jerry watching from thousands of miles away.

But Jerry's attention kept returning to Scarlet, captivated by how easily she'd integrated into his family and the natural rhythm she'd found with his boys. At one point, she knelt beside Emmett, helping him place a flag on top of his castle, and the sleeve of her coverup slipped back to reveal a silver bracelet on her wrist. Jerry leaned closer, recognizing the charms that caught the sunlight: a green wheelchair and a rainbow dinosaur.

The symbols of his sons. His symbols.

The office door swung open, and Jerry startled, nearly dropping his phone as Mac sauntered in, balancing two disposable coffee cups.

"Thought you might need this," Mac said, sliding one across the desk. "You look like ten miles of bad ..." He paused, noting Jerry's expression. "What's wrong?"

He hesitated, then tilted the phone toward Mac and hit play again.

Words felt inadequate for what he was feeling, and even if they weren't, he wasn't sure he could speak them aloud.

Mac watched silently, coffee forgotten as the scene unfolded. When Emmett called Scarlet 'Mom' again, Mac's eyebrows lifted slightly, but he said nothing.

"That's new," Jerry finally said, his voice rougher than intended.

"The 'mom' thing? Not really," Mac replied, setting his coffee down. "He was calling her that at Christmas, remember? Looks like it stuck."

"Yeah, but ..." Jerry trailed off, unable to articulate exactly what felt different. Not wrong, just ... significant. The casual confidence in Emmett's voice when he called for her. The way she responded without hesitation, as if she'd always been Mom.

Mac studied him carefully. "She's good with them," he observed, nodding toward the screen where Scarlet was now helping Marty build a sand turtle. "Really good."

"I know," Jerry said.

"You miss them," Mac said. It wasn't a question.

"Every goddamn day."

"Her too?"

Jerry nodded, surprised by his own admission and the tightness in his throat that accompanied it.

Before Mac could respond, a sharp knock preceded Corporal Barrett's entry. She appeared in crisp ACUs despite the afternoon heat, her expression professionally neutral.

"Sergeant Duncan, Sergeant MacIntyre," she said, "Command Sergeant Major Vega requests your presence. Immediately."

Jerry and Mac exchanged quick glances. Simone Barrett rarely used such formal address unless something serious was happening.

"What's it about?" Mac asked, already standing and adjusting his uniform.

"Above my pay grade, Sergeant," Barrett replied, though her slight grimace suggested otherwise. "She just said to find you both ASAP."

Jerry closed the video and pocketed his phone, suddenly grateful for the distraction from the emotional quicksand he'd been sinking into.

"Probably just wants to admire our beautiful faces," Mac joked as they followed Barrett across the dusty compound. "It's been at least twelve hours since she had the pleasure."

"Your face might get us both disciplined," Jerry returned with a half-smile. "It counts as visual harassment."

"Says the man who looks like he spent the night wrestling Kuwaiti sandcats," Mac shot back, his Louisiana drawl thickening as it always did when he was trying to lighten the mood.

Jerry managed a small laugh, but he couldn't stop thinking about the video, about Scarlet's smile as she helped his sons, about the matching bracelet on her wrist, about the family unit they'd formed in his absence.

The walk to Command Sergeant Major Vega's office was mercifully short. Barrett knocked once before opening the door and announcing them with military efficiency.

Command Sergeant Major Ramona Vega sat behind her desk, her salt-and-pepper hair pulled back in a regulation bun. Decorations from multiple deployments adorned her uniform, but it was her penetrating gaze that always commanded attention.

"Duncan, MacIntyre," she nodded, dismissing Barrett with a slight wave. "Close the door."

Mac, ever the tension-breaker, dropped into a chair with casual confidence. "Whatever it was, Sergeant Major, I can explain."

Vega's lips twitched in what might have been amusement. "Relax, MacIntyre. You're not in trouble ... for once." She shuffled through a stack of papers, extracting two official documents. "I've received your reassignment orders for post-deployment."

Jerry felt a jolt of pressure, like the air had thinned around him.

Reassignment meant leaving his unit. Leaving Mac. Leaving the rhythm and routine that had kept him steady since the divorce.

"Alaska," Vega said, sliding the first paper across her desk. "Fort Wainwright. You're being assigned to a training unit, MacIntyre."

Mac's eyebrows shot up as he reached for the document. "Alaska? Seriously? I'm from Louisiana. I don't even own a real coat."

"Consider it a broadening opportunity," Vega replied dryly, then turned her attention to Jerry. "Duncan, you're heading to Fort Belvoir, DC. Special assignment with the Public Affairs Office."

Jerry accepted the paper automatically, the words blurring slightly as he processed the information. DC. Far from Mac, from the team he'd operated with for years. A new beginning, maybe, for him and the boys.

And Scarlet? What would this mean for them?

"When?" he managed.

"You'll report three months after redeployment," Vega answered. "Colonel Sharp approved extended leave for family reintegration. Plenty of time for leave, getting your dependents settled."

Jerry nodded, trying to process the timeline. Three months of transition after they got home.

"MacIntyre, give us the room," Vega said, her tone making it clear this wasn't a request.

Mac hesitated, glancing between them with uncharacteristic uncertainty before nodding. "Roger that, Sergeant Major." He squeezed Jerry's shoulder briefly as he passed. "Find me after, battle."

The door closed behind him with a soft click, leaving Jerry alone with Vega's penetrating gaze.

"So," she began, leaning back in her chair. "DC. Good assignment for a soldier with your skill set. Stable posting, excellent schools for your boys."

"Yes, Sergeant Major."

"Cut the Sergeant Major bullshit, Duncan," Vega said, her tone shifting to something less official. "We've been through too much for that. I need to know if you're good."

Jerry blinked, caught off guard by the direct question. "I'm fine."

"That's not what I asked." Vega stood, moving to look out the small window behind her desk. "You know why I call you Jelly Donut?"

The apparent non sequitur confused him. "Because of that field exercise where I—"

"Because you're exactly like one," she interrupted, turning to face him again. "Hard exterior, but if someone applies enough pressure, everything soft inside comes spilling out." Her eyes narrowed slightly. "And lately, Duncan, you've been applying that pressure to yourself."

Jerry's jaw tightened, uncomfortable with the sudden shift toward the personal. "With respect, I don't see how—"

"Your work's suffering," Vega cut in again. "Your reports are technically correct but missing the human element that made you good at this job. Your PT scores are down. And according to Barrett, who hears everything, you've been ghosting your family back home."

Heat rushed to Jerry's face. "That's not—"

"You sleeping, Duncan?" Vega asked, shifting tactics abruptly. "Eating regular? Having those nightmares again?"

The precision of her questions hit uncomfortably close to home. Jerry had been managing on three, maybe four hours of broken sleep since arriving in Kuwait, the old hypervigilance from his Iraq tours returning with a vengeance.

"I'm handling it," he said stiffly.

"Like you 'handled' it after your second tour?" Vega's voice was sharp with knowledge. "I've seen your file, remember? I was there for that debrief. The midnight panic attacks. The dissociation episodes."

Jerry felt exposed, raw in a way that made him want to retreat even further. "That was different. That was combat."

"And this is what? A vacation?" Vega leaned forward, her hands flat on the desk. "Listen to me carefully, Duncan. I specifically requested branch pull your name from deployment cycles for the next few years.

Not because you're not a good soldier, but because you need time. Time to get help."

The revelation landed like a physical blow. "You did what?"

"You're showing all the classic signs," Vega continued, ignoring his outrage. "Withdrawal. Isolation. Avoiding emotional connection. The same patterns from your last deployment, except now you've got a woman back home trying to love you through it, and you're shutting her out."

Jerry's hands clenched involuntarily. "You don't understand—"

"I understand perfectly," Vega cut him off, voice sharp but not unkind. "You think you're damaged goods. You think your life is too complicated, your baggage too heavy. You're afraid she'll see all of you and walk away, so you're walking away first." Her eyes pierced him. "How am I doing so far?"

Jerry remained silent, the accuracy of her assessment leaving him without defense.

"Look," Vega's voice softened slightly as she sat back down. "I've been where you are. After my third tour, I couldn't sleep. Couldn't connect. Thought I was handling it, right up until I wasn't." She paused, the admission clearly not easy for her. "I almost lost everything before I got help. Not just my family, but myself."

Jerry looked up, surprised by the personal disclosure from a leader he'd always seen as unshakable.

"Getting help isn't weakness, Duncan," she continued. "It's the strongest damn thing you can do, for yourself, for those boys of yours, for that woman who's holding your family together while you're gone."

Something in her words cut through his carefully constructed defenses.

"You know what happened on my second deployment?" Vega asked, her voice quieter now. "I did the same damn thing you're doing. Figured my husband would be better off without the complications of a deployed wife who might not come home. Started pulling away, making it easier for him to move on without me." Her voice hardened. "By the time I got home, he had. Took our daughter with him."

The blunt admission silenced whatever protest Jerry had been formulating.

"You're not protecting her by pulling away, Duncan," Vega said, returning to her desk. "You're protecting yourself. And those boys of yours? The ones calling your girlfriend 'Mom' while you hide behind deployment? They deserve better. You deserve better."

Jerry's throat felt too tight to speak.

"Not everyone leaves, Duncan," Vega said quietly. "But keep this up, and you'll make sure they do."

The truth of her words landed like a physical blow. Jerry stared at the reassignment orders in his hand, the reality of DC, of what it could mean, suddenly overwhelming.

"When we get back," Vega continued, her voice matter-of-fact, "you're getting help. I don't care if it's a therapist, a psychiatrist, or the chaplain. But you're going to talk to someone. Not just for your sake, but for those kids and that woman who believe in you."

"I don't know how to fix it," he admitted, the words barely audible.

Vega's expression softened, the commanding officer giving way momentarily to the human being who'd known Jerry for four years now. "Start by being honest," she said, her voice quieter. "With yourself first, then with her. You don't have to carry this alone, Duncan."

Jerry nodded, a lump forming in his throat at the unexpected understanding.

"The woman who's got you singing in your truck like a teenager? Yeah, she sounds like she's thinking long-term," Vega said with a small smile, then softened. "You've got three months post-deployment to figure out if you're ready to meet her there."

"Thank you," he managed, voice rough with the effort of holding it together. This wasn't about work. It was about hope, and she'd just handed it to him.

"Take care of yourself, Duncan," Vega said, rising to end their conversation. "Some of us still need you around."

Jerry stood, clutching the reassignment papers in unsteady hands.

Mac was waiting outside, slouched against the wall with studied nonchalance. "So," he began, falling into step beside Jerry. "Alaska, huh? Think they have good bourbon, or will I have to develop a taste for whatever polar bear piss they drink up there?"

"Mac," Jerry said, not slowing his pace toward their CHU, "not now."

Something in his tone must have communicated the depth of his churning emotions, because Mac simply nodded, maintaining a companionable silence for the remainder of their walk.

When they reached their container housing unit, Mac paused at the door. "I've got inventory to finish," he said, the transparent excuse hanging awkwardly between them. "Take some time, man. I'll be back later."

Jerry nodded gratefully, waiting until Mac's footsteps receded before entering the empty CHU.

The cramped space felt suddenly claustrophobic, Vega's words echoing in his mind. *The question is whether you're going to be part of it. Some of us still need you around.*

His eyes fell on his footlocker, where he'd stored every letter from Scarlet since deployment began. Each carefully saved, but many left unopened after the first few weeks. Proof of his gradual withdrawal, physical evidence of his fear taking control.

Jerry knelt beside the footlocker, the metal hinges protesting as he lifted the lid. The stack of envelopes sat neatly organized, Scarlet's precise handwriting visible on each: his name, his unit, his location. The early ones were already worn from repeated reading, but the later ones remained pristine, untouched.

He took the most recent envelope, settling on his bunk as he carefully broke the seal. The paper felt fragile in his hands, as if the weeks of neglect had somehow made it more vulnerable.

Dear Jerry,

I don't know if you're reading these anymore. Sometimes it feels like I'm writing to a ghost of the man I fell in love with. But I keep writing because I refuse to give up on us.

Jade asked me last week if military relationships are always this hard, or if it was just you. I told her the truth, that it's not the distance that's hard, it's the silence. I could handle seven time zones if I still felt connected to you. But lately, it's like you're building walls instead of bridges.

I keep wondering what changed. What I did wrong. If there's something I'm not seeing.

The boys miss you. I miss you. Please don't disappear before you even come home.

I love you, even when you make it hard.

<3 Scarlet

Jerry's vision blurred, the words swimming before his eyes. He set the letter aside, reaching for another from the stack, this one dated three weeks earlier.

The words seemed to blur together, each line revealing the gradual change in her tone as he had pulled away. The cheerful updates on the boys giving way to tentative questions about his silence. Her patient understanding turning to quiet confusion.

He couldn't bear to read more. Not tonight.

Jerry reached for his phone, opening the beach video again. He stared at Scarlet's face, at the joy visible despite the frozen pixels, and felt something give way inside him. The hard exterior Vega had described was breaking under the pressure of his own making.

Jerry watched the video through once more, this time, letting it linger.

Scarlet's steady touch on Marty's back, the twin glint of bracelets, the stillness in her face as she watched the boys.

It was love, unfiltered.

And he hadn't earned it.

Not with silence. Not with distance.

While she filled pages with their life, he gave her fragments.

He lowered himself onto the bunk, feeling the edges of her letter beneath his hand.

The truth was too large to face all at once.

But cracks had begun to form in the walls he'd spent years maintaining.

He wouldn't make the call tonight.

And yet, for the first time in a long while, sleep came gently.

Her words by his side.

Twenty-Seven

Jerry hesitated outside the chapel door, hand hovering over the handle. The modest building stood apart from the utilitarian structures that dominated Camp Arifjan, its white exterior looking almost defiant against the browns and tans of the military base. He checked his watch: ten minutes late already.

Three days had passed since Command Sergeant Major Vega's confrontation, since the beach video that had cracked something open inside him. Three days of restless nights staring at his reassignment papers and Scarlet's unopened letters.

He could still walk away. Tell Vega he'd been too busy with assignments. Given that the unit was always backed up with public affairs requests, it wouldn't be a complete lie.

The door swung open before Jerry could retreat, revealing Chaplain Grant Hayes in PT shorts and an Army T-shirt, looking more like he was heading to the gym than conducting counseling.

"Jerry," Grant said with an easy smile. "I was about to go looking for you."

"Sorry I'm late," Jerry replied, straightening slightly. Despite Grant being technically an officer, their working relationship had always been casual. "Got caught up with some equipment inventory."

Grant nodded, clearly not buying the excuse but not calling him on it either. "No problem. Come on in. I was just making coffee. Fair warning, it's terrible."

The chapel's interior offered blessed relief from Kuwait's relentless heat. Rather than leading Jerry to the small sanctuary, Grant motioned toward his office. It was a cramped space, barely large enough for a desk and two chairs, with a coffee pot heating in the corner.

"Black?" Grant asked, already pouring.

"Thanks," Jerry accepted the chipped mug, grateful for something to occupy his hands.

Grant settled into his chair, propping his feet casually on the corner of his desk. Nothing like the rigid posture of most officers on base.

"So," he began, stirring sugar into his own coffee, "Vega said I should expect you."

Jerry's jaw tightened reflexively. "She didn't give me much choice."

"Yeah, she tends to be ... direct," Grant chuckled. "But between us, I'm glad you're here. Been meaning to catch up anyway." He took a sip of his coffee and grimaced. "God, that's awful. I don't know why I keep making it."

The casual comment eased some of the tension in Jerry's shoulders. This didn't feel like the formal counseling session he'd been dreading. Instead, just two soldiers sharing terrible coffee.

"How're the boys doing?" Grant asked. "Still getting regular video calls?"

The question was innocuous enough, but Jerry recognized the tactical approach. Start with the safe topic.

"They're good," he replied, falling into the familiar patterns of small talk. "With my parents in Utah. Video calls twice a week, though the connection's been spotty lately."

Grant nodded, his expression casual but attentive. "Your mom still sending those care packages with the homemade cookies? The ones Mac always manages to sniff out?"

"Like a bloodhound," Jerry agreed with a small smile. "I've started hiding them."

They talked like they'd done it a hundred times: small updates, familiar faces, the kind of banter that didn't require effort.

When Grant described the chapel losing power in the middle of a storm, Jerry laughed, shaking his head.

It didn't feel like a performance. Just conversation. And that was rare enough to notice.

Then, Grant shifted slightly, his tone remaining conversational but his eyes more focused.

"So, what'd you do to get on Vega's radar? She doesn't usually mandate chapel visits unless something's up."

Just like that, the illusion of casual conversation wavered. Jerry stared into his coffee, searching for the right balance of honesty and restraint.

"Performance issues, she says. Says I'm ... distracted."

"Are you?"

Jerry shrugged, uncomfortably aware of how transparent the gesture was. "Deployment stuff. Nothing unusual."

Grant set his mug down. "Look, Jerry, I've known you since you joined this unit. You're the guy who keeps it together when everyone else is falling apart. The steady one. So when Vega's concerned enough to send you my way, I pay attention."

Jerry's fingers tightened around his mug. "I'm handling it."

"Handling what, exactly?"

The direct question caught Jerry off guard. He hesitated, weighing how much to reveal. "Just ... sleep stuff. Nothing major."

"Not sleeping?" Grant's tone remained casual, but his eyes had sharpened. "Since when?"

"It's not a big deal," Jerry deflected. "Most soldiers don't sleep great on deployment."

"True," Grant agreed. "But most soldiers don't have Vega personally intervening in their mental health."

Jerry shifted in his chair, suddenly feeling cornered despite Grant's relaxed posture. "She's overreacting. I'm fine."

"Sure," Grant said, clearly unconvinced. "That's why you look like you haven't slept in a week and you're checking the door every thirty seconds."

Jerry startled, realizing he'd been unconsciously monitoring the entrance since sitting down. He forced his shoulders to relax.

"Old habits," he muttered.

"From when?"

The question hung in the air between them. Jerry considered another deflection, but something in Grant's steady gaze made him reconsider.

"Second deployment," he admitted reluctantly. "The ... hypervigilance never really went away."

Grant nodded, not pushing for details yet. "What else never went away?"

Jerry stared at the wall behind Grant's head, focusing on a faded map of Kuwait. "Dreams sometimes. Nothing serious."

"Nightmares?"

"Sometimes."

Grant waited, the silence stretching between them until Jerry felt compelled to fill it.

"Look, everyone's got stuff from deployments they carry home," he said, an edge creeping into his voice. "I manage it. It doesn't affect my work."

"Maybe not your work," Grant conceded. "But Vega seems to think it's affecting something else." He paused, watching Jerry carefully. "Or someone else."

Jerry's jaw tightened. "Scarlet."

"Your girlfriend, right?" Grant's tone remained carefully neutral. "Vega mentioned there might be some ... communication issues."

"That's personal," Jerry replied stiffly.

"Most important things are," Grant said with a small shrug. "But in my experience, what happens at home affects us here, and what happens here affects home. It's all connected."

Jerry set his mug down, suddenly wishing for something stronger than coffee. "What exactly did Vega tell you?"

"Just that you've been withdrawing. That it might be related to some unprocessed stuff from previous deployments." Grant's expression softened slightly. "And that there's a woman back home who matters to you, who you might be pushing away."

The accuracy of the assessment sent a flicker of irritation through Jerry. "Vega talks too much."

"She cares," Grant corrected gently. "She's seen this pattern before. So have I."

"It's not a pattern," Jerry insisted. "It's just ... deployment is hard on relationships. The distance. The time zones. It's normal for communication to get ... complicated."

"You lost someone. Previous deployment?"

The chaplain didn't soften the words, just laid them out like a diagnosis.

Jerry stilled.

The question shouldn't have surprised him, but it did.

Not because it was wrong, but because it felt too accurate, like a chorus had been rehearsing this moment in the rafters, just waiting for the cue.

"What makes you say that?"

"You read rooms too fast. You don't sleep. You keep people at a distance once they get past surface level," Grant replied, almost gently. "That kind of vigilance usually has history."

Jerry remained silent, his pulse quickening slightly.

"Was it Iraq? Afghanistan?" Grant pressed gently.

"Afghanistan," Jerry admitted after a long pause. "James Hunter. We were on a foot patrol. He was walking point, I was hanging back to photograph some locals." The memory surfaced with surprising clarity despite his attempt to keep it vague. "IED. One minute he was there, the next ..."

He stopped abruptly, surprised by how easily the words had come. Grant waited, not pushing for more.

"I should have been walking point," Jerry continued, the words emerging despite his intention to remain guarded. "Would have been, if I hadn't stopped to change my camera lens."

"Survivor's guilt," Grant observed quietly. "Heavy burden to carry."

Jerry's defenses rose immediately. "I'm not looking for a diagnosis."

"Not offering one," Grant replied easily. "Just naming what I recognize. Carried plenty of it myself after my tour in Iraq."

The quiet admission of shared experience caught Jerry off guard. Most chaplains he'd known kept their own struggles carefully separate from their ministry.

"How'd you deal with it?" Jerry asked before he could stop himself.

"Not well, at first," Grant admitted with a rueful smile. "Drank too much. Pushed my wife away when she tried to help. Convinced myself I was protecting her from my damage." He paused, meeting Jerry's eyes directly. "Sound familiar?"

Jerry looked away, uncomfortable with the parallel. "Maybe."

Grant leaned forward, setting his empty mug aside. "Here's what I learned the hard way, Jerry. When we push people away to protect them, we're really protecting ourselves. From being seen. From being vulnerable. From risking rejection once they know how broken we really are."

The insight struck uncomfortably close to home, but Jerry wasn't ready to acknowledge it fully. "It's more complicated than that."

"Always is," Grant agreed. "And I'm guessing with your boys, and their special needs, and your ex-wife leaving, it's even more complicated than most."

Jerry stiffened at the mention of his ex-wife. "How much did Vega tell you?"

"Enough to understand you've been carrying a hell of a lot by yourself for a long time," Grant replied. "And that maybe you're afraid of letting someone new get close enough to matter."

"I'm not afraid," Jerry insisted, though the protest sounded hollow, even to his own ears.

"Sure," Grant said, not calling out the obvious lie. "Look, I'm not here to push you into some big emotional breakthrough. That's not how this works." He reached for a folder on his desk, casually sliding it across to Jerry. "But when you're ready, there's a good PTSD program at Belvoir. One of the best in the Army. I made some calls. They've got an opening when you get stateside."

Jerry stared at the folder without taking it. "I don't need—"

"You don't have to decide now," Grant interrupted smoothly. "Just take the info. Consider it. That's all I'm asking."

Jerry hesitated, then accepted the folder, more to end the conversation than from any genuine interest. "Fine."

"And Jerry?" Grant's voice shifted, becoming more direct. "That woman ... Scarlet? If she matters to you, don't push her away because you're afraid of what happens if you let her see all of you. The good parts and the broken parts."

"I'm not—" Jerry started to protest.

"You are," Grant said simply. "And I get it. Believe me, I do. But take it from someone who almost lost everything trying to be the strong, silent type: sometimes the bravest thing you can do is let someone see exactly who you are, damage and all."

Jerry rose to leave, uncomfortable with how accurately Grant had identified his behavior. "I appreciate the coffee," he said stiffly. "And the ... talk."

Grant nodded, not pushing further. "My door's always open. Literally. The lock broke three months ago."

Despite himself, Jerry smiled slightly at the weak joke. "I'll keep that in mind."

"One more thing," Grant added as Jerry reached the door. "When was the last time you actually told Scarlet how you feel? Not just the safe stuff, but the real stuff?"

The question lingered in the air between them. Jerry didn't answer, but his silence was response enough.

"That's what I thought," Grant said. "Might be worth considering."

As Jerry left the chapel, the folder tucked under his arm carried a strange weight that felt both insubstantial and crushing, symbolizing a path he wasn't sure he was ready to take, but couldn't entirely dismiss.

The conversation with Grant followed him through the remainder of the day, fragments surfacing at unexpected moments. He moved through his duties with mechanical precision. Equipment inventory, report filing, the endless paperwork of deployment. But his mind kept returning to Grant's observations.

When we push people away to protect them, we're really protecting ourselves.

He got back to the CHU feeling stripped raw, like silence had done more damage than noise ever could. Mac's bunk was empty, his duty shift running late. It gave Jerry space, but not peace.

Jerry sat heavily on his bunk, eyes falling on his footlocker where Scarlet's letters and his reassignment papers were stored. With deliberate movements, he retrieved both, spreading them across his thin mattress. Twenty-three envelopes in neat chronological order. The official orders placing him at Fort Belvoir, Virginia, in exactly four months.

Two separate futures. Or maybe just one, if he was brave enough to reach for it.

Jerry methodically opened each letter he had left unread, absorbing Scarlet's words with growing anguish. Her initial cheerful updates. Her gradually increasing concern. Her confusion at his withdrawal. Her unwavering love despite his silence.

Midway through the stack, he paused to study his reassignment papers more carefully. Fort Belvoir. Just outside DC. Good schools for the boys. Access to specialized medical care for Marty. Support services for Emmett.

A stable posting. A place to build something permanent.

The image formed in his mind with unexpected clarity: a modest house near the base. A yard where the boys could play. Schools within driving distance. A home office for Scarlet's accounting work, if she wanted it. Morning coffee together before the day began. Family dinners around a table that wasn't temporary.

His breath caught at the vision's simple perfection. Not because it erased the challenges or magically solved everything but because, for the first time, he could see a future beyond survival. Beyond just managing. A future with joy, with connection.

A future with Scarlet.

If she would still have him after months of withdrawal and silence.

Grant's question returned to him with new urgency: *When was the last time you actually told Scarlet how you feel? Not just the safe stuff, but the real stuff?*

The answer was painfully clear, never. Not fully. Not the depths of his feelings, and certainly not the extent of his damage.

Jerry reached for his phone, scrolling to the beach video he'd watched countless times in the past few days. He paused at the frame that had imprinted itself on his heart: Scarlet kneeling beside Marty in the sand, her bracelet catching the sunlight as she helped him feel the water without fear.

That single image triggered something profound inside Jerry, a tectonic realignment of priorities and possibilities. The fear didn't disappear; it remained a familiar presence. But something stronger emerged alongside it: determination. He'd lost too much to trauma already, to his ex-wife's abandonment, to his own protective withdrawal. He couldn't lose Scarlet too, not without fighting for her with everything he had left.

Jerry's eyes fell on the small desk in their CHU, decision crystallizing. He pulled out a notepad and pen, sitting under the harsh fluorescent light. His hand hovered over the blank page, uncertainty momentarily paralyzing him.

What could he possibly say that would bridge the distance he'd created? What words could repair the damage his silence had inflicted?

The first attempt felt stiff, formal. He crumpled it, starting again. The second was too apologetic, focusing on his failings without offering anything forward-looking. The third rambled without direction.

Each discarded attempt littered the floor around him as the hours stretched into night. The words wouldn't come, not in the way he needed them to. Not in a way that could possibly convey every-thing he needed to say.

Finally, exhausted and frustrated, Jerry simply wrote her name at the top of a fresh page and let go of trying to craft the perfect message. Instead, he just wrote what came, raw and unfiltered.

Scarlet,

I don't even know where to start this. 4th try tonight. 5th? Lost count. Keep crumpling papers. Starting over.

I counted them. All of them. All 23 letters you sent. I kept every single one, even when I couldn't bring myself to read them. I laid them out last night. 23 letters and I sent back...

Nothing. Not one fucking word. Just those calls getting shorter and shorter until I barely said anything at all.

I'm sorry. God, I'm so sorry. I don't even know if sorry means anything anymore.

That video my mom sent. Beach day. You and the boys. I can't stop watching it. Can't stop seeing that moment with Marty when the wave scared him and you just ...

You knew exactly what to do. Nobody told you. You just knew.

You were wearing the bracelet with their charms.

I can't ...

Why am I like this? Why do I shut down? I don't understand it myself.

I've been AWOL. Not just Kuwait-gone. ME-gone. Pulling back. Shutting down. I kept telling myself I was protecting you but that's bullshit. That's what Vega said. Complete bullshit. I was protecting myself. Hiding. Like always.

I'm seeing someone here. Oh God, that sounds bad. I mean I'm talking to the chaplain. Grant. Started last week after Vega tore into me. He's helping me figure stuff out. Setting me up with an actual therapist in Virginia when I get to Belvoir. Says there's a PTSD program there. Specialized treatment. He thinks I need it. He's right.

I'm actually going to do it this time. Not just saying the words. Actually doing it. For real. I promised Vega. Promised myself.

I don't do this. The feelings thing. The writing it down thing. But I need to try because I don't want to lose you and I think I'm losing you and it's my fault.

After the boys' mother left I just ...

Shut. Down.

Wake up. Feed boys. Work. PT. Therapy appointments. Sleep. Repeat. No room for anything else. No space for breaking, because if I broke who would hold it all together?

But I am breaking. Been breaking for years. Just hiding it.

There's stuff I never told you

My second deployment

Afghanistan patrol

Lost Hunter. My spotter. One minute walking point, next minute, gone. Just gone. Not even pieces big enough to ...

God, I need to stop.

I still hear it. Still smell it. The nightmares didn't go away. I just got better at hiding them. Knife under pillow. Checking locks three times every night. Panic when I can't remember if I locked the door even though I checked already.

I keep having this dream where I can't find the boys. Like they're gone the way Hunter was gone. Just disappeared.

I never told you any of this because I didn't want you to see how broken I am.

But I'm getting help. Real help. Chaplain says I need meds too. Probably right. I'm done pretending I'm fine. I'm not fine. Haven't been fine in years.

I'm talking to Vega every day. She's been where I am. Says I don't have to carry everything alone. Says it's the strongest thing I could do, ask for help.

I had no right to shut you out like I did. No excuse. None. You deserve better. So much better.

And then there's DC. Our orders. Fort Belvoir. It's a good spot. Great schools. Good hospitals for Marty. Programs for Emmett. Resources for me. It could be good. Really good.

But without you it's just ...

It's just another place I'm trying not to fall apart.

Scarlet, I want you with us. Not because we need you to fix anything. Not because I'm broken. But because I can't stop thinking about you. Every minute. Every second. Because when you're around, everything feels right. Because the boys light up around you in a way I've never seen before.

Because I want you. Not need. WANT. Want with everything in me.

You have your whole life in Miami. Your job. Your family. I know that. I shouldn't ask you to give that up. I know I shouldn't. But I don't know how else to say it.

I want you to come with us. Choose us. We would choose you. We DO choose you. Every day. In every way. Emmett asks about you constantly. Marty looks for you in every video call. And me? I'm so goddamn lost without you it terrifies me.

You set something on fire inside me that I thought was dead. You make me feel alive in a way I'd forgotten was possible. When you walk into a room everything else disappears. When you laugh I can't think straight.

You see through every wall I put up. Every mask. Every bullshit excuse. You call me on it and I fucking love that about you. Nobody else does that. Nobody.

I want to build something with you. A home where I don't have to pretend to be fine all the time. Where I can finally let someone see me. All of me. Even the broken parts.

I keep seeing you there with us. Making coffee in the kitchen with your messy morning hair. Doing homework with Emmett. Rolling your eyes when I try to fix everything myself instead of asking for help. I can't stop thinking about you there. With us. Part of us. Completing us.

You said once you didn't know how to fit in a family that was already built but we're not built, we're still just trying to figure out how to be a family and maybe that's what family actually is. Not some finished, perfect thing, but just people choosing each other every day, especially when it's hard.

I'm going to be better. For the boys. For you. For me. I'm going to do the work. The therapy. The meds if I need them. All of it. And not just for a little while. For as long as it takes. Because I want to be whole again. Or at least less broken.

And I want you there. With us. Building something real.

I'm all over the place, I know. Words coming out wrong.

That morning on the ship. Last day. Sun coming up. You in that blue-green dress. Messy hair. You looked at me like you could see everything. All the shit. All the damage. And you didn't run.

I want that Scarlet. I want real. I want messy and complicated and figuring it out together. I want your laugh first thing in the morning and your voice last thing at night. I want arguments and make-ups and everything in between.

I want YOU. All of you. Not because we need a mother or I need someone to lean on but because there is no one else in this world who makes me feel the way you do. Like I'm more than I thought I could be. Like we could build something extraordinary together.

If you decide this is too much, if this letter makes you finally walk away, I'd understand. I know I'm asking for something huge. I know I've been gone, really gone, even before deployment. I know this might be the thing that makes you realize you deserve better than what I've been giving.

87 days until I'm home. Feels like forever.

I'm not asking you to fix me. I know I have to fix myself. And I'm trying. Really trying this time. But I'm asking if you'll be there while I do. If you'll be part of this weird unfinished family that would choose you in a heartbeat if given the chance.

I don't deserve a second chance. I know that. But I'm asking for one anyway.

Yours (if you still want me), Jerry

He read over the words, not allowing himself to edit or second-guess. It wasn't perfect. It wasn't eloquent. But it was real. Every shaky line, every crossed-out word, every unfiltered thought. It was the truth as he knew it. It was all of him. The damage, the fear, the love, the hope.

It was everything he'd been hiding, laid bare on the page.

Jerry carefully folded the letter, slipping it into an envelope before he could lose his courage. He addressed it with precise handwriting, his fingers lingering over Scarlet's name.

The base was quiet as he walked to the mail drop, the night air carrying the faint diesel scent that permeated everything in Kuwait. The postal clerk looked up in surprise at the late-night visitor but accepted the envelope without comment.

As Jerry watched the letter disappear into the outgoing mail bin, a strange lightness spread through him that wasn't quite happiness but something close to it. Relief, perhaps. Or the particular peace that comes with surrender.

"So, you finally did it."

Jerry turned to find Mac leaning against the doorframe, arms crossed over his chest, a knowing expression on his face.

"How long have you been there?" Jerry asked.

"Long enough to see you staring at that mail bin like it holds your entire future." Mac pushed off from the frame, falling into step beside Jerry as they walked back toward their CHU. "About time you wrote her."

"I told her everything," Jerry said quietly. "Afghanistan. The PTSD. Everything."

Mac's eyebrows raised slightly. "Bold strategy."

"It wasn't strategy," Jerry replied, the distinction important. "It was just ... truth."

They walked in silence for several steps, the gravel crunching beneath their boots.

"Asked her to come to DC with us," Jerry finally added. "After deployment."

Mac whistled low. "That's a big ask."

"I know."

"You think she'll say yes?"

Jerry's thumb brushed absently over the helm charm on his wrist—Scarlet's bracelet, still faithfully worn despite regulations. He thought of her on the beach with his boys, of the easy way she integrated into his family's rhythm, of the silver bracelet she wore with their charms.

"I hope so," he said softly. "God, I hope so."

Twenty-Eight

The August heat hit Jerry like a physical force as he stepped out of the chapel's air-conditioned sanctuary. Kuwait's midday sun seemed determined to remind everyone exactly where they found themselves, in a desert deployment counting down its final days. Eighteen days until wheels up. Eighteen days until he'd be en route back to American soil.

Chaplain Grant Hayes followed him out, leaning against the chapel's doorframe with the casual ease that had initially helped Jerry lower his guard six weeks ago.

"Same time next week?" Grant asked, though they both knew the answer. These twice-weekly sessions had become a fixture in Jerry's schedule since that first reluctant visit.

"Yeah," Jerry nodded, squinting against the brightness. "Thanks, Chaplain."

"You're making good progress," Grant said, his tone casual but his eyes evaluative. "I noticed you mentioned the nightmares are less frequent."

Jerry shifted, still not entirely comfortable discussing his mental health so openly, even after weeks of practice. "Three nights in a row without waking up. That's ... new."

"And the video from Scarlet? That helped?"

The mention of Scarlet's response sent a familiar warmth through Jerry's chest. It had been nearly three weeks since he'd received her video response, sitting on a beach in her business clothes, eyes bright with certainty as she'd said those words that had shifted everything. *Yes. A thousand times yes.*

"Yeah," Jerry admitted, a small smile breaking through his usual reserve. "It helped."

"Good." Grant nodded toward the base entrance visible in the distance. "Remember, the Belvoir PTSD program has intake appointments starting after you settle in January. I've already forwarded your information."

"I remember," Jerry replied, surprised by his own lack of resistance. A month ago, he'd have bristled at the suggestion he needed such help. Now, he simply accepted it as the next necessary step. "Already on my calendar."

He studied Jerry with a glint of approval. "You know, most soldiers I counsel take a lot longer to get where you've gotten in six weeks."

Jerry shrugged. "Had good motivation."

"Family has that effect," Grant agreed. "Speaking of which, any word from Scarlet about her move plans?"

"She quit her job a month ago," Jerry said, still slightly amazed by her decisive action. "She's staying with her parents until I get back. Most of her stuff's in storage already." The reality that she'd made such a major life change for him still felt surreal sometimes.

"Sounds like you've both made some big decisions," Grant observed.

Jerry nodded, a smile breaking through again. "Yeah, looks that way."

He spotted Mac leaning against a concrete barrier about fifty yards away, clearly waiting but making a show of scrolling through his phone.

"That's my cue," Jerry said, gesturing toward his friend. "Mac's got some supply inventory for me to sign off on."

"Sure he does," Grant replied with knowing amusement. "Tell him I said supervision orders don't include escort duty from the chapel."

Jerry chuckled. "I'll pass that along, sir."

He'd gone only a few steps when Grant called after him: "Duncan?"

Jerry turned back, eyebrows raised in question.

"I'm proud of you," Grant said simply. "Not everyone has the courage to do what you're doing."

The comment hit harder than expected. Jerry managed a quick nod of acknowledgment before continuing toward Mac, something lighter in his step despite the crushing heat.

Mac glanced up as Jerry approached, his expression shifting from boredom to mock surprise. "Well, look who's finished with church. Did you confess all your sins, or just the ones I know about?"

"Shut up," Jerry replied without heat, falling into step beside his friend. "And it's not church. It's counseling."

"Same difference," Mac shrugged, shoving his phone into his pocket. "Both involve a lot of talking about feelings, which, until recently, I wasn't sure you had."

Jerry shook his head, used to Mac's particular brand of support. "What's with the welcoming committee? I thought you had inventory duty."

"Finished early," Mac replied. "Thought you might want to grab lunch at the DFAC before they run out of those kabob things you like."

"Sure," Jerry agreed, knowing Mac well enough to recognize the unspoken gesture of companionship.

They walked side by side for a few moments, the gravel crunching beneath their boots. Jerry noticed Mac studying him with uncharacteristic thoughtfulness.

"What?" he finally asked.

"Nothing," Mac said, then immediately contradicted himself. "Just … you look different. Less like you're carrying a Humvee on your shoulders."

Jerry considered this. "Maybe I am."

"Therapy's making you soft," Mac declared, but the small smile that accompanied the words took any sting out of them.

"Not soft," Jerry corrected. "Just … breathing easier."

Mac nodded, suddenly serious. "Good. About time." Then, shifting tone, "Weird to think in a few months I'll be freezing my ass off in Alaska while you're setting up house in DC."

"January," Jerry confirmed. "Three months in Texas first, then Belvoir. Gives the boys time to finish their semester before the move."

"And time for you and Red to figure things out," Mac added meaningfully.

Jerry didn't respond, but the gentle texture of Scarlet's bracelet against his wrist felt more significant than usual.

They rounded the corner past the supply depot, and Jerry noticed colorful canopies and makeshift stalls had transformed the normally empty space near the MWR facility into an unexpected hub of activity.

"What's going on over there?" he asked, gesturing toward the commotion.

Mac's face brightened. "Oh yeah, I forgot to tell you. Command approved a local vendor day. Happens every few months. They let some approved civilians bring crafts and stuff onto base. Builds goodwill with the locals and gives us a chance to buy authentic souvenirs instead of the overpriced junk at the PX."

Jerry raised an eyebrow. "And you're interested in authentic Kuwaiti crafts now?"

"No," Mac grinned, "but I'm definitely interested in authentic Kuwaiti food. The guy who makes those date pastry things is back. I've been dreaming about those since last deployment."

"Of course it's about food," Jerry chuckled. "Lunch can wait, then. Let's check it out."

The impromptu market consisted of about a dozen stalls, each manned by local vendors carefully vetted by base security. The offerings ranged from handwoven textiles to intricately carved wooden boxes, semi-precious stone jewelry to traditional foods. Soldiers wandered between the stalls, examining wares and making purchases with a mix of dollars and Kuwaiti dinars.

"I'm going to find my pastries," Mac announced, already drifting toward a stall where several soldiers had gathered. "Meet you back here in twenty?"

Jerry nodded, content to browse the market alone. He moved between the stalls with casual interest, examining carved wooden camels and handwoven scarves, mentally cataloging potential gifts for his parents and the boys.

At the far end of the market, a small table caught his attention. Unlike the more elaborate displays, this one featured a simple black cloth covering and a modest arrangement of metalwork. An elderly Kuwaiti man sat behind it, hands weathered by decades of craftsmanship, working intently on a small piece of metal.

Jerry approached, drawn by the quiet dignity of the old craftsman. The table displayed an array of handcrafted jewelry: intricate silver pendants, copper bracelets, and several rings, each unique in design.

"Salaam alaikum," Jerry greeted, using one of the few Arabic phrases he'd picked up during deployment.

The old man looked up, his eyes brightening at the respectful address. "Wa alaikum salaam," he replied with a nod. "You look. Good pieces."

His English was limited but clear enough. Jerry examined the display, genuinely impressed by the craftsmanship. Each piece showed remarkable attention to detail, with geometric patterns and flowing Arabic script incorporated into the designs.

Among the jewelry, a small collection of rings caught his attention. They weren't flashy, just simple bands with intricate engravings. One in particular stood out: a silver ring with a subtle pattern of interwoven lines and small Arabic script flowing along its surface

Jerry picked it up. The silver caught the light as he turned it, the inscription seeming to come alive with the movement.

"Beautiful work," he said, looking up at the craftsman. "What does it say?"

The old man smiled, pointing to the inscription. "It say ..." he paused, searching for the words. "In Arabic, 'Al-quloob al-muttasila, walaw ba'udat, laa taftareq.'"

Jerry waited patiently as the man found the translation.

"In English ... 'Hearts connected across distances never truly separate.'" The craftsman nodded with satisfaction. "For love that is ... far but still close."

Jerry stared at the ring, the words resonating deeply. How many miles had separated him from Scarlet over these months? How many times had he tried to create even greater distance, only to find her steadfastly present despite his efforts?

"For wife?" the craftsman asked with a knowing smile.

"Not yet," Jerry answered honestly, turning the ring to examine it from all angles. "But maybe soon."

The old man nodded as if this made perfect sense. "Silver good for promise. Shows journey." He tapped his weathered finger against the woven pattern surrounding the script. "See here? Pattern never end, never break. Like good love."

Jerry studied the pattern more closely, seeing how the lines interwove in a continuous flow that circled the entire band, with no clear beginning or end. Like their own journey, it was complicated and interconnected, but unbroken despite the challenges.

"I can size," the craftsman offered, gesturing to his tools. "Not take long."

Jerry realized he was still holding the ring, had been turning it between his fingers for several minutes. His thumb brushed over the inscription again, feeling the engraved words that spoke of hearts connected across distances. The message seemed written specifically for him and Scarlet, for the path they'd traveled and the future they were building.

In his pocket, his phone vibrated with a text, probably Mac wondering where he'd disappeared to. But Jerry couldn't look away from the ring, from the promise it represented.

Eighteen days until he'd be home. Eighteen days until he could see Scarlet, hold her, thank her in person for not giving up on him even when he'd nearly given up on himself. Eighteen days until they could truly begin building the life they'd committed to across continents and time zones.

The craftsman watched him with patient eyes, seeming to understand the significance of the moment. "Some decisions," he said softly, "the heart makes before the mind knows."

Twenty-Nine

The familiar rattle of the bus as it crested into Fort Cavazos hit Jerry like a memory at full volume, bringing comfort laced with disbelief.

Outside, Texas looked impossibly lush after so many months of sun-scorched beige.

He sat too still, back straight, heart not. His fingers kept brushing the small box in his pocket, like he needed to remind himself it was still there.

"You're gonna wear a hole in that seat, brother," Mac observed from beside him, his characteristic drawl somehow both amused and calming. "Relax. Operation Future Mrs. Duncan is locked and loaded."

Jerry shot him a sidelong glance. "Never should have let you name the mission."

Mac grinned. "Too late now. We've got twenty-three men using the codename on comms." He gestured to the soldiers surrounding them, most pretending not to eavesdrop while failing spectacularly.

The plan had started simply enough. After receiving Scarlet's video response to his letter, watching her breathlessly say "Yes, a thousand times yes" while standing on that Miami beach, Jerry had known two things with absolute certainty: he wanted to marry her, and he wanted to ask properly the moment he saw her again.

What had begun as a personal mission had somehow, with Mac's enthusiastic involvement, evolved into what amounted to a full tactical operation involving half their unit, Colonel Sharp himself, and a military-grade sound system.

"Run through the timeline again," Jerry said quietly, needing the comfort of structure, of details, of a plan. Executing missions with precision and care was what he did best. Even if this particular mission involved a ring and spotlights rather than cameras and protective gear.

Mac sighed dramatically but complied, knowing his friend's need for reassurance. "Bus arrives at 1400," he began, slipping into briefing mode with practiced ease. "We form up outside, standard procedure. At 1405, we enter the gym to AC/DC. Sharp confirmed with the DJ this morning. Formation holds until dismissal, then chaos erupts."

"And you'll—"

"Find Scarlet and position her at grid point Charlie," Mac finished, referencing their hastily drawn gymnasium map. "Your brothers-in-arms create a perimeter, ensuring operational security. DJ gets the signal, cuts to the song, hits the spotlight, and then boom! Sergeant Romantic drops to one knee."

The soldiers around them nodded in confirmation. What had started as Jerry nervously confiding in Mac about his proposal plan had somehow spread through the unit like wildfire, each man offering to help without hesitation. The brotherhood of deployment had transformed his personal mission into a collective effort.

"What if she's not where you expect?" Jerry asked, voicing one of the dozen concerns cycling through his mind. "What if—"

"Duncan," Specialist Rodriguez interrupted from across the aisle, his normally serious face breaking into a rare grin. "The woman quit her job and is planning to move across the country for you. She's going to say yes."

"That's not what I'm worried about," Jerry muttered, though in truth, a small voice of doubt had been whispering in his ear since he'd purchased the ring in Kuwait. What if she'd changed her mind? What if the reality of his PTSD, of raising neurodiverse children, of military life had finally sunk in during his absence?

Mac seemed to read his thoughts, leaning closer. "She's been visiting the boys every chance she gets," he said quietly. "Your mom says they're practically inseparable when she's there. Scarlet's not going anywhere."

Jerry nodded, drawing strength from his friend's certainty. Nine months ago, he'd been so afraid of his own vulnerability that he'd nearly pushed Scarlet away completely. Now, he was planning to ask her to stay forever, in front of everyone who mattered.

The bus slowed as they approached the gymnasium entrance, and an electric murmur swept through the returning soldiers. Through the windows, they could see the gathered crowd, hundreds of eager families waiting to welcome them home.

Colonel Sharp stood from his seat at the front of the bus, turning to face them. "Men, in about five minutes, you'll be reunited with your families," he announced. "But first, I understand we have a special operation to execute." His typically stern face softened with a knowing smile as his eyes found Jerry. "Sergeant Duncan, is everything in order for Operation ... what was it again, MacIntyre?"

"Future Mrs. Duncan, sir," Mac supplied with a grin.

The Colonel shook his head, but the amusement in his eyes was unmistakable. "Right. I've coordinated with the DJ. Thunder entrance, quick dismissal, then Lady in Red for the main event. All clear?"

"Yes, sir," Jerry replied, surprised by the steadiness in his voice despite the adrenaline coursing through him.

"Good." Sharp's expression grew more serious. "It's been an honor serving with all of you. Welcome home."

As the buses parked and the soldiers prepared to disembark, Jerry felt a hand on his shoulder. Staff Sergeant Peterson, a usually stoic man with three deployments under his belt, gave him a solemn nod.

"We've got your back, Duncan," he said simply. "Form a perimeter tighter than a diplomatic convoy."

Jerry swallowed against the unexpected emotion rising in his throat. "Thank you," he managed.

They filed off the bus with practiced precision, the Texas sun warming their faces as they formed up outside the gymnasium. The muffled sounds of music and cheering leaked through the building's walls, the anticipation almost tangible in the air around them.

"Nervous?" Mac asked, falling into position beside him.

Jerry considered the question, surprised to find that beneath the anxiety lay something stronger ... certainty. "Terrified," he admitted. "But ready."

"That's my boy," Mac grinned. "Just don't puke on her shoes when she says yes."

"Your confidence is overwhelming," Jerry replied dryly, but felt some of the tension ease from his shoulders.

Colonel Sharp stepped to the front of the formation, conducting a quick uniform inspection more out of habit than necessity. When he reached Jerry, he paused, his voice lowering.

"Ring secured, Sergeant?"

Jerry patted his pocket in confirmation. "Yes, sir."

Sharp nodded. "My wife says this moment changes everything. Twenty-seven years later, she still remembers exactly how I asked." A rare smile crossed his face. "Make it count, Duncan."

"Plan to, sir," Jerry replied, the box feeling heavier with each passing second.

The Colonel moved on, completing his inspection before returning to the head of the formation. Jerry took a deep breath, centering himself as he had countless times before missions. Muscle memory took over, pushing aside personal thoughts as they prepared for entrance.

"Third Brigade Combat Team," Sharp called out, his voice carrying easily over the assembled soldiers. "Prepare to move out."

The double doors to the gymnasium opened, revealing a brief glimpse of the decorated space beyond. The opening riff of "Thunderstruck" blasted through the speakers, carrying with it a wave of cheers from the waiting families.

"Forward, march!"

They surged forward as one body, training transforming their entrance into something more akin to athletes taking the field than soldiers returning from duty. Jerry felt the shift as they crossed the threshold, discipline momentarily yielding to the pure, unfiltered joy of homecoming.

The gymnasium exploded with sound and color. Smoke machines created a dramatic effect, confetti rained down, and hundreds of voices joined the chorus of "Thunder!"

The sensory overload was immediate and overwhelming after months in the controlled environment of deployment. Jerry blinked against the spotlights, his eyes already scanning the crowd for Scarlet.

The formation came to a halt in perfect unison, but Jerry barely registered Colonel Sharp approaching the microphone. His focus had narrowed to a single priority: finding her.

A flicker of red stopped him cold. Jerry's eyes found her instantly.

Scarlet stood in the heart of the crowd with one hand steady on Marty's wheelchair and the other holding Emmett's. Jerry's chest squeezed when he spotted the bright earmuffs protecting Emmett's head from the overwhelming noise. She'd thought of everything, anticipated his son's needs in a way that spoke louder than any words could about who she'd become to his family.

She hadn't just accompanied them. She'd prepared. She'd cared.

His family. All three of them, together, waiting for him.

Their eyes met across the gymnasium, and nine months of distance compressed into a single electric moment of connection. Everything he'd carried crystallized into absolute certainty. The fear, the longing, the gradual healing. This was right. She was right. They were right.

Colonel Sharp's abbreviated welcome barely registered as Jerry maintained his position, muscles tense with the effort of not breaking formation early. When the dismissal finally came, the choreography they'd rehearsed on the bus kicked into motion with military precision.

Mac slipped away immediately, his mission clear. The soldiers who'd agreed to help spread strategically through the crowd, maintaining visual contact as they navigated the chaos. Jerry held position momentarily, allowing the initial wave of reunions to create the necessary diversion.

Specialist Rodriguez appeared at his side. "Perimeter team is in position, Sergeant. Waiting for your signal."

Jerry nodded, his hand closing around the ring box in his pocket. The silver band with its Arabic inscription felt warm against his palm, as if charging with energy for its unveiling.

Through the moving bodies, he caught glimpses of the operation unfolding. Mac intercepting Scarlet, guiding her toward the predetermined spot. The soldiers gradually forming the human perimeter, their movements casual to avoid suspicion. Colonel Sharp conferring with the DJ, who grinned and gave a thumbs up.

All systems go.

Jerry moved then, sliding through the crowd with purpose. The gymnasium became a blur of kaleidoscopic reunions, tears and laughter, and the beautiful chaos of homecoming swirling around him. But his focus remained singular, unwavering.

He reached the center of the perimeter unseen, shielded by his brothers-in-arms as planned. Through the small gaps between shoulders, he could see Scarlet's confusion as Mac positioned her, could hear her questions beneath the celebration's roar.

Jerry dropped to one knee, the movement as natural as if he'd practiced it a thousand times. The velvet box opened in his hands, revealing the ring that had traveled from a Kuwaiti craftsman's stall across an ocean to this moment.

The signal passed wordlessly through the circle of soldiers. The DJ's announcement cut through the noise. The music shifted. The spotlight hit.

The perimeter parted, and there she was; Scarlet, stunning in a navy dress, her vivid red hair catching the light, her eyes widening in beautiful shock as she registered the scene before her.

The moment expanded, stretching to contain their entire journey: the cruise where they'd met, the gradual building of trust, his withdrawal during deployment, her steadfast patience, his eventual surrender to vulnerability, her immediate acceptance of all he was, broken pieces included.

"Scarlet," he began, and was surprised by the steadiness in his voice despite the emotion threatening to overwhelm him. "I had a whole speech planned, but seeing you here ..." The words he'd rehearsed evaporated, replaced by the simple truth that had guided him home. "All I want to say is thank you. For waiting. For not giving up. For loving the boys like they were always yours."

Tears formed in her eyes, but she made no move to brush them away. They stood as perfect counterpoints to the joy radiating from her face.

"You saw me at my worst," he continued, finding the words as they came, "and somehow still wanted me at my best. I don't know why fate put us on that cruise, but I thank God every day that it did." He took a deep breath, steadying himself for the question that would change everything. "I want to build a life with you. A real one, with all the messy, beautiful, hard, wonderful parts. Scarlet Bellari, will you marry me?"

The gymnasium, the crowd, the mission all faded into nothing as he waited for her answer, his heart suspended between one beat and the next.

"Yes," she whispered, her voice strengthening as emotion broke through. "Yes. A thousand times yes."

Jerry got to his feet, his hands steady despite the storm stirring beneath his ribs.

The ring slid into place as if the moment had been waiting for them both.

Its quiet inscription pressed against her skin, invisible to the world but shining in the soft curve of silver and the certainty in her eyes.

After nine long months, this kiss wasn't tender … it was a *declaration.*

A collision of time, distance, and everything they hadn't said.

The crowd around them erupted, joy cascading like confetti, wrapping them in a celebration that honored not just survival, but return.

But Jerry heard none of it. In that moment, with Scarlet in his arms and the taste of her tears mingling with his own, nothing else existed beyond this perfect completion of the longest deployment of his life, and the beginning of everything that mattered.

Epilogue

The afternoon sun streamed through the balcony door of Mac's cabin, casting long rectangles of light across the floor. Jerry stood before the mirror, fingers fumbling with his bow tie for what must have been the third time. The same cabin. The same ship. But everything else had changed.

"You're making this way harder than it needs to be," Mac said from his perch on the bed, still in his suit pants and undershirt. He looked annoyingly relaxed for a best man, one leg crossed over the other.

"Easy for you to say. You're not the one getting married in ..." Jerry glanced at his watch, "less than an hour."

Mac stood, crossing to the mirror. "Here, let me. Before you strangle yourself on your wedding day."

Jerry dropped his hands and surrendered to Mac's surprisingly deft fingers. As Mac worked, Jerry caught himself in the reflection. There was a steadiness in his eyes now that hadn't been there when they'd first boarded the Elysian Serenade two and a half years ago. Back then, he'd been running on fumes, held together by routine and obligation. Now ...

"So," Mac said, voice deliberately casual as he adjusted the tie. "How've the sessions at Fort Belvoir been going? Still twice a week?"

"Down to once," Jerry answered, grateful for Mac's straightforwardness. Anyone else might have avoided mentioning therapy on his wedding day. "The EMDR's been ... it's been good. Really good. Doc says we can move to monthly check-ins soon."

Mac nodded, eyes on his work. "Nightmares?"

"Better. Not gone, but ... manageable." Jerry paused. "The stuff with Iraq, with feeling responsible for ..." He cut himself off, not needing to rehash the details. "It doesn't own me anymore."

Mac finished with the tie and stepped back, appraising his work. "Scarlet's been good with all of it?"

Jerry thought of the countless nights Scarlet had sat with him after he woke up gasping for air. How she'd learned exactly when to ask questions and when to simply exist beside him. How she never made him feel weak or broken.

"She never pushed, you know? Just held space. Knew when to ask and when to let me breathe."

Mac's usual smirk softened. "That's why you're standing here today. You both did the work."

Jerry nodded, emotion catching in his throat. "Still am. Still have rough days. But ... I'm in a good place. Ready for this."

Mac clapped him on the shoulder, then quickly pivoted, emotional moment apparently over. "Speaking of good places, you'll never guess who I ran into after your bachelor party last night."

"Subtle, Mac. Real subtle."

"What? I'm just saying, some of us need to keep our options open. Not everyone finds their soulmate on some cheesy singles cruise."

A knock at the door saved Mac from further interrogation. Jerry opened it to find his father standing there in a charcoal suit, looking more put-together than Jerry had seen him in years.

"You clean up nice, Dad."

Thomas Duncan stepped inside, eyebrows rising when he saw Jerry's bow tie. "Impressive. Did you actually manage that yourself?"

"Mac's hidden talents," Jerry said.

"Mind if I steal my son for a minute?" Thomas asked Mac.

Mac glanced between them. "Take your time. I need to finish getting dressed anyway."

Once Mac disappeared into the bathroom, Thomas reached into his jacket pocket. "I wanted to give you these before the ceremony."

He held out a small velvet box. Inside lay a pair of silver cufflinks, weathered with age, engraved with the Duncan family initials.

"Grandpa's," Jerry said softly, running a finger over the worn silver.

Thomas nodded. "He wore them when he married Grandma. I wore them when I married your mother." A shadow passed across his face. "Figured it was time for them to keep moving forward."

Jerry carefully removed the cufflinks he'd been wearing and replaced them with these. As Thomas helped him secure the second one, he cleared his throat, and Jerry immediately recognized the gravity in his posture.

"Compassion," Jerry said before his father could begin, the hint of a smile playing at his lips.

Thomas's eyebrows rose. "You've heard this a few times."

"Never gets old, though."

Thomas's weathered face crinkled with a smile as he continued. "The Duncan men live by three principles in marriage: communication, commitment, and compassion." He fastened the second cufflink, his hands steadier than his voice. "Communication: because the hardest truths spoken gently are better than the kindest lies. Commitment: because love isn't just a feeling that comes and goes, it's a choice you make every morning. And compassion:"

"... because you'll both be wrong sometimes," Jerry joined in, "and forgiveness matters more than being right."

Thomas's eyes glistened. "I failed at these with your mother. Especially the last one. But watching you with Scarlet, with the boys ... you already live these principles. You've figured out what took me decades to learn."

Jerry swallowed hard. "These saved us during deployment. When it would've been easier to let distance win. When it felt like we were drifting. It was choosing to communicate even when it was hard. Staying committed even when it was easier to withdraw."

"You've already lived these principles in the hardest ways," Thomas said, straightening Jerry's lapels. "Now you get to live them in joy."

Another knock interrupted them, this one lighter, followed by the distinct sound of Marty's delighted squealing. A smile broke across Jerry's face as he opened the door to find his mother holding both boys' hands, all three dressed in their finest.

"Look at you," Maggie breathed, taking in Jerry in his tuxedo. "My handsome boy."

He lost track of the conversation the moment his eyes found his boys.

Dressed in matching suits, they looked impossibly grown.

Emmett pushed Marty's chair with practiced ease, the pillow secured to the tray, rings catching the light. The small boy dwarfed by the chair in the photo Jerry still kept close was gone, replaced by this confident young man.

And Marty? He was grinning like he was leading a parade.

Emmett, solemn as ever, studied Jerry with careful eyes. "After today, Mom will officially be our mom forever, right?"

The word *mom* rolled so naturally from Emmett's lips, even after two years of calling her that, it still caught Jerry in the chest every time. The way both boys had embraced Scarlet, how she'd slipped into their lives like she'd always belonged there.

Jerry placed a hand on Emmett's shoulder. "Yes, buddy. After today, she'll officially be your mom forever and ever. But you know what? She's been your mom in all the ways that matter for a long time already."

Emmett nodded seriously. "I know. But now everybody else will know too."

"That's right," Jerry agreed, throat tight. "The whole world will know we're a family."

The adults laughed, the tension of the moment breaking. Mac emerged from the bathroom, fully dressed now, nodding approvingly at the boys. "Looking sharp, gentlemen. Ready to go make it official?"

The walk to the ceremony space seemed to pass in a blur of familiar landmarks. The ship felt different now, no longer the escape hatch Mac had forced him through, but a place of beginnings. They passed the bar where he'd first really talked to Scarlet, the hot tub where something deeper had sparked between them. Each spot held memories, fragments of who they'd been when this journey started.

The ceremony space on the upper deck was simple but elegant. White chairs arranged in intimate rows, an arbor woven with white flowers, the endless blue of the ocean stretching behind it. Only their closest family and friends were present, exactly as they'd wanted it.

Jerry took his place at the altar with Mac beside him, Emmett and Marty standing proudly nearby. A flash of recognition pulled his gaze to the second row where Ramona—formerly Command Sergeant Major Vega—sat with her husband.

"Glad you could make it, sergeant major," Jerry said, genuine warmth in his voice.

"Wouldn't have missed it," she replied with a smile. "And it's Ramona now, remember? I've been retired for nine months."

"Still getting used to that."

The ship's captain, resplendent in a formal pink tux, nodded respectfully to Jerry as he took his position at the altar. "Beautiful day for a wedding, especially for Valentine's Day."

Jerry hadn't planned the date intentionally, it had simply worked with their schedules. But there was something fitting about it now.

A change in the music signaled the beginning of the procession. Conversations quieted as everyone rose, turning toward the path that led to the back of the ceremony space. Cami appeared first, stunning in a deep teal dress, her usual confidence somehow softer today. She caught Jerry's eye and gave him the smallest of winks before taking her place opposite Mac.

Jade followed, her dress a near match to Cami's, looking happier than Jerry had ever seen her. Both women assumed their positions as co-maids of honor, their expressions a mix of joy and barely contained emotion.

Jerry didn't miss the way Mac's eyes tracked Cami's every movement, nor the way she pretended not to notice.

Then the music shifted again, and every head turned.

There she was. Scarlet, on her father's arm, haloed by sunlight that set her vibrant red hair ablaze. The same red that had caught his eye across the atrium that first day, when he'd been drowning in the crowd. The same red that had become a beacon throughout their story.

Her dress was simple and elegant, with clean lines and subtle shimmer. But it was her eyes that held him, locked on his from the moment she appeared, unwavering and certain.

Time slowed as memories cascaded through him, including that first moment of connection in the Topaz Lounge, paddle boarding in Grand Turk when he'd first risked telling her about the boys, the way she'd looked at him in her cabin when he finally let her see all of him. The ache of deployment, the joy of reunion, the thousand small moments that had led them here.

Emmett stepped forward, solemn in his duty, and took Scarlet from her father. Leo kissed his daughter's cheek, then stepped back, visibly emotional. Jerry watched as his son led the woman who would be his wife the rest of the way to him, his chest swelling with a pride he couldn't contain.

Two and a half years ago, I wasn't a whole person. I was fragments: soldier, father, survivor, held together by duty and fear. I never questioned if I deserved more. Never thought to ask. Just kept my head down and pushed through each day, convinced that sacrifice was the only love I had to offer.

I boarded this ship back then because Mac wouldn't take no for an answer. Couldn't imagine deserving a break, let alone finding someone who would choose the complicated mess that was my life. My boys. My baggage. My broken pieces.

Then, she happened. That first real conversation at the bar, I felt something unlock. Something I'd buried so deep I'd forgotten it existed. She didn't look at my life with pity or fascination. She just saw me. And kept seeing me, even when I tried to hide.

She taught me that vulnerability isn't weakness. That asking for help isn't failure. That compassion starts with yourself. The first time I let her see me break down after a nightmare, I was terrified she'd run. Instead, she stayed. Not to fix me, but to remind me I was worth fixing.

Because of her, I finally got help. Faced what war had done to me. Started putting myself back together into someone new, not the man I was before. Someone better. Someone who could be present for his sons instead of just physically there. Who could feel joy without waiting for the other shoe to drop.

Dad talks about communication, commitment, and compassion. But Scarlet taught me a fourth C: courage. Courage to believe I deserve happiness. Courage to love without limits. Courage to be whole.

I used to think being a good father meant carrying every burden alone. Now I know it means showing my sons what real partnership looks like. What healthy love can be. Not only do Emmett and Marty have a mom now, but they have a father who's fully present. Who knows how to laugh. Who can show them that strength lives in softness too.

Before her, I existed. Because of her, I live.

The man standing at this altar is nothing like the one who first stepped onto this ship. That man was surviving. This one is thriving. That man was afraid to want. This one knows how to hope. That man believed duty was all he deserved. This one understands he's worthy of joy.

Scarlet didn't change me. She reflected back the man I could be until I finally saw him too. And now, watching her walk toward me, I'm not just choosing her. I'm choosing the man I've become because she loved me. The man who knows that home isn't a place, but the people who see your whole truth and stay anyway.

I've finally stopped living in fragments. I'm whole. I'm here. I'm hers.

Afterword

Dear Reader,

Thanks for reading to the end of *Golden Shores.*

It means you've been with Jerry through the mess and the mending, through mistakes, reckonings, and quiet moments of truth.

Whether his journey felt familiar or foreign, I hope it offered something worth sitting with.

There are scenes in this book that are intentionally raw. Moments that may have felt heavy. Uncomfortable. Maybe even too familiar. That was deliberate. Jerry's story isn't just fiction, but deeply personal.

I know these struggles because I live them too.

Post-Traumatic Stress isn't just a plot device: it's part of my reality, and of many others like me. For some of us, it came from combat. For others, from entirely different kinds of trauma. Regardless of where it starts, PTSD doesn't always present in the loud, visible ways the media often portrays. It can be quiet. Internal. A constant hum of hypervigilance. A long-held breath. A version of yourself you keep carefully hidden from even the people who love you most.

The symptoms don't always disappear for good.

They can show up long after you thought you were past them.

That doesn't mean you're back at square one.

It means healing is ongoing and being human is messy.

As someone who has walked this path, I want you to know:

It is not weakness to seek help. It is not quitting if you can't carry it all alone.

Whether you're a veteran, a survivor, a loved one trying to understand ... it's okay to need support.

You are not alone. You never have been.

If you or someone you love is struggling with mental health, trauma, or suicidal thoughts, please consider reaching out. Help is real. Healing is possible. You are worthy of both.

Here are some resources that can help:

Emergency Help

- National Suicide & Crisis Lifeline (24/7): Dial 988 (in the U.S.) 988lifeline.org (Support for anyone in emotional distress, not just suicidal ideation)

Veterans Crisis Line

- Veterans & Service Members (24/7): Dial 988, then Press 1 www.veteranscrisisline.net Text: 838255

Mental Health & Support Resources

- NAMI (National Alliance on Mental Illness): Helpline: 1-800-950-NAMI (6264) www.nami.org/help

Give an Hour:

- www.giveanhour.org (Free mental health care for those affected by military service, mass violence, and more)

The Trevor Project (LGBTQ+ Youth Support):
- 1-866-488-7386 | Text "START" to 678678 www.thetrevo rproject.org

SAMHSA (Substance Abuse and Mental Health Services):
- 1-800-662-HELP (4357) www.samhsa.gov/find-help/nati onal-helpline

And these are just a few.

From community clinics to survivor networks, school counselors to veterans' groups, help is out there—genuine and ready. Don't let the need for the "right" solution keep you stuck.

Reach out. You'll find someone ready to answer.

If you're reading this and something inside you is aching, please know that your pain matters. Your story matters. And help is out there.

This world is better with you in it.

With all my heart,

J.D. Harbor

Author. Veteran. Work in progress.

About the Author

I'm J.D. Harbor, a romance novelist drawn to love stories set on the high seas. A former military photojournalist, I discovered my writing voice through capturing real-life moments and now channel that same sense of intimacy and adventure into fiction. My novels invite readers aboard cruise ships filled with possibility, where love often arrives in unexpected tides.

The RomantiSea Serenades series began with Emerald Tide and Sapphire Seas and continues with Scarlet Wave and Golden Shores, companion novels that explore the same love story from two perspectives. These newest releases are loosely inspired by my own love story of meeting my wife at sea and finding a future neither of us had planned.

I now live in Central Florida with my wife and two kids, always dreaming up our next adventure on the open water. I believe the best love stories begin with self-discovery, because only when we truly know ourselves can we fully open our hearts to love.

Set Sail with the RomantiSea Serenades Series: A Voyage of Love and Self-Discovery

RomantiSea Serenades is an ever-expanding world of love stories set aboard the luxurious Elysian Serenade cruise ship. Each novel is designed to capture the transformative magic of travel, connection, and the open sea. Whether it is through laughter at the pool deck or quiet moments under starlight, these books explore how love can be discovered when we finally give ourselves permission to be seen.

Every romance unfolds as a complete story told across a companion pair of novels, each one offering a distinct perspective on the same relationship. Readers can choose either side of the story or read both for the fullest emotional journey. In addition to these duet voyages, the series also features bonus standalone novellas that spotlight unforgettable characters and moments from the Elysian Serenade community.

While the novels connect through shared settings and cameos, each book stands entirely on its own and can be enjoyed in any order. The heart of RomantiSea Serenades is simple yet profound: new places, new faces, and the unexpected power of love to change everything.

Scarlet Wave

Scarlet Wave is the companion to Golden Shores, offering her side of the love story that blossoms on the Elysian Serenade. Scarlet Bellari appears to have everything figured out, with a career in Miami that looks flawless from the outside, yet beneath the shine she is restless and worn thin. Joining a singles cruise with her best friend, she hopes for nothing more than a break from the life she has built.

Onboard, she meets Jerry Duncan, a single father and soldier whose quiet steadiness draws her in. Their chemistry unfolds slowly, through banter, vulnerability, and unexpected tenderness. The cruise becomes a place where Scarlet is forced to confront the truth she has long avoided—that success means little without fulfillment and that love cannot grow unless she stops performing long enough to be present.

Scarlet Wave is a journey of letting go, of finding worth beyond achievement, and of daring to trust her heart with someone who sees past the polished surface. Read alone or together with Golden Shores, it is a romance that proves real connection thrives when walls come down.

Emerald Tide and Sapphire Seas

Emerald Tide and Sapphire Seas introduced readers to the sweeping world of RomantiSea Serenades with the unforgettable love story of Harper Brooks and Aidan Murphy. She is a driven New York advertising executive who has built her life on success yet feels hollow inside. He is an Irish chef who has sacrificed his own ambitions to carry the weight of family responsibility. Their chance meeting aboard the Elysian Serenade sparks a connection that challenges them both to question the lives they have accepted.

As their relationship unfolds, Harper and Aidan discover that love is not only about finding someone to share the journey but about daring to hope again. Together they awaken dreams they thought had slipped away, encouraging each other to imagine a future beyond the safe but unfulfilling paths they had been walking. Their story is tender, transformative, and filled with the promise of second chances.

Emerald Tide tells the story through Aidan's eyes, while Sapphire Seas offers Harper's perspective. Each novel stands on its own, yet when read together they reveal the full depth of two people learning that the truest love is the one that helps you grow into who you were always meant to be.